Praise for the novels of

LAURIE BRETON

"Breton skillfully balances the suspense and romance."
—*Publishers Weekly* on *Final Exit*

"Breton keeps the readers guessing from
the first page to the last...a great read."
—*Romantic Times BOOKreviews* on *Final Exit*

"Gritty and realistic, *Mortal Sin* is a powerfully written
story...a truly exceptional book on many levels."
—*Romantic Times BOOKreviews*

"Breton's way with characters—and her knack
for giving her tales a twist—elevates
this story above most."
—*Romantic Times BOOKreviews* on *Lethal Lies*

LAURIE BRETON

POINT OF DEPARTURE

MIRA®

ISBN-13: 978-0-7783-2427-0
ISBN-10:   0-7783-2427-3

POINT OF DEPARTURE

Copyright © 2007 by Laurie Breton.

All rights reserved. Except for use in any review, the reproduction or
utilization of this work in whole or in part in any form by any electronic,
mechanical or other means, now known or hereafter invented, including
xerography, photocopying and recording, or in any information storage or
retrieval system, is forbidden without the written permission of the publisher,
MIRA Books, 225 Duncan Mill Road, Don Mills, Ontario, Canada M3B 3K9.

All characters in this book have no existence outside the imagination of the
author and have no relation whatsoever to anyone bearing the same name
or names. They are not even distantly inspired by any individual known or
unknown to the author, and all incidents are pure invention.

MIRA and the Star Colophon are trademarks used under license and registered
in Australia, New Zealand, Philippines, United States Patent and Trademark
Office and in other countries.

www.MIRABooks.com

Printed in U.S.A.

This one's for Jay and Jen
who've grown up to be amazing people.
I love you both more than words can say;
you are the joy in my life.

Prologue

Thank God for October.

Right through the end of September, Boston had been so ungodly hot that she'd come close to melting into a puddle on the sidewalk. But October, Kaye Winslow decided as she cruised Comm Ave in search of a parking space, was as close to perfection as it was possible to be. The days still warm, the nights comfortably cool, the sky a vivid blue, unmarred by summer's haze, patches of it visible through an overhead canopy of green smudged here and there by daubs of brilliant red and gold.

Luck was with her. She spied a parking space on the opposite side of the street. At Dartmouth, she took an illegal left at the red light, cutting off a delivery van, whose driver blared his horn in token protest. She circled the pedestrian mall and reversed direction, swooping with practiced ease into the empty parking space in blatant disregard of the sign not ten feet away designating it for Back Bay residents only.

Kaye cut the engine, checked her reflection in the rearview mirror and rubbed a splotch of lipstick from her front tooth. Flinging her meticulously streaked blond hair over her shoulder, she gathered up her Gucci briefcase and slid smoothly from the BMW's soft leather upholstery.

The house stood half a block away, a grand old pile of bricks and mortar situated on Boston's most elegant thoroughfare. Commonwealth Avenue was the city's finest jewel, a broad, tree-lined, old-world-style boulevard, bisected by a strip of lush green that rendered it unique in this city of narrow, congested streets. It was one of the most prestigious addresses in Boston. As her associates were fond of saying, location, location, location.

The Worthington house—and calling it a house was a great understatement—had been built by Gerald Worthington in 1886 and handed down through several generations of the Worthington family. When the reigning matriarch had died six months ago and rumors had flown that the heirs were interested in dumping the place and splitting the cash, the Boston real estate world had perked up and taken notice. There wasn't a broker out there who wouldn't have gladly sacrificed an appendage to get his or her hands on the property. By some miracle, it had been Kaye Winslow the Worthington heirs had called when they were ready to put the place on the market.

Selling this house, with its six-point-five-million-dollar price tag, would show the world that Winslow & DeLucca was capable of standing its ground against the big agencies: ERA, Coldwell Banker, Century 21. This sale, with a motivated seller and the right buyer, would cement her reputation as a major league player, and then she'd finally be able to put her farce of a marriage to Sam Winslow behind her.

Thinking about her soon-to-be-ex-husband always caused tiny frown lines to bracket her mouth, and Kaye made a conscious effort to relax her facial muscles. At thirty-three, she was too young to be getting wrinkles. But Sam knew just which buttons to push, and he pushed them with clocklike regularity. Two years they'd been married. Two years during which she'd catered to his every whim; two years when she'd been there on his arm, the consummate hostess, the perfect little faculty wife; two years of playing the loving stepmother.

Enough was enough. Sam's usefulness had come to an end. Kaye had gotten what she wanted from him: respectability. As his wife, she'd gained the kind of acceptance she'd spent her entire life seeking. But now that she'd built a name for herself as a respected member of the real estate community, she didn't need him anymore. It was time to slough him off like an old skin. Time for a new beginning, a new life. One that didn't include Professor Sam Winslow or his crazy, anorexic daughter.

Kaye walked up the granite steps and unlocked the massive double front doors, letting herself into a sweeping two-story foyer. With its brass wall sconces and its majestic, winding staircase, both fanciful and uncommon in a Back Bay home of this vintage, the foyer never failed to take her breath away. Right now, it was bathed in light as bright afternoon sunshine poured through the antique leaded panes of the fanlight above the door.

As the clicking of her heels on the hardwood floor echoed through all that empty space, she walked from room to room, raising window shades to let in the light. The house possessed the stuffy feel that all houses seemed to acquire when they'd been closed up for any time, as though the lack of bodies moving about left the air too still and stagnating. She set down her briefcase on the kitchen island, flipped it open and took out the secret weapon she always carried. A quick spray here, another quick spray there, and she transformed stuffy into deliciously subtle vanilla. She knew all the tricks for making a house appealing, had learned most of them from her mentor, Marty Scalia, the man who'd taken her under his wing and taught her everything he knew about real estate. A few of them, including the vanilla spray, she'd figured out on her own.

She tucked the spray back into her briefcase and returned to the foyer, to take a last look at herself in the mirror there. Power suit. *Check.* Hair. *Check.* Makeup. *Check.* Everything was in order. The doorbell rang, and Kaye glanced at her Rolex. Two-thirty, just as scheduled. Promptness always garnered extra points with her. Pasting on a professional smile, she opened the door to greet her client.

Her smile wobbled and faltered at sight of the man who stood on the top step, his hands shoved into the pockets of his lightweight jacket. *Shit,* she thought frantically, her stomach instantly balling into a hard knot. *Oh, shit.* She'd thought she was rid of him, thought she'd given him what he'd wanted and that he would go away. Thought she'd made it abundantly clear that they had nothing more to say to each other, that she'd made a mistake, and now she was trying to rectify it.

Apparently, she'd failed to make him understand. "What are you doing here?" she demanded.

"You know what they say, Kaye." He smiled, but there was little humor in it. "Sooner or later, the chickens always come home to roost."

"What the hell is that supposed to mean?"

"It means that you and I need to talk."

"I have nothing to say to you. Get out of here. I have a client due any minute."

"This won't take long. Are you letting me in, or do I have to strong-arm my way into the house?"

"If you don't leave, I'll call the police."

"I don't really think you'll do that. Too many awkward questions to answer. All I want is five minutes of your time. If you don't let me in, I could make things pretty nasty for you. I could screw up that rosy future you have planned. I could screw up a whole lot of things."

Glancing past his shoulder at the empty sidewalk, Kaye tried to figure out a way to stall him until reinforcements arrived. But her client was nowhere to be seen. They were alone, the two of them, and if she refused to talk to him, he could destroy her life. He'd have no qualms about it. He was the only person she'd ever known who had fewer scruples than she did.

Damned if you do, damned if you don't.

"Five minutes," she snapped. If he scented fear in her, like a wild animal he would chew her up and spit her out. "And if my client shows before then, you leave. Understood?"

Arrogance propelled his smile, and she wanted to slap it from his face. "I thought you'd see it my way," he said.

Kaye opened the door wider and her visitor stepped across the threshold. Hands flat against the door as she closed it, she took a deep, calming breath. This would all work out. If she was careful, if she used the right words, she could talk her way out of anything. After all, she was Kaye Winslow. She possessed the gift of gab, the power of persuasion. It was what had allowed her to rise so quickly from a nothing little secretary to a respected real estate broker, somebody in whom people like the Worthington heirs were willing to place their trust. As long as she re-membered that, as long as she kept a cool head and made no missteps, her carefully constructed little world wouldn't come crashing down on her head.

Raising her chin in a gesture of defiance, she turned and crossed her arms. Back pressed firmly against the closed door, she said, "I'm listening. Start talking."

One

Doug Policzki was late for the party.

Here on Comm Ave, where town houses routinely carried seven-figure price tags, the presence of a half-dozen emergency vehicles had brought out the neighbors. They stood in small, hushed clusters, chatting quietly and casting nervous glances toward the house. One of the local TV stations had already caught wind of the situation. If this had been Dorchester, where kids were shot dead on the street daily—black kids, of course—the media wouldn't have bothered to show up. Murder in Dorchester wasn't news. But to nobody's surprise, murder in this staunch bastion of WASP prosperity was deemed newsworthy. Policzki recognized the on-air reporter, a striking redhead who stood with shell-pink compact in hand, checking her makeup before the camera started rolling. She glanced up, met his gaze and studied him for a little longer than was necessary before she decided he was nobody of any importance, and returned to checking her makeup.

The house was impressive, one of those brick and stone monstrosities that the wealthy had built before the turn of the last century as a stronghold against the plebeian masses. He paused to gaze up at it for a moment before he showed his ID to the uniform whose job it was to keep away anybody who didn't know the secret password. "Policzki," he said. "Homicide."

The uniform waved him on. Policzki climbed over the yellow tape that had been used to secure the scene, and sprinted up the granite steps.

At the broad double door, another uniform glanced without interest at his ID and gave him a curt nod. Policzki opened the door and stepped inside the house. Above his head, a massive chandelier threw a million crystalline particles of light over a foyer bigger than Rhode Island. Brass wall sconces highlighted the most spectacular staircase he'd ever seen. Most Boston homes of this vintage had narrow stairways steep enough to test the hardiest Puritan constitution. Whoever had built this house had deviated from the norm, building a wide, graceful spiral that seemed to hang in midair of its own free will.

The rooms were empty. Following the echo of voices to the back of the house, Policzki took in the scene in a single, sweeping glance: the corpse that lay in a crumpled heap on the kitchen floor, one arm outflung, palm up as if pleading for mercy; the forensic tech who whistled tunelessly as he dusted the briefcase on the broad granite island for prints; the paunchy, middle-aged man in a Ralph Lauren suit who sat, seemingly forgotten, on a folding canvas stool, mopping his bald pate with a snow-white linen handkerchief.

Two women knelt beside the corpse, studying it with clinical detachment. As Policzki approached, Lorna

Abrams said without looking up, "About time you got here."

Policzki crouched beside the body and studied with interest the hole drilled into the dead man's temple. Beneath the man's head, a pool of blood had started to congeal on the slate floor. "No need to be testy," he told his partner. "Our friend here's already dead."

Neena Bhatti, the doe-eyed assistant M.E., glanced at him, eyes alight with humor, and made a valiant, if unsuccessful, attempt to suppress a grin. "Hey, Doug," she said.

He was always surprised to hear that nasal Queens accent coming from the lovely and exotic Bhatti. It was like expecting Princess Grace and getting Fran Drescher instead. "Neena," he acknowledged. "What do we have here?"

"What we have here," Lorna said briskly, "is a John Doe."

Policzki raised an eyebrow. "No ID?"

"No wallet, no wedding band, not so much as a sticky label on his shirt that says, Hi. My name is Bruce."

"As you can see for yourself," Neena said, "it appears that he died from a single gunshot wound to the head. Small caliber. Nice, neat entry hole. Exit wound's a little messier. The bullet tore off a chunk of his skull on its way out."

"Nice visual," Policzki said. "Any idea who he is?"

"Not a one," Lorna said. "But the house is for sale. The guy over there in the corner? His name's Philip Armentrout. He had a two-thirty appointment with Kaye Winslow, of Winslow & DeLucca Realty, to look the place over. He was running a little late, got here at approximately two forty-eight. The house was unlocked, so he walked in and found Mr. Doe here. What he didn't find was Ms. Winslow."

Policzki rocked back on his heels. "Any indication of where she might be?"

"Nope," Lorna said cheerfully. "But the briefcase O'Connell's dusting for prints belongs to her."

Policzki glanced briefly in the direction she indicated and said, "So she was here at some point."

"It sure looks that way."

Which they both knew thrust Kaye Winslow into the unenviable position of prime suspect, a position she shared with Philip Armentrout, at least until the evidence cleared one or the other of them. Policzki had learned early in his career to take nothing at face value, to question everything, no matter how it looked on the surface. Just because Armentrout said he'd stumbled across the corpse didn't mean he was telling the truth.

Doug gave the body another long, searching glance and said to Neena, "Do we have an estimated time of death?"

"Need I remind you that fieldwork is an inexact science? I can give you a more accurate assessment once we get Mr. Doe into the lab."

"Ballpark?" Lorna asked.

"Couple of hours, tops. I'd say he died no more than a half hour before Mr. Armentrout found him." Neena stood and pulled off her rubber gloves with a snap. "I'm done here."

"Thanks," Lorna said. To Policzki she added, "And I actually thought I might get home on time tonight."

"With your vast experience, you of all people should know better than that."

She rolled her eyes. "Right. Thanks for setting me straight. I have to get somebody out there to talk to the neighbors. Find out if anybody saw or heard anything. Then we'll try to locate Ms. Winslow. If we don't find her lickety-split, we'll have to issue an APB. She could be the perpetrator. Or..." Lorna paused, met Policzki's eyes and shrugged.

The message that passed between them was unspoken, but clear. If Winslow wasn't the perpetrator, chances were good that she was either dead or in serious trouble. "Want me to talk to Armentrout?" he said.

"Have at it. After that, you can check Winslow's ID for next of kin."

While Lorna headed outside to rally the troops, Policzki considered how best to address Philip Armentrout. The gentleman in question sat hunched over, his elbows braced on his knees, his head hung low between his shoulders. Obviously not a happy camper. Straightforward and sincere seemed the most appropriate route. "Mr. Armentrout?" Policzki said.

Armentrout looked up, focused on his face, recognized that this was yet another stranger, and scowled. "When can I leave?" he said.

"I'm Detective Policzki. Mind if I ask you a few questions?"

"I already answered questions. Twice. Don't you people ever talk to each other? This is ridiculous. I already told you everything. I'm a busy man. I have work to get back to."

Policzki hunched down in front of him, balancing on the balls of his feet. "I understand how busy you are," he said. "And I realize this has inconvenienced you. But it won't take long, and when we're done, you can get back to your busy life. Unfortunately…" he paused, and in the silence he heard the rasp of a zipper as one of the EMTs maneuvered the DOA into a body bag "…the victim over there won't be able to do that."

Armentrout winced and closed his eyes. Sighing, he said, "Fine. What do you want to know?"

"Why don't you tell me everything that happened, starting with the time you arrived?"

"We had a two-thirty appointment. I was twenty minutes late because my one o'clock meeting ran over. I got here about ten of three, knocked on the door. Nobody answered. It was unlocked, so I let myself in. I figured the Winslow woman was somewhere in the house and hadn't heard me knock. I called her name a couple of times, came down the hallway and around the corner and saw this guy's feet sticking out from behind the kitchen island. Hell of a shock."

"I imagine it was. What did you do then?"

Armentrout rubbed the back of his neck with a beefy hand. His eyes were a little bloodshot. "I walked around to check. I thought somebody'd passed out or something, and maybe needed medical attention. I didn't realized the guy was dead until I saw the blood."

"How'd you know he was dead?"

Armentrout gave Policzki a long, level look. "I wasn't born yesterday. It was pretty obvious."

Fair enough. "What did you do when you realized he was dead?"

"I got the hell out. If there was a killer on the premises, I wasn't about to hang around and wait to become his next victim. I hightailed it out of there and called 911 from the park across the street. I waited there until the cops arrived."

"All right. Did you, at any time, touch anything?"

"Just the doorknob."

"Were you acquainted with the victim? Was he anybody you'd met before?"

Armentrout shook his head. "I figured he was one of Kaye Winslow's associates. I don't know who the hell he is. Maybe she can tell you."

She probably could, Policzki thought, if they could just

locate her. "All right, Mr. Armentrout," he said, "I think we're done. I'll need verification of your whereabouts earlier this afternoon, and a number where I can reach you in case I have more questions."

"Verification of my—what the hell, am I a suspect?"

"It's routine, sir. You're the person who found the body. In the absence of a smoking gun or a signed confession, we have to consider you a suspect until we can rule you out. Hopefully that'll happen sooner rather than later."

"I don't believe this." Armentrout fished in his pocket for his wallet. He pulled out a business card and shoved it into Policzki's hand. "I go out to look at a house and end up in the middle of a mess like this. My whole goddamn afternoon's been screwed up. You'd better believe I'll be crossing this mausoleum off my list of possibilities." Glowering, he slid the wallet back into his pocket. "Matter of fact, I wouldn't buy a house in Boston if somebody paid me to take it off their hands. Not after this insanity. Maybe I'll find something in Newton or Andover. I hear Lexington's nice."

He left in a huff, this short, self-important businessman whose schedule had been hopelessly derailed by his discovery of a dead body. Hell of an inconvenience, Policzki thought as he watched him go. A real shame that murder had disrupted the guy's busy day.

The door slammed shut behind Armentrout. Across the room, O'Connell, the forensics tech, closed up his fingerprint kit. "That went well," he said.

"Right," Policzki said. "He didn't pull a weapon on me, or threaten to have me fired, so I guess in the greater scheme of things, it could have been worse."

"Oh, yeah. It could've been a lot worse." O'Connell

nodded in the direction of the black plastic bag the two EMTs were wheeling toward the front door. "You could've been that guy."

The setting sun poured like honey through the closed windows of the lecture hall, infusing it with the ambience of a sauna. The dog days of summer were a thing of the past, but so was the air-conditioning that had rendered them tolerable. Cheap construction, minimal insulation and a simpleminded administration that insisted the heating system be turned on according to the calendar instead of the thermometer all conspired to ensure that learning take place in the most hostile environment imaginable. In the midst of this tropical paradise, Assistant Professor Sam Winslow sat reading the latest Dan Brown paperback while his art history students waded through the first exam of the semester. Fifty-eight heads leaned over fifty-eight blue books as fifty-eight pens scratched diligently against paper.

Sam had come to this job six years ago with the zealous idealism of a new convert. It had taken him awhile to accept the irrefutable truth that ninety-eight point eight percent of his students simply didn't give a shit. Back Bay Community College wasn't the kind of place that bred art majors. His classes were well attended because everybody who graduated from BBCC needed nine hours of humanities credit. They'd heard that Professor Winslow was an easy grader, and how hard, after all, could art history be? With a few notable exceptions—primarily those few students who signed up each semester for his introductory painting class—his students were here for one reason only: the three credits that would magically appear on their transcripts if they paid attention in class, showed up on exam days and regurgitated his words back to him in some kind of meaningful form.

This was what his life had come to: he trafficked in regurgitation. Not a particularly pretty realization, especially at four forty-five on a sticky Indian summer afternoon when the only thing he'd eaten since breakfast was a couple of purple Peeps that had been left to petrify on the table in the faculty lounge. Judging by their cardboard consistency, they'd been there for a while.

At a soft rap on the door, Sam glanced up from his book and saw the face of Lydia Forbes, Dean of Arts and Sciences and his immediate supervisor, framed in the tiny window. Setting down his book, he got up from his chair, crossed the room and, with a slow sweep of his gaze over the classroom—his students were supposed to be adults, but it didn't hurt to give them the impression that he had eyes in the back of his head—he opened the door and stepped out into the corridor.

"Lydia," he said, leaving the door open just a crack behind him.

"Sorry to interrupt, but you didn't look busy." Six feet tall in her conservative two-inch heels, Lydia met him nearly eye to eye. Thin almost to the point of emaciation, she wore a brown tweed suit, her gray hair pulled back in its customary severe chignon. Eyebrows that were a dark slash in her pale face gave her a look of perpetual surprise. The first time he'd met her, he'd thought she looked just like Miss Grundy, the schoolteacher from the Archie comics. It hadn't taken him long to see that the outer package was merely professional camouflage for a woman with an infectious laugh, a bawdy sense of humor and a relentless addiction to unfiltered cigarettes. "Take a walk with me," she said.

He glanced back at the classroom. Reading the uncertainty in his gaze, she said, "For Christ's sake, Sam, pull that big stick out of your ass. They're adults. Let them be responsible for their own actions."

Sam latched the classroom door and fell into step with her, matching her leggy stride along the silent corridor and out into the crisp October afternoon. The sun's rays, angling between brick buildings, bathed the entire scene in a muted pink glow. Lydia walked two steps from the entryway, fired up a Pall Mall and took a drag. Eyes closed in ecstasy, she exhaled a cloud of blue smoke and said without rancor, "Damn idiotic state laws."

Behind her back, Sam discreetly waved away the smoke. She took another drag and said, "I forwarded your tenure application to the committee yesterday."

Moving upwind of the toxic blue cloud, he took a breath of fresh air. Or as fresh as it got on a weekday in downtown Boston. "And?"

She turned and studied him with shrewd blue eyes. Took another puff and said, "I'm worried about Larsen."

Professor Nyles Larsen was Sam Winslow's nemesis. He was also the chair of the tenure committee. In theory, if a professor didn't achieve tenure, there was nothing forcing him to move on. In reality, being denied was a slap in the face, best responded to by making a rapid retreat with tail tucked firmly between legs. There was just one problem with that: Sam didn't want to retreat. He might have come to teaching by a circuitous route, but now that he was here, he had no intention of going anywhere.

Sam furrowed his brow. "You think he'll give us trouble?"

"I think Nyles Larsen would take great glee in denying your tenure application. He's had it in for you since the day you first walked through the door of this place."

It was true. Larsen had been a member of the search committee that had hired Sam, and when the man had taken an immediate dislike to him, he'd come close to losing out to another candidate. If not for the staunch ally he'd made in Vince Tedeschi, Professor of Mathematics, he'd have ended up standing on a street corner, selling pencils from a cup. Fortunately for Sam, majority vote had ruled the day, but Nyles Larsen continued to wage a one-man campaign against what he claimed were Sam's mediocre standards and slapdash teaching methods.

"He's jealous," Lydia said. "Your students think you walk on water. Nyles puts his students to sleep."

A pair of twenty-something young women carrying backpacks passed them, talking animatedly, and entered the building through the wide double doors. "So how do we counteract his influence?" Sam said.

"We've done as much as we can do," Lydia said. "I've read your materials all the way through. Proofed them twice. Just to be sure. Your tenure packet's thorough. You've provided good documentation. Your student evaluations are top-notch. Your publication record is a little thin, but it's outweighed by other factors, like your outstanding committee work. Your peer recommendation was stellar."

Of course it was. If not for him, it would have been his peers sitting on all those mind-numbingly tedious committees. They'd do whatever it took to keep him on board so they could continue nominating him to do the dirty work they were all so desperate to avoid. He figured it was worth the sacrifice. No matter what he was asked to do, he accepted the job with a smile. Damn little ever got accomplished in those committee meetings, but membership always looked good on paper.

"Christ, Lyd," he said, hating the thread of desperation that ran through his voice, "I *have* to get tenure. If I can't make it in this place…" The rest of the sentence went unspoken, but they both knew what he meant. When you started at the bottom, there was nowhere left to fall. "I can't make a living from painting. And I'm not trained for anything else. If they boot me out of Back Bay, I'll end up waxing floors at the bus station."

Lydia took another puff of her cigarette, held in the smoke and exhaled it. Flicking an ash, she said, "You've done everything we asked you to do. There's no reason on God's green earth why you should be turned down. Not unless Larsen starts flapping his gums, and even then, the rest of the committee should ignore him. The man is irrational, and everybody knows it. They also know he's determined to hang you out to dry. If anything goes wrong at this point, I'm holding Nyles Larsen personally responsible. If that happens, the little weasel won't want to cross my path."

The lowering sun slowly leached the afternoon of its warmth. Just beneath the surface of that golden glow lay October's surprisingly sharp little teeth, nipping unexpectedly when a sudden arctic gust caught and lifted a strand of Sam's hair.

"I appreciate the support," he said. "I owe you."

"You don't owe me a thing. I just wanted to give you a heads-up." She dropped the butt of her cigarette onto the ground and crushed it out with her foot. "And to let you know that I'm watching your back."

Detective Lorna Abrams had a headache.

She fumbled in her black leather purse for the emergency bottle of Tylenol she always carried, opened the bottle and popped two capsules into her palm. Snapping the cap back on the bottle, she glanced around the interior of the car for something liquid, then said, "To hell with it!" and swallowed them dry.

Policzki, his hands at ten and two on the wheel and his eyes focused on traffic to prevent them from becoming yet another highway statistic, said, "I don't know how you do that."

"Easy. I just work up a mouthful of spit and—"

"Thanks," he said, "but you really don't have to go into detail."

"Stop being so spleeny. You're a cop, for Christ's sake. Act like one."

Policzki didn't respond. It was just as well. When she was in this kind of mood, heads were likely to roll, and Doug Policzki's head, being the nearest one, was in danger of becoming her first victim.

None of the three telephone numbers listed on Kaye Winslow's business card had yielded results. The first, her cell phone number, was useless because in the abruptness of her departure, Winslow had left her BlackBerry behind. The second, her private line at Winslow & DeLucca, rang twice and then went directly to voice mail. Lorna had left an urgent message, but the chances of getting a response were probably zip and zilch. That left door number three. But by the time they'd finished up at the scene, it was well past closing time, and the realty office answering machine had directed her to call back after eight o'clock in the morning.

"Three strikes and you're out," she muttered.

Policzki glanced at her out of the corner of his eye. "Having a bad day, are we?"

"They postponed the court date on the Moldonado case. Again."

Arturo Moldonado, a soft-spoken supermarket meat cutter who'd lived in the same East Boston apartment for two decades, was known for taking in strays—both the human and the animal variety—and handing out penny candy to the neighborhood kids. One day last October, he'd come home early and discovered his wife in bed with a twenty-two-year-old college dropout friend of their son. Upon seeing his inamorata engaged in steamy passion with another, much younger and more virile man, Moldonado had tiptoed to the kitchen and taken out a meat cleaver— which, in consideration of his occupation, he kept razor sharp—then returned to the bedroom and the still unsuspecting couple, and proceeded to hack them into a jillion pieces. Afterward, he'd called 911, then sat calmly on the couch with the bloody cleaver and waited for the authorities to come and take him away.

"You can't control the court calendar," Policzki said. "They'll do what they're going to do. All we can do is roll with it."

His logic was flawless. And maddening. "That isn't even the worst of it," Lorna said, rubbing at her throbbing temple. "It's those crazy people I call relatives that have me one step from the edge and peering down into the abyss."

"Oh," he said as the light dawned. "Wedding stuff."

"Yes, wedding stuff! You know what I did today? I spent my lunch hour watching my nineteen-year-old daughter try on wedding dresses. Do you have any frigging idea how much those things cost?"

Policzki made a noncommittal grunt of sympathy. Of course he was noncommittal, she thought irritably. He didn't have a clue how much wedding dresses cost. He lived at home with his mother and banked all his money. "Too damn much," she said, answering her own question. "That's how much. All for a kid who has her head in the clouds and doesn't have a clue what life is really about."

And that was the crux of the matter: Krissy was too young to get married. She was nineteen years old, barely out of high school. A baby. She was also headstrong and determined, so the wedding preparations rolled merrily along, gathering momentum and gaining in size, until they threatened to crush anybody who failed to jump out of the way.

"Silk and taffeta," Lorna grumbled. "Tulle and organza. What the hell is organza, anyway?"

"I haven't a clue."

She glanced out the window, down a darkened side street. "Ed and I got married at city hall. I wore a navy-blue suit and carried a bouquet of carnations. We spent our wedding night at a hotel in Revere, then got up and went to work the next day. We did not—I repeat *not*—spend two weeks on Maui. Who the hell was the idiot that decided the bride's parents are supposed to pay for the wedding?"

"The tradition dates back to ancient times," Policzki said, "when the bride's family was expected to provide a dowry to the family of the groom, presumably in payment for taking her off their hands."

Lorna snorted. "If I'd known that was all it took, I'd have gladly paid Derek to take her off my hands. He's welcome to all of her—the nose ring, the messy room, the *Real World* addiction. The posters of Heath Ledger and Orlando Bloom. He's an easygoing kid. I could've paid him off for a tenth of what this wedding will cost me. They could've eloped. Think of the money I would have saved."

"I think this is it." Policzki pulled up to the curb behind

an aging Volvo wagon. Soft light spilled through a bay window of the South End town house onto the shrubbery below, giving the place the cozy, inviting look of a Thomas Kinkade painting. A shadow moved behind a curtained window. Policzki turned off the engine, and by silent agreement, they simultaneously opened their doors and stepped out of the car.

The day's warmth had given way to a crisp, clear evening. As they moved briskly toward the front door of the house, Lorna said, "So I'll be good cop and you can be bad cop."

"How come I never get to be good cop?"

"Are you kidding, Policzki? With that grim expression of yours, you'd scare people half to death. Tell me. Do you take the face off when you go to bed at night, or is this a 24–7 kind of thing?"

"Hey, that's not fair. I love babies and flowers and puppies."

"I know. You're just incredibly earnest. Or incredibly dedicated. Or incredibly something."

They climbed the steps and Lorna rang the bell. Muffled footsteps approached and the door opened.

Lorna's first thought was that Sam Winslow—if, indeed, the man standing in the open doorway, outlined by soft lamplight, was Sam Winslow—was a sinfully handsome man, with coal-black hair worn to his shoulders, electric blue eyes and a lean, craggy face topped by cheekbones sharp enough to slice diamonds. Somewhere in the vicinity of forty, if the wisps of gray at his temples were any indication, he could be a model—or a stand-in for George Clooney—if he ever tired of teaching. She could imagine him in a magazine layout, standing in a room full of glamorous and playful people, wearing Armani and sipping from a glass of Chivas Regal.

Christ on a crutch. His female students must be tripping over their own feet just to get close to him. Probably a few of the male ones were, too.

He eyed them warily. "Yes?"

"Sam Winslow?" Policzki said.

"Yes."

The young detective held up his badge. "Policzki and Abrams, Boston PD. Is your wife home, sir?"

"My wife? I—no, actually, she's not. What's this about?"

"May we come in?"

"It's dinnertime. I really don't think—"

"Professor Winslow," Lorna said, "there was an incident this afternoon involving your wife. I think you'd better let us in."

"An incident?" He hesitated, looked momentarily nonplussed. Then he nodded and moved away from the door.

Winslow closed the door behind them, cleared his throat and ran a hand through his perfectly coiffed hair. "What's this about?" he repeated.

"Professor Winslow," Lorna said, "when was the last time you spoke with your wife?"

"This morning," he said. "We had breakfast together. Then she went her way and I went mine. You still haven't told me what's going on. What kind of incident?"

"It's almost seven o'clock," Policzki said. "Your wife isn't home, and you haven't spoken to her since this morning. Is this your typical daily routine?"

"Kaye works crazy hours. Look, I wish you people would tell me what the hell is going on. Is Kaye in some kind of trouble? Has something happened to her?"

"Your wife had an appointment this afternoon to show

a house on Commonwealth Avenue," Lorna said, watching his eyes carefully for even the merest flicker of recognition. Or guilt. But she saw neither. "When the client arrived, Mrs. Winslow wasn't there."

Winslow wrinkled his brow in puzzlement and ran a hand along his jaw. "I don't understand. You mean she never showed up?"

"Oh, she showed up," Policzki said. "Her briefcase was there. Her PDA and her wallet were there. But no Kaye. We did find somebody else there, though."

Winslow crossed his arms. "Who?"

"That's what we're trying to figure out," Lorna said. "Whoever he was, he'd been shot in the head. Does your wife own a gun, Professor?"

Two

Winslow's color wasn't good. He sat on a cream leather sofa, directly across from Lorna, who'd snagged herself a comfy armchair, while Policzki wandered the room, taking a casual inventory of its contents. The professor had loosened his tie and unbuttoned his collar, but to Policzki he still looked like something that should be hung out to dry on a wash day morning. His pallor might be due to the shock of learning that his wife was missing. On the other hand, it could be traced to a more sinister source. Guilt had a way of taking its toll on a man.

"The very suggestion is ludicrous," Winslow said.

Lorna leaned back in her chair. "Why is it ludicrous?"

"A, we don't own a gun. And B, even if we did, there's not a chance in hell that Kaye would ever shoot it. She'd be too worried about breaking a nail or getting her hands dirty."

His ears attuned to every nuance of their conversation, Policzki studied the collection of African tribal masks that hung on the wall above the fireplace mantel. They looked like the genuine article. Somebody—presumably the good professor—had done a good deal more traveling in his lifetime than had Douglas Policzki of Somerville, Massachusetts. Six semesters spent at an Arizona university was hardly in the same league as a trip to the Dark Continent.

The Winslows had eclectic tastes. An antique open-fronted china cabinet housed a large collection of Hummel figurines. At least the Winslows kept them all in one place. Policzki's mother collected Hummels, and she had dozens of them scattered all over the house, an excess of cuteness so saccharine it made his teeth ache.

"My wife did not kill anybody," Winslow said. "There has to be some other explanation. Have you talked to the owner of the building? Maybe this dead guy is one of the Worthingtons."

Policzki picked up one of the offending objects, a dimpled boy in knee pants and tight curls who carried a shepherd's crook. Odd, he thought, absently running his thumb over its cool, smooth surface, that Winslow should seem more interested in the dead man than in his missing wife.

"Technically, the house is owned collectively by the Worthington heirs," Lorna said. "The executor of the estate, Bruce Worthington, is out of the country right now, traveling in Europe. We're trying to reach him."

Policzki set down Little Boy Blue, leaned against the china cabinet and crossed his arms.

"Maybe…" Winslow's brows drew together in concentration. "Maybe she witnessed something that frightened her. Maybe she saw the killer." His skin, taut across his cheekbones, seemed almost too small for his face. Too tight. "Maybe," he said, "she's hiding from someone."

Policzki met Lorna's gaze and held it for an instant. She

leaned closer to the professor, elbows braced on her knees. "What makes you say that?"

Winslow loosened his tie a little further, but it did nothing to heighten his color. He still looked like somebody's washed-out bed linens. "No particular reason. I'm just thinking out loud. Trying to come up with some logical explanation."

"Have you noticed anything unusual about your wife's behavior lately? Any personality changes? Has she seemed more irritable than usual? More nervous? More secretive?"

"None of the above," Winslow said. "Kaye's just been her usual self."

"Which is?"

"I'm not sure I understand the question, Detective."

"If you could describe your wife to me in one word, what would it be?"

"Ah. I see. I'd probably say driven."

"Driven?"

Winslow shifted position, digging his backside deeper into the sofa's plush cushions. "My wife's enough of a workaholic to make the rest of us look like slackers. I know it sounds like a cliché, but Kaye eats, drinks and breathes real estate. She's never off duty. Evenings, weekends, holidays. If she's not out showing properties, she's on the phone, drumming up business."

"I'd think," Policzki said, "that might cause friction in the household."

Winslow blinked a couple of times, as though he'd forgotten there was a third person in the room. "Friction?"

"Well," Policzki said, his gaze focused directly on the professor's face, "if my wife worked 24–7, after a while I'd start to feel neglected."

"I'm not neglected. There's nothing wrong with my marriage, if that's what you're implying. Kaye and I are adults. I understand the importance of her job, and she understands the importance of mine. We do our best to accommodate each other's needs."

Across the room, Lorna crossed shapely legs and adjusted the hem of her skirt. "Then you don't fight at all?" she said.

"Of course we fight. All couples fight."

"Of course," she agreed. "About what?"

Had Winslow gone even paler, or was it a trick of the light? "I don't know," he said. "What does any couple fight about? Maybe I left the toilet seat cover up again, or she left the cap off the toothpaste. Or I forgot to pick up milk on the way home."

Policzki stepped away from the china cabinet and stood behind Lorna's chair. "Tolstoy once said that all happy families are alike, but each unhappy family is unhappy in its own way."

Winslow's mouth thinned and his eyes lost some of their warmth. "We're not unhappy, Detective."

Soothingly, Lorna said, "Nobody said you were."

"He implied it. I'm trying to be cooperative."

"And we appreciate it," Lorna said. "Let's change direction for a minute. What was your wife wearing when she left the house this morning?"

"Ah…let me think." Winslow ran the fingers of both hands through his hair while he thought about it. "A red suit," he said finally. "Yeah, that's it. A red suit and matching heels. White silk chemise top underneath."

"Any jewelry?"

"Just her wedding ring. A wide gold band with a single

marquise-cut diamond. One carat. Oh, and her Rolex. She never leaves the house without it."

"Just like American Express. Karl Malden would be proud. And she was driving her car this morning? The red 2005 BMW?"

"That's right."

"Dr. Winslow," Policzki said, "where were you this afternoon between, say, two and four?"

He wasn't imagining the hostility he saw in Winslow's eyes. It was real. But he had to give the guy points for control. "I was in my office," Winslow said. "Working. I teach two classes every Tuesday. I spent the time between classes doing online research for a paper I'm presenting at a symposium in Kansas City next month."

"Is there anybody who can vouch for your presence? Did anybody see you there? Did you talk to anybody, take any phone calls, while you were there?"

A muscle twitched in Winslow's jaw. He looked at Lorna as if seeking support. When it didn't come, he said, "No. I kept the door shut to discourage interruptions. If I leave it open, I don't get any work done."

"So you have no alibi for the time in question. That could pose a problem, Professor, if we don't locate your wife."

"Look…" Winslow's eyes suddenly went damp. "You have to know how worried I am about Kaye. If something's happened to her—" He closed his eyes and shook his head. A single tear escaped from the corner of his eye. Policzki watched in fascination as it trickled down his cheek. "No," he said after a moment of silence, "I won't even go there. Not yet. I refuse to believe that anything's happened to her. There's a reasonable explanation for all of this. I don't know what it is yet, but we'll find it."

Gently, Lorna said, "Does your wife have any enemies, Professor? Anybody you can think of who might wish her harm?"

He looked at her, blinked a couple of times. "Enemies? What possible reason could anyone have for wishing my wife harm?"

"I don't know. That's why I'm asking you."

Winslow had begun to perspire profusely. The underarms of his shirt were ringed with sweat. "No," he said, his voice a little shakier than before. "I'm not aware of any enemies who might wish her harm."

"She hasn't mentioned anything about problems at work?" Lorna said. "A tiff with a co-worker, a disgruntled client? A deal that went south? A competitor who thinks Winslow & DeLucca is horning in on his territory and wants to even the odds?"

"She hasn't said anything to me. You should probably talk to Mia. If anything like that was going on, Mia would know."

"Who's Mia?"

"Mia DeLucca. My sister. She and Kaye are business partners."

Lorna and Policzki exchanged glances. "Call her," Lorna said. "Get her over here."

Mia DeLucca sat in a line of cars at the tollbooth, inching her way forward, one car length at a time, in mortal danger of being asphyxiated by exhaust fumes. Ahead of her, Boston rose like the Emerald City, a breathtaking vista of twinkling lights and soaring buildings. Behind her lay ninety miles of turnpike, ninety miles of brutal, bumper-to-bumper traffic, ninety miles of crazed Massachusetts drivers, at least half of them fueled by road rage.

The trip from Springfield had been a nightmare. After eight hours of tedious real estate seminars, all she wanted was to go home and soak in a hot bubble bath. But she'd been expected to eat dinner with the rest of the presenters before they went their separate ways, so she'd made the best of it and splurged on a meal of shrimp scampi and a single glass of white wine. Even taking into account the ninety minutes that dinner took from start to finish, she still would've made it home by seven-thirty if fate hadn't intervened in the form of a semi truck that had jackknifed and overturned on the Mass Pike somewhere near Framingham. It had taken over an hour for emergency personnel to right it, while Mia and nine trillion other drivers sat at a standstill.

When she realized how late she would be, she'd called Kevin from her cell phone so he wouldn't worry. She should have known better. Her son had expressed sympathy in typical unfocused teenage fashion, meaning he was wrapped up in some computer game and hadn't been thinking about her at all. He'd undoubtedly forget her existence again the instant he hung up the phone. It was a good thing that she planned to amass a fortune in real estate before she retired. If Kevin was responsible for taking care of her in her old age, she'd probably end up living in a refrigerator box on some downtown street corner. Her son would be too busy playing Grand Theft Auto to remember the aged crone who'd given birth to him all those years ago.

The line of cars inched closer to the tolls, and as her engine shuddered in protest, Mia drummed her fingernails on the steering wheel. Somewhere between Springfield and Boston, her odometer had rolled past three hundred thousand miles. It was nearing time to send the ancient Blazer to the boneyard, but she was loath to spend the money on a new car. At least the old girl was paid for. Embarrassing to drive, but paid for. The previous owner, a twenty-year-old kid from Revere, had pimped it out with shiny black paint, chrome wheels and opaque, black-tinted windows. Kev, of course, loved the damn thing. He called it her Mafia staff car.

Kaye, on the other hand, was forever hounding her to buy a new car. Her sister-in-law was a strong proponent of the you-have-to-look-successful-to-be-successful philosophy. That might work fine for Kaye, who drove a flashy BMW and dressed like Ivana Trump. But Kaye wasn't feeding and clothing a seventeen-year-old boy with a hollow leg and feet that wouldn't stop growing. She wasn't paying off student loans and a killer mortgage. And she certainly wasn't going it alone. She had a husband to help pay the bills, a husband who was solid, respectable and gainfully employed.

Mia finally reached the tollbooth. The toll taker, a sallow-faced man in his sixties, wordlessly took the five-dollar bill she offered, and shoved the change into her hand with sullen impatience. Checking her rearview mirror, she pulled away from the tolls, changed lanes and shot across town through the Big Dig tunnel in a quarter of the time it had taken back in the days of the elevated expressway. She took a downtown exit and quickly found herself in the heart of the North End. Boston's Little Italy, with its narrow, congested streets, its restaurants and its pastry and butcher shops, possessed an old-world charm and a warm, neighborhood feel Mia hadn't known existed until she had married Nick and moved here. Now, she couldn't imagine living anywhere else.

She climbed the hill and turned onto her street, found a tiny opening at the curb only two houses down from her own, and squeezed into it. Shutting off the engine, she studied her house, assessing its curb appeal, admiring the brick and stone exterior, the bay windows, the freshly painted front door. She'd bought the house seven months ago, and still the sight of it sent a tiny thrill down her spine. She hadn't been in the market for a house; she'd originally brought a client here, a thirtyish yuppie banker looking to invest in the recently fashionable North End. He'd wanted something he could buy cheaply, renovate and turn over in five or six years. The house had just come on the market, and the asking price, while a little steep, still didn't reflect the skyrocketing prices she'd been seeing all over the Greater Boston Area.

The house hadn't been what her client was looking for. Too expensive, too much work to be done. But Mia had walked through the front door and fallen instantly in love. The house might need work, but she was handy with a hammer and a paintbrush. She'd walked from room to room, picturing what she could do with the place even as she extolled its virtues to her client and prayed he wouldn't love it the way she did.

It was the courtyard that sold her. It was exquisite, a sun-dappled oasis tucked away behind the house, accessible to the street only by a narrow alley that ended in a locked wrought-iron gate. Although it had been a blustery February day when she'd looked at the house, she had seen the tiny courtyard's potential. She could picture it blooming in a riot of color, with tubs of pink and white impatiens and long wooden planters overflowing with red geraniums. A park bench over here, maybe some kind of water fountain over there, with cascading sprays of greenery everywhere.

She'd grown up without flowers, without any of the feminine touches a mother would have brought to her life. Johnny Winslow hadn't exactly been Martha Stewart. Mia's old man had been too busy drinking and committing the petty crimes that kept him on a first-name basis with various members of the local constabulary to place any stock in something as frivolous as flowers. Or any home decor more exotic than a tableful of empty Pabst Blue Ribbon bottles.

Mia had gone home that night and spent hours crunching numbers. Winslow & DeLucca was doing well, but she and Kaye had agreed at the start of their partnership not to bleed it dry. They lived on their personal commissions and filtered most of the agency's share right back into the firm. The real estate business was notoriously unpredictable, and she had to be sure she had enough money tucked away to cover the next dry spell. In another year, Kevin would be off to college, and Mia didn't even want to think about what that would cost.

She'd weighed her options and her finances carefully. It had been close, but in the end, the little courtyard, with its old-world charm, had won out. In the morning, she'd gone into the office, called the listing Realtor and made an offer. It had been accepted immediately. Four weeks later, she'd signed papers and the previous owner had handed over the keys. Now she had a home that belonged to her (or would, after 356 more payments), a never-ending renovation project that filled every hour of her spare time, and a hefty mortgage that kept her awake at night thinking up creative ways to put more cash into her bank account. Fear of starvation, she'd discovered, was a powerful motivator.

She found Kevin at his desk, his lanky six-foot-three

frame hunched over a gargantuan computer monitor. He handled the joy stick with rapid and accurate movements as the *vroom-vroom* of racing automobile engines, accompanied by squealing tires and a frenzy of gunshots, poured from the wall-mounted speakers. Pausing in the open doorway, Mia made a sweeping assessment of his room: the empty pizza box beside his desk; the clunky size-thirteen sneakers—bought a month ago and probably already outgrown—carelessly discarded in the middle of the floor; the dog-eared *Star Wars* poster; the dirty socks collecting dust bunnies beneath the unmade bed. Kev's housekeeping skills might be lacking, but this was his space. As long as there were no drugs hidden in his underwear drawer, as long as the dirty socks eventually got washed and nothing was growing under the bed, she let him keep his room the way he wanted it.

Leaning against the door frame, she said, "Killed any bad guys lately?"

"*Shit!* I mean, shoot." Kevin glanced warily over his shoulder. "Geez, Mom, you just got me killed. Now I have to start all over again."

She raised an eyebrow. "Forgive me for the intrusion."

"You could at least knock first. You scared the crap out of me." Finally remembering the manners she'd drilled into his head since birth, he leaned back in his chair, swiveled in her direction and said, "So how was the seminar?"

"Have you ever watched paint dry? Multiply that times ten, and you'll have an idea."

His grin was quick and broad. "Sorta like sitting through Miss Crandall's English class."

"Sorta like that."

"So," he said, "I have something to ask you."

Cautiously, she nodded. "Okay. Ask."

"Michelle's family is flying down to Tampa for the Columbus Day weekend. They're leaving on Thursday night. They invited me to come along. Can I go?"

"They're flying all the way to Tampa for three days?"

"Three days, four nights. They do it all the time. They have a condo down there, and it's right on the beach. There's plenty of room. I'd have my own room and everything. It would be really cool, Mom. The sun, the sand, the swaying palm trees."

The sex, she thought, but didn't say it. What kind of supervision would the Olsons provide? Would it be sufficient to keep Kevin from sneaking into Michelle's bedroom while the rest of the family was asleep? She knew the kids were deeply involved, and she'd spoken to Kevin some time ago about safe sex. Mia wasn't sure if their relationship had reached that level yet, but if it hadn't, it was bound to in the near future. Anybody who looked at the two of them together could tell. One of Mia's biggest fears was that Michelle would get pregnant and both their young lives would be ruined. Could she trust her son to exercise good judgment?

Mia took a deep breath. "Who's paying for your plane ticket?"

It wasn't the question she wanted to ask, and they both knew it. But because it was the opening she'd provided, he jumped into it eagerly. "Don't worry, Mom, I already told them I'd pay for it myself. I knew you wouldn't want me to let them take on the extra expense. This time of year, a ticket to Florida's pretty cheap if you buy it online. I have enough money saved up. I already talked to Denny. He says I can have the time off from work. And all my teachers are giving me my assignments early so I won't miss anything important."

Her son was one clever boy. He'd covered all the bases. "Let me think about it," she said. "How soon do you have to have an answer?"

"Tomorrow. Mr. Olson needs to know how many tickets to buy."

"I'll let you know in the morning. Right now, I'm taking a hot bath."

She started to move away from the doorway, but his voice stopped her. "Mom?"

Mia turned back to her son, waited. "I know what you're worried about," he said, raising his gaze to hers. "Michelle and I are seventeen years old. We're smart and we're careful." A flush spread across his cheeks, but he bravely continued. "We respect each other, and we don't take chances. We know how much we have to lose. So please don't worry about us. We know what we're doing, and we're acting like responsible adults."

Well. It looked as if she had her answer. Something tightened inside Mia's chest, and she felt a momentary urge to cry over the realization that her son was sexually active. He was so young. It seemed just yesterday he was taking his first steps, learning to ride a bike, becoming an Eagle Scout. Was he emotionally mature enough to handle a sexual relationship? Who would guide him through those shark-infested waters? For the first time in Kevin's young life, she felt totally inadequate as a parent. She'd done well, raising him alone after Nick died, but there were times when a boy needed a father, and this was one of them.

Mia stepped back into her son's room, leaned over his chair and gave him a hug. "I'm proud of you," she said.

Most kids his age, male kids anyway, would have struggled to escape, but not Kevin. He hugged her back with the same enthusiasm with which he faced everything in life. "Thanks, Mom," he said. "I'm pretty proud of you, too."

Kevin DeLucca was his own person. He didn't let peer pressure influence him, and he didn't give a rat's behind that it wasn't cool to actually like your parents. Most adolescents were sullen and sulky, but Kevin was sunny and upbeat. His and Mia's relationship was based on trust, mostly because he had never given her any reason not to trust him. Mia knew how lucky she was to have a son like that.

"I'll talk to you in the morning," she promised. "Don't stay up too late."

She'd just started to run her bath when the phone rang. It was past ten o'clock, late for a phone call, and for an instant, the old fear crept up through her, fanning out in a wall of flame across her chest and tightening around her throat. Back in the day, back when she was a kid, a call after 10:00 p.m. invariably meant that Dad was in trouble again. Back in jail on a D&D, occasionally something worse.

But those days were in the distant past. It had been fifteen years since she'd last seen Johnny Winslow, nearly as long since a late-night phone call meant trouble. It was probably just Bev, calling to remind her about an early morning appointment. Or one of Kev's buddies who'd chosen to ignore her no-calls-after-nine-o'clock rule.

Kevin's voice yanked her back to the present. "Mom," he yelled, "it's for you."

Tying her soft flannel robe more tightly around her, she eyed the claw-foot bathtub with great longing before turning off the taps and padding barefoot into her bedroom.

"I've got it," she said into the telephone receiver, and heard the click as Kevin hung up. "Hello?"

But it wasn't her administrative assistant's voice she heard. It was her brother's. "Mia," he said, "it's Sam. Can you come over to the house? The police are here, and Kaye's missing."

Three

A single unmarked police car sat at the curb behind Sam's Volvo. Mia parked three houses down and locked the Blazer. Adjusting the soft leather gloves she'd worn to ward off the evening chill, she walked up the three steps to the door and rang the bell. A plainclothes cop wearing a shoulder holster and a deliberately neutral expression answered the door. Beneath the police academy stiffness, he was cute as the proverbial button. Tall and lanky and handsome. But he looked so young that she felt like a pedophile for the salacious thoughts that raced through her head. She shoved them aside and followed him into the living room, where her brother sat on the cream-colored leather couch. His hair was mussed, as though he'd been running his fingers through it.

In the armchair across from him sat another plainclothes cop, a fortyish woman in a gray suit, her chestnut hair clipped in a short, no-nonsense style. Her blue eyes were sharp and intelligent as she gave Mia a thorough once-over.

Sam glanced up, looking unfocused and weary. When he saw Mia, his entire face changed. Warmth flooded his eyes, and one corner of his mouth turned up in a half smile so loaded with gratitude it was almost painful to witness. He looked like a drowning man who'd just been thrown a life preserver. "Mia," he said, standing and crossing the room. He took her in his arms and hugged her, hard. "Thank God you got here so quickly."

She glanced past his shoulder at the cops and whispered, "Sam? What the hell is going on here?"

"Ms. DeLucca," the female cop said in a brisk voice as no-nonsense as her hairstyle. "Detective Lorna Abrams." She gave a brief nod toward the younger cop. "Detective Policzki. We'd appreciate it if you could sit down with us and answer a few questions."

Mia stepped free of her brother's arms. Policzki, her erstwhile doorman, stood in front of the bay window, feet planted firmly apart, arms crossed, his silent demeanor rivaling that of the guards at Buckingham Palace. Mia had an overwhelming urge to tickle him, just to see if he was human.

Squelching it, she removed her coat and gloves and, tossing them over the back of the couch, took a seat. "Kaye is missing?" she said, her gaze moving back and forth between the two detectives.

"It's a little more complicated than that," Abrams said.

"Meaning?"

"This afternoon," she explained, "Kaye Winslow had an appointment to show one of your listings. The Worthington house on Commonwealth."

"Yes, of course. She mentioned it this morning."

"When the buyer arrived, nobody answered his knock, but the house was unlocked, so he walked in——" Abrams and Policzki met each other's eyes before she turned her gaze back on Mia "——directly into a homicide scene."

Mia felt the color draining from her face. "Homicide," she whispered. "Is Kaye—"

"We don't know where Kaye is, Ms. DeLucca. The victim was a male, and so far we've been unable to identify him. Mrs. Winslow wasn't at the scene." Abrams paused. "But her briefcase was."

"Oh, God." This was every Realtor's secret nightmare, the fear that they would place their trust in the wrong person and end up paying the price for the mistake. How many hours had Mia spent alone with some stranger in an empty house? Every time she met a new client, the fear was there, hovering at the periphery of her mind. Some of her peers had taken to carrying stun guns for protection. Just last week a fellow broker had shown her the Taser she kept hidden in her purse.

"What about the buyer?" Mia demanded. "Has anybody talked to him?"

Policzki spoke up. "Philip Armentrout. CEO of Geminicorp in Cambridge. They manufacture medical equipment. Mr. Armentrout has been questioned, and his whereabouts prior to arriving at the Comm Ave residence verified. He's still not off the hook, but he looks clean."

"He looks clean? What the hell does that mean?"

Policzki's eyes were brown, a soft, rich shade that was completely at odds with his cool demeanor. "It means," he said, "that we have no reason to believe Philip Armentrout was involved."

"That's just ducky," she said. "In the meantime, what are you doing to try to find Kaye?"

It was Abrams who answered. "We're following standard protocol—"

"Standard protocol? What the hell does that mean? My

brother's wife is missing. A man is dead. She could be in terrible danger! While you're sitting here talking to me, the trail could be going cold. She might be—"

"Mia," Sam warned, "please. Just listen to what she has to say."

"Let me finish," Abrams said, not unkindly. "We're pouring all our available resources into locating Mrs. Winslow. But these things take time. In the absence of a crystal ball, we need to talk to a lot of people, ask a lot of questions. Which is why I'm sitting here talking to you right now."

Mia reminded herself to keep her cool, reminded herself that these two people were supposed to know what they were doing. They were professionals who did this kind of thing every day, and they weren't frazzled and frightened like she was. As Johnny Winslow's daughter, she'd learned early that it didn't pay to antagonize the cops. Taking a deep breath to quell her rising temper, she said, "I'm sorry. But I've never been faced with a situation like this before. Go ahead. Ask me anything. I'll answer as best I can."

From across the room, Policzki inquired, "Ms. De-Lucca, can you think of any reason why Kaye Winslow might want to disappear?"

"You're kidding," she said. "Right? You're not suggesting she disappeared of her own free will?"

"We have to look at all the possibilities."

He was too damn cool, and her temper began to flare again. "There is no reason. I'm sure Sam has already told you that."

Policzki barely gave Sam a glance. "We've heard what Dr. Winslow had to say. Now we want to hear your point of view."

"You just heard it. This is preposterous. Tell me, Detective, exactly what do you know so far?"

"Three things," Policzki said, with such unflappable cool that he reminded her of the infamous Mr. Spock of *Star Trek* fame. All that was missing was the pointed ears. "Number one," he said, "a man is dead. Number two, Mrs. Winslow's briefcase was found at the scene. Her BlackBerry, her wallet, her credit cards and identification were all there. Number three, Mrs. Winslow herself was absent." He paused, those brown eyes of his burning a hole in Mia. "You do the math."

"It's all circumstantial. It means nothing."

"Which is why," Lorna Abrams said, "we have to ask so many questions. That's how we find the truth."

"Fine," she said. "Here's the truth. I have no idea why Kaye might want to disappear. She leads a charmed life. Look around you, Detectives. She has a successful business, a lovely home, a picture-perfect family. What possible reason could she have for wanting to leave that behind?"

"Homicide," Policzki stated, "is a pretty compelling reason."

"But there's no reason why she would be involved in a homicide! Not unless she happened to be in the wrong place at the wrong time!"

"That's a possibility we're looking into," Abrams said. "What about enemies? Anybody you can think of who doesn't like her?"

Mia clasped her hands in her lap and tried to find a diplomatic way of answering the question. "We all have people who dislike us," she said. "Nobody's universally loved. Kaye is a strong, vibrant, forceful businesswoman. A salesperson, with all the attendant clichés that go along with the title. She's good at marketing, good at persuasion, good at manipulating people into doing what she wants. She's a bit ruthless, and I mean that only in the most positive of ways. Because of that, she moves a lot of real estate. In our business, that's the ultimate goal. Kaye can be very charming. She can also be—" she shot a glance at Sam "—shall we say difficult? A little abrasive at times. She goes after what she wants, and sometimes her methods aren't quite conducive to winning friends and influencing people." Mia gave an apologetic shrug of her shoulders. "But as far as anybody wanting to do her harm, no. That I can't imagine."

"Do you think you might come up with any names? People she may have had problems with in the recent past? Anybody who thought they got cheated in a real estate deal? Somebody she had words with? Somebody she cut off in traffic?"

"No. You're going on a wild-goose chase. Whoever this dead man is, he was obviously the target. Not Kaye. Otherwise—" She shot another glance at Sam, took a deep breath and continued "—otherwise, you'd have found two victims. Or a different one. Am I not correct?"

"Possibly," Abrams said. "Possibly not. It's too soon to start theorizing about what happened. We have to look at all the information first, and we just don't have that yet."

"And while you're gathering information, my sister-in-law could be dying. Or already dead." Mia glanced at her brother, who sat beside her on the couch, his hands in his lap, his expression slack, as though he was in shock. "Has it even occurred to you people that she might be injured?" Mia turned her attention back to the cops. "That she might have driven herself to the hospital? Have you checked the local emergency rooms?"

"We have somebody looking into that."

"I'd like to backtrack a minute," Policzki said. "You said that people sometimes found Kaye to be difficult. In your personal dealings with her, have you found that to be true?"

Mia didn't like the direction this was headed. Coolly, she said, "Only occasionally. I'm more of a soft sell than Kaye. For the most part, our personalities mesh in a way that works for us. We have good chemistry. Surprisingly few disagreements. We work well together."

"Okay," Abrams said. "She's married to your brother. You worked together. You saw each other every day. Women in relationships like that often share the intimate details of their lives. Did she have any deep, dark secrets? Maybe something—" Abrams eyed Sam "—she didn't want her husband to know about?"

Mia didn't like the way the woman spoke of Kaye in the past tense, as if it were a foregone conclusion that she wasn't coming back. "Kaye and I aren't that close," she said, deliberately using present tense. "We have a good working relationship, but we don't share the intimate details of our lives with each other. She isn't the type to share confidences. And neither am I."

Don't trust, don't tell. That was what she'd learned at Johnny Winslow's knee. The less said to outsiders, the better. The fewer people you trusted, the safer you were. She'd learned it as a little girl and still, at thirty-six, she hadn't been able to erase it. *If you don't tell anybody your secrets, they stay secret.* They still resonated in her head, the philosophies of the petty thief and small-time crook whose DNA she shared. Johnny Winslow's legacy to his kids.

Thanks, Dad.

The policewoman's cool blue eyes elicited in her an inexplicable desire to squirm like a little kid sitting on the miscreants' bench outside the principal's office. Mia hadn't done a thing wrong, yet the woman's intense scrutiny made her feel guilty. "Would you call her a friend?" Abrams asked.

Again, she pondered how to answer, finally decided on the truth. "We're friendly," she said.

"Which isn't quite the same thing as being friends."

"There are different levels of friendship, Detective."

"Interesting answer. How long have you and Kaye been partners?"

"Three years. I started the agency four years ago. The market was strong and, as the business grew, I found myself with more work than I could handle. So I decided to take on a partner. It was a good business decision. Kaye's brought in a tremendous number of new clients. Both buyers and sellers. As I said, she's a real go-getter."

"And has the agency been lucrative?"

"Lucrative enough. There are always start-up costs involved in running your own business, and it takes a year or two before you really begin to see any profits. But yes, the last three years, since Kaye came on board, we've done quite well."

"And she's been married to your brother for how long?"

"Two and a half years. They met at a dinner party at my house."

"So you knew Kaye before your brother did."

"Yes. Over the years, we'd met two or three times—real estate's a small world. Even in a city the size of Boston, you keep running into the same people. But we didn't really know each other as anything more than nodding acquaintances. She was recommended to me by Marty Scalia, a close friend of mine. He runs the Scalia Agency.

I worked for five years for Marty before I left to start my own agency. When I realized I needed a partner, I turned to Marty because I knew he had his finger on the pulse of the local real estate world. Kaye had come to work for him after changing agencies a couple of times. She was a rising star, on her way up. He recommended her to me. It's a decision I've never had reason to regret."

"Is that common?" Policzki said. "Hopping from agency to agency?"

"It's not uncommon. An agent can sell real estate anywhere, but like anything else, it's better to have the right fit."

Policzki crossed the room and sat on the arm of the couch, uncomfortably close to her. "Where were you today, Ms. DeLucca?"

Another facet of Johnny Winslow's legacy sprang to life in full Technicolor: rampant paranoia. "Excuse me?" she said. "Are you implying that I might have had something to do with this—this mess? Because if you are, Detective, I resent the implication."

"It's a routine question," Abrams said. "You're one of the most significant people in Kaye Winslow's life. The homicide, and her disappearance, took place at one of your real estate listings. We have to ask."

Mia raised her chin. "I was at a conference in Springfield. I left at six-thirty this morning and got back about a half hour ago."

Policzki said, "Is there anybody who can confirm your whereabouts?"

Every time the young detective opened his mouth, she liked him a little less. Of their own volition, her fists clenched. Forcing them to relax, she snapped, "Just the hundred and fifty real estate agents who attended the seminar I ran from two to four this afternoon, 'Maintaining Strong Sales in a Troubled Economy.' I can give you a brochure if you don't believe me."

Abrams scribbled something on a notepad. Ignoring Mia's sarcasm, she said, "If we need it, we'll ask." She dropped the pad into her briefcase and snapped it shut. Rising from the chair, she said, "Dr. Winslow, we'll need a recent photo of your wife. A good, clear one."

"Check the agency Web page," Mia said. "You'll find a recent photo."

Policzki reached into the **inside** pocket of his suit coat, briefly flashing his service revolver in its underarm holster, and pulled out a couple of business cards and a pen. He handed one of the cards to Mia, then flipped over the second one and wrote the URL she gave him on the back.

"That'll do for now," Abrams said. "I trust you'll both be available if we have any more questions."

To Mia, it sounded vaguely like a threat. She glared at Abrams, then at her stone-faced partner. "So what happens next?"

"We keep doing what we've been doing, and hope we get a break. We'll contact you if there's anything you need to know. We'd appreciate you doing the same. If you think of anything, no matter how small or insignificant it might seem, please call. Oh, and one more thing. We'll need you to make up a list of Kaye Winslow's friends, coworkers, people she sees on a regular basis. Names, addresses, phone numbers if you have them. Everybody who's a significant part of her life. We'd like it as soon as possible."

Was there any end to the woman's demands? Mia followed them to the front hall and held the door for them. Abrams breezed out without so much as a goodbye, but Policzki paused at the threshold. His eyes met Mia's and stayed there for an instant. "Have a nice evening," he said.

"Right," Mia said. "You, too."

And she slammed the door behind them.

The house seemed too quiet. Even the movement of traffic on nearby Tremont Street seemed hushed and distant. Sam returned to the living room, his footsteps silent on the Aubusson carpet. His coloring was ashen, his hair a mess from his habit of raking nervous fingers through it. "Can I get you a drink?" he offered. "Glass of wine? Something stronger? You look like you could use one."

"That goes double for you," Mia said. "Scotch, if you have it. What the hell is this all about, Sam?"

He moved to the bar, dropped ice from a bucket into a pair of squat glasses and poured two fingers of Glenlivet into them. Crossing the room, he handed one to her. "I don't know," he said.

"Who is this dead guy? Is there something going on that I don't know about?"

He sat down across from her, in the chair that Lorna Abrams had used. "Of course not," he said. But he didn't meet her eyes, and Mia felt a flicker of fear.

"Sam?" she prodded.

He let out a long-suffering sigh and closed his eyes. "Fine," he said, opening them again. "I might as well tell you. We had a terrible fight the other night." Still avoiding her gaze, he lowered his chin to his chest and studied the movement of the ice cubes swirling around in his glass. "I said reprehensible things to her. Every one of them true, but still—" He raised the drink and knocked it back in a single swallow. "I didn't tell them."

"The cops? Why?"

His troubled eyes finally met hers. "There's no sense in confusing the issue," he stated. "I don't want Abrams and Policzki wasting their time focusing on me. They need to find her."

This wasn't adding up. "Why would they focus on you?"

"Are you kidding? The husband's always the first person they look at. And I don't have an alibi for the time in question. If only I'd known she was going to disappear—" He choked back a laugh. "I could have managed to manufacture one."

"Oh, Sam."

Darkly, he said, "Good thing Mom never lived to see this day."

Their mother had died far too young. Johnny Winslow had seen to that, and Mia still hated him for it. But Mom's death had nothing to do with this situation. Bringing it up was Sam's way of redirecting Mia's attention.

"Now you're feeling sorry for yourself," she said.

"Damn right, I'm feeling sorry for myself! Yesterday, my life was rolling along the way it always does. Stale and boring and comfortably predictable. Now my wife is missing, she might have been involved in a homicide, and I can't even tell the cops the truth for fear of tying a noose around my neck."

"You don't think her disappearance has anything to do with your fight?"

"I don't know what the hell to think."

"What was the fight about?"

He lifted clear blue eyes to hers. "Please. Allow me a little dignity. Let's just say it wasn't pretty."

"When was any fight ever pretty? But why keep it from

the cops, if you don't have anything to hide?" She gave her brother a long, considering look. "You don't have anything to hide, do you?"

"For God's sake, Mia. Don't you know me better than that?"

She'd thought she did. But something wasn't adding up here. Were there problems in the relationship? Issues she wasn't aware of? She'd always believed that Kaye and Sam's marriage was solid. Neither of them had given her any reason to believe anything else.

But now, he'd planted a seed of doubt. She wanted to prod, wanted to shake him if that's what it took to get the truth out of him. But she knew her brother too well to push. If he'd thought it was any of her business, he would have told her. It would be pointless to pry. Instead, she asked, "Have you told Gracie yet?"

Sam shook his head. "She's upstairs. I suppose I have to tell her something, don't I?"

"Do you want me to do it?"

The ambivalence in his eyes told her he wanted to say yes. But to his credit, he shook his head again. "She's my daughter. It's my job. But thanks for offering."

"What are you going to tell her?"

"I don't know. I don't know what to say. Or, for that matter, what to do." He rose from the chair, walked to the bar and poured himself a refill. This time, he didn't bother with ice. "I have a job I need to get to tomorrow morning. Classes to teach. Exams to grade. The semester won't grind to a halt because my wife has disappeared."

For the first time, the enormity of the situation landed squarely on top of her. Mia set down her untouched glass. "I think you should tell the police about the fight," she said.

"Better they should hear it from you than from some loud-mouthed neighbor."

"How the hell do you propose I do that? Call Abrams up and tell her I forgot one tiny detail? That'll go over big."

"Abrams won't be happy no matter how she hears it. But if she has to find out from someone else, it'll make you look as if you're trying to hide something. And they'll waste precious time trying to prove that you had something to do with Kaye's disappearance. Time they could spend on finding out what really happened. We don't know who this dead man is. Or where Kaye is. If somebody's taken her…" Mia paused, her own words sounding implausible "…there might not be much time."

Gracie Lee Winslow was fat.

Kàye kept telling her it was all in her head, but Gracie knew the truth. She saw it every time she looked in the mirror. She was chunky. Hideous. In response to this catastrophe, Gracie had tried every diet under creation: Atkins, South Beach, low-fat, low-carb, grapefruit, watermelon, vegetarian and plain old starvation. She'd even tried that crazy Bible diet, the one where you only ate foods that were mentioned in the Bible. She'd joined an online chapter of Weight Watchers, had bought a totally gay workout video and exercised until she grew so weak she nearly passed out. She'd even given laxatives a try. But nothing she'd attempted had managed to change the reflection gazing back at her from the mirror. All she could see were her chipmunk cheeks, her pudgy belly that curved out instead of in, and the thunder thighs that rubbed together when she walked. Gracie hated her oversize nose, hated her frizzy hair, hated her snooty private school with its cliques of skinny girls with their perfect hair and their perfect faces and their perfect bodies and their perfect lives. She hated that her mom was dead, hated that her dad barely noticed she was alive. Hated everything about her wretched life.

Most of all, she hated her stepmother.

If Kaye had been a nicer person, Gracie might have been willing to tolerate her. But there was something about the woman that set her teeth on edge. Not that she didn't understand why her dad had married Kaye. Like those perfect girls at school, her stepmother was drop-dead gorgeous. The woman exuded sex like a cloud of perfume. Pheromones. What man could resist? Even though it was beyond gross to imagine her dad having sex with Kaye, Gracie understood that he was a man, and men were all alike. They all wanted the same thing, and any woman who looked like Kaye Winslow would always have men groveling at her feet.

It made Gracie want to hurl.

For the last two years and seven months, her stepmother had been destroying her life. Like Casper the Friendly Ghost, Kaye tiptoed around the house, silently following Gracie from room to room, spying on her. Watching. Listening. Judging. Kaye had snooped in her bedroom while she was at school; she'd pawed through Gracie's backpack, looking for God only knew what. She'd even gone through the call list on Gracie's cell phone to find out who she'd been talking to. The bitch undoubtedly would have read all her e-mails, too, if Gracie hadn't password protected her computer.

It was infuriating. At fifteen, she was entitled to her privacy. But Kaye was determined to know every move her stepdaughter made. Determined to turn over every rock and uncover every last one of Gracie's secrets.

But if Kaye thought she held the upper hand, she had another thing coming, because Gracie wasn't the only one with secrets. Her darling stepmother had more than her share, and the secrets Kaye held would blow her marriage right out of the water if Dad ever found out about them. Thanks to the floor register in her bedroom, Gracie had a front-row seat to everything that went on downstairs. All she had to do was roll back the Oriental carpet and lie on the floor, and she could see and hear everything through that register. Kaye was so damn stupid she didn't even notice. Which meant that Gracie had accumulated a lot of dirt on her stepmother. A *lot* of dirt.

None of which meant diddly-squat compared to what she'd just heard. This was some serious shit.

When the cops had first come to the door, she'd freaked, afraid they were here about her. Afraid they knew what she'd done. But that hadn't been it at all. Something had happened today, something bad. Kaye was missing, and a man was dead. There was talk of a gun. Murder. And Gracie had the sick feeling that she might have been the one to set all this in motion.

He was only supposed to follow Kaye. Find out where she went, who she saw, what she did when she was away from the house. Gracie's directions to him had been very clear: *Be discreet. Whatever you do, don't let her know you're following her.*

Something had gone horribly wrong. Dad was downstairs right now, pacing the floor and drinking Glenlivet straight from the bottle. That wasn't a good sign; Dad wasn't much of a drinker, and that stuff tasted like crap. She knew how awful it was because she'd been taking the occasional nip since she was thirteen, since the day Dad first brought Kaye to the house and he'd looked at the woman *that way.* Like she was some piece of meat on a stick. That was the night Gracie's life had started its downhill slide. It was also the first time she'd ever gotten shit-faced drunk. She'd woken up the next day with the mother of all hangovers, but at least she'd remembered to refill the bottle with water so nobody would notice how low the level of the liquid inside had dropped.

She flipped the carpet back over the floor register, went to her desk and logged on to her laptop. *Please let him be online,* she thought as she signed into AIM. *Please, please, PLEASE let him be online.* She typed in his screen name, then checked his availability.

AIM told her: Magnum357 is not currently signed on.

Gracie let out a hard breath as dread bottled up inside her chest. She swallowed a couple of times, just to make sure her throat still worked. She didn't know any other way to reach him. They'd only started hanging out together a couple of months ago. She didn't know where he lived, didn't have his cell phone number. All she knew was his screen name—Magnum357—and his real name—Carlos—which, for all she knew, might not even be the real deal.

This was bad. This was really bad. If Dad found out she'd been seeing Carlos, who was definitely on the wrong side of twenty, not to mention *dangerous,* she'd be grounded for the next thirty years. And if the cops thought she knew something about Kaye's disappearance—not that she did, but if they found out what she'd done it would make her look pretty damn guilty—she could go to jail. For a really long time.

This was a lose-lose situation, and guess who the loser would turn out to be? Sooner or later the truth would come out about what she'd asked Carlos to do. When it did, the shit would hit the fan.

And at that point, no matter how you looked at it, she was toast.

Four

"You got in late last night."

Doug Policzki stood in a square of morning sunlight, his gaze focused intently on the shiny stainless toaster as he awaited the arrival of two perfectly browned squares of whole wheat bread. "New case," he said. The toaster popped. He pulled out his toast, tossed his necktie over his shoulder to keep it clean, and picked up the butter knife.

"When you gonna get a chance to mow the lawn? It's starting to look like *Wild Kingdom*."

Policzki opened the dishwasher and dropped the butter knife into the basket. "I don't know," he said. "This is a complicated case. It'll probably suck up a lot of my time."

"They're all complicated."

He felt a twinge of guilt. His mother was right. From earliest childhood, he'd been made to understand that his primary obligation was to the people who'd raised and nurtured him and tried to mold him into a civilized and decent human being. And he'd been a dutiful son; after his dad died, he'd moved back home to take care of his mother. But over the last year or two, he'd been increasingly remiss in those duties. The truth was that homicide took up most of his waking hours. And it was hardly fair to his mother that he always seemed to place her lower on his list of priorities than the dead bodies of strangers.

"Maybe Bernie could do it," he suggested. "Or one of the boys." His oldest sister, Debbie, and her husband, Bernie, lived three houses down and had a new lawnmower and two strapping teenage sons, neither of whom ever lifted a finger to help out their grandmother. Under the circumstances, one of them should jump into the breach before the lawn reached shoulder height.

Sounding exasperated, Linda Policzki said, "Doesn't it ever bother you?"

Policzki shot her a quizzical glance before he sliced the toast in half with a quick incision from corner to corner. "You mean *Wild Kingdom?*"

"Oh, for the love of all that's holy. I'm not talking about the lawn!" His mother's strong and capable hands momentarily stopped kneading the meat loaf she was preparing for dinner, and she gave him the evil eye. Which wasn't good news. Strong men had been known to weep when Linda Policzki turned the evil eye on them. "I'm talking," she said, "about the fact that all the people you meet are dead."

"Oh." He relaxed a little and leaned against the counter. "I meet live people all the time." He punctuated his sentence with a bite of toast.

His mother snorted. "Right," she said. "Cops and murderers."

"And lawyers, and judges, and—" he took another bite of toast, briefly considered the lovely and sophisticated Mia DeLucca, who'd looked at him last night as if he were the lowest form of pond scum "—other people."

"All that talk of autopsies must make for scintillating dinner conversation."

"They're my colleagues, Ma. These are professional relationships. We don't do dinner."

Linda went back to kneading, pouring all her energies into a meal he likely wouldn't be here to eat. Guilt gnawed at him. That was probably why she did it. She wanted him to feel guilty. It was what kept her going. His mother needed something to complain about, and she'd been blessed with a son who always managed to excel at filling that need.

It was nice to know that he excelled at something, but he wished fervently that she'd find somebody else to focus on. Anybody else. He had three sisters. Why couldn't she meddle in their lives for a change? All of them were married and, between them, they'd given her seven grandchildren. Managing the lives of seven kids should be more than enough to keep her busy. Especially Jake and Jesse, who could definitely use a little more management. Deb and Bernie were both lawyers, which meant that the boys had been raised by a series of housekeepers. Which was pretty much the equivalent of being raised by a pack of wolves. There'd been little structure and less discipline. Jake and Jesse could undoubtedly benefit from a little of Gram's influence.

But no dice. Linda Policzki had apparently decided her mission in life was to focus all her attention, all her energy, on her youngest child and only son.

A few months ago, he'd tried to convince his mother to take a cruise. Fantasies of a shipboard romance had played in his head like an old-fashioned movie reel: Linda meeting up with some lonely widower and being swept off her feet. Then traipsing around the world on a once-in-a-life-time honeymoon. He could picture his mother backpacking through the rugged terrain of the Himalayas or riding a camel across the desert. The woman was as solid and invincible as concrete.

He'd brought home a stack of brochures. He'd even gone so far as to offer to pay for her ticket. But she'd laughed at him. He needed her here, she'd said, and that had been that.

Policzki had a suspicion that somebody had gotten a raw deal. He'd moved back home to take care of his widowed mother, but it seemed that more and more, it was his mother who was taking care of him. Whether he wanted her to or not. He wasn't sure which of them had gotten the short end of that stick. But one of them surely had. And he'd begun to wonder if, when his sisters had ganged up on him and practically begged him to move back home, that had been their intent all along.

Without looking up from the meat loaf she was spooning into a baking pan, his mother said, "I need a favor."

Policzki froze, his morning cup of coffee halfway to his mouth. This could mean only one thing. He could feel it coming, could feel the change in the air, like the stillness before a storm. An electrical charge that hadn't been there a moment ago. *No,* he screamed silently. *Please. Don't say the words. Don't do this to me.*

But it was too late. "Brenda Petrucci's niece is visiting," she said. "Melissa. She's never been to Boston before. Brenda says she's a nice girl, maybe a little backward socially, considering that she was raised on a farm in Iowa. She just graduated from veterinary school, and since Brenda doesn't know anybody else who's Melissa's age, I told her you'd be happy to show her the town."

He closed his eyes. Sighed. "Ma," he said.

"What?" She carried her mixing bowl to the sink and filled it with hot water. "You're too good now to do a favor for my oldest and dearest friend?"

"You know it's not that."

"Then what is it?"

"You have to stop playing matchmaker. I'm fully capable of finding my own women."

"I'm not playing matchmaker. I'm just trying to help out a friend. I asked your sister to invite her over for dinner. Maybe that's matchmaking, too?"

"Stop trying to confuse the issue. I can see right through you. I'm thirty years old. You have to stop treating me like I'm twelve."

Linda washed her hands at the sink. Drying them on a dish towel, she said, "If you don't want to do it, fine. Brenda will be disappointed, but she'll understand."

"I'm in the middle of a messy case. I have an unidentified corpse and a missing woman who's probably either the perpetrator or the victim of a homicide. Even if I did manage to find a few free hours, what would I talk to this girl about? I don't know a thing about veterinary medicine, and I highly doubt that she's familiar with police procedure."

"You're right. I know you're right. I'll just tell Brenda you can't do it."

He closed his eyes, knowing he was defeated. "I didn't say I wouldn't do it."

"Thank you." She tossed down the dish towel and took his face between her hands, and Policzki felt the noose tighten around his neck. "I'm not asking you to marry the girl. Just spend a little time with her. Get to know her. Show her a good time."

He didn't dare to ask just how far he was expected to go to ensure that Brenda Petrucci's niece, the Iowa farm girl who'd just graduated from veterinary school, had a good time during her first visit to Boston. It was probably better if he didn't ask. He might not like the answer.

But he'd do what his mother asked. It wouldn't hurt to escort Brenda's corn-fed niece to a play or two, maybe to the Museum of Fine Arts, or even on a harbor cruise. It would make his mother happy, and it would assuage his guilt about being derelict in his familial duties.

Policzki picked up his travel mug and kissed his mother on her smooth, scented cheek. "Tell Brenda that unless somebody else dies an untimely and violent death, I'll be happy to show her niece the town. And I'll call one of the boys about mowing the lawn. Oh, and don't hold dinner for me tonight. I might not make it home."

Her voice followed him out the door. "Am I supposed to be surprised by that?"

Sam Winslow unlocked the door to his office and flipped the light switch. The overhead fluorescents sputtered to life, casting harsh blue light over a cinder block room just big enough for his desk, a file cabinet, a narrow bookcase and a single straight-backed visitor's chair painted a hideous mauve. Sam set a steaming cup of McDonald's coffee on his desk, dropped the exam booklets he'd taken from his mailbox, and pulled the door closed behind him. He prayed that he'd managed the ten-second sprint from the department office to his cubicle without being seen. The story of the unidentified homicide victim and the missing Realtor had been front-page news this morning, and he'd fielded a half-dozen phone calls before breakfast. Reporters looking for an exclusive. Friends who'd heard the news and wanted to offer their support. The last thing he wanted was to socialize, and if he didn't hide behind closed doors, Nikki Voisine, the newly hired French instructor, was bound to stop by with her own cup of coffee to get the rest of the story right from the horse's mouth.

He hadn't slept worth a damn. Who could, under the circumstances? He kept picturing Kaye's face the last time he'd seen her, the accusation in her eyes. The disbelief. The fear. And the guilt he'd felt so deep in his stomach that it had been an actual physical ache.

Ever since the cops had shown up at his door, he'd been a wreck. Just how much did Abrams and Policzki know? Who had they talked to? Even his sister didn't know the truth, and he wasn't about to tell her. He couldn't cope with the disappointment on her face when she found out that her brother had feet of clay. Unless he could find a way of bringing the investigation to a halt, it was only a matter of time before Abrams and Policzki discovered the truth about him. When they did, his life, the life he'd worked so hard to build, would implode with the force of a ton of TNT.

Sam picked up his coffee with hands that trembled like his father's had the morning after a drinking binge. He raised the cup to his mouth and took a slug of coffee. He had to stop this. Had to stop the shaking, had to stop the thinking, had to stop the endless going around in circles, the perpetual game of what-if and if-only. If he didn't, he'd make himself crazy. *Normal,* he told himself. *You have to keep up the pretense of normal.*

Okay, so he could do normal. He *would* do normal. Sitting down behind the desk, Sam pulled out his red pen, tuned the stereo to a classical station and began grading exams.

Not his favorite job, but a necessary one. His students came from all walks of life and from a mix of age groups, but the vast majority of them shared one thing in common: they were monumentally unprepared for college. Most of their papers were riddled with spelling and grammatical errors. At some point before they entered his classroom, every one of his students had managed to graduate from high school. Yet invariably, in every class he taught, when he assigned the first three-page research paper, he had to waste valuable class time teaching them how to write one.

But this morning, he just couldn't concentrate. Couldn't differentiate between good grammar and bad, couldn't seem to remember the difference between Doric, Ionic and Corinthian columns. He checked his watch for the third time in five minutes, set down his pen and rubbed his bleary eyes. Acting as-if wasn't working. He could pretend until the cows came home, but normal didn't exist anymore. Not in his life.

And he had nobody to blame but himself.

He pulled open the bottom drawer of his desk where, tucked away beneath six years of grade books, he'd hidden a framed photo of Rachel. Kaye wouldn't have liked it if she'd known he kept his first wife's photo in his desk. She would have liked it even less if she'd known he took that photo out regularly and had long, rambling conversations with his dead wife.

It still hurt to look at her. After eight years, it should have stopped hurting. But every time he gazed at her face, his chest ached with a pain no medicine could take away.

"I've really botched things up this time, haven't I?" he told her. "Christ, Rach, I wish you were here to impart a little of your worldly wisdom. I know just what you'd say.

'Snap out of it, Winslow. Life's too short to waste it worrying.' That's what you used to tell me. I guess you were right about the short part. At least for you it was short.

"I'm scared," he murmured. "I'm not sure what to do, Rach. Maybe I should be wearing a sign that warns women away from me—Don't Marry Sam; You'll Never Survive the Marriage."

Rachel didn't answer. She never did. No matter what he told her, she just smiled at him in that loving, nonjudgmental way.

"Everything's falling apart," he said. "My marriage, my life. Payback, I guess, for past sins. I guess you'd know about that, wouldn't you?"

Rachel smiled silently back at him. Sam swiveled in his chair, stared out the window at a passing cloud. "I've been a terrible husband. I haven't even made an effort. What does that say about me? A man who lets his marriage disintegrate without even bothering to try to repair it doesn't have much of himself invested in that marriage, does he?"

Somebody knocked on his door, and Sam winced. Maybe he should just pretend he wasn't here. But pretending had gotten him nowhere so far, and he couldn't hide forever. It was better to brazen it out than to look more guilty than he already did. So he tucked Rachel's photo back into the drawer, pushed away from the desk and said, "Come in."

The door opened and Vince Tedeschi stuck his head in. "Hey, buddy," he said, his face etched with concern. "Want some company?"

Not particularly, he thought, but this was Vince, his closest friend. Sam couldn't turn him away. "Come on in," he said wearily.

Vince closed the door behind him, pulled the visitor's chair from its corner, spun it around and straddled it. "I just heard about Kaye." He folded his arms across the chair back. "This is unimaginable. Have you had any news?"

"No."

"Man, that's hard. How's Gracie taking it?"

"Gracie's the same as always. Quiet as the tomb. She and Kaye don't get along. For all I know, she could be jumping for joy about this. But there's no way to tell when she keeps it inside. Half the time I think she hates me, too."

"She doesn't hate you. She's a teenage girl. At that age, nothing you do or say is going to be the right thing. Believe me, I speak from experience. Kari and Katie barely acknowledge me. Unless they want something, and then the Bank of Dad is their favorite place for one-stop shopping."

They fell silent, both of them contemplating the mystery that was teenage womanhood. "We can't even carry on a conversation," Sam said. "We haven't been able to for years. It's as though I'm speaking English and she's speaking Swahili."

"She'll grow out of it. Until she does, good luck trying to have any kind of normal relationship with her." Vince got up from the chair and stood there awkwardly. "Do the police have any theories about where Kaye might be?"

"If they do, they haven't bothered to share them with me."

Vince shuffled his feet a little. "Listen," he said, "if you need a babysitter, or if Gracie gets lonely, she's welcome at our house anytime. Day or night."

Vince and his third wife had a young daughter. Every summer, the two families spent a couple of weeks together in a rented beach house on the Cape. Gracie thought of five-year-old Deidre as a younger sister, and always loved spending time with her. "Thanks," Sam said. "I appreciate the offer."

With false heartiness, Vince said, "Well, I'm off to slay the dragons of ignorance." He tucked the chair back into its corner and paused, hand on the doorknob. "Hang in there," he said. "If you need anything, Ellen and I are just a phone call away."

When he was gone, Sam buried his face in his hands and exhaled a hard breath. How had his life deteriorated to this point? It just kept getting worse and worse.

There was a knock at the open doorway. He looked up. The man who stood there, dressed in jeans, a navy windbreaker and a Red Sox cap, was unfamiliar. "Dr. Sam Winslow?" he said.

"Yes?"

"This is for you." He handed Sam an envelope. "Have a nice day."

Sam looked stupidly at the envelope, picked up his letter opener from the desk and slit it open. He pulled out a thick sheaf of papers and unfolded what appeared to be some kind of official-looking documents. It took his sleep-deprived mind a couple of seconds before the words in bold print at the top of the page took on form and meaning.

Petition for Divorce.

Five

The squad room was noisier than a junior high cafeteria at noon, abuzz with conversation, ringing phones and the deathly slow *ka-thunk ka-thunk* of the photocopier that was the bane of Lorna's existence. At the desk across from hers, Policzki was on the phone. "Thanks, guy," he said. "I really appreciate it, and so does Gram. Give me a call this weekend, and we'll catch that movie. Maybe pick up some pizza afterward."

Policzki hung up the phone, caught her watching him. "My nephew," he explained. "My mother's on my case about mowing the lawn. I bribed him."

"That always seems to work at my house," she said. "Just be careful you don't go overboard. By the time you're done paying for two movie tickets, popcorn and soda for two, and a teenage-boy-size pizza afterward, you could've paid to have it done by a professional."

"True, but it's worth more brownie points if I keep it in the family."

"Christ, Policzki, you need a life. Matter of fact, what you really need is your own place. How long have you been living with your mother?"

"Six years," he said. "Six long and—did I mention long?—years."

"Lord love a duck. If I had to spend six years living with my mother—or worse, *Ed's* mother—I'd tie a rope over the nearest rafter and end it all."

"She's not that bad. She means well."

"Of course she means well. She's your mother. It's part of the job description. So is making your kid's life hell if he's past twenty-five and still living at home."

"It wasn't my idea to move back home."

"Which is why you need to move out. Listen to me, kid. I know what I'm talking about. You've paid your dues and then some. If you don't cut the apron strings pretty soon, you're going to wake up some morning and realize you're forty and still living at home with Mom. Get a clue, Policzki. You must have enough money saved up by now for a down payment. Buy yourself a condo. Something small, something you can turn over in a few years if you get married and need more space."

"And leave my mother alone? I'd never be able to live with myself. The guilt would do me in."

"Oh, but you see, Policzki, there's where you're wrong. That's one more thing about mothers. We're really good at playing the guilt card. But you know what? You're not helping her by living there."

"How do you figure that?"

"You're creating an unhealthy dependence. She needs to reclaim her independence. She's a strong woman. You step back a little and watch what happens. I bet you'll see her bloom."

"You've been watching *Oprah* again, haven't you?"

"I'm serious, Policzki. The two of you need some space

between you or you'll never figure out that you're two separate people. And how convenient for you—you just happen to know a genuine, card-carrying Realtor."

"Mia DeLucca? Be serious. She hates my guts."

"I wouldn't be so sure. To know you is to love you."

"Not if I'm eyeing your brother as a possible murder suspect."

Lorna thought about it, shrugged. "I suppose that would tend to put a damper on my enthusiasm," she said.

"You think?" He leaned back in his chair and stretched his arms over his head, then lowered them. "So, tell me. Did you have any luck with the M.E.'s office?"

"Nothing yet," she said, "although not due to a lack of badgering on my part. How about you?"

"Salvatore's starting work on the BlackBerry. He'll fax us over a list of all Winslow's calls, all her appointments. We should have it by noon. Delvecchio just e-mailed me a couple photos of the victim. Maybe they'll help us with the ID."

"Shit. Can't Salvatore put a rush on it? I have a feeling we need to move fast on this one."

"That is his version of a rush. Just because you eat Wheaties every morning, Abrams, doesn't mean the whole world does. Some of us have to sleep occasionally."

Dryly, she said, "I'll try to remember that."

"I just shot the photos of the vic to the laser printer. And while you were on the phone with the M.E.'s office, I went to the Winslow & DeLucca Web page and pulled Kaye Winslow's photo. I'm having copies distributed even as we speak. I also have Jiminez working his way through the list of Winslow's friends that Mia DeLucca dropped off this morning. If he runs across anything worth more than a phone call, he'll let me know and I'll follow up with a visit in person."

Lorna rested her chin on her hand. "You know," she said, "something about this really bothers me."

Policzki leaned back in his chair and studied her with interest. "Besides the obvious?"

"Besides the obvious. Kaye Winslow fled the scene. What does common sense tell you?"

"That she's more than likely the perpetrator. But since when is homicide supposed to make sense? And we don't know for sure that she fled the scene. She may have been coerced."

"There's something about Sam Winslow. I don't like the guy. He's hiding something."

"Which might or might not be germane to the case."

"You did see the tears, right? Tell me I didn't imagine them."

"I saw the tears."

"Crocodile tears. That guy is as substantial as toilet tissue, not to mention insincere."

"Polite and cooperative on the surface," Policzki said, "but, yes, I could see a boatload of hostility in those eyes."

"Oh, yeah. The body language was a dead giveaway that something's rotten in Denmark."

"He certainly didn't seem too distraught for a guy whose wife is missing."

"Missing and possibly dead. Almost as bad as missing and possibly responsible for somebody else being dead. He didn't even bother to worry about Kaye until he realized he'd better make it look good if he wanted us to believe him. That's when the crocodile tears came into play." She mentally chewed on it awhile longer. "What's your take on the sister?"

"DeLucca? She struck me as pretty straightforward. A little protective of her brother."

"Interesting," Lorna said, "how she danced her way around saying that she and Kaye Winslow were friends."

"I caught that. What do you suppose that's about?"

"Beats me. She seemed genuinely concerned about Winslow's welfare, and she admitted they have a good working relationship. But she wasn't about to commit to anything as intimate as friendship."

Policzki considered for a moment. "You think there's something there?"

"Something. Might not have anything to do with what's gone down, but it's there. Her body language didn't scream guilt, but there was something I couldn't put my finger on. She's maybe not as fond of her sister-in-law as she'd like us to think."

"If it was a crime to dislike your in-laws, half the population of the United States would be behind bars."

"Good point. Understand, I'm not ready to write her off completely. But I like the husband better for this."

"So you think he did her?"

"I dunno." Lorna picked up a pen from her desk and began doodling on the desk blotter. "Scott Peterson was polite and cooperative with the authorities, too. At least he was at first. Handsome son of a bitch, too. Just like Winslow. Didn't seem particularly distraught, either, if memory serves me."

Policzki nodded slowly. "Mark Hacking reported his wife missing and then went out, cool as a cucumber, and bought a new mattress."

"Lot of wives going missing these days."

"Lot of guys who seem tired of being married."

"Guy reminds me of Chuck Stuart. Slick, sincere, good-looking. With a dark side lurking underneath the surface."

"I know I'll hate myself later for asking this, but who's Chuck Stuart?"

Lorna grinned. "I forget you're just a baby. You were probably in diapers when the Stuart murder came down."

"Hey, watch it. I'm not that young. The name's vaguely familiar. I just can't place it."

Lorna got up, walked to the coffeepot and poured herself a cup of sludge. Perching on the corner of her desk, next to the stack of empty paper cups that were starting to resemble antique collectibles, she crossed one leg over the other and said, "Guy's driving back from Lamaze class with his pregnant wife. They're somewhere in Mission Hill when he calls 911, says they were robbed and shot by a black man. He's got bullet wounds in the leg, the abdomen. Wife was shot in the head. She never stood a chance. Baby was born by C-section, but he never really had a chance, either. The case started one hell of an uproar. Black perpetrator, middle-class white victims just minding their own business. Everybody was, 'Poor Chuck this,' and 'Poor Chuck that.' Except that poor Chuck's story started unraveling after his kid brother admitted he'd ditched a gun for big brother that night. Once the story fell apart, so did Chuck. A couple months after his wife and kid died, he took a header off the Tobin Bridge. And if you think racial tension was bad before he jumped, imagine how much hotter things got when the truth came out that there was no black man, that Chuck's gunshot wounds were self-inflicted."

"Sounds to me like the plot to a bad *Lifetime* movie."

Lorna took a sip of coffee. "Now that you mention it," she said, "I believe they turned it into one."

Policzki tapped his PaperMate against the edge of his desktop. "So you think Winslow's tired of being married?"

"I couldn't say for sure, but you know what they say. If it walks like a rat and smells like a rat, has a long, skinny tail and likes cheese—"

"Chances are pretty good," Policzki said, "that it's a rat."

"Exactly. I think w̄e should do us a little checking up on the good professor. Open a few closet doors, see if we rattle any skeletons."

The show must go on.

The old showbiz cliché ran through Mia's head all Wednesday morning. No matter how hard she might wish it, the real estate industry wasn't about to grind to a screeching halt because there'd been a homicide and her partner was missing. Mia still had to check the Multiple Listing Service for new listings, still had to answer a raft of e-mails and wade through a dozen voice mail messages. She had to finish the comparative market analysis she'd promised a new client who was in a rush to put his condo on the market because he'd just been transferred to San Francisco and had to move in three weeks. She had to make follow-up calls to touch base with contacts she'd met at yesterday's seminar who might prove useful to her in the future. A closing to attend at eleven-thirty, which meant she probably wouldn't get a copy of the settlement statement until ten forty-five, at which time she would have to call the client to make sure everybody was on the same page before they all converged on the title company. She had to follow up with a nervous buyer who needed a gentle nudge to commit to bidding on the house she'd looked at three times but couldn't quite make up her mind about.

In her spare time, Mia had to deal with the fallout re-
sulting from Kaye's absence. The story had hit the papers
this morning, and the phone was ringing off the hook. The
ever-competent Bev was a godsend, juggling phone calls
and walk-ins, routine paperwork and the random crisis
with a finesse so smooth it seemed choreographed. She
gleefully hung up on reporters, then, in an abrupt Jekyll-
and-Hyde, offered warm reassurance to clients who
phoned to inquire about Kaye's welfare.

Yolanda Lincoln, the part-time agent Mia and Kaye had
brought in six months ago, did her best to help pick up the
slack. But Yolanda and Mia both had their own busy schedules to keep, so plugging the holes Kaye left was a challenge.
She'd been scheduled for two closings today. Mia sent Yolanda to the nine o'clock in her place, but Yolanda was already tied up midday, and Kaye's own one o'clock was too
close to Mia's eleven-fifteen to guarantee that they wouldn't
overlap. So Mia conveyed her regrets to the title company
via Bev, then called the buyer and spent twenty minutes
calming his fears and convincing him that everything was
in place, just as it should be, and that he'd make it through
the closing just fine without his Realtor by his side.

The closings were the only piece of Kaye's schedule
that Mia was privy to. Because they worked in a small office with only three agents, she knew many of Kaye's clients, just as Kaye knew quite a few of hers. But without
access to the woman's electronic date book, she had no way
of knowing where Kaye was expected to be or when, not
until a disgruntled client phoned to complain, or a stranger
walked through the door to announce that he had an appointment with her.

Mia forwarded Kaye's calls to her own phone and left

a message on her partner's voice mail saying that she was away from the office until further notice. This thing would probably blow over, or at least that was what she tried to tell herself. Kaye would come home, everything would be explained satisfactorily and her disappearance would turn out to be just a simple misunderstanding.

Kevin called from school around ten o'clock. "You didn't give me an answer about Tampa," he said.

With all the chaos surrounding Kaye's disappearance, Mia had completely forgotten about Tampa. Or maybe it was just unconscious avoidance. She glanced at her watch and said sharply, "Why aren't you in school?"

"Relax, Mom, I have a free period. I'm sitting in the cafeteria right now, drinking an orange juice. You should be proud of me. It's not even carbonated."

It was a not-so-subtle dig at her determination to save her son from the self-imposed junk food diet he was equally determined to live on. They'd had a number of go-rounds on the topic. She'd lectured him on good nutrition and he'd pointed out that he was a teenager and that junk food went with the territory. They'd finally reached a compromise. He agreed to eat the healthy, nutritious meals she prepared for him at home, and she agreed not to ask what he was eating when he walked out the door. What else could she do? Soon he would be eighteen, and her flimsy parental control, such as it was, would be ended for good. She might as well start getting used to it. Once he went off to college, she'd be an empty nester, rattling around that big old house all by herself. She might as well start getting used to that, too.

"Well?" he said. "Can I go or not? They need an answer today."

She'd loved him since the first moment she'd laid eyes on him. It seemed only yesterday. Hard to believe that seventeen years had passed, harder to believe that it was time she started loosening the apron strings. She knew she was an overprotective mother, but she couldn't seem to help it. "Fine," she said. "You can go. But I'll want to talk to Mrs. Olson before you leave. And you'll have to promise to call me while you're gone."

"Mom, it's only four days."

"And you're the only kid I have. Humor me."

"Thanks, Mom. Listen, I gotta run, the bell just rang. If I'm late for English class, Miss Crandall will have a bird. See you tonight."

And he was gone, the connection broken, leaving Mia holding a dead telephone receiver. She should be glad he was growing up, should be proud of the man he was turning into. And she was. It was just happening so soon. She wasn't ready. Maybe she never would be.

She'd just hung up the phone when her brother burst into her office, looking like a wild man, his hair awry, his shirt wrinkled and blind fury in his eyes. He flung a sheaf of papers on her desk and demanded, "Did you know about this?"

"What's going on?" she said. "Have they found Kaye?"

Her brother planted both fists on the edge of her desk and loomed over her, his face dark with fury. "You heard me, damn it! Did you or did you not know about this?"

She'd never seen Sam like this, not even when they were kids and he'd had one of his weekly go-rounds with their dad. Fury didn't set well on her brother's handsome features. His complexion was mottled with rage, his eyes bloodshot and wild. Like some kind of caged animal.

"I don't know," she said, reining in her own too-short

fuse. "Maybe it would help if I knew what 'this' refers to." She fumbled for her reading glasses, slid them onto her face and peered through them at the paperwork he'd so unceremoniously deposited amid the sales contracts and the flyers and the gazillion notes that littered her desk. "'Petition for Divorce,'" she read. "'Katherine Bradford Winslow, plaintiff.'" Mia raised startled eyes to his, then continued reading. "'Samuel L. Winslow, defendant...' Christ, Sam. I had no idea."

He continued to sway over her desk, so close she could smell the coffee on his breath. And something else, something slightly medicinal. Had he been drinking? At ten-fifteen in the morning?

"No idea," he said. "You're her business partner. Her sister-in-law. You see her, you talk to her, every blessed day of your life. And you want me to believe she decided to file for divorce and didn't bother to mention it to you?"

Mia's anger caught up to her. "Believe what you want," she snapped, removing the reading glasses and tossing them down on the desk. "But you might want to take a look in the mirror before you attack me. Because it seems she didn't bother to share her plans with you, either."

"Jesus Christ." He wheeled away from the desk, raked his fingers through his hair as he paced to the window and back to Mia's desk. Through the open doorway, she saw Bev watching, her hand on the phone and her face etched with concern.

Behind Sam's back, Mia frowned and shook her head. Bev took the hint, discreetly moving to another corner of the office, where she pulled out a file drawer and focused intently on her filing.

"Shut the door," Mia ordered him.

His mouth set in a grim line, Sam closed the door with a little more force than was called for. "This is a place of business," she snapped. "You can't just come storming in here, roaring like a lion and sending people running for cover. Around here, we act civilized."

"How could she do this to me? After all the shit I've gone through with that woman, how could she do this now? I'm on the verge of getting tenure. The least little thing rocking the boat could end it all. I could strangle her."

Mia just stared at this wild-eyed stranger who looked like her brother, walked like her brother, even sounded like her brother. Except that the words coming from his mouth made no sense. "Under the circumstances," she said, "that's a pretty unfortunate choice of words."

"If I don't get tenure, my career is over!"

"Your wife is missing," Mia said. "Maybe dead. And all you can think about is your career? I don't think I know you anymore, Sam. I don't think I want to know you anymore."

He deflated abruptly, like a balloon stuck with a hatpin. "Shit," he said.

"Will you please sit down? Have you called Detective Abrams yet?"

He slumped onto the chrome-and-tweed chair opposite her desk. "I'll get to it."

"You'll get to it," Mia repeated. "While your wife is out there God knows where, maybe hurt or kidnapped or dead, you'll eventually get around to telling the cops about evidence you've been withholding?"

"I'm not withholding evidence!"

"You lied, Sam. That's withholding evidence."

"I didn't lie. I just didn't tell Abrams everything. It

shouldn't matter anyway. My fight with Kaye is not relevant to any of this."

"How the hell do you know that?"

"Because! Because I just know!"

"Oh, so now you have a crystal ball? Tell me, oh great one, what are my odds of winning the lottery next week? Probably one hell of a lot better after you look into your crystal ball and give me the numbers ahead of time."

"Oh, shut up."

"Listen to me, shit-for-brains. I hate to tell you this, but relevant or not, that divorce petition is a matter of public record. It'll take the cops about ninety seconds to unearth it. When they do, you can be sure they'll come knocking at your door again. If you're on their short list—which we don't know for sure yet—right now all they have is suspicion. Once they get their hands on that—" she indicated the legal papers "—then they'll have motive. In my experience, cops are quite fond of motive."

"You know damn well I didn't do anything to Kaye."

"Well, the cops don't know it, and they're the ones that matter. It's time to come clean with them, Sam, before this gets any worse than it already is." She eyed him speculatively. "Unless there's some reason you don't want her to be found."

"Jesus, Mia, I can't believe you'd say that."

"Why not? Your wife just filed divorce papers. Maybe she's leaving you for another man. Maybe your ego can't take it. Maybe she's threatening to take you to the cleaners. Leave you with nothing but a toothbrush and a pup tent. Take away your daughter. Lie to the courts and tell them you're an abusive husband, a lousy father. So maybe you decide there's only one way to shut her up, and that's to get rid of her—"

"Stop it!" he shouted. "Just stop it!"

"What do you expect, Sam? That's exactly what the cops will be thinking once they find out about the divorce petition. You have to tell them before they stumble across it."

"You don't know, do you?" he said. "You really don't know."

There was more? Awash with dismay, Mia clasped her hands in front of her and stared at him, not sure she wanted to hear it. She hadn't slept worth beans last night. She'd skipped breakfast, she was exhausted, and it wasn't yet ten-thirty. She still had a lot of day to get through. "What?" she said wearily. "What is it I'm supposed to know now?"

"If the cops start digging, they'll find ample motive. Kaye's been cheating on me."

"What?"

Her brother's eyes softened. "You really didn't know, did you?"

"Come on, Sam. You must be wrong."

"She admitted it, Mia. I confronted her, and she admitted it to my face."

"Oh, Sam," Mia said. "I'm so sorry."

He tucked his hands into his pockets, walked to the window and stared out at the back of the brick apartment building across the alley. "Yeah, well, it's not the first time."

"She's done it before?"

He turned away from the window, his eyes as bleak as a January afternoon. "The first time—or at least the first time I know about—was last winter. I found out about it in March, but by the time I discovered it, the affair'd been going on for months. His name was Mickey Slattery. She met him at work. He was a client."

Her brother paused, as if waiting for a response from

Mia. What the hell did he expect her to say? "I don't know him," she said, resenting the defensiveness she heard in her own voice, "if that's what you're asking." She had nothing to feel defensive about. It wasn't her fault his wife hadn't been able to keep her knickers on.

"We had one hell of a go-round over it. I yelled a lot and threw a few of her precious knickknacks. She cried and swore to me that she was sorry, promised she'd clean up her act and kick Slattery to the curb. Promised it wouldn't happen again. Being the sucker that I am, I believed her."

"But…?"

"A week ago, I found condoms in her purse. And before you ask, no, I wasn't snooping. She'd borrowed my car that day because hers was in the shop. I needed to run to the store to pick up milk. She was busy doing paperwork in her office, and she told me the keys were in her purse. I went to get them. I wasn't expecting to pull out a fistful of Trojans along with the keys."

Mia didn't know what to say. Because she didn't, she said nothing. The Kaye Winslow she knew was not the kind of woman to allow herself to be derailed by stupid slipups, not the kind of woman to be blindsided by unfortunate, avoidable little accidents. She conducted her life with deliberation and forethought, leaving nothing to chance. She would never have forgotten those condoms were in her purse. Which led to an obvious conclusion, one Mia hated to even consider because it seemed so cruel: Kaye had wanted her husband to find the evidence of her infidelity.

This wasn't a burden Mia'd expected to have dropped in her lap. She didn't want to become entangled in her brother's marital difficulties, didn't want to find out that her sister-in-law wasn't the woman she'd thought her to be.

But Sam had been carrying this burden alone, and he needed to share it with somebody. It was only natural that he'd turn to her. Even though he was three years older, Mia had been taking care of him for most of their lives. She'd been the one who protected him from their father when he became drunk and violent. She'd been the one who stepped into the breach when Rachel died, leaving Sam alone with a seven-year-old daughter. And now, like it or not, she would be the one to see him through this.

"How much sleep did you get last night?" she said.

"An hour. Two at the most."

"Go home, Sam. Get something to eat, take a sleeping pill if you have to, and get some rest. I'll call you later. Okay?"

He stood in front of her, shoulders quivering, a pathetic wreck of a man. Nodding, he said, "Fine." He scooped up the divorce papers and, without another word, strode from her office, leaving her sitting there with her mouth hanging open. The bell over the front door jangled when he opened it, sounding slightly less melodic and slightly more affronted when he slammed the door behind him.

"Damn it," she said. "Damn it all to hell." And for lack of any other solution to her frustration, she picked up a fat black marker from her desk and hurled it at the wall.

Six

Back Bay Community College was located in a butt-ugly post–World War II cinder block building that had probably started out life as a warehouse. Tucked away on a narrow side street just off Kenmore Square, its campus sat within spitting distance of Fenway and the bars and clubs that lined Lansdowne Street. Lorna hadn't thought it was possible to find a building less aesthetically pleasing than Boston City Hall, but she might have been wrong about that.

They stood on the sidewalk for a moment, breathing in the school's ambience. Policzki cleared his throat and said, "It has a solid, no-nonsense, academic look to it."

She glanced over at him, but his eyes, hidden behind dark lenses, gave away nothing. "Looks like a junior high school," she said. "Or a penitentiary."

"Which, if memory serves me, is pretty much the same thing."

They went inside. The interior wasn't much of an improvement over the exterior. The lobby sported cracked green-and-white floor tiles. Somebody had made an attempt to brighten up the place by painting the walls a pale yellow. It was a dismal failure. Instead of sunny and cheerful, the walls looked sallow and jaundiced, like somebody in the advanced stages of liver disease. It wasn't a look that BBCC wore well.

Lorna walked up to the reception desk and asked a corpulent woman in a fuchsia dress and a black telephone headset where she could find Sam Winslow. "Down the hall on the left, Arts and Sciences Department," the woman said, and segued back into her telephone conversation without missing a beat. The two detectives followed her directions, passing a room full of vending machines, a couple of empty classrooms, then a bulletin board laden with notices: a reminder about the annual flu shot clinic; an announcement of a poetry reading taking place on Sunday afternoon at a nearby café; a photo of a 1999 Toyota Celica. *Runs great, low mileage. $1500 or B.O. Call 555-3372.*

The Arts and Sciences office was marginally more welcoming than the lobby had been. The secretary's desk was sleek and modern. The overhead fluorescents had been left off in favor of the gentler, more muted glow of floor lamps, and the carpet, while an ugly dirt-resistant brown, appeared to be relatively new. A slender young woman with a magnificent head of red curls sat behind a flat-screen Gateway computer. She glanced up, gave them both the once-over. Lorna could see it in her eyes, the instant she recognized them as cops. It didn't seem to faze her too much. Red's gaze returned to Policzki. In spite of his aloof manner—or perhaps because of it—women always took a second look at Doug Policzki. Being a pretty boy was sometimes useful.

"Can I help you?" she said to him, pretending Lorna didn't exist.

"Detective Policzki." Doug held up his badge. "This is Detective Abrams, and we're looking for Professor Winslow."

"Sam? Is he in some kind of trouble?"

"No, ma'am," Policzki said in that earnest, by-the-book manner that women seemed to find irresistible. "We just want to ask him a few questions. If you could point us in his direction, we'd greatly appreciate it."

"I'd love to," she said, "but I'm afraid you won't find him. He came in earlier and worked in his office for a while, then he left. He isn't scheduled to teach today, so I don't have any idea where he went or when he'll be back."

Neither of them bothered to tell Red that they already knew they wouldn't find the good professor on the premises. She might have turned really frosty if she'd known they'd seen him leave a half hour ago, then sat in a parking space halfway down the block and waited until they were pretty sure he wasn't coming back.

"In that case," Lorna said, "we'd like to speak to his supervisor."

Red looked a little surprised by this rude reminder that there were three people in the room instead of two. Tearing her gaze away from Policzki, with his lantern jaw and his pure heart, she said, "That would be Lydia Forbes. Dean Lydia Forbes."

"Is the dean in?"

"She's in, but I'm not sure she's available. I'll have to check."

The secretary left them alone, disappearing down a short corridor that led deeper into the suite of offices. Lorna took advantage of her absence to take a look around. There wasn't much to see. A potted palm in a corner. A row of battered gray file cabinets. A wooden shelving unit that upon closer inspection turned out to be mail cubbies. She scanned the names beneath the boxes, pausing when she reached Sam Winslow's. The professor's mail slot was empty.

Red returned to say, "Dean Forbes has a busy morning, but she can talk with you for a few minutes. It's the second door on the right."

They walked down the corridor and paused in the open doorway, waiting to be acknowledged. Lydia Forbes was in her late fifties, with graying hair, a tweed suit and ramrod-stiff posture. She was studying the open file on her desk with intense concentration. Lorna cleared her throat and the dean glanced up, saw them and closed the file. "Detectives," she said in a brisk, no-nonsense voice. "I understand you're here regarding Sam Winslow."

"That's right." Lorna edged into the office, with Policzki behind her. "We're working a homicide case, and we have a few questions for you. If you have a minute."

"I'm aware of the case," Forbes said. "Considering the media coverage, it would be difficult to miss the story."

"Then you know that we're trying to locate his wife."

Lydia Forbes drew her eyebrows together in a line that suggested displeasure. "Are you looking for my opinion? Because if you are, I'll be glad to offer it. As far as I'm concerned, he's better off without her."

She gestured to a couple of straight-backed chairs that looked as though they'd been pilfered from a dentist's waiting room. "Sit," she said. "I'm at an unfair psychological advantage with the two of you towering over me like this."

Lorna sat. The chair was about as comfortable as it looked. Forbes reminded her of her fifth-grade teacher, who wasn't averse to applying a wooden ruler to tender knuckles if that's what it took to get her point across. Nowadays, that kind of behavior would get a teacher fired, and possibly arrested for assault. What a crazy world this had turned out to be.

Policzki said, "Why do you feel Professor Winslow would be better off without his wife?"

Neither his bluntness nor his steady gaze had any noticeable effect on Forbes. "Because," she said, "the woman's been nothing but trouble for him since the day he married her."

Lorna raised an eyebrow and leaned forward as if eager for the next juicy piece of gossip. "What kind of trouble?"

"I assume you haven't met Kaye Winslow. If you had, you wouldn't be asking that question."

"Would you care to elaborate?"

"She's a very attractive woman," Forbes said. "Salon-perfect hair, meticulous makeup. Drives a bright red BMW. Dresses like her net worth puts her in the Jackie Onassis category."

"Those aren't exactly crimes."

"You're right. They're not. But they're just the tip of the iceberg. There are other issues."

"Such as?"

"You're the detective. Draw your own conclusions. Sam is too damn easy. She walks all over him. Why he lets her get away with it is beyond me. He should dump her and find himself a woman who appreciates him. But I think he's scared to make the move. There's a certain measure of security in staying. The devil you know being better than the devil you don't know. That kind of thing."

Policzki said, poker-faced, "So you consider Kaye Winslow to be a devil?"

The dean smiled. "It was a figure of speech, Detective."

"Exactly how does she walk all over him?" Lorna asked.

"It's not my business to air Sam Winslow's dirty linen. If you want an answer to that question, you should ask him."

"We'd love to ask him," Policzki said. "There's just one little problem with that. According to Sam, his marriage is a match made in heaven."

"Not my problem," Lydia Forbes said, opening her desk drawer and pulling out a pack of Pall Malls. She drew one from the pack and lit it up with an old-fashioned Zippo lighter. The lighter clicked shut. She took a long drag and exhaled a cloud of blue smoke through her nose.

Policzki coughed discreetly. Lorna refused to acknowledge the challenge. The dean took another drag, exhaled. And smiled. "At least once a week, I like to practice flagrant disobedience. Insurance against boredom-induced senility. Want to cuff me and drag me off?"

Lorna held back a grin. Lydia Forbes was a formidable opponent, and she kind of liked the old girl. "What we'd prefer," she said, "is to look at Professor Winslow's office."

Forbes dropped the cigarette into a huge crystal ashtray. Blue smoke rose, swirled and danced. "Got a search warrant?"

"Not yet."

"That's a shame. What, exactly, are you looking for?"

She wasn't the kind of woman who tolerated bullshit, so Lorna settled for the truth. "If I knew the answer to that, I'd already have that warrant."

"In other words, you don't have a clue what you're looking for. You're just shooting in the dark, hoping you hit something."

It was a pretty accurate assessment of the status of their

investigation. "Be serious," Forbes continued. "You can't honestly believe Sam Winslow had anything to do with his wife's disappearance or this man's murder."

"From what you tell me, it sounds like he'd have plenty of reasons to want Kaye out of his life."

"True. But I trust that Sam's intelligent enough to realize divorce is a far better choice than foul play. Presuming, of course, that foul play is what you're suggesting."

"We're not suggesting anything," Lorna said. "But just in case something unfortunate has happened to Mrs. Winslow, don't you think it would be better to eliminate Dr. Winslow from the list of possible suspects as quickly as possible?"

"And just how is searching his office going to eliminate him from your list of suspects? Which I imagine at this point is a rather short list."

"We won't know that until we've looked."

Forbes grinned. "You know," she said, "I'd love to stay and chat with you, but I'm late for a meeting. If you'll excuse me." She took another drag on the cigarette, crushed it out in the ashtray and stood. Standing, she was an Amazon. "You want to ransack Sam's office, get a search warrant."

"It's a shame," Policzki told her, "that we'll have to mark you down on record as being uncooperative with our investigation."

The dean hoisted a huge black purse over her bony shoulder and uttered a whiskey-throated laugh. "I'm shaking in my shoes," she said. "Have a nice day."

Red's real name was Maureen Grogan; and while Policzki worked his wiles on her, Lorna wandered the corridor. She passed an open classroom where a short, stocky man was trying to impart his algebraic wisdom to a class of perhaps thirty students who ranged in age from late teens to mid-forties. A couple of the students were nodding and taking rapid notes. Most of the others looked mildly confused.

Farther down the hall, she found the library, its door propped open with a big yellow jack-o'-lantern. Lorna stepped inside and looked around. Private study carrels lined one wall. Students sat at big wooden tables, notebooks open as they leafed through the pages of the tomes piled in front of them. Other students milled about the stacks. On a corner table sat a nice display of handmade ceramics from Guatemala, bowls and vases and cups in cheerful, vibrant colors.

Every spare inch of wall space was covered with posters. Travel posters of the Eiffel Tower at night, twinkling above the city of Paris, and of the ancient and mysterious Great Pyramids of Egypt. Posters reminding students of the importance of literacy, and posters that were reproductions of great works of art: the *Mona Lisa*, and others Lorna recognized as pieces by Rembrandt and Van Gogh. Obviously the folks here at BBCC were determined to encourage students to broaden their horizons beyond the giant Citgo sign that towered over Kenmore Square. This place might not be Harvard, but at least it was giving it the old college try.

She stepped back out into the corridor and found Policzki waiting for her. "What'd you get?" she said.

"Winslow's teaching schedule, his office hours and the name of one David Briggs, who runs the painting studio."

"Great work, Policzki. Maybe I should consider letting you play good cop once in a while."

They found the painting studio on the second floor, squeezed into a tiny room with a dozen easels scattered about, most of them holding canvases in various stages of completion. Shelves built into the side wall held art supplies, and on the windowsill, a dog-eared pile of *American Artist* magazines lay yellowing in the sun. At the back of the room, a young woman sat on a stool in front of one of those easels, paintbrush in hand, studying the canvas before her with the same absorption Lorna's kids usually showed for an MTV video. At the front of the room, a thirtyish man in a paint-spattered smock sat at the teacher's desk hunched over a comic book, with a Diet Pepsi and a half-eaten sandwich nearby.

Lorna cleared her throat. The guy looked up, focusing on them through the lenses of wire-framed glasses. "David Briggs?" she asked.

"That's me. What can I do you for?"

Lorna flashed her badge. "Detectives Abrams and Policzki, Boston PD." She took a look around the room. "Nice studio you've got here."

"Professor Winslow pulled it all together a couple of years ago. The room used to be a storage closet. I guess the powers that be took a little convincing. Budget constraints, all that kind of political mumbo jumbo. But Sam finally convinced them that after the initial outlay, the studio would pretty much run itself. And the students would flock to it. He was right. The class fills up every semester. So here we are."

"Here you are." Lorna stepped in front of a nearby easel and studied the half-finished still life. She was no art critic, but to her eyes, the painting seemed to show talent. "Nice work," she said.

Briggs got up from his chair, leaving his sandwich behind. "That's Julie Coulter's work. Pretty impressive, don't you think? Until she started this class, Julie was totally self taught. Sam's been helping her to refine her skills. You'd be surprised by how much raw talent we see here at BBCC. Considering that we're not an art school."

Lorna wandered, checked out a couple more works in progress. "Of course," Briggs said, "our students possess varying skill levels. This is a beginner's class. Anybody with an interest in painting can get in."

"I see. And Winslow's in charge of this place?"

"It's his baby," Briggs said.

"Does he teach upper-level classes as well?"

"He's been trying for three years to get the administration to let him offer Advanced Painting. The administration keeps on saying no. It's a shame, because so many students finish this class and have nowhere to go."

"So Winslow's a painter?"

"A damn good painter. That's one of his works, hanging on the wall over there. I've never known anybody who uses color and motion quite the way he does. There's so much going on in his paintings."

She turned and studied the piece. It was one of those abstract things, full of bright colors and asymmetric shapes in wild juxtaposition that made no sense at all. She just didn't get abstract art. Take, for instance, Picasso, who was as likely to place a woman's breast on top of her head as on her chest, where it belonged. How the hell did Briggs know it was a good painting? How were you supposed to judge the relative merits of something that looked as though the artist had just stood there and randomly flung paint at a blank canvas?

Because she didn't know what she was expected to say, Lorna changed the subject. "You work here with Winslow?"

"For him, actually. He's my supervisor."

"What's your job?"

"Studio assistant. I help out during classes, keep the place cleaned up, monitor it during certain times of day so the students can come in and work on their paintings."

"How long have you been here?"

"Three semesters," Briggs said. "I'm a work-study student. Hired on a semester-to-semester basis. It's part of my financial aid package."

"You know Winslow pretty well, then."

"Pretty well."

"What's he like to work for?"

Propping a sneakered foot on a chair rung, Briggs said, "Easygoing. Fair. Pretty much the same as he is in the classroom. Laid-back, but he still has expectations of the students. He has a little bit of a temper, but he keeps it well hidden."

Lorna and Policzki exchanged glances. Policzki said, "Tell us about that. Have you ever been on the receiving end of his temper?"

"Oh, no. Not at all. He's never been anything but great with me. Or his students. They all love him." Briggs leaned forward and added, in a confidential tone, "It's just that I heard him on the phone with his wife the other day. I don't know what she'd done, but he sounded ready to kill her."

"Really," Lorna said. "Do you happen to know Mrs. Winslow?"

"No. But I've heard a lot. You could say her reputation precedes her."

"What reputation is that?"

Briggs waggled his eyebrows. "Let's just say that the lady's hotness quotient is legendary."

"Winslow brags about how hot his old lady is?"

"No, that's not what I meant. He's not that kind of guy. But people talk." Briggs shrugged. "The academic world's pretty dull. If people couldn't gossip, they'd probably die of boredom." He eyed them with curiosity. "So," he said, "what's this all about? Why are you here asking questions?"

Obviously the guy didn't read the newspapers. Or watch the Channel 5 news. Deliberately ignoring his question, Lorna said, "When was the last time you talked to Dr. Winslow?"

"Not today," Briggs said. "And yesterday was my day off. I guess I haven't seen him since Friday."

"He seem okay then? His usual self?"

"Yeah, sure. Except…" Briggs rubbed his chin while he thought it over. "Now that you mention it, he did seem a little…I don't know, I guess distracted. I went down to his office to ask him something, and I had to speak to him three times before he heard me. He was just sitting there, staring at the wall. Like he was in a daze."

"And he's not usually like that?"

"Never. He's usually right on the ball. I just figured he had a lot on his mind. It was the same day I heard him arguing with his wife. I figured they hadn't settled whatever the problem was between them."

"Thanks for talking to us," Lorna said. She gestured toward the sandwich. "Sorry we interrupted your, uh…"

"Hey, no prob."

When they walked out the door, Briggs had already returned to his comic book.

* * *

Gracie Winslow sat in the high school cafeteria, using her fork to roll a single pea from one side of her tray to the other. When she was satisfied with its placement, she rolled a second pea over beside it, and then a third. Slowly, and with meticulous precision, she lined them all up in a row and counted them. Eleven peas, the mushy kind, the kind they put in a can and then pressure-cooked until they were a sickly vomit-green and the consistency of sewer sludge.

She'd been trying since Tuesday night to track down Carlos, but he might as well have dropped off the face of the earth. The cops still hadn't located Kaye, still hadn't figured out who the dead guy was. And Dad was drinking so much—she'd actually smelled alcohol on his breath this morning at breakfast—that if things didn't get back to normal pretty soon, she was going to call in reinforcements in the form of her aunt Mia. Mia would give Sam the ass-kicking he needed. Gracie'd seen her do it before. On the outside, Mia was every inch the lady. But she could kick some serious ass. Next to her mother, who Gracie could barely remember because she'd been dead for eight years, Mia was the person she most admired in this world.

At the other end of the ugly gray cafeteria table, Ashlee Jordan was holding court. "So, he was, like, 'you know that's not what I meant' and I was, like, 'right, that's why you lied to me about dating Bunny' and he was, like, 'I told you that was before I ever asked you out' and I was, like, 'take a hike, you loser.'"

Amanda Elkins and Kim Farrell nodded solemnly, their little blond heads moving in unison like twin bobble-head dolls in the back window of an old Ford. Gracie rolled her eyes, picked up her fork and delicately stabbed pea number one, hearing in her mind its death screams as she eviscerated it. She took it in her mouth and chewed it slowly, seventeen times, before she swallowed. That was the magic number. Seventeen. If she chewed every mouthful of food seventeen times before she swallowed, God would grant her the thin thighs and the flat stomach she craved.

"So what will you do?" Amanda was asking Ashlee. "Now that you don't have a date for the Halloween dance?"

"Who cares?" Ashlee said. "I am *so* done with him. There must be, like, eight hundred other guys out there who'd hook up with me in a New York minute. You know everyone says I look just like Jessica Simpson."

Gracie stuck a tine of her fork into pea number three, leaving number two sitting on the tray in all its puke-green, glistening glory. Beneath her Modest Mouse T-shirt, her stomach growled. Gracie took the pea into her mouth, moved it around from left to right and began to chew. *One, two, three, four, five, six—*

"Hey, Gracie. I heard about your stepmother."

Her chewing interrupted, Gracie stared stonily at Victoria Roberts, who sat down across the table from her, looking all hot and totally awesome in her Hello Kitty crop top and acid-washed jeans. Vicky sat wide-eyed and expectant as she peeled open her carton of milk. Exactly what was she expecting Gracie to say? Her comment hadn't been phrased as a question. She'd simply said, *"I heard about your stepmother."* Hardly a promising conversational opening.

So Gracie continued chewing until she reached seventeen, then picked up her bottle of Evian water—in this fancy-schmancy private school, they served your basic, inedible cafeteria food, but they couldn't commit the unpardonable faux pas of stocking up on ordinary Poland Spring water—unscrewed the cap and washed down her lunch.

Vicky took a sip of milk and smirked at her. "So I heard that guy was her boyfriend and he wanted to break up with her. And they were doing it, you know, like a last fling or something, and she just pulled out the gun and shot him. *Right while they were doing it.* And he was all bloody and gory and covered with brains and stuff."

Good Lord. So this was how quickly rumors reached urban legend status. Instead of responding to Vicky's asinine story, Gracie took another slug of Evian.

"You know," Vicky said as she tore open a ketchup packet and squeezed it out onto the slab of mystery meat that lay atop an open bun on her tray, "you really are weird. Are you a mutant or what?"

"What," Gracie said.

Vicky's eyes narrowed as she tried to figure out how to respond. "Yeah, well," she said, "you sure are some kind of freak. You're probably a murderer, too. Just like your mother."

Gracie said, "She's not my mother."

Vicky shrugged her slender shoulders. "Whatever."

"But she did teach me a thing or two about killing people."

"Riiight."

"I've been endowed with special powers, you know. I can use them for good or for evil. If I like you, I might help you out of a jam. If I don't like you, well…" She shrugged, as if to say, *Comme ci, comme ça. You win some, you lose some. That's the way the chocolate chip cookie crumbles.*

Sniffing, Vicky said, "I don't even know how you got into this school in the first place."

"I went through the same rigorous selection process as

you, Einstein. It's called my dad could afford the tuition. Have you ever read *Carrie?*"

"Who the hell is Carrie?"

"Not who, dimwit, what. It's a book by Stephen King. Or have you never read a book?"

"Isn't that the guy who writes that weird stuff? It figures you'd like him."

"You see, Carrie had these telekinetic powers, and—"

Vicky crinkled up her cute little nose. "Teleki-whatic?"

"It means she could make things happen just by thinking about it."

Vicky appeared agog at the vast possibilities. "You mean, like winning the lottery? Or like making Jake Gyllenhaal fall in love with her?"

"Like killing people, twit. You see, the kids at school treated Carrie like shit. They tricked her into going to the prom, then they dumped a bucket of pig's blood over her head. It really pissed her off, so much that she ended up destroying the whole town and pretty much everybody in it. It was awesome."

Vicky's brow wrinkled in puzzlement. "What's your point, mutant?"

Gracie stood and picked up her tray, grabbed her backpack and slung it over her shoulder. "Be careful who you piss off," she said.

She dumped her uneaten food in the trash and stacked her empty tray with the others. Outside the swinging cafeteria doors, the hallways were deserted. Gracie headed purposefully down the corridor toward the media room. She still had ten minutes before lunch period was over, which should give her ample time to check her e-mail to see if there were any messages from Carlos.

She wasn't supposed to be running around out here without a hallway pass. The administration in this place treated the students like four-year-olds. You weren't supposed to go to the freaking bathroom unless you had a pass giving you permission to tread these hallowed halls. But there was nobody around to see her. And if she ran into one of the teachers, she'd just hold up her head and smile with such an air of confidence that God himself wouldn't question her right to be here. As her aunt Mia liked to say, if you can't dazzle them with brilliance, then baffle them with bullshit.

Gracie reached the door of the media room. The place was dark, lit only by the glow of a dozen flat-panel computer monitors. She looked left, then right. Nothing. She tried the door, breathed a sigh of relief to find it unlocked. Gracie opened it, and was about to step inside when the voice of doom—otherwise known as Felicia Marlowe, the academy's sour-faced director—stopped her dead in her tracks. "Gracie Winslow," she said in that imperious tone that would have made the strongest man quake in his boots, "just what do you think you're doing?"

Seven

Mia's late-morning closing dragged on forever. As the listing agent for the property, Mia represented the sellers, a sweet elderly couple who were selling the family home and retiring to Florida to spend their golden years playing golf and tennis. The Bennetts had been a dream to work with. It was the buyers who presented the problem. Brett Gunderson was an investment banker and his wife, Brenda, was an accountant, and they both insisted on exercising their right to read every line of fine print before they signed anything. As a result, what should have taken forty minutes took nearly two hours. Marty Scalia, their Realtor, kept sneaking glances at his watch, while the title company attorney, Greg Dubrowski, drummed manicured fingernails on the conference room table. In spite of the wedding ring he wore on the third finger of his left hand, Dubrowski had a major reputation with the ladies. Darkly handsome, he wore Armani suits and carried himself with the air of somebody who was confident about his own importance and liked to remind people of it. Although he'd hit on her more than once, Mia had never found him particularly attractive. His ego—and the gold band he didn't bother to hide—kept getting in the way. But she knew that other women did. She'd heard rumors of fellow Realtors who closed one kind of deal with Greg around a conference table, then closed a more intimate kind of deal with him over champagne and silk sheets. Now that she knew the ugly truth about Kaye, she wondered if her sister-in-law had been one of them.

Mia immediately felt guilty. Was she doomed to spend the rest of her life wondering, every time she looked at a reasonably attractive man, whether or not Kaye had slept with him? It was pointless, but she couldn't seem to help it. Regardless of his failings, Sam didn't deserve that kind of treatment. How had she missed seeing what was going on? She and Kaye had worked together five days a week for years. Was she so self-absorbed that she couldn't see past her own nose? Or was she simply in denial about the possibility that a woman she'd trusted enough to go into business with might be chronically unfaithful to her husband? Especially when that husband was Mia's own brother?

The Gundersons finally finished signing papers. Greg gathered them up, and there were handshakes and congratulations all around. Mia made her escape, half-starved and desperately needing a bathroom to rid herself of the five gallons of coffee she'd ingested since breakfast. She made a beeline for the restroom, took care of business, then frowned at herself in the mirror as she stood washing her hands at the sink. Her pale face and the dark circles under her eyes gave away her state of mind and announced her lack of sleep to the world. She could have tried to salvage the situation with makeup, but she just didn't have the heart. No amount of makeup would change the situation. Until her sister-in-law was located, Mia was destined to walk around with bags under her eyes.

She waited by the bank of elevators and caught the first car that was headed to the lobby. It was empty, and while it made its descent, Mia called her voice mail in case there was news about Kaye.

There wasn't. Discouraged, she flipped her phone closed and headed across the lobby toward the revolving door that led to the street. Marty Scalia caught up with her halfway across the granite-floored lobby. "Hey, gorgeous," he said. "Want to buy your biggest admirer a cup of coffee and a sandwich?"

Without breaking stride, she said, "Your clients were horrible, Marty."

"I know, I know. Luck of the draw. Anal retentive, the both of 'em. I'm sorry, babe. It won't happen again."

"Don't make promises you can't keep." If any other man had called her "babe," she would have punched his lights out. But Marty had been calling her that since the first week she went to work for him, nine years ago, after Nick died and she'd been lost and alone, with no idea where to turn. Marty, with his own peculiar brand of tough love, had saved her.

They went through the revolving door together and melted into the crowd that thronged the sidewalk. Glancing across the street, she spied a hot dog vendor's cart near the Park Street T entrance. Even from this distance, she could smell the fried onions, mingled with exhaust fumes from the midday traffic. Mia's stomach rumbled. It was past her lunchtime. She needed to eat; Marty needed to eat. If they ate together, she could kill two birds with one stone. Marty had eyes and ears everywhere. He might know something that would help them locate Kaye. At the very least, Mia could bounce her thoughts off him without worrying that they'd be broadcast to everyone within hearing distance.

"Tell you what," she said. "If we can make it a hot dog and a Pepsi, and eat it in the park, I'll take you up on your offer."

"I eat a hot dog, it'll be barking all afternoon. But for you, I'll risk it." Glancing sideways at her as they stood waiting for the light, he said, "You're not looking so hot today, kid. Rough night?"

The light changed, and they started across Tremont Street with the crowd. "Marty, you have no idea."

"Maybe a little. I heard the news about Kaye. Listen, there's something I have to talk to you about."

They reached the other side, stepped up onto the curb. "I'll buy the dogs," Mia said. "You find us a bench. I'll be right back with lunch."

Sam wasted a half hour driving aimlessly around the city, muttering under his breath, talking to himself like a crazy person, wondering aloud why his life had derailed in such a spectacular manner. Okay, so he wasn't a saint. But then, who was? Nobody, not when you dug underneath the smooth, shiny facade everybody wore and went straight to the slimy underbelly. He might be flawed, but was he any worse than the next guy who'd done something really stupid and paid dearly for it?

It wasn't until he ran a red light and came within inches of being broadsided by a moving van that he decided he'd better park the car before he ended up in the morgue. So he parked on a side street, fed the meter, bought a cup of coffee at a 7-Eleven on Boylston, and walked off his mad.

The foliage in Boston's Back Bay was spectacular in October. Normally, he would have appreciated the color. But today, he barely noticed it. His life was tanking with a vengeance. He was, as his sister might say, up to his ass in alligators. In hot water, with no discernible way out.

His cell phone rang, and Sam's heart rate doubled. It didn't slow until he pulled the phone from his pocket and saw that it was Lydia calling. He glanced over his shoulder as he flipped the phone open. There were no monsters here, at least none that he recognized. But who knew? That Asian kid with the backpack who looked like every other college student in the city could have an ulterior motive for being on Newbury Street this afternoon.

Or maybe Sam was just losing his mind.

"Hey, Lyd," he said into the phone. It seemed almost surreal that, heedless of his own private calamity, the planet continued to spin. Back at BBCC, it was just another day. Students still chatted in the corridors. Professors still gave pop quizzes. Secretaries still typed memos and faculty committees continued to make inane decisions that would alter the ultimate fate of the institution. Nice to know things were still normal somewhere.

But normal didn't last long. "Why the hell didn't you tell me?" Lydia said.

Sam closed his eyes and fought back the nausea that had been with him ever since those two cops came to his door and told him his wife had disappeared. "I suppose I was still in shock," he told her. It was only a partial lie. He was in shock, but that wasn't why he'd avoided her. "None of this seems real to me, Lyd." At least that part was the honest-to-God truth.

"If you'd told me this morning, I might have been able to do some damage control. It's a little late for that now."

"What kind of damage control?"

"For once in your life, Sam, ditch the absentminded professor routine and use your head. Did you really think that Nyles Larsen and his merry band of henchmen wouldn't jump on this the minute they heard about it?"

"Oh, Christ," he said. "The tenure committee." The sick feeling in his stomach intensified. "How bad is it?"

"Bad enough. After Officer Friendly and her stone-faced sidekick finished their little campus-wide survey about your character, or lack thereof, Larsen couldn't wait another minute to put your neck on the chopping block. He rushed to call an emergency meeting of the committee. They voted five-to-one to put your tenure application on hold until this whole mess is cleared up. After all, we wouldn't want to be granting tenure to somebody of questionable character, would we?"

"I don't believe this."

"Believe it. Look, Sam, your life is unraveling at the seams. I'll do what I can as far as the tenure committee is concerned. Maybe I can go behind Larsen's back and talk to some of the other committee members. But, Sam…" Her silence was somehow more frightening than her words had been. "You need to get this mess cleaned up, and you need to do it fast. If you don't, I'm afraid you might as well flush your future here at BBCC right down the john."

It was early afternoon when Rafferty called Lorna into his office. Outside his window, the sky was a brilliant blue, and the sunlight, slanting in through the blinds, fell in narrow strips on the floor. "Close the door," the lieutenant said. "Talk to me. Comm Ave. What's going on with that?"

Lorna closed the door and perched casually on the corner of his desk. She and Conor Rafferty went a long way back, all the way to the police academy. He was godfather to her last two kids and, as rookie detectives, she and Conor had been partners. She'd known him too well, and for too long, to be intimidated by his rank.

"Jiminez has been talking to Kaye Winslow's friends and acquaintances. The consensus there seems to be that Winslow wasn't the type to involve herself in a homicide."

"You and I both know there's no such thing as type."

"Hey, don't shoot the messenger. I'm just reporting what I've been told."

"Fine. Keep talking."

"The evidence—what little there is of it—might actually support that conclusion. Although there was no sign of a struggle at the scene, the fact that she'd been there and left without taking her briefcase strongly suggests that she left with somebody else's assistance. I don't know about you, but if I were to suddenly find myself in the presence of a fresh corpse and a smoking gun, I probably wouldn't leave behind my name, address and driver's license photo."

"I've seen some pretty stupid criminals do some pretty stupid things."

"Granted. But Kaye Winslow wasn't stupid. She's a rising star in the real estate world. That doesn't spell stupid."

"Anybody can be stupid under the right circumstances. Any ID on the corpse?"

"None yet. We're still waiting for the autopsy report. If that doesn't pan out, I'll get Policzki looking into missing persons reports."

"What about her car?"

"We haven't located it yet, but if it's in Massachusetts, we should find it soon."

"And no strong suspects?"

"Not yet, although we're looking pretty closely at the husband. He seems a little shaky."

"Shaky in what way?"

"Shaky as in I'd bet my firstborn male child that he's lying about something."

"Any idea what?"

"Nope. But we'll get to it eventually. We just have to peel away a few layers first."

Conor thought it over. "Unidentified DOA, no murder weapon, no solid leads of any kind. This case isn't endearing itself to me. What about the sister-in-law?"

"Probably not involved, not unless she hired somebody to do her dirty work for her. Has a rock-solid alibi. At the time of the homicide, she was in Springfield, presenting a seminar to a hundred and fifty real estate professionals."

"Move her to the bottom of your list, but don't take her off until I tell you to." Conor spread his hands on top of his desk. "You might as well know that a group of neighbors from Comm Ave has been making a lot of noise down at city hall. They want this case solved yesterday. Make the streets safe again for their wives and daughters. I had a call from the mayor himself a half hour ago, asking what progress we're making."

"And I bet he just wants it to go away."

"You'd win that bet. He wants it to go so far away it's like it never happened."

"Well, then, we'll just have to give him what he wants. Keep the man happy. You know how the saying goes—you can't fight city hall."

"Yadda yadda yadda."

She grinned. "I love it when you go all eloquent on me."

"Just get the case solved. I have gangbangers shooting each other dead in the streets all over Dorchester. One or two a week. Kids, for Christ's sake. I have husbands killing wives. Wives killing husbands. Random strangers killing other random strangers for no reason that's comprehensible in the known universe. And I have two of my best detectives tied up over a DOA who just dropped out of the sky into the kitchen of a six-point-five-million-dollar house."

"Boggles the imagination, doesn't it?" Lorna slid off the desk and smoothed her skirt. "Something'll pop soon. I'll bet you six months of lunches that we'll get a break within the next twenty-four to forty-eight."

"I'd take you up on that bet, but your idea of lunch is usually something that gives me heartburn for three days afterward. I'd never survive the six months if I had to let you pick the restaurant."

There was a rap at the door. "Yes?" he said.

A massive bouquet of yellow roses stepped through the door, followed closely by Isabel, Rafferty's secretary and right appendage. "They're for you," she told Lorna in the sultry Puerto Rican accent that had been known to drive men to silly adolescent behavior and worse. "Some delivery guy just brought them. That husband of yours, he really knows how to treat a woman right."

Lorna took the bouquet from Isabel and stared at it in disbelief. Yellow roses? She'd given birth to four of Ed's children—if she hadn't lost count somewhere along the way—and he'd never yet sent her flowers. He was either feeling damn guilty about something, or there'd been a monumental mix-up at the florist shop.

"Go ahead," Isabel urged. "Read the card. I want to hear what he has to say."

Lorna dug into the center of the bouquet and pulled out the small white envelope. She set the flowers down on the corner of Conor's desk while she opened it. "'Dig deeper,'" she read aloud. Puzzled, she glanced up, met Conor's scowl, registered that and the rapt expression on Isabel's face before she returned her attention to the card. "'Dig deeper,'" she read again. "'Check out Rachel Winslow, August of 1999.'" She raised her eyes to Conor's and said, "Who the hell is Rachel Winslow?"

Mia balanced her hot dog on her knee, pulled a tissue from her purse and scrubbed the top of her Pepsi can. "Have the cops talked to you yet?" Marty asked.

"Oh, yes." She checked to make sure the can was clean, tore open a straw, then crumpled the wrapper into a ball and dropped it into her pocket. "Bumbling idiots, if you ask me. They had the nerve to question Sam and me as if we were crime suspects."

A gust of wind blew up, setting Marty's necktie flapping around his face. He grappled with it while juggling his hot dog and his can of Mountain Dew. Mia reached out and took the soda from him before he could spill it in his lap. "Well," he said, "it doesn't seem unreasonable to me. You want her found, they have to start somewhere." He got the necktie under control, rubbed at a speck of mustard before tucking the tie into the pocket of his shirt and reclaiming his soda. "It would seem to me that they'd check out the people closest to her first. Then, if nothing pans out there, they'd start widening their net."

"It was insulting, Marty. They had the nerve to ask me where I was Tuesday afternoon and whether or not I could prove it."

"Oh, Christ. You must be having a cow."

"I'm angry. I'm scared. I'm confused. I'm feeling so many conflicting emotions right now that I'm about to burst. And I feel utterly helpless."

"That's gotta be tough. How's the kid taking it?"

"I don't know. I haven't talked to her. But they've never been close, so God only knows what Gracie's thinking. She's a good kid, but she wears this mantle of hostility that Kaye's never been able to break through." Mia fell silent, watching a homeless man move from bench to bench, bumming pocket change and cigarettes. "I just don't know what to think anymore, Marty."

He crossed his legs and leaned back on his tailbone. Studying the toes of his loafers, he said, "Do you think she killed this guy and then disappeared?"

"No. I've looked at it from every possible angle, and I refuse to believe that Kaye would have committed a murder and then walked away into the sunset. For starters, I can't imagine her blithely tossing aside a possible commission on a multimillion-dollar property. I suspect she wouldn't have left unless she was dragged away, kicking and screaming all the way. Which leaves us with a glut of unanswered questions."

"The biggest of which is, if she was dragged away kicking and screaming all the way, who did the dragging?"

"Exactly. Where the hell is she, Marty? She's not in any of the area hospitals. Nobody's seen her car, nobody's seen her. But she *was* in that house. She was in there when something really nasty went down. Then she vanished. Somebody has to know where she is."

"Next question—did that somebody happen along in the form of a random and opportunistic stranger—"

"Or has she managed to get herself into some kind of trouble she can't get out of?" Mia set her Pepsi on the bench beside her. "That, my friend, is the million-dollar question."

"And the cops haven't identified the dead guy?"

"Not as far as I know."

Marty took a big bite of his hot dog and chewed thoughtfully. Blotted his mouth with his napkin. He leaned forward and took a breath, as if he was on the verge of saying something, then shook his head and took another bite of hot dog.

"Marty?" she said. "Is there something I should know?"

He swallowed the mouthful, washed it down with Mountain Dew. "Who does your bookkeeping?"

Surprised, she said, "Bev does. Why?"

"And you trust her?"

"Absolutely. Why?"

"Bottom line looking good? Nothing funky going on?"

"No," Mia said. "Nothing funky's going on. Marty, why are you asking me this?"

"Keep an eye on your money. That's all I'm saying."

"What do you know that I don't?"

"It's just rumors, you know? Gossip. People talk."

"About what?"

He gave her a sideways glance before tossing the remains of his hot dog on the ground, where it was immediately set upon by a dozen pigeons with iridescent, rainbow-tinted neck feathers. "If I was one to gossip," he said, "and I'm not one to gossip—but if I was, I might've heard something about a real estate deal that smelled worse than Boston Harbor before the cleanup."

She caught a sharp breath. "And?"

"Rumor has it that your sister-in-law may. have allegedly been involved in this alleged deal that might be truth and might be nothing more than speculation."

"I see. And who else might have allegedly been involved in this mysterious and mythical deal that may or may not have even happened?"

Marty picked an invisible speck of dirt from his sleeve. "Now, I'm not saying this is anything more than gossip. But in case you want to check it out, you might want to talk to Grant Ashford."

Grant Ashford was the too-pretty-for-his-own-good vice president of First Boston Savings Bank. Great-grandson of the bank's illustrious founder, Grant was a spoiled-rotten rich boy who now was in charge of the bank's loan department. Since they specialized in mortgage loans, he worked closely with the local real estate community. Mia had heard rumors that his second cousin on his mother's side was some Big Dig contractor who'd gotten the job through family connections. She'd also heard something to the effect that Ashford was acquainted with a number of local Mafia figures. Some legends even linked his father to the infamous mobster Whitey Bulger. But who the hell knew what the truth was? There were so many rumors circulating about Grant Ashford that it was impossible to differentiate truth from lies.

It took a moment for her anger to catch up to her. "Goddamn it, Marty, if she's got herself mixed up in something illegal, I'll kill her."

Marty turned his face up to the warm afternoon sun. "Gotta find her first," he murmured.

"What's wrong with me?" Mia said. "Do I live under a rock? Maybe in a cave? Do I go through life with blinders on, or am I simply so stupid and self-absorbed that you could set fire to my living room couch and carry it out the door right past my nose, still aflame, and I'd hold the door for you without even smelling the smoke?"

He gave her knee an avuncular pat. "Don't be so hard on yourself, kid. You're not stupid or self-absorbed. You're just a little naive. You're one of the good guys, and you expect everybody else to be the same way."

Naive. It wasn't quite how she thought of herself. In her line of work, you couldn't afford to be naive. Thinking out loud, she said, "So if this alleged deal really did take place, there must be a paper trail."

"More than likely. But good luck finding it."

"When was this supposed to have taken place?"

Marty shrugged. "Sometime last year. I heard about it a few months ago."

"Why the hell didn't you tell me about it then?"

"It was just a rumor. It's still just a rumor. Could be a grain of truth to it, or it could be just smoke and mirrors."

"Who else was involved?"

"Sorry, kid, I don't have the foggiest. The only names I ever heard were Grant Ashford and Kaye Winslow. I did hear it said that there were some people who weren't particularly pleased with the outcome. Or with either of them."

"I have to go, Marty." Mia stood abruptly and tossed the remains of her lunch in a trash can. "I have to look into this."

"Yeah, well, don't do anything stupid."

"Me? When have I ever done anything stupid? Never mind, don't answer that question." She leaned and planted a quick kiss on his cheek. "Thanks for listening."

She was already thirty feet down one of the paths that crossed the Common when she heard him call her name.

She swung around, raised a hand to shield her eyes from the sun, and picked him out of the crowd, an aging man in a bland gray suit, necktie still tucked into his pocket.

"You be careful!" he yelled. "You hear me? Be careful!"

Eight

First Boston Savings Bank was a venerable institution with none of the flash of Boston's modern office towers and all of the dignity that was missing from those late twentieth century glass-walled monstrosities. A solid edifice fashioned of New Hampshire granite and Italian marble, First Boston Savings had stood for four generations on the same plot of land in downtown Boston. It was rumored that the bank's founder, Jacob Ashford, had been a close confidant of the infamous Isabella Stewart Gardner, whose eclectic Fenway home had been turned into a museum that was one of Boston's big tourist draws. The rumor might even have been true; it was acknowledged fact that they were contemporaries, and obviously acquainted, occasionally turning up in the same group photographs taken during an earlier, simpler era.

The lobby boasted an oil portrait of the man himself. Painted at the height of his prosperity by the illustrious John Singer Sargent, it showed a handsome man of middle age, sporting muttonchop sideburns and a handlebar mustache, who sat stiffly in a wooden armchair with red velvet cushions. Old Jacob had been a self-made man who'd put in an honest day's work for every penny he earned. He would probably roll in his grave if he knew that his great-grandson, who at thirty-six held the enviable title of vice president, was just waiting for his own father to retire so he could take over the presidency and begin mismanaging the place. Grant Ashford had inherited none of Great-Granddad's thrift, none of his work ethic. But he had inherited the money, as well as the family resemblance. If you took away the sideburns and the mustache and dressed Jacob in contemporary clothes, he'd be a dead ringer—no pun intended—for his great-grandson.

At this time on a weekday, the place was a tomb. The security guard in the lobby was sitting on one of the uncomfortable-looking wooden chairs drinking a cup of coffee. A lone customer stood at one of the teller windows conducting a transaction. The air felt heavy and stale, as if the building lacked proper ventilation. Mia crossed the lobby, her footsteps swallowed up by the thick carpeting, and pressed the button for the elevator. It, too, was vintage, an elaborate, gold-painted wire cage that reminded her of a prison cell once the doors were closed. She knew it was irrational, but every time she stepped into that elevator, she had visions of some ancient threadbare cable snapping, releasing the cage and sending her plummeting to a horrible and untimely death.

But today, as it always did, it took her without mishap to where she wanted to go—Grant Ashford's third-floor office suite. His secretary, a toothy young black woman named Deondra, smiled at her as she entered. "Afternoon, Ms. DeLucca."

"Hello, Deondra. Is Himself in?"

"He is. Just got back from lunch. Hang on and I'll buzz him for you."

Within seconds, the door to the inner office opened, and Grant Ashford blew through. Dressed in his usual somber uniform of black suit and red tie—an attempt, she supposed, to look as though he were competent to hold the position of VP—he looked more like an undertaker than a banker. But the radiant smile was genuine, illuminating his blue eyes and enhancing his strong features: the solid line of his jaw, the full lips, a nose straight as a ruler, flared perfectly at the end. Grant had inherited not only his great-grandfather's good looks, but also his unruly dark hair. He kept it tamed with a crisp haircut that ended just above his collar.

"Mia!" he said. "What a nice surprise!"

"Grant. Do you have a few minutes?" The vice presidency of a bank sounded like a big deal, but in Grant Ashford's case, she suspected it was more a titular position than one that carried any real power or influence. His days were likely boring and filled with busywork. He probably had plenty of minutes to give her.

"Of course. Come in. Coffee? Tea?"

Her business with him wasn't the kind you generally conducted over a nice, civilized cup of Earl Grey. But it would give her a minute to compose herself, a brief reprieve while she tried to figure out what she was going to say. In spite of the fact that he was about as deep as a Kleenex, she'd always sort of liked Grant Ashford. Grilling him about a crime he may or may not have committed would be awkward.

"Thanks," she said. "I'd love a cup of coffee. Cream, no sugar."

While he was gone, she took a good look around his office. She'd been here before, more than once, but always for business reasons, and she hadn't paid much attention to the decor. Above his desk was his framed degree from Harvard Business School. Beneath that hung a collection of photos. Grant shaking hands with the mayor. Grant again, standing at some construction site with the governor. Again shaking hands, this time with a woman Mia didn't recognize, while holding a giant check made out for a large sum of money to the local Big Brothers Big Sisters organization.

On the wall to her left, a mahogany display case with locked glass doors held Grant Ashford's pride and joy: a baseball autographed by Red Sox legend Carl Yastrzemski. He'd acquired it as a kid, shortly before Yaz retired. Grant had told her once that he'd had several offers for it over the years, but that he'd never sell. He fully intended to pass it on to his son someday.

He returned with two coffees, handed one to her and sat down behind his desk to gaze at her with eager curiosity. Mia took a slug of coffee to bolster her courage and jumped in feetfirst. "When was the last time you saw Kaye?"

Something flickered in his eyes, but his smile never wavered. "Two, three weeks ago?" he said. "I don't remember exactly." He took a sip of coffee and grew solemn. "I heard that she's missing, Mia. You have my condolences."

She wasn't sure condolences were in order just yet, but she bowed her head in silent thanks.

"So do the police have any leads?"

"I don't think so."

"This is just so unbelievable. Do you think she's…" He paused meaningfully and didn't finish the sentence.

"Dead?" Mia finished for him. "That's one theory."

He drummed his fingertips on the desktop. "There are other theories?"

"At least one. She could have killed the mystery guy and walked away."

Grant wrinkled his brow. "Walk away from her job, her family? Her life? Why on earth would she do that?"

Things were about to get sticky. Mia took another slug of java, wishing it were something stronger. Watching Ashford's eyes, she said, "She may have been involved in something shady."

He didn't blink. "What makes you think that?"

"A little bird told me about a rumor that's been circulating for a few months. About my sister-in-law being involved in a crooked real estate deal."

"And you're telling me this because?"

"Because that same rumor says you were also involved."

His response wasn't what she'd expected. She'd been prepared for anger. Vehement denial. Maybe even to be ejected from his office. But he did none of those things. Instead, he laughed. He laughed so hard he nearly spilled his coffee. "I'm sorry," he sputtered. "It's just so ludicrous. Oh, Mia." Humor twinkled in his eyes. "You've just made my day."

She didn't know how to respond. He'd thrown her off guard. Had he done it deliberately? "That little bird," he continued, "wouldn't happen to be Marty Scalia, would it?"

Her eyes widened. "How'd you know that?"

"The guy hates me, Mia. He'd say anything to try and get me in trouble. Crooked real estate deal. Oh, God, that's priceless."

"So you weren't involved? At all?"

His expression was indulgent. Fond. As though she were a particularly charming, particularly naive infant. One who'd just performed a clever, highly entertaining trick. "No," he said. "I wasn't involved. At all. Of course—" amusement once again took over his features "—I can't speak for Kaye."

Mia felt like the world's biggest fool. It wasn't a feeling she was accustomed to. Or one she much liked. Being laughed at hurt, no matter what the circumstances. "Look," she said, a flush climbing her face, "this isn't personal. I'm just going on what I was told. I have to ask this, you understand? Because if Kaye was involved in something crooked—"

"You need to know." His expression sobered instantly. "I understand. Really. It's okay, Mia. No offense taken."

"Listen, Grant, I've known Marty for nine years. You may have your personal differences with him, but I know him well, and there's no way he would have made up something like this. The rumor has to be out there or he wouldn't have passed it on to me. How do you suppose something like that got started? Who would do it? And why?"

"Who the hell knows? Professional jealousy? Somebody wanting to discredit one or the other of us? Somebody who wants revenge for some real or imagined injustice? Or somebody who just likes to stir things up and see how much trouble they can cause? Take your pick." He rotated his coffee cup in slow circles on his desk. "I hate to say it, but there are a lot of people who don't like Kaye."

He had a point, but it seemed unprofessional in the extreme for somebody to start a vicious rumor like the one Marty'd passed on just because he or she had a problem with Kaye. That was junior high school reasoning, and these were businesspeople, for Christ's sake, not seventh graders. It just didn't play right for her.

Mia needed more time to mull this over. "Thanks for your input," she told him, getting up from the chair.

Behind the desk, he stood. "You're welcome. I hope they find Kaye soon, and in one piece."

He escorted her out, walked her all the way to the elevator to show he bore no ill will toward her for the bizarre and unjustified accusation she'd hurled at him. While they waited for the car to arrive, he held out his hand. "Still friends?"

She studied him closely, looking for any sign of duplicity. But his blue eyes just stared back, steady and unflinching in their ingenuousness. She saw not a trace of guilt in their depths, nothing but sincerity, concern and mild amusement.

The elevator doors slid open. "Still friends." She shook his hand, then stepped into the elevator and waited for the door to close.

And wondered, as the elevator started to descend…if he was so damned innocent, why were his palms sweaty?

Rachel Winslow.

The name sounded familiar to Lorna, but she couldn't place it. It was Rafferty who made the connection. "Remember that T stop shooting seven or eight years ago?" he said. "Orange line. New England Medical, I think. There were a few minor injuries. One DOA. I believe the vic's name was Rachel Winslow."

"Right," she said. "Now it's coming back to me. The case was never solved, was it?"

"It was before I made lieutenant, and I wasn't directly

involved, so I'm relying on memory here. But I think you're right. And I suspect that by some miraculous coincidence, Rachel Winslow will turn out to be related to Kaye Winslow."

"Gee, you think?" When he scowled, Lorna rolled her eyes and said, "More likely related to Sam. Kaye wasn't a Winslow until she married Sam, about three years ago. But he has a fifteen-year-old daughter, which means there must be another wife hiding in the woodpile somewhere. Who worked the case?"

"I think it was Ted Rizzoli and Jan Harding."

"Well, Rizzoli's out of the question. Where's Harding located these days?"

"Last I heard, she was working Vice. She should be easy enough to track down, if she hasn't retired yet."

Glancing at the bouquet of roses, Lorna tapped her fingernail against the card in her hand. "So who do you suppose our concerned citizen is? And why choose this method of getting to me? Why not just call me up and put a bug in my ear? Isabel, did you get a look at the guy who delivered this bouquet?"

"No. He left it with the desk sergeant. Hinkley. He called me to come down and pick it up."

"Call Hinkley," Rafferty said. "Find out if anybody got a good look at the guy. There's nothing here to indicate which florist it came from?"

Eyeing the bouquet as though she expected a giant python to jump out of it at any minute, Lorna said, "Nothing. It's just a blank white card. Could've come from anywhere."

"Lovely."

"Might not even be a real florist. Methinks somebody

doesn't want us to know where it came from. If Rachel Winslow was Sam Winslow's wife, somebody's going to an awful lot of trouble to draw our attention to that fact. Why the heavy-handed approach?"

"Concerned citizen?"

"Could be."

"Either Winslow's guilty of something—"

"Or," Lorna said, "somebody wants us to think he is."

Isabel flounced back into the room, a living, breathing ball of energy. "Hinkley says he was on the phone when the flowers arrived," she said breathlessly. "They were delivered by a young guy wearing dark glasses and a baseball cap. A black one. The cap, not the guy. Hinkley didn't even talk to him. That's all he could tell me."

"That narrows it down," Lorna said dryly. "And I suppose nobody else saw anything."

"Sorry." Isabel looked far too cheerful for genuine regret. "Too bad these aren't from your husband." She sniffed the flowers and glanced coyly at Lorna. "If you don't want them…"

"They're evidence. We have to dust the vase for prints."

Isabel looked momentarily disappointed, but she managed to recover with amazing speed. "It's a shame," she said, "for something so pretty to end up in an evidence room somewhere."

"You want flowers," Lorna told her, "go buy your own."

She put Isabel to work tracking down the file on the Rachel Winslow homicide, then stopped by Policzki's desk. He'd just come back from talking to the Winslows' neighbors, and now he was eating a strawberry yogurt. "What's that gross-looking stuff on top?" she asked.

"Wheat germ. Good for what ails you."

"And my body is a temple. Spare me. I've already heard it. Give me a nice, greasy pork chop any day. Did you get anything?"

"One of the neighbors overheard the Winslows fighting the other night. He said they were pretty loud."

"Did he hear what they were saying?"

"Nope. They weren't that loud."

"What night was it?"

"He wasn't sure, but he thinks it was Saturday."

"Three days before she disappeared. Isn't that interesting." Policzki ate a spoonful of yogurt. "We already knew they'd been fighting. David Briggs told us that."

"True. But maybe something happened Saturday night. Maybe the tension between them was simmering, ready to boil over. Maybe something made it boil over."

"Yes, but—" He swallowed another spoonful of yogurt. "If things boiled over on Saturday night, why would it take Winslow until Tuesday afternoon to act on it? Kaye Winslow was alive and well up until that time. If he killed her, it couldn't have been a crime of passion."

He had a point. "Maybe the fight wasn't over on Saturday," she said. "Maybe he followed her to Comm Ave on Tuesday and started it all over again."

"So who's John Doe? How does he fit in?"

"I don't know. He could be the key to our whole investigation. Without him, our hands are tied."

"Hard to uncover motive until we find out who he is."

"Where the hell is that autopsy report? I'm going to call the M.E.'s office and ream them a new one."

"Don't bother. I just talked to Neena. We'll have the report sometime this afternoon. That's the good news."

"What's the bad news?"

"The bad news is that there was no match on the prints. Our friend John Doe isn't in the system."

"Fuck. Fuck, fuck, fuck."

"Uh-huh."

"How is that possible, Policzki? This guy, who just happened to end up dead with no ID on him, has never been arrested, never been in the military, never been to freaking grade school? I was printed in grade school. Weren't you?"

"Sixth grade." Policzki took a final bite of yogurt, licked the spoon clean and tossed the container into the trash. "Maybe Mr. Doe was absent that day."

"That's just ducky. What about the rest of the prints? The ones from the scene?"

"Nothing yet. Forensics says maybe later today. By the way, the info Salvatore sent over on the BlackBerry's sitting on your desk. I skimmed it. It'll take some time to work through it. A lot of names and numbers. There was one thing that jumped out at me. Winslow made a phone call right about the time she disappeared. So I called the number."

"And?"

"And I got the switchboard operator at Back Bay Community College."

"Son of a bitch. Sam said he hadn't talked to her since breakfast."

"Uh-huh."

"And he said he didn't take any calls."

"Right again."

"Liar, liar, pants on fire."

"Maybe. Maybe his voice mail took the call. Maybe he really was working. Maybe we're barking up the wrong tree."

"And maybe my great-uncle Alfred was a chimpanzee. You don't think Winslow did it?"

"I didn't say that. I'm just playing devil's advocate."

"Goddamn it, Policzki. I like him so much for this. Besides, he's all we've got. Don't take him away from me."

"I'm not taking him away. I'm just saying we don't have the big picture yet. Only pieces of it. We need more information."

"Which is why I want you to run a background check on DeLucca and the Winslows. Credit check, priors, lawsuits filed by or against. Any unusual banking activity, any recent major purchases made by credit card. You know the drill. I want to know what they fucking ate for breakfast yesterday."

Policzki was a tireless and meticulous researcher. If there was anything to be found, he would find it. "How deep should I dig?"

"As deep as you can go."

While Policzki busied himself digging up dirt on the Winslows, Lorna tracked down Jan Harding. "I remember the case well," Harding said. "Damnedest thing. Guy just winged those two people. They walked away with no more damage than what a Band-Aid could cover. But Rachel Winslow took a bullet direct in the heart. The perp couldn't have done a neater job if he'd painted a bull's-eye on her chest. I always had a funny feeling about it. Was it dumb luck, or deliberate and unerring accuracy?"

Lorna let out a hard breath. "You mean Winslow might not have been a random target?"

"I told myself it was my imagination. That it was a gang thing and Rachel Winslow just happened to be in the wrong place at the wrong time. But it's odd. We interviewed every witness who was there that night. Nobody who was standing outside that subway station at that particular time on that particular night had any gang affiliations that we could find. They all seemed to be just ordinary citizens, minding their own business."

"So," Lorna said, thinking out loud, "why did Winslow end up dead while every other ordinary citizen walked away?"

"Exactly."

"Was she married?"

"Yes. And she had a young daughter. We checked out the husband, but he was never a serious suspect. The poor guy was devastated. And that poor little girl, left motherless like that. She couldn't have been more than six or seven years old."

"What was his name? The husband?"

"Let me think…it's been awhile. Sid? No. Sam? Yes. That was it. Sam Winslow."

Bingo. "And there were never any serious suspects?"

"Nope. It's like the shooter performed his appointed deed and then vanished into thin air."

"You're not thinking professional job?"

"I didn't know quite what to think then, and after eight years, I still don't. But I wouldn't rule out anything. I still think about the case every now and then. They haunt you, the ones you couldn't put to bed no matter how hard you tried. Those are the ones that stay with you the longest. The successes are what they are. It's the failures you can't let go of."

After Lorna hung up the phone, she propped her chin on her palm and pulled a notebook from the rubble that covered her desk. Pen in hand, she doodled while she thought about what Harding had told her.

She examined the situation from every angle: straightforward, upside down, sideways and inside out. Compared Kaye Winslow's disappearance and Rachel Winslow's homicide, considered the years separating them, looked for parallels and similarities. Pondered possible motives, wondered about the mathematical probability of coincidence. So many unanswered questions, scattered about like a jigsaw puzzle waiting to be pieced together. Sam Winslow's first wife had been murdered. The killer had never been caught. Now his second wife had simply vanished, in broad daylight. Leaving behind her briefcase, her BlackBerry and an unidentified corpse.

And nobody had seen a damn thing.

Across the way, Policzki sat straighter in his chair and said, "This is strange."

"What?" Lorna said. "Did you find something?"

"More like I didn't find something. Everything I've been able to dig up on Kaye Winslow is from the last five years. Before that, nothing. No credit report, no previous address, no place of employment. It's as if, five years ago, she spontaneously generated. Before that, she didn't seem to exist."

"Hunh. The big bang theory of existence."

"Pretty much."

"Sort of the opposite of how she disappeared five years later."

They looked at each other for a while. "What the hell is that supposed to mean?" Lorna asked.

"I'd say it means we need to dig a little deeper." Policzki returned to his computer and began clicking keys with admirable speed. "Looks like our friend Kaye might have a few secrets. If only we can unearth—whoa. What's this?"

"What?" Lorna said impatiently. "What?"

"The day before she disappeared, Kaye Winslow filed for divorce."

They looked at each other again. "I'll be damned," she said. "If I didn't know better, I might think that was a clue. So now we have both opportunity and motive. Not to mention Winslow has no alibi, and a first wife who died under mysterious circumstances."

"It's not enough. It's all circumstantial. Unless we can find something solid to tie him to the case, it would never stick. The D.A. would laugh at us."

"But we're making progress. According to Winslow, theirs was a marriage made in heaven. I told you he was a lying sack of shit."

"Maybe it's time we put a little more heat on him."

"Maybe. Maybe we'd have better luck with DeLucca. She's got that mother hen thing going, but I think underneath it, she's a straight arrow. Maybe you could work a little of that charm of yours on her, see if you can get her to spill."

"I don't know," he said. "She doesn't seem to like me much."

"Maybe I'll let you play good cop. Maybe that'll thaw her out."

The phone rang, and Lorna scowled at it. Some days, she wanted to rip the Christless thing out of the wall and stomp up and down on top of it. Rolling her eyes, she picked it up and barked, "Abrams."

"Mom?" It was Krissy, and she was crying.

Lorna's heart began hammering as the mother in her trumped the cynical cop and she immediately began cataloging all the disasters that could have befallen one of her nearest and dearest. Heart attack. Auto accident. School shooting. "What?" she demanded. "What's wrong?"

"Derek and I…we had a f-f-f-fight." Her daughter snuffled louder than a pig rooting for truffles. "We broke up. The wedding—it's…" she paused, snuffled again "…it's off." And she began wailing like a hurricane off Nantucket.

Lorna closed her eyes and counted to ten while she waited for her heart rate to return to normal. She should have remembered that at nineteen, tears didn't necessarily signify tragedy. At nineteen, every cross word, every squabble, meant the end of the world. But it had been too long since she'd been her daughter's age. Too long since she'd been innocent enough to think those were the things that mattered. Her memory of those years had dulled and faded. All Lorna understood now was that true disaster wasn't the kind that reversed itself once things cooled off.

But Krissy was too young to understand that. Covering the mouthpiece, Lorna said to Policzki, "Family crisis. I have to deal with it. Go." She rooted around, one-handed, in the mess on her desk until she found the keys to the cruiser. Tossing them to him, she said, "You're on your own, kid. See what you can get out of DeLucca."

Nine

Mia had an even dozen phone calls to return, an ad to lay out for next Sunday's *Globe* and a list of possible properties to pull together for a repeat client. Instead of doing any of those things, she was wasting her time—and decimating the office budget—staring out the window and viciously snapping paper clips in two. Thinking. Wondering. Speculating about possibilities she didn't want to think about. But like a rubbernecker at a traffic accident, she couldn't seem to tear herself away from them.

Grant Ashford had seemed so sincere. Almost too sincere. And it seemed to her that an innocent man would have protested a little harder. Shown a brief flash of anger. Been at least mildly insulted by her suggestion that he'd participated in a crime.

But Ashford had done none of those things. Instead of defending himself, he'd turned the tables on her. By making a joke of the whole situation, by implying it was the most ludicrous thing he'd ever heard, he'd put her on the defensive instead.

It could have been the genuine response of an innocent

man. Or it could have been his clever way of taking the wind out of her sails. Using ridicule to make her doubt herself and her convictions. It had certainly been effective.

Until that damp handshake. The room hadn't been hot. As far as she knew, he didn't have any medical conditions that would cause sweaty palms. But Grant Ashford had been sweating, and if she were a gambling woman, she would have bet a month's income that he was lying to her.

She brutally ended the life of another paper clip. "For God's sake," Bev said, "give those to me." She marched up to Mia's desk like an avenging angel and scooped up the ceramic mug of paper clips that Kevin had made years ago in fifth-grade art class. "You keep eating up the profits that way, we'll be holding a bake sale to pay the electric bill."

The bell over the door jingled, and they both glanced up. "Can I help you?" Bev called out to the visitor who stood inside the entrance.

The anonymous somebody mumbled a few words Mia couldn't hear, and right before her eyes, the über-competent Bev turned a lovely shade of peach like some smitten adolescent. "Of course," she said. "Come in. She's right here."

The man who paused at the threshold to Mia's office wore a crisp white shirt with a gray suit coat, and Ray-Ban sunglasses that completely hid his eyes. Who did he think he was, James Bond? In his dreams, maybe. Bev stood clutching the ceramic mug of paper clips and, behind his back, waggled her eyebrows. Mia scowled at her and said, "Well, if it isn't one of my two favorite people. Where's your other half? Out flogging shoplifters?"

"We're not joined at the hip," he said. "We're partners. Just like you and Kaye."

Score one for the Vulcan. Mia must have hit a nerve.

"Bev," she said, "this is Detective Policzki. Detective, my administrative assistant, Bev Constantine."

Bev juggled the mug and extended her newly freed hand. Policzki stared at it for an instant before he seemed to realize what she wanted. Probably on the planet he'd come from, people greeted each other by waving their antennae or something. He shook her hand and said, "Nice to meet you."

"Nice to meet you, too," Bev said. "I assume you're working on Kaye's case?"

"That's right. I was hoping you and Ms. DeLucca would have a few minutes to talk to me."

Bev questioned Mia with her eyes. "Go lock the door," Mia said, "and flip the sign." To Policzki, she added, "I suppose you might as well sit down. You're bigger than I am, and you carry a gun and a badge. Asking you to leave wouldn't be worth the effort."

He chose the chair nearest the window, the one that afforded him a view of the door. She'd always heard that cops never sat with their backs to a door. It must be true. Bev returned minus the mug and sat in the remaining chair. Perfect, Mia thought. Now they could all have a nice little tea party.

"How's the investigation going?" she asked.

Policzki removed the sunglasses and lost a little of that extraterrestrial air. "You know I can't answer that question."

"But you can certainly ask a lot of them yourself."

"That's my job," he said. "I can't help it."

"You know," she said, "I'm not generally rude. You just seem to bring out the worst in me."

For an instant, she almost thought he was going to smile. He might actually look human if he ever smiled. She waited, anticipation shortening her breath, as the corner of his mouth succumbed to several suspicious twitches. But to her disappointment, he managed to wrest control of his runaway emotions, and his tough-guy mask remained intact. "I have that effect on a lot of people," he said.

Mia checked her watch. "As much as I'd love to sit here all afternoon with you, exploring my latent tendency toward masochism, I do have work waiting to be done. So if you have something to say, please say it now and get it over with."

"All right. Let me throw something out, and we can chew on it. The day before she disappeared, your sister-in-law filed for divorce."

Mia glanced at Bev, whose eyes signaled her surprise. Which meant that after Sam closed the door yesterday morning, Bev hadn't been hovering on the other side with a drinking glass pressed up against the wood. "I know," Mia said. "Sam told me."

"Ahhh," Bev said as the light went on over her head. "That's why—" She broke off abruptly, glanced at Policzki and clamped her mouth shut.

"You knew?" the detective said to Mia.

"Sam was served with divorce papers. He came here right afterward. He was a little…" Mia glanced out the window for inspiration, but all she saw was the brick wall of the building across the alley. Shrugging, she said, "I guess *distressed* would be the most appropriate word. He hadn't expected it."

"That's what he told you? That he hadn't expected it?"

"Not in those exact words," she said, "but that was the gist of it."

"So he had no idea that his wife was unhappy with their marriage. No clues, no little alarm bells going off? They just went from honeymoon to divorce in one fell swoop?"

"Look, I wasn't a fly on the wall, okay? I only know what Sam told me. That's hearsay evidence, isn't it? I thought you couldn't use that in court."

Again, that almost smile. "We're not in court," he said. "There's no judge here, no jury. No criminal charges, no defendant. I'm just trying to get a feel for what was really going on. Generally, when a marriage is on the rocks, there are symptoms."

"Thank you, Dr. Phil."

Ignoring her sarcasm, he continued. "Excessive fighting. Excessive silence. Increased time spent apart and less time spent together. Sleeping in separate bedrooms. One or both parties suddenly putting in a lot of overtime at work. Money hoarding, or, at the other end of the spectrum, extravagant spending. Unexplained credit card charges. Increased irritability with friends and coworkers." He paused. "Infidelities on the part of one or both spouses."

Bev made some kind of noise, and they both turned to look at her. "Are you suggesting that my brother was unfaithful to his wife?" Mia said, drawing Policzki's attention back to her. "Because if you are—"

"I'm not suggesting anything. I'm just thinking out loud. Your brother tells me everything in his marriage is hunky-dory. Meanwhile, his wife has just filed for divorce. Which leaves me with an obvious question—was he lying to me, or is he deaf, dumb and blind?"

Mia picked up a pen from her desk and began scribbling viciously on a notepad. "There's something you should know about my brother," she said. "He's a bit of an idiot savant. He got straight A's in school, but he never had a lick of common sense. He whizzed through college and graduate school. He now has a head overloaded with information, which I understand he's pretty good at disseminating to students. But when it comes to any practical application of his knowledge, he's a dismal failure." She stopped scribbling and met Policzki's eyes. "He can expound for an hour on a critical analysis of Michelangelo's painting of the Sistine Chapel, but he can barely manage to tie his own shoelaces."

"Meaning, I presume, that if his wife was showing signs of discontent, he might have missed seeing them."

"Exactly."

Policzki turned back to Bev. "Ms. Constantine?" he said. "Was there something you wanted to say?"

Shit. Mia thought she'd sufficiently distracted him. Apparently she'd underestimated him. Young and cute didn't necessarily equate to stupid. Bev, obviously torn between loyalty and some innate sense of right and wrong, looked to Mia for help. Mia sighed, rubbed her temple and gave her assistant a brief, almost imperceptible nod. She'd always been a big proponent of truth. If Bev knew something she didn't, it probably needed to come out.

"I don't like to gossip," Bev said. "I don't like saying things about my coworkers. I have to keep a roof over my head and make sure the bills are paid. I need my job. And usually, the fastest way to lose a job is to bad-mouth the boss." She shot a rapid, guilty glance at Mia. "The other boss," she clarified.

Mia nodded. Policzki waited patiently while Bev took a breath. "I shouldn't even be saying this. Especially under the circumstances. I mean, Kaye could be dead, and I'd never wish anything like that on her. But the truth is—" again, that guilty look "—the truth is that if it weren't for you, Mia, I would've quit a long time ago."

It was the last thing she'd expected to hear. "Why?" she said.

"You always treat me with respect. Like an equal. Kaye doesn't do that. She can be demanding and bossy. Not that there's anything inherently wrong with that. I mean, she *is* my boss, and she has a right to certain expectations of me. But she likes to remind me that she's the one with the college education, the prestige and the fat bank account, while I'm the peon who works for an hourly wage and is here for no other purpose than to do her bidding."

"I had no idea. Why didn't you tell me?"

"Be serious. What was I supposed to do, run to one of my bosses and tattle on the other one? This isn't junior high school. I'm a professional. I know there will always be people out there in the working world who make life difficult. I'm not a whiner. I suck it up and deal with it."

"You're certainly not a whiner," Mia said indignantly. "What you are is my right arm."

"See what I mean? You show appreciation for what I do. Kaye treats me like a piece of office machinery, placed on this planet exclusively for her use."

"I'm so sorry."

"Don't lose any sleep over it. I haven't. But it isn't just that. She's two-faced. I've caught her playing Little Miss Bountiful with clients to their faces, then bad-mouthing them the minute they walked out the door. I've also heard her making promises over the phone, then turning around and doing the exact opposite of what she'd said." The administrative assistant's mouth thinned. "I understand that in any kind of sales, there's a certain level of manipulation that goes on. But this goes beyond that. Quite honestly, I don't trust the woman. Her ethics are questionable at best."

For the first time, she hesitated. "There's more. I'm not even sure I should bring it up. It's not work-related, it's really none of my business and I'm uncomfortable discussing it. But something you said—" she nodded in Policzki's direction "—just struck a chord with me, and I don't think I can keep quiet about it."

"Go ahead," the detective said. "We all want the same thing here."

Do we? Mia wondered. Policzki wanted his case solved. Bev wanted to get something off her chest. While she herself wanted—what? If anybody had asked her two days ago, she would have said she wanted to find Kaye, safe and sound and innocent of murder. But two days ago, her brother hadn't been served with divorce papers. Two days ago, she hadn't known about Kaye's mistreatment of their office assistant. Two days ago, she'd never heard of Mickey Slattery.

Bev was speaking to her, and she forced herself to focus on her assistant's words. "You remember those red roses Kaye got last Valentine's Day? The ones we teased her about, saying Sam must be one hell of a romantic?"

"Of course."

"They weren't from Sam."

Mia closed her eyes, expelled a breath and muttered a curse.

"Remember how she clammed up and turned red and wouldn't talk about it? She tore up the card and tossed it in the trash. I, uh…" Bev looked abashed, but she quickly got over it. "I sort of fished it out and pieced it back together. They were from somebody named Mickey."

Policzki leaned forward. "Mickey?" he said. "Mickey who?"

"I don't know," Bev said. "The name doesn't ring a bell, although I suppose he could be a client. We could look through the files…." She trailed off, apparently realizing what a daunting job that would be.

Acid began to gnaw at the lining of Mia's stomach. She was probably getting an ulcer. Wearily, she said, "There's no need for that."

They both looked at her as though they'd forgotten she was in the room. "You know who he is?" Policzki said.

Mia sighed. "His name is Mickey Slattery," she said. "Sam told me about him, too."

The instant the door closed behind Policzki, Bev leaped on her like a starving lioness taking down a gazelle. "That man is totally hot," she said. "How come you didn't tell me about him?"

"That man," Mia said, "is totally annoying. Besides, he's about twelve years old."

"Nah. Probably somewhere in his mid-twenties. Besides, you know what they say about younger men. Fewer wrinkles, more stamina—"

Mia shuddered and closed her eyes. "Please."

"—plus they treat older women with respect, and they won't die fifteen years before we do."

"Stop making me feel geriatric. I'm not looking for a boy toy. Even if I was, it wouldn't be someone like Policzki."

"What's wrong with him? I think he's a total hottie."

"Great. You go after him, then. This topic is now closed. Damn it, Bev, why didn't you tell me about the way Kaye was treating you? And how come I never noticed?"

"I told you, I'm not one to tattle. And she mostly did it when you weren't around."

"Oh, God." Leaning over her desk, Mia cradled her head in her folded arms. "How am I going to get through the rest of this day?"

"I don't know about you, hon, but I'm voting for caffeine. Chocolate wouldn't hurt any, either."

Mia thought about all the caffeine she'd already ingested today, decided a little more wouldn't make much of a difference. She raised her head. "Starbucks?" she said hopefully.

"Starbucks works for me."

"Good. Get me the biggest mocha latte you can carry. It won't solve all my problems, but it'll make them a little easier to deal with."

"Two mocha lattes coming up. And if I catch you with one more paper clip in your hands, I'm locking your mug in my desk and sending you to a twelve-step program."

The bell over the front door jangled merrily as Bev left the building. The mocha latte probably wouldn't help Mia's gnawing stomach, but what could you do when one need superseded another? You had to go with your strengths. And she was a world-class coffee drinker.

While she waited for Bev to return with that vital jolt of caffeine, Mia killed time cleaning off her desk. She usually kept it neat, but in the chaos of the last couple of days, the clutter had begun to take over. Mia stacked papers and tucked them in a drawer to be dealt with later, lined up her stapler, her tape dispenser, her desk organizer. She swept the broken paper clips into the trash, then picked up a file folder and was halfway to the filing cabinet when the telephone rang.

She hesitated, took an instant to work herself into business mode, and reached for it. "Good afternoon," she said with false cheerfulness, "Winslow & DeLucca."

"Mia DeLucca?" The voice was scratchy, little more than a whisper.

"Yes?" she said.

"I have a message for your brother."

At first, she thought she'd heard wrong. "My brother?"

"Yeah. Tell him we're watching him."

Her heart rate skyrocketed as the file she held slithered free and fell to the floor, scattering papers in a ten-foot radius. "Excuse me?" she said.

"You heard me. Just tell him. He'll understand."

Gracie was waiting on the sidewalk in front of Bellerose Academy when her dad pulled up in the thirty-year-old Volvo that was an embarrassment compared to the Beemers and the Lincoln Navigators driven by the parents of her classmates. She opened the passenger-side door, tossed in her backpack and slumped onto the seat.

"Hi, sweetie," he said. "Did you have a nice day?"

Gracie looked at him out of the corner of her eye. Sometimes he reminded her of the William H. Macy character in the movie *Pleasantville*. Too naive to be real. Didn't he remember that high school was like a POW camp, only with better clothes? Or had he gone through adolescence wearing the same blinders he wore as an adult?

"Sure, Dad," she said. "Whatever you say."

Apparently missing her sarcasm, he turned on the radio, most likely so he wouldn't have to talk to her. Which was fine with Gracie, but she would've appreciated it if he had better taste in music. All he listened to was this god-awful classical stuff that made her teeth ache and her eyeballs bleed. Mozart and Tchaikovsky and God only knew what else. A little kick-ass rock and roll would be an improve-

ment. The Darkness, maybe, or Aerosmith. Even something from the eighties, like AC/DC or some early Spring-
steen. When she was twelve, she'd discovered her mom's
old record collection in the attic. Some of it was pretty lame
(Adam Ant, anybody?), but most of the stuff was amazing.
Ever since then, classic rock had been her favorite music.
It confused the hell out of those twits at school, and it sure
beat most of the stuff they called music nowadays.

But her dad was clueless. Not just about music, but
about everything that had happened since 1962. Gracie
loved him, but he was pretty much a failure as a parent.
Their relationship existed on a purely superficial level, and
their interactions as father and daughter were depressingly
routine. "What's for dinner?" and "Please pass the salt"
were perennial favorite conversational topics. She was
pretty sure he couldn't have named her favorite color, or
her favorite band, or her favorite book, not even if he had
a gun to his head. Dad was so far out of touch with reality,
he'd probably never even heard of Madonna. Matter of fact,
Gracie suspected that the last female recording artist who'd
entered his radar screen was probably Carly Simon.

He didn't look good. His skin was pasty, and he hadn't
shaved this morning. If he'd been a seventeen-year-old
boy, his unshaved look might have been attractive, if you
were the kind of girl who went for that macho, testoster-
one-driven type. But on a grown man, it just made him look
like he belonged on a park bench somewhere, clutching a
bottle of Wild Turkey wrapped in a brown paper bag. Gracie supposed it was understandable that he should look a
little rough around the edges, considering that his wife
was missing and God only knew what had happened to her.
Except that for some reason, he'd been looking kind of

squinty around the eyes for a couple of weeks now. Long before Kaye took a powder. Maybe it had nothing to do with her stepmother's disappearance.

And that idea scared Gracie half to death.

She sniffed the air inside the car, but didn't detect any lingering scent of alcohol. At least she could be grateful for that. It meant he wasn't likely to kill them both between Bellerose Academy and Union Square. Or if he did, it would be due to an act of God, instead of an act of drunkenness.

She supposed she had to ask the inevitable question, even if the answer wasn't what she wanted to hear. She leaned forward and turned down the radio. "Have they found Kaye yet?"

Her dad's knuckles were white on the steering wheel. "No."

"And the cops haven't told you anything more?"

His eyes stayed glued to the road as he maneuvered in and out of traffic. "No," he said again.

"Do you think something's happened to her?"

"Of course not."

His response, so immediate it must have been rehearsed, was undoubtedly his way of trying to protect her. Gracie might have been touched, if she hadn't found it so annoying. "Look," she said, "I'm not some four-year-old who'll believe everything's okay because her dad says it is. I'm old enough to understand the ramifications of the situation. Old enough to know the truth. So if you're trying to protect me, you're about eight years too late."

Her father's face, when he turned to look at her, was pallid, his cheeks hollow beneath prominent cheekbones. For the first time, Gracie could see signs of aging in him. She'd never considered the passage of time, particularly not in connection with her father. He'd just been Dad, tall and good-looking, ineffectual but for the most part well-meaning. But it seemed as though he'd aged ten years since yesterday. She knew that wasn't possible, knew it was an illusion. But the haunted look in his eyes cut her to the bone, and the truth hit her like a lightning bolt. It wasn't her he was trying to shield from the truth; it was himself he was protecting.

He'd already lost one wife. The prospect of losing another must be terrifying. Gracie hadn't really thought about it from his point of view. She might consider her stepmother to be the spawn of Satan, but for better or for worse, Kaye was Dad's wife. The woman he'd vowed to cherish until death did them part. Regardless of Gracie's own feelings about Kaye, it wasn't fair to him to have to go through something like this a second time.

And what if it really was all Gracie's fault?

Guilt gnawed at her, a guilt so strong that she had to look away from her father. *No way,* she told herself vehemently. No way was this her fault. She was being paranoid. That was the conclusion she'd come to after lying awake half the night, thinking it through. Just because she couldn't track down Carlos didn't mean he had anything to do with her stepmother's disappearance. Or with that guy's murder. It was just coincidence. Carlos was probably just busy. Working or something. That was why he hadn't been online in a couple of days. She'd let her own vivid imagination run wild, that was all.

But a seed of doubt still remained, big enough to feel like a heavy weight lodged in the pit of her stomach.

When they got home, Gracie went directly upstairs. Her cat, Ralph, sat at the top of the steps, waiting for her, just as she did every day. Gracie picked Ralph up and cradled the misnomered kitty to her chest. When they'd first adopted the tiny kitten from some lady who worked with her dad, they'd been assured that Ralph was a male. By the time they found out the truth, the name had stuck, so Ralph she remained, in spite of her anatomy.

Gracie buried her face in the cat's fur. "Hey, babe," she whispered. "I bet you missed me today."

She was rewarded with a loud purr. Ralph avoided Sam and tolerated Kaye, but it was Gracie she loved, Gracie whose bed she slept in every night. Gracie might not have many human friends, but she and Ralph were tight.

She sat down at her computer with the cat in her lap and logged on. "Come on," she muttered. "You have to be there."

But he wasn't. It was like he'd disappeared into thin air. Just like her stepmother had. And that really freaked Gracie out. Trying to dam the fear that kept threatening to drown her, she visited a couple of chat rooms where she knew he liked to hang out. Hey, she wrote, anybody seen Magnum357 around lately? Been trying to hook up with him, but he's MIA.

The response was negative. Nobody had talked to Carlos in several days. Discouraged, she logged off the computer and sat stroking Ralph's soft, warm fur. There were a couple of real-world places where she knew he liked to hang out. The food court at the Prudential Mall was one of them. Harvard Square was another. He liked places where he could be anonymous in the middle of a crowd. Maybe she should check them out. The Pru was just a few blocks away. If he wasn't there, she could hop on the red line to

Cambridge. She could patrol the Square and see if he was hanging there.

Downstairs, the doorbell rang, three short, angry bursts. Gracie dropped Ralph to the floor and got up from the chair. She stepped out into the hall with the cat trotting along behind her, and waited at the top of the stairs, one hand clutching the newel post. Downstairs, there was another short, sharp series of buzzes, and her dad sprinted the last few steps to the door.

When he opened it, her aunt Mia blew through, looking like a fashion model in tight black pants tucked into high-heeled ankle boots. Mia had her own distinct style, one that Gracie would have given her right arm to copy. But on her, Mia's sophisticated wardrobe would have looked ridiculous; she didn't have the panache to pull it off.

Her aunt's mink-colored hair was disheveled, as though she'd run all the way over here in a high wind, and it was clear, even from this distance, that she was armed for bear.

"You'd best shut the door," Mia snapped, "unless you want your neighbors to know all your business."

Gracie lowered herself to the floor and shrank back into the shadows. Ralph twined her slender body around Gracie's forearm as Mia dragged her fingers through her hair in an unsuccessful attempt to neaten it. "I don't know what the hell is going on," she said, "but you and I are going to talk, Sam Winslow. And this time, you're going to tell me the truth!"

Ten

Mickey Slattery was a fry cook at a seafood restaurant called the Beachcomber near the docks in Southie. The restaurant's name conjured up images of hot sand, warm breezes and piña coladas. In reality, the Beachcomber was a dark, dank, unpainted shanty that sported red-and-white-checkered plastic tablecloths and smelled of rancid grease. Squeezed in between two warehouses, the restaurant's only connection to the briny deep was the faded buoys and dead starfish somebody had tacked up on a dirty fishing net strung on the wall behind the bar. It was a solidly blue-collar establishment that served a solidly blue-collar clientele.

At this time of day, the dinner rush—such as it was—hadn't yet started, and the place was deserted. A middle-aged waitress with wary eyes paused, cleaning rag in hand, and watched the two detectives walk through the door. She didn't reach for menus. Policzki and Abrams weren't the first cops she'd seen in here, and they wouldn't be the last. "Help you?" she said in a voice devoid of warmth. Funny, Policzki thought, how few truly welcoming greetings they received.

"We're looking for Mickey Slattery," he told her.

"Kitchen," she said, and went back to wiping down the counter.

They found their way to the kitchen without a road map, stepped through a swinging door into a space the Health Department would have shut down if they'd seen it. After his initial stunned reaction, Policzki forced himself to close his eyes to the lack of sanitation. Although it was tempting, that wasn't why they were here. In the background, a radio was playing an old country classic, Ray Price singing "Crazy Arms" in that inimitable Texas twang. A skinny kid with one eye that looked off in the wrong direction was sweeping the floor, hands grasping the broom like a lover, on his face a dreamy expression as he swept in time to the music.

Doug and Lorna exchanged glances, then moved in unison toward the man who was busy scraping the grill while he sang along with Ray in a surprisingly clear, sweet tenor. His sleeves rolled up to reveal tattooed forearms, Mickey Slattery was a reasonably good-looking guy in a rough-hewn, thuggish sort of way. Tall and solidly built, he had sandy hair and a redhead's complexion, and the kind of body that in ten years, if he wasn't careful, would run to fat.

He looked up, saw them and went still for an instant. "Mickey Slattery?" Policzki said.

"Depends on who wants to know."

He was dicking them around. There was no way in hell he didn't know they were cops. Lorna held up her badge and said, "Maybe this will clarify it for you."

"In case you hadn't noticed, I'm working here."

Policzki turned and, through the pass-through window, surveyed the empty dining room. Eyes widened in mock surprise, he turned back to Slattery. "And just look at all those customers out there, clamoring for their dinner."

Lorna said, "We just want to talk to you, Mick."

"About what?"

"Two words. Kaye Winslow. Any idea where she is?"

Slattery eyed them emotionlessly. "Any reason I should?"

"When was the last time you saw her?" Lorna asked.

"Why?"

"Just answer the question," Policzki said.

"I haven't seen Kaye in months. I don't know where she is. If she's been out whoring around again, it must be somebody else's bed she's warming, because it sure isn't mine."

"You read the papers?" Policzki said.

A muscle twitched in Slattery's jaw. The movement was minuscule, but Policzki saw it. "Sometimes," Slattery replied.

"You read them this morning? Maybe you saw the article about the missing Realtor."

"I didn't have anything to do with it. I already told you."

"Oh. So you did read the paper this morning."

Lorna said, "We checked your record, Mick. We know about the aggravated assault charge."

"That was eight years ago. I already did my time. Talk to my parole officer. He'll tell you I'm clean."

"We already did," Lorna said. "You still have eight months to go before you're in the clear. Don't screw it up. Talk to us."

Glancing at the kid with the broom, Slattery set down his spatula, picked up a rag and wiped his hands on it. "Keep an eye on things," he told the kid. "I'm taking a break." He gave a nod of his head toward the back door. The two detectives followed him through the filthy kitchen, past the kid, who stared at them without a flicker of interest and then went back to sweeping.

The screen door slammed behind them. The alley beside the restaurant was littered with garbage. A shiny green housefly dive-bombed them, and Doug swatted at it. Beside him, Slattery lit a cigarette and took a puff. "So," he said.

"Where were you Tuesday afternoon?" Policzki said.

"Gee, let me check my appointment book, see if I was taking tea with the queen. Nope, looks like I was here, slaving over a hot grill, same as I am every other day."

"You got people," Lorna said, "who can vouch for you?"

"Edith out front. And Lenny. That's the kid with the—you know." He crossed his eyes, took a draw on his cigarette, then tossed it down and ground it out with his foot. "Trying to quit," he said.

"Tell us about Kaye," Policzki suggested. "How'd you meet her?"

"I was in the market for a house. I called her, she started taking me around to look at properties. One thing led to another and…" He shrugged.

"Forgive me for saying this," Lorna said, "but you don't seem her type. Compared to her husband."

Slattery laughed. "I clean up pretty good. Besides, I don't know as I'd say Kaye has a type. You got the equipment, baby, she's ready to rock and roll. And that husband of hers is a loser. He may be good-looking, but holy shit."

"So you've met him?" Policzki said.

"I've heard about him. And I've seen him. Kaye brought him here a couple of times. Just for shits and giggles, you know? I think it was a turn-on for her, having us both in the same place at the same time. Her little secret. Know what I mean? Hell, I almost feel sorry for the guy. But he should've known better. Guy like that, with a little four banger under the hood, should've known better than to take up with a woman like Kaye. That lady is a V8, firing on all cylinders. She's way out of his league."

"She out of your league?" Lorna said.

"There's a big difference. I wasn't in it for keeps. I knew better than to think she was in love with me."

"So you were just in it for the sex," Policzki said.

"Man, have you seen her? A woman like that could make the Pope change his mind about celibacy."

"Did she ever express any fear of her husband?" Lorna asked. "She ever say he roughed her up, or threatened her in any way?"

"Nope. **Just** that he was kind of dense. And he wasn't meeting her needs, if you get my drift. That lady has a lot of needs."

"Did he know about your affair?"

"He found out toward the end. I guess it wasn't pretty."

"What happened?" Policzki said.

"She broke it off with me. The edge was starting to wear off, anyway. I knew it was in the Dumpster before she did."

"The edge," Lorna said. "Explain what you mean by that."

"Kaye was a risk-taker. One of those—what do you call it? Adrenaline junkies. That was the whole trip for her." Slattery lit another cigarette, blew out the smoke. "We did it in empty houses."

"Empty houses," Lorna said. "You mean abandoned buildings?"

He laughed. "I mean people's houses. I was in the market for a house. We looked at a lot of 'em. We did it in the bedrooms while nobody was home. Sometimes the kitchen, or the living room. Put everything back together afterward, and nobody knew the difference."

The ramifications of what he'd said, just in terms of professional ethics, were astounding. If what Slattery said was true, Kaye Winslow had risked not only her marriage, but her reputation, the reputation of her business—and Mia's—and the loss of her broker's license.

"Weren't you afraid," Policzki asked, "that you'd get caught?"

"That was the point, man. The risk was what made it all worthwhile. At least for her it was. I was just along for the, uh…" he grinned "…ride."

They decided the alley was the lesser of two evils, and picked their way through assorted refuse, skirting unidentifiable puddles and stepping over broken beer bottles on their way back to the street. Spotting the cruiser parked at the curb, Lorna wasn't sure when she'd ever seen such a welcome sight. Without discussing it with Policzki, she made a beeline for the passenger door. It might be awhile before she regained enough strength to drive.

Policzki climbed in behind the wheel and started the engine. But instead of going anywhere, they sat there in silence, both of them digesting what they'd just learned, neither quite able to articulate an appropriate response to the overwhelming ick factor.

After a few minutes of psychological decontamination, Lorna said weakly, "Do you suppose we could file that under the heading of Things Your Realtor Will Never Tell You?"

"How about under More Information Than You Ever Wanted?"

"I'm never putting my house up for sale. Ever. And if I ever do, I'm delousing the place after every showing."

"Do you suppose anybody ever found—never mind. I'm not going there."

"Please. Whatever you do, don't go there."

"Gives a whole new meaning to the story of Goldilocks and the Three Bears, doesn't it?"

"Somebody's been sleeping in my bed." Lorna fought back a snicker, wasn't quite successful. "Oh, shit, Policzki. This isn't funny."

"It certainly isn't."

She braved a glance at him, saw the humor in his eyes. "Shut up," she said, even though he hadn't said a word. "Just shut up and drive."

"Can I just say one thing? Since we need to check out his alibi, I'd be more than happy to turn that critical piece of the investigation over to you."

"What's wrong, Policzki? You didn't like the ambience of the place? Or was it the roaches hiding in the corners that put you off?"

"I just think you're better than I am at dealing with certain elements of society."

"I'm not sure how to take that."

"Take it any way you want. It was meant as a compliment."

"Why, Douglas. Are you trying for brownie points?"

"That depends," he said. "Is it working?"

The kid had mellowed in the time they'd been partners. It had been torture at first, being paired with Dudley Do-Right. Policzki had been pain-in-the-ass proper, following the rule book to the nth degree, while she was used to cutting corners when circumstances warranted. Their styles hadn't exactly meshed. It had taken her a couple of years and some major excavating before she'd unearthed Policzki's rebellious side. That inner rebel might have been overpowered by the Boy Scout exterior, but every so often, he peeked through. With a little more seasoning, Policzki would turn into an exceptional cop, even if he did look more like Elwood Blues than Elliot Ness every time he put on those god-awful sunglasses he couldn't seem to step outdoors without.

"So why do you need brownie points?" she said.

"So you won't scream bloody murder when I tell you I'm cutting out early tonight."

"You mean you're actually leaving on time for once? Geez, Policzki, the sky might fall. Tell me you have something exciting planned. I have to live vicariously, you know."

"I don't have anything planned. Yet. I'll get back to you on that."

When they strode into the chaos that was headquarters, Lorna took a deep breath. This was more like it. This was home, more so even than the little three-bedroom ranch in Quincy that she'd never live long enough to pay off. Even the air in here was different. Electrified, somehow, and smelling of burned coffee and stale air-conditioning.

The autopsy report was waiting on her desk, where Isabel had left it. "About time," Lorna muttered, and plunked down into her chair to read it. Across from her, Policzki removed his jacket, hung it neatly over the back of his chair and picked up the telephone.

She tried to concentrate on what she was reading, but it was hard not to eavesdrop when he was sitting just five feet away. When he asked for someone named Melissa, Lorna raised her head and studied him surreptitiously over the top of the autopsy report. The kid was just full of surprises.

"Hi," he said into the telephone receiver. "This is Doug Policzki. Linda Policzki's—yeah, that's right. I know this is short notice, but if you don't have plans for tonight, I thought we might—good. That's good." He glanced up and caught Lorna watching him. She quickly ducked back behind the report. "I thought we could grab a quick dinner and then maybe do a little sightseeing. Six o'clock? Excellent. I'll see you then."

He hung up the phone. Behind the autopsy report—which held no surprises and no clues to John Doe's identity—Lorna hummed a breathy little tune.

"Before you ask," Policzki said, "no, it's not a real date."

"I didn't say a thing."

"It's a family obligation. Melissa from Iowa. She just graduated from veterinary school. Her aunt and my mother are best friends. I've never even met the girl."

Lorna dropped the autopsy report and all pretense of indifference. "Woman," she corrected cheerfully. "I hear that even in Iowa, they're politically correct." At the sight of his mournful expression, she added, "Hey, kid, cheer up. Maybe she'll be cute."

"Right. That's just what I need, cute. So is there anything worth reading in that report?"

"Nope. Our DOA remains a John Doe for now."

"In the morning, I'll start checking missing persons reports. What about you? Are you staying late tonight?"

"I don't know." She swiveled restlessly in her chair. "I'll probably hang around here for a while. I want to go over Rachel Winslow's file. See if anything jumps out at me."

"You should go home to Ed. There's always tomorrow."

"Says the guy who's usually here until 10:00 p.m. every night."

"Which means I should know the signs of workaholism."

"Get out of here, Policzki. Go pick up Miss Iowa and have yourself some fun. Get yourself laid or something."

He stood, picked up his jacket and shrugged into it. "Does your husband know about that potty mouth of yours?"

She grinned. "Are you kidding? Why do you think he married me?"

In her brother's front hall, Mia tugged off her jacket and tossed it on the antique telephone table. Furious, she said, "I just had a very interesting phone call."

"From who?"

"You know, Sam, that's just the thing. I don't have a clue who he was. But he asked me to deliver a message to you." A noise at the top of the stairs drew her attention, and she glanced up just in time to see Gracie duck back into the shadows.

"Kitchen!" she whispered to Sam. "Now!"

The kitchen table was littered with toast crumbs, and a sticky butter knife lay beside an open jar of grape jelly. The sink was stacked with dirty dishes. Kaye would have gone ballistic if she'd seen the mess. The kitchen was equipped with a dishwasher. Didn't the man know how to operate it?

"Do you have any coffee in this place?" Mia said irritably. After the anonymous phone call, she'd been so rattled that she'd written a note to Bev and then driven directly to her brother's house without waiting for her mocha latte. The caffeine would probably keep her up all night, but right now the prospect of it was the only thing preventing her from slapping her brother right across that movie-star-handsome face.

"Tell me," he demanded.

"First the coffee. Then we talk."

Her brother scowled, but he moved to the coffeemaker. Mia stood there with her arms crossed, watching him slam things around. A box of coffee filters. A bag of ground Colombian coffee. The water faucet.

"Keep that up," she said, "and you'll be calling a plumber."

Instead of answering, her brother flipped the switch on the coffeemaker, leaned with both hands braced against the edge of the counter, and took a deep breath. "All right," he said, facing her. "You'd better tell me what's going on."

"I was about to ask you the same question."

"Don't screw around with me, Mia. I'm not in the mood for it."

"Just like I'm not in the mood to be getting creepy calls from some guy with his voice disguised, telling me he has a message for my brother. Quote, 'Tell him we're watching him,' end quote. Care to explain that, big brother?"

Sam's face went ashen, and he looked as though at any minute the contents of his stomach would backfire in a spectacular eruption. Mia actually took a step backward, to get out of the way, just in case. The emotions that crossed his face—shock, bewilderment, guilt, coming full-circle right back to shock—were terrifying.

"What the hell is going on?" she said.

"I don't know."

"Bullshit! How can I help you if you won't tell me the truth? Did you—" She closed her eyes for an instant, unable to bear the thought. "Did you do something to Kaye? Did you kill her?"

"No."

"Do you know where she is?"

"No."

"Damn it, Sam, you're not telling me anything. Are you involved somehow in her disappearance?"

His eyes, when he opened them, were red-rimmed and bloodshot. In their depths, she saw something unidentifiable. Guilt? Fury? Bewilderment? "I can't talk about it," he said.

The thin thread of hope she'd been clinging to snapped. "Then you are involved."

"I didn't say that."

"Well, which is it, Sam? Either you are or you aren't. You can't have it both ways."

He squared his jaw and refused to answer.

None of this made any sense. Sometimes her brother was his own worst enemy. Mia had spent most of her childhood, and a fair portion of her adult life, protecting him from himself. He'd always been a little different from everybody else. A little quieter, a little more fragile. A little weirder. She felt disloyal even thinking it, but what if her brother had a dark side she'd never seen? He'd admitted that he knew Kaye was unfaithful. What if he hadn't been able to handle her infidelity? What if he'd followed her to the house on Commonwealth Avenue? What if, upon seeing her there with another man, something inside him had snapped?

Icy fear washed over Mia. Not fear of her brother, but fear *for* him.

"I'm not a killer," he said, apparently reading the doubt in her eyes. "You have to trust me."

"How can I trust you? You're lying to me, Sam!"

"I've already said too much. Forget I ever said anything. And for God's sake, whatever you do, don't go to the cops. I have to handle this myself."

The scent of fresh-brewed coffee wafted around them. Suddenly weary, and more disillusioned than angry, she watched him pour coffee into a thick white mug, the kind used in roadside diners. "I have sugar," he said brusquely. "No milk. Kaye didn't buy groceries, and I've been a little busy."

It wasn't until he held out the mug that Mia realized she'd lost all interest in its contents. She took it from him anyway, hoping the simple feel of it in her hand would restore some semblance of normalcy to her life. But normal no longer existed; everything had been turned upside down, and she no longer trusted her own perceptions. "All right," she said to nobody in particular as she paced the length of the kitchen, coffee in hand, and tried to think her way out of this mess. "All right," she said again, knowing that nothing was all right and probably never would be again.

"So you won't tell the cops?" her brother was saying. "You won't tell them about what we just talked about?"

"How can I when I don't even know what it is that we just talked about?"

His mouth thinned. "It has to be that way."

Mia walked to the window, stood there staring out at nothing, her mind a jumbled mess. She absently massaged her wrist with the fingers of her other hand while she debated sharing the rest of it. Finally deciding she didn't have a choice, she said, "There's something I have to tell you. There are rumors circulating that Kaye was involved in some kind of shady real estate deal."

Mia waited for him to tell her she was crazy. Waited for him to say there was no way his wife would do anything like that. When he didn't, a heavy weight settled inside her chest. "I had lunch with Marty Scalia," she said, turning away from the window. "He told me about it. He couldn't tell me if the rumors were true, just that he'd heard them. But you know what they say. Where there's smoke, there's generally fire."

Sam didn't say anything, just stood there with that hang-dog look of his, as though he were a pup that she was in the process of cruelly beating. "I think I'm going to go through her files," she continued. "Snoop around, see if I can find anything that seems a little off. It could take some time. But I can't just sit on my duff and wait for Winslow & DeLucca to go belly-up."

"If this is true," he said, "if Kaye really did do something illegal, what does it mean for you?"

Mia gave up on the coffee. Setting it on the table, she said blithely, "Oh, not all that much. Maybe just financial ruin. Bankruptcy. The loss of my real estate license. Starvation and homelessness. Maybe a year or two or five in prison." She gave him a tight smile. "Nothing serious."

He looked as wretched as she felt. "You know how gossip is," he said, sounding unconvinced of his own words. "When there isn't anything interesting to talk about, people make it up. Just because they're saying it doesn't necessarily make it true."

"And maybe there's some sunny corner of the globe where pink and purple unicorns run wild and free. But I can't risk my business—the business I've spent years building, the business that's paying Kevin's college tuition and my mortgage and hopefully will support me in my old age—on maybes. I have to do what I can to protect myself now."

"I'm sorry."

"Is that all you can say?" She raked a hand through her hair. "Damn it, Sam, we are in major crisis mode here, and you're acting like—like…" She paused in utter frustration, unable to find the right words to express herself. Abruptly changing topics, she asked, "How's Gracie taking this? You haven't said a word about her."

"She seems fine to me."

Mia thought about strangling him. Actually weighed the pros and cons of wrapping her hands around her brother's neck and squeezing until he turned blue. But he out-weighed her by at least fifty pounds. And killing him wouldn't solve anything. It would give her immense satisfaction, but it wouldn't solve any of their problems.

Wearily, she said, "She's not fine, Sam. Her stepmother has disappeared. She has to be feeling something."

"Well, I don't know what she's feeling. The two of them don't get along."

"You don't know how she feels about it because you haven't bothered to ask. It's easier to just pretend everything is fine, and let the kid suffer in silence."

"She's not suffering. I told you, she doesn't even like Kaye."

"What the hell does that have to do with it? So she's not in deep mourning. Her life is still in upheaval. You may have a Ph.D., but you don't know anything about people and what makes them tick. Academic theory. That's all you know. You can name every goddamn dead artist since the beginning of time. You can dissect their work until the cows come home. But when it comes to actual living, breathing humans, you suffer from profound retardation."

She could see the hurt in his eyes, but at this point, she no longer cared. "Go talk to your daughter," she told him. "Tell her you love her, and let her know that no matter how things turn out, it'll be okay."

"I don't know—"

"That things will be okay? Lie if you have to. You seem to have become pretty good at that."

"That's not what I was going to say. I was going to say that I don't have any idea how to talk to her."

"Figure it out. She's just a kid. You're the one who's supposed to be the adult."

Mia left him standing in his kitchen, and drove home with her hands shaking in fury. What was wrong with the man? What had happened to turn him into an emotional cripple? He'd been raised in the same environment she had, by the same drunken, sadistic bastard of a father. Yet she'd survived that twisted childhood and had become stronger because of it, while Sam had just sort of faded away, hiding behind a Ph.D. and a pair of wire-rimmed glasses.

Oh, God. The sky was falling around her in pieces, like a crazy quilt, each shred that fell more tainted with madness than the last. Her sister-in-law was missing, and her brother was lying about something. The thought that he might be involved—in his wife's disappearance, in a homicide—was heartbreaking. He might be an idiot, but he was still her brother, and he expected her to protect him, the same as she always had. Shelter him, as she always had, from the harsh realities of life.

Now, those harsh realities had affected her. Her agency might be going down the tubes. If what Marty said was true, Kaye had been playing a dangerous game, risking not only her own ass, but Mia's as well. If her sister-in-law had done something illegal and the truth came out, Mia stood to lose everything. The business she'd worked so hard to build. The home she loved. Even Kevin's future could be jeopardized. If she lost everything because of Kaye, who would pay his college tuition?

Certainly not Sam. Especially if he was languishing in a prison cell somewhere.

Mia parked her car at the curb in front of her house. When she unlocked the front door and stepped inside the house, the silence was overwhelming. Kev was working tonight, and wouldn't be home until sometime after ten. Without him, the house was too empty, too confining. She needed to get out, needed to be someplace where there was light and sound and motion. Someplace where she could think this through, try to make some sense of it, try to figure out her next move.

She showered and changed her clothes, wrote Kevin a note, just in case he got home early, grabbed her denim jacket and her car keys.

And headed for the Prudential Mall.

Eleven

Melissa from Iowa turned out to be an outspoken, dark-haired beauty, a vegetarian with a pierced eyebrow, a tiny koi tattooed on her collarbone, and an interest in Buddhism. Well-read and even better traveled, she kept Policzki entertained through dinner with tales of her recent backpacking trip to Kashmir. "I hope I haven't bored you," she said finally, dabbing her lips with her napkin and dropping it on the table. "Sometimes I tend to run off at the mouth without intending to. I don't even notice until I realize everybody is sitting there looking glassy-eyed."

"Of course not," Policzki said. "I found it fascinating." In truth, he'd hung on her every word, enchanted by the verbal pictures she painted of foreign and exotic places. The fertile fields of the Kashmir Valley and the rugged majesty of the Himalayas sounded like paradise to a guy who'd spent his entire life—with the exception of those six college semesters in Arizona—living in the cramped, working-class town of Somerville, Massachusetts.

"I'm sorry I got foisted off on you. I tried to tell Aunt Brenda that if I could find my way around the Himalayas,

I could probably navigate Boston without getting lost or abducted, but I suspect there was more going on than she was telling me."

"As in I might turn out to be something more than a mere tour guide?"

"Exactly. A little bit of matchmaking going on, do you suppose?"

"I don't have to suppose. I know. My mother denies it, but she's a lousy liar. There's this twitch thing she does with her left eye. Really ugly." He examined Melissa's face. "You're not what I expected."

"You were expecting a blue-eyed milkmaid with blond pigtails?"

Policzki felt foolish. "Maybe," he admitted.

"Don't feel bad. That's what a lot of people expect the minute they hear the words *Iowa* and *farm*. I grew up in a town so small that when I was nine, they closed down the elementary school and bused us to the next school district. Nothing but cows and corn for as far as the eye could see."

"And now you play doctor to all those cows."

"That's me," she said. "A regular Doctor Dolittle. Believe me, you haven't lived until you've spent an afternoon with your arm buried to the shoulder inside the hind quarters of a laboring bovine."

"I think I'll stick to homicide."

Melissa grinned. "Any juicy cop stories you can tell me?"

"I suppose that depends on your definition of juicy."

"What's the most bizarre case you've worked?"

He thought about it for a while. "Well," he said, "there was the senator's daughter who shot her husband because she was tired of him borrowing her makeup and panty hose all the time."

"Oops."

"Of course, it was all hushed up. We worked our tails off, but in the end, his death was ruled an accident, and they just swept the whole thing under the rug."

"Well, of course. Money talks. So now that we've completed the dinner portion of the evening, what did you have in mind for the sightseeing portion?"

"I thought I knew, but after hearing about the places you've visited, I'm afraid you might be a little underwhelmed."

"Are you kidding? Judging by what I've seen so far, I think Boston's fabulous."

"In that case," he said, "I thought we'd go upstairs."

Melissa glanced at the ceiling with avid curiosity. "Upstairs?"

"Way upstairs. The Skywalk may not rival the Himalayas, but if you visit Boston without seeing it, you're missing out on something really special."

"Sounds exciting. Let's go."

They took the express elevator to the fiftieth floor, along with a solemn-faced young Japanese couple. The woman carried a city map, and the man had an expensive 35 mm camera strung around his neck. While the elevator rose at breakneck speed, the young couple studied the map, whispering back and forth in Japanese.

At the Skywalk ticket counter, Melissa insisted on paying their admission. "You paid for dinner," she said. "That means it's my turn to pay for the entertainment."

"That's not necessary."

"Oh, but it is." She handed a twenty to the middle-aged man behind the counter, who watched their exchange with interest. "I'm a firm believer in equality between the sexes."

"But—"

"No buts. You're a very nice man, Doug. I don't expect you to spend your hard-earned money on me."

The guy behind the counter grinned as he counted out Melissa's change. "Take my advice," he said to Policzki. "Never argue when a woman offers to pay."

"See?" she said, tucking the change into her purse. "Listen to the man. He gives good advice."

Had this been a real date, instead of something engineered by his mother and Melissa's aunt, Policzki probably would have argued. But because it wasn't, and because it seemed the only reasonable and courteous response, he backed down.

He didn't like it. But he backed down.

"I need to use the powder room," Melissa said. "Go ahead and wander around. I'll catch up with you."

There wasn't much else he could do. Hands tucked into the pockets of his dress pants, he walked over to the window and looked out at the view that had been taking his breath away for decades. Down there, on the street, was reality, with every gritty truth the term entailed. But up here, fifty floors above the traffic jams and the exhaust fumes, fifty floors above the muggers and the whores and the crack dealers, it was a different story. Up here, with the lights of Boston spread out before him like some giant, glittering carpet, the city was magic.

Through the upper half of the picture, the I-93 Expressway cut a twisting line north and south of the city. In the downtown area, it disappeared underground, part of the much maligned and perpetually troubled Big Dig. In spite of the hour, lights twinkled in the downtown office towers. He imagined rooms occupied by cleaning crews, and by others like him, workaholics who didn't have the good sense to go home when everybody else left for the day.

A movement at the edge of his vision caught his eye. Twenty feet away, a solitary figure stood studying the scene before her with unnerving intensity. He felt a quick jolt of recognition. Elegant even in denim, she radiated an élan that few women ever achieved. Mingled with that sophisticated chic was an air of loneliness that stirred something inside him, some protective instinct he'd worked hard to bury. As a cop, he had no business feeling anything for this woman. He was supposed to remain objective. Maintain a professional distance at all times.

But she looked so damn vulnerable.

For far longer than was advisable, he studied her, common sense warring with something else he couldn't quite identify. The woman hated him. He should leave well enough alone. Walk away. Track down Melissa and escort her to the opposite side of the observatory, where he could show her the view of Fenway Park from fifty floors up.

Policzki glanced hopefully in the direction of the women's room, but there was no sign of his date. He took a deep breath and refocused his attention on the jets waiting for takeoff on the runway at Logan. At this distance they were little more than pinpricks of light, lined up like toy soldiers headed into battle. He stared at them so intently his eyes blurred. He wouldn't look at her again. The woman hadn't asked for anything from him, and she wouldn't welcome his attention. He'd only be starting something that was better left alone.

Twenty feet away, she raised a slender hand to her temple. Her fingers were long and elegant. She wore a diamond solitaire on the third finger of her right hand, a narrow gold watch on her wrist. Her left hand, he already knew, was bare. She'd been a widow for nine years. He wondered why she was still single. Maybe the answer was simple; maybe no man she'd met was good enough for her.

While he watched, she brushed a strand of dark hair away from her face. Policzki made a final sweeping search of the area for his date, but she was nowhere to be seen. There was nobody here to save him from making a fool of himself.

He was on his own.

Against his better judgment, and probably in violation of twenty-seven different departmental policies, he let his legs carry him directly to Mia DeLucca.

"Makes you feel small and insignificant, doesn't it?"

The voice, coming from so close to her shoulder, yanked her out of her thoughts and back to reality. Mia glanced up, recognized its owner and felt a shock run through her. What the hell was he doing here? Hadn't he already done enough damage? Weren't there laws to protect her from this kind of harassment? Maybe if she closed her eyes, he'd go away.

It didn't work. When she opened them again, he was still there. But he wasn't looking at her. Instead, he was focused exclusively on the view. "All those people," he said. "All those lives. Makes you realize that you're just one of six billion inhabitants of this rotating chunk of rock. Really puts your problems into perspective, doesn't it? It's a humbling experience."

Mia took a deep breath. "Are you stalking me, Policzki? Because there are laws that cover that kind of thing."

He finally looked at her. "Relax," he said. "I'm here with someone."

She narrowed her eyes. "What kind of someone?"

"If you must know, a date."

Her eyes made a slow, deliberate sweep of the surrounding area. "I don't see any date."

"She's in the powder room. I'm as surprised to see you as you are to see me."

"Sorry, Detective, but I don't believe in coincidence."

"Neither do I. So maybe we should call it fate. Maybe we were meant to run into each other this way."

Mia gave a most unladylike snort. "For what possible purpose?"

He turned his attention back to the view. "I don't carry a crystal ball. I'm not that good a detective."

She continued to glare at him, not sure whether she should believe him. "This is how you dress when you're off duty?" she said. "You still look like a cop to me."

"I know," he said unapologetically. "There doesn't seem to be anything I can do about it."

"Maybe you should hire a fashion consultant."

"I'm not sure about this, but I suspect I could go Goth, pierce everything that shows and a few things that don't, and I'd still look like a cop. It seems to be an internal thing."

"Ah, yes. That law enforcement inner glow. Try smiling once in a while. You're too young to be so grim."

"I'm not grim. And I'm not as young as you think I am."

"Of course not. You must be at least twenty-four or twenty-five."

"Try thirty. Almost thirty-one."

"In your dreams, Policzki."

His eyes, dark and intent, pinned her, and Mia's heart stuttered. He reached into his hip pocket, pulled out his wallet, flipped it open to his driver's license and tossed it to her.

She caught it in midair. It was warm and smelled of leather, and he'd been carrying it around long enough so it had molded to the contours of his backside. There was something peculiarly intimate about holding it in her hands. Mia shot him a quick glance, then studied his license photo. Not a bad likeness. His first name was Douglas, and according to the official ID that had been issued to him by the Commonwealth of Massachusetts—who ought to know—he was three months shy of his thirty-first birthday.

"Well, golly gee," she said. "Look at that."

"In case you're having a little trouble with the math, that makes me five years younger than you."

She narrowed her eyes. "Why is it that you know my age?"

"I'm a cop. It's my job. Want to hear what else I know about you?"

"I shudder to think about it." In the slot opposite his license, displayed behind clear plastic, was a photo of two teenage boys holding soccer balls. "Who's this?" she said.

"My nephews." Warmth flooded his voice, and she glanced at him in surprise. He sounded almost…human. "Jake and Jesse," he said, apparently not noticing the skepticism on her face. "They're great kids. Typical teenagers, with all the issues that entails. But great kids nevertheless."

Intrigued, Mia paged through more photos. "This is Hannah," he said proudly. "Heather. Bobby. And the twins, Owen and Olivia."

"Big family."

"I have three older sisters. They all have kids."

"Uncle Doug," Mia said, trying to imagine him kicking around a soccer ball with the two teenagers. Handing him back the wallet, she said, "I'm a little disappointed to discover you're not a Vulcan."

"A Vulcan?"

"You know, with the pointed ears?" She gestured. "Like Spock? A master of logic, but incapable of human emotion."

"Oh. That kind of Vulcan. You know, Mia, I'm not the enemy. I'm just a guy, doing his job."

She felt slightly abashed. The man symbolized everything that had gone wrong with her life. He could be arrogant and pushy, and she was pretty sure he wanted to put her brother behind bars. But he was probably a good cop. He seemed sincere as hell. And he had nice eyes. Warm and compassionate eyes that were completely at odds with his standoffish cop exterior.

Damn it all. She didn't want to like him. If she liked him, there'd be nobody left to pin her anger on except her brother. And his missing wife, who might or might not be dead, and who may or may not have sold Mia down the river.

"There you are."

They glanced up in unison. The woman who approached them was young and supple and exotic. "Melissa Hardesty," she said, holding out her hand to Mia.

"Mia DeLucca." She shook the hand of this woman who was a good decade younger than her, this woman who was stunningly beautiful and obviously well bred. Policzki's stock immediately shot up a good hundred points in her estimation. The man had to have something going for him, besides his looks, to snag the interest of a woman like this.

"Nice to meet you," Melissa said. "Are you a friend of Doug's?"

"Actually—"

"Mia's a Realtor," Policzki said. "I'm thinking about buying a condo, and I was asking her advice."

He lied with such ease, Mia thought. Not like her brother, the stumbling fool. Of course, Policzki was a cop. It was probably part of the training he'd received at the police academy. Lying 101, The Art of Deception for the Greater Good.

"That's right," Mia said. "Give me a call, Detective, and we'll look at your options. I'm sure we can find something in your price range." She nodded to Hardesty. "Nice to meet you."

And she made her escape.

The elevator seemed to take forever, and for an instant, she was afraid he might follow her. When he didn't, she breathed a sigh of relief. The elevator arrived, Mia stepped inside and the doors closed. She shut her eyes as she always did when sealed inside one of these death traps, and wondered whether the sick churning in the pit of her stomach was the result of the rapid descent or her encounter with Doug Policzki. The man made her antsy. Uncomfortable. Hyperaware of the very molecules of oxygen floating in the air between them. He was too intense. Too challenging. Too good-looking.

Too damn young.

The elevator reached ground level, and Mia headed for the mall food court. She needed something to settle her churning stomach. A cup of tea. A doughnut. Even a soda would help. She reached the food court and got in line at the first kiosk she came to. At this time on a weeknight, the place wasn't doing much business. Mostly teenagers and a few matronly types. While she waited her turn, she absently watched a young girl dressed in an army jacket and a black beret. The teen stood with her back to Mia, scanning the room as if trying to locate somebody.

There was something familiar about her. The way she stood. The way her shoulders slumped when she didn't find whoever she was looking for. The girl turned, their eyes met and Mia saw the shock of recognition in her niece's eyes an instant before Gracie said, "Aunt Mia! What are you doing here?"

In summer, the Newbury Street ice cream parlor served its wares on an outdoor patio shaded by a green awning. Patrons sat at cute little wrought-iron café tables topped with pink-and-white-striped umbrellas. At this time of year, the umbrellas were put into storage, the tables and chairs were chained together on the patio to discourage thieves, and all the action had moved indoors.

They settled on opposite sides of a wooden booth set snug against the building's granite foundation. "I'll have a hot fudge sundae," Mia told the waitress. "With the works." Ice cream was a luxury she seldom allowed herself, and she fully intended to savor every delicious bite. "Gracie?"

"I just want a single scoop of frozen yogurt. Plain vanilla. In a cup instead of a cone."

"Plain vanilla?" Mia said. "You come to a place like this, I give you carte blanche to buy the most expensive, gooey concoction on the menu, and you pick vanilla yogurt? Girl, you are denying yourself one of life's simple pleasures."

A flush colored Gracie's cheeks. "I'm watching my weight."

Mia looked her up and down. "You watch it much harder, hon, nobody else will be able to see it at all."

"So why were you at the mall tonight?"

Clever change of topic. Mia filed it away in her mental record book. "I just needed a change of scenery," she said. "I'm glad we ran into each other. I was feeling a little blue tonight. I needed some company to cheer me up."

"Then you probably should've found somebody who's better at cheering people up, because I'm about as cheery as a heart attack." ·

"You have good reason to be down. Your life is in turmoil."

Gracie shrugged. "Yeah, well. Stuff happens."

"Yes, and in your short lifetime, you've had more than your share of 'stuff' happening."

"You don't know the half of it."

"Is there something I should know?"

Gracie's hesitation was brief, but it lasted just long enough to register as a blip on Mia's internal radar screen. "It's just…school, and Dad, and this thing with Kaye. I haven't slept much, and—" Gracie shrugged with such careless indifference that Mia, who'd been a mother for seventeen years, instantly recognized that her niece was lying. Something was going on, something more than what Mia knew already.

Their ice cream arrived. Mia picked up her spoon. Eyes carefully trained on the swirl of French vanilla topped with fudge sauce that she spooned into her mouth, she asked, "Everything okay?"

"Everything's okay," Gracie said. "I'm fine. Really."

Which meant, in the universal language of teenagers, that she wasn't fine at all. But Mia didn't dare push it, for fear of alienating her. The time might come in the near future when Gracie needed someone to talk· to. It wouldn't be Sam, that was pretty much a given. Even if his daughter did try to open up some kind of meaningful dialogue with him, maintaining it long enough to get to the heart of the issue would be nearly impossible. Mia never doubted that Sam's heart was in the right place. It was his head that gave him trouble. It would be pointless for Gracie to use him as a sounding board. The girl's mother was dead, and her stepmother wouldn't have been any help even if she hadn't been among the missing. That pretty much left Mia.

Gracie took a single tiny spoonful of frozen yogurt and rolled it around in her mouth before she swallowed it. "You know," she said, "one of the things I like best about you is that you never talk down to me. You don't treat me like a kid. Sometimes Dad really ticks me off. He keeps things from me, like he thinks he might injure my fragile sensibilities if he tells me what's going on. I'm fifteen, for God's sake. Hardly a kid anymore."

She made fifteen sound ancient. In so many ways, Gracie *was* just a kid. And her father, overprotective as daddies had been of their daughters since they wore animal pelts and carried clubs, wasn't ready yet to admit that his little girl was growing up. Or maybe he simply hadn't noticed.

"Your dad means well," Mia said.

"Yeah, well, he's living in the Dark Ages." Gracie moved a spoonful of frozen yogurt from one side of her bowl to the other. "He thinks I'm too dumb to notice that he and Kaye are always fighting."

"They fight a lot?" Sam hadn't said that; he'd intimated, or perhaps she'd inferred, that there'd been a single big blowout. Not a series of smaller battles.

"Maybe fighting's too strong a word," Gracie said, using her spoon to systematically decimate her yogurt until it was little more than slush. "They snipe at each other. And they sulk, and they give each other the silent treatment, and they generally act like the kids I see at school. Except that the kids at school are supposed to act like they're fifteen years old. Dad and Kaye are supposed to be adults."

Mia remembered Policzki's laundry list of symptoms that generally accompanied a rocky marriage, and her stomach soured. "So things have been rough for a while?"

"A while? Try right from the beginning."

"Really? I had no idea."

"Nobody does. They put on a good show when they're in public. They wait to fight until they get home."

Which meant that Gracie had front-row, season tickets to the show. Mia scowled. Her brother ought to have his head examined. Except that if they X-rayed it, they'd probably find nothing but a big, empty shell.

She shoved aside her sundae and picked up the check the waitress had left. "I don't know about you," she said, "but I'm not really in the mood for ice cream. Are you planning to eat that mess?"

"No." Gracie seemed almost relieved to be able to set down her spoon, as though she'd been performing under pressure. "I'm really not very hungry."

"Me neither. What do you say we blow this joint? I need to stop by the office to pick up something. I could use your help, if you think your dad wouldn't mind me keeping you out late on a school night."

For the first time in longer than Mia could remember, she saw enthusiasm on Gracie's face. Determined to camouflage it with teenage disdain, her niece said, "I suppose I could do that. Anything beats staying at home and watching Dad mope around the house."

* * *

Gracie had always loved the realty office. It had such a warm, welcoming feel, the exact opposite of the ugly building where her dad worked in that tiny prison cell of a cubicle. Like Mia herself, this office was classy. Gracious. That was an old-fashioned word, but it seemed to fit. The building was constructed of redbrick. The sign read Winslow & DeLucca in a tasteful gold script on a black background. Beneath the sign, a door painted glossy black to match was bracketed by bay windows, their trim painted the same black enamel. Inside, asparagus ferns in hanging ceramic pots draped green fronds over display boards that presented photos and descriptions of some of W&D's current listings.

Mia unlocked the door and swung it open. They both dropped their jackets on a chair in the reception area, and Mia led the way to the supply closet. It wasn't really a closet, but a room that had been deemed too small for an office. The supply closet was home to the photocopier, the fax machine, the laser printer and the coffeemaker. Adjustable shelves lining one wall held the assorted supplies and detritus necessary to the running of a business.

"What are we looking for?" Gracie said.

"Empty boxes. Probably two will do it." Her aunt glanced around, spied a couple cases of copier paper on the floor beneath the shelving. Designed to hold heavy reams of paper, the boxes were sturdy, with reinforced corners, and rugged enough to hold up under the strain of being carted hither and yon. "Bingo," Mia said. "Run out to Bev's desk and bring me the scissors."

When Gracie returned with them, Mia was busy rearranging the contents of the shelves, shoving things aside, stacking and consolidating. When the bottom shelf was empty, she said, "Snip the plastic bands that hold the covers on the boxes, then start handing me blocks of paper."

They worked quickly and efficiently as a team, Gracie emptying the boxes while Mia neatly stacked reams of paper on the shelf. When they were done, they stood back and admired their handiwork. "Geez," Mia said, "I hope these flimsy-looking aluminum shelf brackets hold up under the weight of all that paper. If Bev comes in tomorrow morning and finds two cases of paper scattered all over the floor, she'll think I've lost my mind."

Gracie tried to wiggle one of the brackets, but it seemed to have a firm grip on the wall. It didn't budge. "They'll hold," she said.

She followed her aunt to Kaye's office, where Mia flipped on the overhead fluorescents, dropped the empty boxes on the desk and unlocked Kaye's file cabinet. She opened the top drawer, studied the contents, then opened the second. More files. The third drawer held office supplies, and the bottom drawer was empty. "Good," Mia said. "What I need you to do is pull all these folders and put them in the boxes. Neatly. Both drawers." She paused to study Gracie speculatively. "We'll have to carry them to the car. How strong are you?"

"Strong enough to carry a little old box of files, if that's what you're worried about."

"Let's hope the boxes hold up. If we drop an armload of these puppies in the street, it'll take six months to sort out all that paperwork. Don't overload the boxes. If two won't do it, we'll pilfer one from somewhere else."

Gracie studied the drawer of files, then glanced at the empty boxes. "Why are we taking files out of the office?"

Mia squared her jaw and said, "I'm going on a fishing expedition."

Which was pretty cryptic, and told her absolutely nothing. Her aunt added, "I have to make a couple of phone calls. Give me a holler if you have any questions."

She left, and Gracie started pulling files from the top drawer and squeezing them into one of the boxes. Did Mia actually intend to read all these things? Cover to cover? Holy shit. Why would she do that? Especially when they weren't even her files. They were Kaye's. And just what had she meant about being on a fishing expedition?

She must be looking for something, something she expected to find buried in this half ton of paper.

In Kaye's files.

The same Kaye who'd vanished without a trace.

The lightbulb went on over Gracie's head. She might be a little slow, but eventually she caught on. She watched all those cop shows. *CSI. NYPD Blue. Veronica Mars.* Step-mommie Dearest must have gotten her hands dirty. Kaye had been up to something, or at least Mia suspected she had. And now Mia was looking for evidence. Just like they did on TV.

Well, well. Wasn't this an interesting turn of events?

Mia's first phone call was to her brother. "In case you're wondering where your daughter is, she's with me. I thought I'd let her spend the night, if it's not a problem for you."

"It's fine. Look…I'm sorry I was such an ass earlier. I'm a wreck right now. There's too much going on, between this mess with Kaye, the divorce papers and those damn cops harassing me." He sounded indignant. "They had me so tied up in knots, I was starting to doubt myself."

"It's their job to befuddle you to the point where you're ready to confess to everything from the Lindbergh baby kidnapping to being the second gunman standing on that grassy knoll in Dallas. Sam…" She hesitated, torn between her earlier anger and the concern that always hovered just beneath the surface. He might be three years older, but she'd probably never outgrow playing the mommy role with her brother. Right now, there were so many things she wanted to say to him, she wasn't sure if she should toss a coin or just jump in and start listing her concerns. "I'm worried about you," she said.

"Don't be."

"I know something's going on. Something you're keeping from me."

"There's nothing you can do about it. I'm dealing with it. Listen, is Gracie okay? She crept out of here so quietly I never realized she was gone."

"She do that a lot?"

"No, of course not. I—oh, hell." He sighed, and she could hear the weariness in his voice. "Who am I kidding? For all I know, she's going out every night, smoking crack and selling her body on the street."

"She's too smart to do that. And yes, she's fine, at least at the moment. But…"

"What?"

"I took her for ice cream. She ordered a single scoop of nonfat yogurt. And, at best, she ate maybe two spoonfuls of it. She told me she's watching her weight."

"What weight?"

"My point exactly. I'm wondering if there are some body image issues we don't know about. Does the kid ever eat?"

"Of course she eats."

"Have you actually seen her do it? Have you actually sat down to a meal together at any time in the past year?"

The silence at the other end of the line answered her question. "You have a teenager," he said at last. "You know what it's like. She's going in one direction and you're going in another. Kaye and I have erratic work schedules. Even when we're all home, we make a meal and inevitably Gracie doesn't like it, so she finds something else and takes it up to her room. Welcome to twenty-first century family life."

"She's too damn skinny, Sam."

"You don't think she's anorexic?"

"Maybe. If not, she might be headed that way. I think the girl could use counseling."

He let out a hard breath. "I feel like the village idiot."

"You're not an idiot. Well, sometimes you're an idiot. But mostly, you just need to pay closer attention to what's going on with your daughter."

"Thanks. Thanks for the heads-up."

"Have you eaten? Slept?"

"I'm capable of taking care of myself."

She didn't believe him. She'd seen, with her own eyes, too much evidence to the contrary. But she was too tired to argue. "Get some sleep," she said. "I'll talk to you tomorrow."

She disconnected, waited for a dial tone, then punched in another series of numbers.

"Marty?" she said into the phone. "It's Mia. I'm going through Kaye's files. What should I be looking for?"

Twelve

When Gracie offered to help with the files, Mia automatically said no. Not because they contained confidential material; somehow she doubted that her niece had even a smidgen of interest in the financial dealings of adults she'd never met. And certainly not because she thought Gracie wasn't smart enough to understand what particular needle to look for in that paperwork haystack. But Mia felt it was too big a burden to lay on the shoulders of a fifteen-year-old girl. Gracie's family was falling apart. She already had enough to deal with. Mia couldn't see any benefit to adding to her niece's woes by letting her know that before Kaye disappeared, she might have been involved in something shady. It just wasn't appropriate to lay something like that on a young girl.

Gracie, of course, had other ideas. "I know what you're trying to do," she said. "You're trying to protect me. Just like Dad does. But I'm not stupid. You brought home all Kaye's files because you're looking for something. And if it's something you can't look for during business hours—which must be why you brought them home—then it has to be something bad. Am I getting warm?"

Taken aback, Mia said, "It might not even be there. I don't even know that there's anything wrong. Just that there's a possibility. I'm not accusing Kaye of anything, and neither should you. Not without any kind of evidence. But if there is something to be found in these files—"

"You need to find it. Listen, Aunt Mia, I know things about that woman—" Gracie pursed her lips in distaste "—that would curl your hair. There's nothing we could find in these files that would shock me. So you might as well let me help you. The work will go twice as fast that way. Just tell me what we're looking for, and let's get to it."

Mia stared at her, dumbfounded. Was it really possible that the girl was only fifteen years old? With a few sentences, she'd demolished all her arguments and rendered them silly and pointless.

"Well," Mia said, at a loss for words. "Well."

"I'll take one box, you take the other." Gracie plunked down on the living room floor, dragged a box over between her knees and pulled off the cover. "I imagine I can figure this out. I made it through *Moby Dick.* After wading through all that symbolism, reading an insurance policy would be a cakewalk."

Mia couldn't argue with that kind of logic. "All right," she said, settling down on the opposite side of the coffee table. "I'm not sure how much you understand about the real estate business—"

"Quite a bit, actually," Gracie said. "Living with Kaye, it's hard to avoid."

"Okay, then we'll skip the preliminaries and jump right in. If there's something you don't understand, or you have any questions, speak up."

"Okay."

"I called Marty Scalia right after I called your dad. He's been in the business a lot longer than I have, and Marty's sharp. He sees and hears everything. I asked him to give me the fifty-cent lecture on what he knows about real estate fraud." Mia wiggled to adjust her body into a more comfortable position on the hard floor. "According to him, there are a couple types of fraud that are quite common. First, there's property flipping. That involves buying a property for a little nothing, slapping on a coat of paint and turning around and selling it for an inflated price without making any improvements that would justify the higher price. A lot of people buy property, fix it up and resell it in a year or two at a profit. There's nothing wrong with that—it's how people make money in real estate. The kind of flipping Marty's talking about is the dark side, if you will, of profiting by investing in real estate."

She tapped her fingernail against a file folder while she ruminated. "I don't see that as a viable alternative," she said. "If Kaye had been buying and selling property, I should have known it. Plus, it's risky. There's no guarantee that the property will sell, and if it doesn't, then you're stuck with a white elephant on your hands."

"Okay," Gracie said. "What's the other type?"

"The other one's a little more complicated, because it involves more than one person. To pull that off, you'd need to have your Realtor, your appraiser, your buyer and the title company attorney all in on the scam. Basically, what you do is obtain a property appraisal that's inflated way above true market value. Then you prepare two sets of settlement statements. Do you know what a settlement statement is?"

"That's the paper you bring to the closing with all the

numbers on it. Sale price, down payment, financing, all that stuff."

"Very good. So the first statement, the one you present to the seller, is the real one. It shows the real selling price, based on the genuine property appraisal. The second statement, the one that goes to the lender, shows the inflated price. The lender, assuming everything's on the up-and-up, makes the loan to the buyer based on the fraudulent appraisal. The seller gets his money and walks away from the table without ever knowing a fraud was perpetrated, and the rest of the crew split the difference among them. In a strong market, that can amount to a significant wad of cash that the IRS will never know about. Then the buyer, who usually applies for the loan using false credentials, defaults on the property and walks away scot-free, leaving the lender stuck with a property that's worth considerably less than what they financed it for. If you're clever, you can pull it off. If you're really, really clever, you can pull it off more than once, getting a little richer each time. But if you're not so clever, all those pretty greenbacks won't do a thing to buy your way out of five to ten years in prison."

"And you think Kaye was involved in something like that?"

"I never would have thought so. Not in a million years. Until Marty told me about the rumors he'd heard. I know the whole thing sounds far-fetched, but according to Marty, it's pretty common. Of course, she'd have to have coconspirators. At least three of them." Mia's brow wrinkled as she considered the possibility. "Thinking of the appraisers and title attorneys I'm familiar with, I find it hard to imagine any of them pulling something like that."

"Greed," Gracie said, "changes people. It turns them into something other than what they started out to be."

"You're right," she said. "How'd you get to be so smart at your age?"

"I lived alone with Dad for five years before he married Kaye. Somebody had to be the adult. So what are we looking for, then? Dual settlement statements?"

"Any numbers that don't add up. Any irregularities, anything that stands out as unusual or that seems just a little bit off. Noticeable patterns that can't be easily explained. Like an overly large number of transactions involving the same Realtor, the same appraisal company, the same title company. Or, as you said, dual settlement statements."

"Wouldn't it be risky to keep two sets of statements in the same file?"

"The whole thing is risky, but the chances of being caught in the process of perpetrating the scam are a lot higher than those of being caught afterward because you kept incriminating evidence in a file folder. Once those files land in the drawer, they're pretty much forgotten. Nobody ever looks at them again."

"Wow."

"Yeah. Wow. There is one more thing I want you to look for. I'm particularly interested in any transactions that might have involved Grant Ashford or First Boston Savings Bank, so set those files aside, in a separate pile."

"Who's Grant Ashford?"

"Vice president of First Boston. He's in charge of the loan department. The same rumor that mentioned Kaye's possible involvement also mentioned Grant Ashford as a coconspirator."

So while the clock ticked and their Diet Pepsis grew warm, Mia and Gracie waded through a half ton of paper, searching for God only knew what. Progress was slow, hindered by the complexity of the paperwork. Mia was inundated with names and numbers, buyers and sellers, offers and counteroffers, cash deposits and contingency clauses. Before she settled on a career as a Realtor, she'd always supposed that selling real estate primarily involved showing houses to prospective buyers. But in truth, that was only a small piece of what she did each day. On the outside, the job might look glamorous, but in reality, it involved an inordinate amount of drudge work. If you were good at it, and if market conditions were favorable, you could make a lot of money. But every penny of that money was earned with countless hours spent shuffling papers, dialing the phone, negotiating deals and pounding the pavement. Real estate sales was not for the faint of heart.

Beside her, Gracie turned a page. Mia glanced at her watch. Two hours had passed, and her hind end was numb from sitting on the floor, but she was no closer to finding that elusive something that she hoped she'd recognize when she saw it. Upstairs, the shower was running. Kev had come home some time ago, taken a look at all those stacks of paper and wisely headed up to his room before they could enlist his help. It was past ten-thirty, probably time to quit for the night. But these were extraordinary times, and any kind of normal schedule had fallen by the wayside the day Kaye disappeared.

"Find anything interesting?" Gracie said.

"Unfortunately, no. You?"

"Just the same old same old." She closed the file she'd been reading. "Aunt Mia?" she said. "Do you think it's important to always tell the truth?"

Was this some kind of trick question? "I'm a big fan of the truth," Mia said guardedly. "But I suppose it depends on the situation. How big a truth? Who will it hurt? Most everything in life, you see, is relative."

"What if you did something, and somebody maybe got hurt because of it, only that's not how you meant it, and then you didn't know what to do?"

A heavy sense of dread filled her insides. "Gracie?" she said. "What's going on?"

The adult facade cracked, and the fifteen-year-old girl who'd been hiding behind it finally surfaced. "I did something awful," her niece blurted out. "If I tell Dad, he'll kill me. But I'm afraid it's all my fault that something's happened to Kaye."

Rachel Winslow's file was three inches thick and coated with dust. Lorna wiped the cover clean and opened it. Inside she found a jumble of typed memos, crime scene photos and handwritten notes. She paged through them slowly, skimming reports, examining the photos, giving careful attention to the interviews with witnesses.

The details were stark and straightforward: Rachel Winslow had been standing outside a crowded subway stop on a frigid December evening when some sociopath with a loaded gun had decided to play target practice. Two people had been wounded, neither of them seriously. Rachel had been the only fatality.

They'd never caught the shooter. It had been dark, and nobody'd gotten a good look at him. In the ensuing panic and chaos that followed the shooting, he'd simply melted away into the night. The cops had questioned witnesses, but none of them could seem to agree. The guy had been black; he'd been white. He'd been tall; he'd been short. He'd been a scrawny teenager; he'd been a middle-aged guy with a paunch. After a year with no progress whatsoever, the detectives had retired Rachel's murder to the cold case files, and that had been that.

As a homicide cop, Lorna had hardened herself against violent death, but every once in a while a case managed to break through her brittle outer crust and get under her skin. This was one of those times. Everything in the file highlighted the senselessness of Rachel Winslow's death. A young wife and mother, gunned down in public for no apparent reason except that she happened to be in the wrong place at the wrong time. She'd left behind a seven-year-old daughter, a grieving husband and two parents destroyed by the death of their only child.

It made Lorna think about things she usually tried to avoid thinking about: the fleeting, ethereal quality of life; the way happiness can be snatched from you in an instant, only to be replaced by a grief that would follow you around for the rest of your days, no matter how fast or far you tried to run. It reminded her of her own kids and how precious and brief her time with them really was, reminded her of how little of that time she'd spent at home with them lately.

Take tonight, for instance. It was almost ten o'clock, and here she was, still at her desk. Police work was easier, somehow, for her male colleagues, easier because society was more accepting of men who devoted their entire lives to the job, easier because they never suffered from mommy guilt. The crazy hours were the downside to being a cop. Your life was never your own. She'd lost count of the number of dinners she'd missed, the number of family vacations that had been cancelled because somebody was murdered at an inconvenient time. It had been Ed who'd raised the kids, Ed who attended the parent-teacher conferences and the school plays, Ed who'd carted them to basketball and Little League and dancing lessons and to the doctor for their shots.

Sometimes the mommy guilt nearly drove Lorna crazy. Sometimes she thought about turning in her gun and her badge and walking away from it. But something inside her refused to quit. She was an addict, as bad as any junkie, except that her drug of choice was homicide. There was no high that could compare to the one she got when a case was moving along and her instincts told her she was about to get a break any minute. It could come in the form of an unexpected confession, or a piece of new information that tumbled into her lap. She'd gotten breaks when a suspect was pulled over for some minor traffic infraction, like a broken taillight, and upon closer inspection was found to be in possession of a prime piece of evidence she'd been looking for. Sometimes the break came when, after staring and staring at the evidence until her brain went numb, suddenly she saw two pieces of the puzzle in a new light and realized they fit together in a way she hadn't previously recognized.

That was the payback. That was the reason she kept doing it, day after day, year after year. That was the reason every cop did.

On the corner of her desk, the portable radio poured soft jazz into the night. It was time to go home, time to pack it in before Ed thought she'd left him for good. He was the glue that held her world together, the man she knew was dozing on the sofa in front of the TV, waiting for the sound of her key in the lock. She'd married young and she'd married well, and she sometimes wondered why he kept doing it. A lot of men would have given up by now. But Ed just stayed by her side, steadfast, and never questioned any of the decisions she made. Not all women were so lucky.

Her phone rang and she picked it up. "Abrams," she said wearily.

"Lorna, you sexy thing, I knew I'd find you there with your nose still to the grindstone. It's a wonder that husband of yours hasn't divorced you by now and found himself a nice little hausfrau to chase after all those rug rats you have running around."

The voice was all too familiar. It was a little creepy the way he'd echoed her thoughts. Tommy Malone had made a name for himself digging up dirt and printing it in a sleazy rag known as the *Boston Tribune*. The *Trib* made the *Boston Herald*'s sensationalism look as tame as Little Bo Peep and her sheep. Malone was an overachiever when it came to ferreting out information, and not averse to making it up if he couldn't find what he was looking for and it made for a good story.

"Malone," she said dryly. "Don't you ever go off duty? Or are you some kind of vampire, spending your nights sucking the blood out of innocent victims?"

"Au contraire, my sweet. Few of my victims are innocent. Most of them are guiltier than Whitey Bulger. So how are you, light of my life?"

"Since I know you're not calling to inquire about my health," she said, "exactly what is it you want?"

"Simple. I want you to leave Ed and run away with me."

"Nice try, Malone. I'm giving you one more chance before I hang up on you."

"You have no sense of the absurd, Lorna. None at all.

Listen, a source told me you were working on the case of one Kaye Winslow, Realtor extraordinaire, who seems to be among the missing. That same source tells me that her husband, a college professor at that hallowed bastion of higher education, Back Bay Community College, is the front-runner in the suspect department. True or untrue?"

"No comment."

Malone uttered a deep sigh. "I'm hurt, Lorna. Sorely injured to think you don't trust me enough to throw me just a bone or two for tomorrow's story. What would it take to bribe you? How about an extra-large slice of something wonderful from the Cheesecake Factory?"

The man was outrageous, so full of blarney that it was difficult to take him seriously. But that was his secret weapon. Malone might give the appearance of a lightweight, but in truth he was sharp as the edge of a well-honed razor. Tommy liked to charm his intended victim into thinking he was some buffoon, while keeping the steel-trap intellect hidden. Because people underestimated him, he was able to glean information from them that they would otherwise never have revealed. "I'll give you this," she told him. "Yes, we're working on the case. But I won't confirm anything beyond that."

"Just think about that cheesecake I'm metaphorically waving under your nose. It could become the real thing in time for lunch tomorrow. I bet Ed doesn't buy you cheesecake."

It ticked her off that she was tempted. It ticked her off even more that he'd heard Sam Winslow was her prime suspect. The only people who were supposed to know that were her partner and her lieutenant, and she knew damn well neither of them had blabbed.

"How about I ask you a question instead?" she said. "I'd really love to know the identity of that source."

"No can do. You know reporters don't have to reveal their sources. I have another question. In a fascinating aside to the case, a remarkable coincidence, if you ask me, Sam Winslow just happens to have been the husband of Rachel Winslow, shot to death outside the New England Medical T stop one summer night eight years ago."

Lorna leaned forward a little. "Who told you that?"

"Well, well. Is that a sudden spark of interest I'm hearing? I assume that means you're already in possession of this information. So that leads to my next question. Is there any connection between the first wife's death and the current wife's disappearance?"

"No comment. Go home, Malone. I think I hear your mommy calling."

"Just one more question. Do you think that the professor—"

"Good night, Thomas."

Malone was still talking when she hung up the phone.

He'd just gotten into bed when his cell phone rang. He reached out in the dark, made contact with it effortlessly and checked the digital readout. The number wasn't familiar. Flipping it open, he brought the phone to his ear and said, "Policzki."

"It's Mia DeLucca. I'm so sorry to bother you at this time of night, but I have an issue, and I don't know what to do about it. Well, actually, it's my niece who has the issue, and it might be relevant to the case or it might be nothing more than silliness. But I don't feel qualified to make that judgment and—oh, hell, I can't explain this over the phone."

Policzki sat up on the edge of the bed and rubbed a hand over his jaw. "Do you want me to come over?"

"I hate to ask. You're probably still with what's-her-name, and I really, *really* hate to disturb the two of you—"

"It's okay," he said. "I'm home. In bed. Alone."

There was no reason he should have added that last part. He didn't owe her any explanations about his sex life. Or the lack thereof.

"Oh," she said.

"I'll be there in twenty minutes."

"Don't you want to know where I live?"

"I know where you live."

At the other end of the phone, she sighed. "Of course you do. Tell me, Detective, do you also know what brand of lingerie I wear?"

"I don't know you well enough to answer that question," he said. "Yet." And hung up the phone.

He got lost a couple of times on the constricted side streets of Little Italy before he found it, a typical North End row house separated from its neighbor on one side by a brick-paved alley with a wrought-iron gate at the side-walk. It looked like the kind of place where she'd live, elegant in an unpretentious, old-world manner.

She'd been waiting for him; the door opened before he reached it. She was still wearing the clothes he'd seen her in earlier. In black jeans and a black silk shirt, with her dark hair and narrow gold hoop earrings, she looked like a gypsy. "Thank you for coming," she said. "Maybe I should have waited until morning, but I couldn't be sure that this was no more than a false alarm, and Gracie's so worried about it, I had to do something. You're the only person I felt I could trust, so—" She came to an abrupt halt. "I'm running off at the mouth again, aren't I?"

"Yes," he said, "but I like what you're saying. Especially that last part."

"Don't let your ego run away with you, Policzki. It's called process of elimination. I only know two cops, and your partner's a wild card. I bet she eats her young. Alive."

"Lorna? She's all bluster. Underneath it, she has a heart the size of Texas. She's just embarrassed to show it to the world."

"Right. I bet that's what they said about Attila the Hun."

"I'm flattered to be higher on your list than Attila."

Mia fought back a smile. "Gracie's in the kitchen," she said.

He got a quick glimpse of a cozy living room painted a soft rose color as he followed her down a narrow hallway to the kitchen. "Excuse the mess," she said. "I'm renovating the place one room at a time, as money and time allow. Right now, the kitchen's taking its turn."

It certainly was. The old flooring had been ripped up and a new subfloor had been installed. Someone had peeled the walls down to the bare plaster and begun patching holes. A new granite countertop ran around two walls, lined with a copper backsplash and topped by beautiful ash-blond cabinets. Copper-bottomed pots hung above a matching center work island that also served as a breakfast bar. The woman had good taste. A new graphite sink had been installed, but the appliances still screamed 1948. They looked like the ones his mother had used right up until the mid-1990s. Linda Policzki never discarded anything that had an ounce of life left in it.

A young girl sat on a wooden stool at the center island. A little too slender—didn't the kid ever eat?—she wore her dark hair chopped off in some sort of flattering spiky arrangement around her face. It was easy to see that she was Sam Winslow's daughter. She had the same pale complexion, the same startling blue eyes. The same eyes that Mia had. This, he imagined, was what Mia had looked like at her age.

The girl raised those blue eyes to his. He saw the terror in them, and Policzki's heart contracted. Whatever she was about to tell him had her scared shitless. This was his chance to play good cop. He didn't have much of a choice about that; if he said or did the wrong thing, the kid would probably run like a scared rabbit.

"Hi, Gracie," he said. "I'm Doug." He held out his hand. She looked at it for a minute, then tentatively reached out and shook it. Her grip was solid, but he could feel her trembling.

Withdrawing her hand, she said, "You're one of the detectives who came to my house the other night and talked to my dad."

"That's right." He rested a palm on the empty stool beside hers. "Mind if I sit here while we talk?"

"It's fine."

He sat, close enough for an intimate conversation but not so close that she'd feel he was invading her personal space. "I hear you have a problem," he said. "Want to tell me about it?"

The kid looked at Mia, who hovered nearby, slender arms crossed and a tiny frown on her face. Mia nodded, and Gracie said, "I met this guy online. In a chat room. His screen name is Magnum357."

"Okay."

"His real name is Carlos. At least that's what he says. We hit it off. I'm always complaining about Kaye—" she had the grace to blush "—and he's a really good listener. His folks divorced when he was little, and he has a step-mother, so he knows where I'm coming from. A couple of months ago, we met at the Prudential Mall. And we started hanging out. My dad would freak if he knew. He'd say I don't know anything about this guy. Which I suppose is true. Even after all this time, he hasn't told me much of anything about himself. Except that he's from East Boston, and his dad and stepmom have three other kids, all of which get treated better than he does."

She took a breath. "The other thing Dad would freak about is that Carlos is older. He's somewhere in his twenties. But he understands me, you know? The kids at school are so…" She shrugged. "Immature. And snotty. A little pathetic, although they'd probably tell you that I'm the one who's pathetic. But Carlos isn't like that. He's nice to me."

In spite of her fear, those blue eyes met his openly. Not sure where this was headed, Doug waited. "It's nothing sexual," she continued, "if that's what you're thinking. We're just friends. We like the same music, we have a similar sense of humor. We laugh at things other people don't think are funny. We're comfortable with each other."

Policzki glanced at Mia and found her watching him. He held her gaze for an instant before he turned his focus back to Gracie. This was her moment, and she deserved his undivided attention.

"A week or so ago," she said, "Dad and Kaye were fighting again, and I was complaining to Carlos. I know Kaye cheats on my dad. She's brought men to the house when she thought I wasn't home. Look, my dad's no prize, but he's my father, you know? I care about him, and I'm tired of that woman making his life miserable. I told Carlos I wished I could get some kind of proof of what she's been doing. Something I could give to my dad, to prove to him that he'd be better off without her. Carlos offered to follow her around for a few days with his digital camera. He said if he caught her doing something, he could take pictures, and then we'd have proof to show Dad. I thought it sounded like a good idea, so I said okay."

Quietly, Policzki said, "So what happened?"

"We talked online Monday night. He said he'd followed her around for a couple of hours that day, but all she did was real estate stuff. Business. So he said he'd try again the next day. Which was Tuesday."

"The day she disappeared."

"Right. Except that I haven't been able to reach him since then. He hasn't been in the chat room, and he hasn't answered any of my e-mails. It's as if, when Kaye disappeared, so did Carlos. Which has me really freaked out. What if he had something to do with her disappearing like that? What if—I don't know, what if he was there, and something happened to him, too? I don't like Kaye. She's the worst thing that ever happened to my family. But I couldn't live with myself if I was responsible for her, like, dying or something." Gracie paused, and for the first time he saw the sheen of tears in her eyes. "Or if I was responsible for something happening to Carlos."

He and Mia again exchanged glances. Policzki cleared his throat and said, "What does Carlos look like?"

Gracie gazed down at her hands, knotted tightly in her lap. "Medium height, I guess. Dark eyes, like yours. Good-looking. And he has dark hair, but right now, his head's shaved bald, so you really can't tell."

Which described half the young men in Boston. Policzki gave Mia a barely perceptible shake of his head. She let out a breath as relief blanketed her features. John Doe was six feet tall and had a full head of sandy hair. Gracie's friend wasn't a corpse. At least he wasn't a corpse on Policzki's watch.

"What about a job? Does he work somewhere?"

Gracie shrugged. "I think he said something once about making deliveries."

"Did he say where? Or for whom?"

Eyes still focused resolutely on her hands, she said, "No."

Needle in a haystack. Carlos—or whoever the hell he was—could be a long-haul trucker or a bicycle courier, a drug runner or an obstetrician. Or even a professional liar. There were a lot of professional liars running around. The job didn't pay much, but it allowed a lot of free time to spend trolling the Internet for young victims.

Gracie sniffed. The kid was really suffering. Guilt had a way of doing that to a person. Although he hated to, Policzki was about to make that guilt worse. "Gracie," he said sternly, "look at me."

He had to admire her guts; the kid raised her head and looked him straight in the eye.

"What you did was wrong," he said. "I don't want to hear that you did it out of love for your father. That's a lousy excuse, and we both know it. What you did, or what you had Carlos do for you, is called stalking. Stalking is illegal. You may not like your stepmother, but that doesn't give you, or anybody else, the right to invade her privacy. Are we clear on that?"

She didn't flinch. The kid was one tough cookie. "Yes," she said in a clear, strong voice.

"Good. Now I expect you to tell your dad what you did, and I expect you to apologize to him."

Her mouth fell open. Aghast, she said, "He'll kill me!"

"He won't kill you. He'll probably be disappointed by your behavior…" Policzki paused deliberately, long enough to allow the sting from his words to sink in "…but he won't kill you. Irresponsible behavior generally isn't punishable by death. So you'll tell him. Tomorrow."

It wasn't phrased as a question, and the girl knew it. "Fine," she said, the single syllable awash in misery.

"There's one more issue we have to deal with. What were you thinking, getting together with some stranger you'd met on the Internet? You're a smart girl. You must know that those chat rooms are rife with predators."

"Carlos isn't like that! He's not a predator."

"So you got lucky this time. Maybe next time you won't be so lucky. Maybe next time I'll be fishing your body out of a garbage Dumpster in some alley in Chinatown."

His words were deliberately cruel, and they had the desired effect. Policzki steeled himself against the single tear that escaped from the corner of her eye and trickled down her cheek. She swiped furiously at it. "What do you want me to say?"

Quietly, he said, "I want you to pull your head out of your ass and tell me you'll never do anything that stupid again. Your dad loves you. Your aunt Mia loves you. How do you think they'd feel if something happened to you?"

"Fine. I get the message."

He relaxed his tensed muscles, surprised to realize he was sweating. "Good," he said. "There's one other thing I want you to do. I want you to stop worrying about this. It's not your concern anymore. It's mine now. That's my job, and I'll try to track down Carlos and find out what the deal is. If he had anything to do with what happened to your stepmother, I'll handle it. But I want you to drop this heavy burden you've been carrying and go back to being a kid. Think you can do that?"

She shrugged. "Whatever." And returned to studying her hands.

Policzki got up from the stool. "Gracie?"

She gave a heavy sigh, then raised her tearstained face and glared at him. "What?"

"Thanks for telling me this stuff. It took guts."

He saw the surprise on her face in the instant before she masked it behind that tough-as-nails exterior. "Whatever," she said again, but this time, some of the tension was gone from her voice.

Mia walked him to the door. They paused in the foyer. "Thank you," she said in a low tone that wouldn't carry to the kitchen. "Thank you for coming, and thank you for putting the fear of God into her."

"You probably think I was too hard on her."

"I think it hurt you more than it hurt her. She needed to hear it, Detective. Maybe coming from you, it'll sink in."

"I hope so. She's smart, and she's tough, but so is the average pedophile who trolls the chat rooms looking for fresh meat."

Mia shuddered, and Policzki saw gooseflesh on her forearms. She took a breath and folded slender arms around her chest, seeming to draw her courage around her like an invisible cloak. "Do you think there's a chance this Carlos was involved?"

"Honestly? I think the chances are somewhere between slim and zero. But we'll look into it. Sometimes we get surprised. Guy like that, picks up young girls on the Internet, he sounds kind of shady. For all we know, he could be a gangbanger. Especially with a screen name like Magnum357. On the other hand, he might just be using the name to sound tough and impress the girls."

"That must be it," she said. "It certainly impresses me."

They fell silent, the air around them growing heavy with something he couldn't quite identify. "Your girlfriend," Mia murmured. "She's stunning."

"She is," he agreed, "but she's not my girlfriend. She's here visiting her aunt. My mother's best friend. Our date tonight was the result of two sixtyish ladies with too much time on their hands and a burning desire to play matchmaker."

"I see."

He cleared his throat. "What I mentioned earlier, about buying a condo? I was serious."

"Well," Mia said. "Then call me during business hours. We'll talk about what you're looking for, and I'll see what I can do for you."

It was clearly a dismissal, but he made no move to leave. She stood there looking at him, those blue eyes questioning. "Was there something else?" she asked.

Nothing he could give voice to. Not without sounding like a nutcase. "I'll call you," he said, pulling open the door and fleeing before he could make more of an ass of himself than he already had.

Thirteen

The telephone dragged Sam Winslow from sleep. In the dark, he fumbled for it and brought it to his mouth. "H'lo," he mumbled.

"Sam?" The voice was light and sweet, utterly feminine, inarguably familiar. But in his sleep-fogged condition, he couldn't quite place it.

He opened one eye and focused on the bedside clock. It was a little past three. "This is Sam," he said. "Who is this?"

"I can't believe you don't recognize my voice." She sounded petulant, slightly miffed. He could almost picture the pout on her face. Almost. But he couldn't quite picture the face that went with that pout. Like a fleeting memory, a name hovered on the tip of his tongue, almost there but for some reason impossible to retrieve.

"You really don't know who this is?" she said, petulance giving way to disbelief.

"No. And I don't appreciate guessing games at three in the morning, so unless you want me to hang up right now, you'd better identify yourself and tell me why you're calling."

"I'm calling because I miss you. You and Gracie. It's been so long, Sam."

"Who the hell is this?"

"Oh, Sam." Sorrow ran so deep in her voice that he could feel it through the telephone line. It reached out and wrapped itself around his heart, icy fingers clutching and squeezing. *"Don't you know?"* she said. *"This is Rachel."*

Stunned and confused, he rose up on one elbow and glanced around the darkened room. "Rachel's dead," he said.

"I assure you, Sam, I'm very much alive."

It was Rachel's voice. He recognized it now, and a plethora of bittersweet emotions rolled through him. Agony. Ecstasy. Bewilderment. "I don't understand," he said. "I identified your body. I watched them put you in the ground."

"It was all a lie, Sam. All a terrible lie. That wasn't really me. I've been alive all this time, waiting for you to come after me. Waiting for you to figure out the truth. But you didn't." Her voice grew dark and petulant again. *"The truth is, you don't need me anymore, now that you have Kaye."*

"You don't understand, Rach. I thought you were dead. I was alone. I needed somebody. Gracie needed somebody. We were so lost after you left us."

"If you really loved me, you would have known I was alive. You would have felt it in your bones. You would have gone to the ends of the earth to find me."

"I didn't know where you were!"

"I don't believe you, Sam. I think you just didn't care. You let my daughter call some other woman 'Mother,' and you forgot all about me."

"No." Panicked now, he tried desperately to make her

understand. "Rach, it's not like that at all. I never forgot you. I've thought about you every day of the last eight years. You were the best thing in my life. Then you went away, and it almost killed me."

"I'm leaving now, Sam. I just called to say goodbye."

Dread shortened his breath until it was a searing pain in his chest. "Wait! Rachel! Tell me where you are. I'll come and get you. Anywhere. Just tell me!"

"I'm sorry. It's too late. I have to go now. Goodbye, Sam."

"No! Damn it, Rachel, don't leave me again!"

He shot bolt upright, brutally torn from sleep, his heart hammering and his chest heaving, a river of sweat streaming down his back. The glowing red digits of the alarm clock read 2:27 a.m., and the telephone receiver lay untouched in its cradle.

"Jesus Christ," he said, his breath coming so hard it felt like a six-ton elephant sitting on his chest. "Jesus Christ Almighty." He buried his face in his hands, combing fingers through his tousled hair. Even awake, it was still with him, the gut-wrenching mix of elation and panic and profound sorrow that had been such an integral part of the dream. It had felt so real, so vivid, that if he'd reached out to the other side of the bed and found Rach lying there, breathing deeply and evenly in restful slumber, he wouldn't have been surprised. But then, that was the nature of dreams, where the impossible happened on a regular basis.

He'd dreamed about Rachel occasionally in the years since she died, but never like this. This mess with Kaye had stirred up old baggage he'd tried to bury. Old fears, old guilts. God help him, the same old hatred of the monster that lived inside him.

The temptation was strong to go to the cops and tell

them everything. Let them put him in front of a firing squad. It was what he deserved. But there was Gracie to think about. How would it affect her if the truth came out? He was no candidate for Father of the Year. But he wondered how many blows one little girl could endure before she turned bitter and twisted, the way he had. One? Two? Twelve? He might not be much of a father, but he couldn't let that happen to her. Not if there was any way he could prevent it.

Sam swung his legs over the side of the bed, stripped off his pajamas and left them in a sodden pile on the floor. Naked, he fumbled his way in the dark to the ostentatious master bath that was Kaye's pride and joy. He flipped the light switch, blinked a couple of times, then stood with his hands braced against the marble vanity and stared at his reflection in the gargantuan mirror.

His skin was sallow, his pupils dilated, his five o'clock shadow evolved into early morning bristle. Bewhiskered and bedraggled, he looked as if he'd just come off a three-day bender. His hair was too damn long. At the ripe old age of thirty-nine, he was years beyond the age when he should be wearing it to his shoulders. He looked like a reject from a 1980s hair band.

He turned on the shower and stepped inside, adjusted the tap until it was as hot as he could take it, and just stood there with the water pounding against his shoulders and streaming down his body. After a while, the tension began to dissipate, and Sam wondered just how much stress a man could endure before he started to crack.

He was toweling himself off when the telephone rang. Sam met his own startled eyes in the mirror. This time, he wasn't dreaming. This time, he was wide awake. It was two forty-five in the morning, the cops were looking for Kaye and his telephone was ringing. This couldn't be good news. Fastening the towel around his hips, Sam strode across the room and snatched up the ringing phone.

"Hello?" he said.

Nobody spoke. Nobody breathed. Instead, he was greeted by that odd anticipatory silence that signaled an open connection. Irritated, he said again, "Hello?"

"Sammm." It was little more than a whisper, his name spoken in a soft caress in the dark. He couldn't even tell if it was a man or a woman.

Like some kind of scaly serpent, a shiver slithered down his spine. Because it pissed him off, he demanded, "Who is this?"

Again, that soft whisper. *"Sammm."*

"What the hell do you want?"

"You know what we want." From the other end, there came a breathless little laugh, and then a click as somebody broke the connection.

Trembling, he dropped the phone back into its cradle and sank onto the edge of the bed. He couldn't take much more of this. The guilt and the fear were bad enough without the phone calls. Short of having his telephone disconnected, he had no way of stopping them. What would happen if one of these times Gracie answered? What if whoever it was said something to her? How the hell would Sam explain it?

He got up from the bed and crossed the room to the bottle of Glenlivet he'd started keeping on his bureau for occasions like this one. He was drinking way too much lately, but it was the only thing that took the edge off the anxiety, the only thing that kept him sane. He picked up the bottle, scouted around in the rubble on the bureau for a clean glass. When he didn't find it, he unscrewed the cap, tipped the bottle and chugged it down straight.

The warm glow was almost instantaneous. As it hit all the right spots, he wondered what the tenure committee would think if they saw him now, standing in his bedroom at two forty-five in the morning, stark naked and swilling whiskey straight from the bottle.

With the dawning of the day came a measure of sanity. Gracie was still at his sister's, so Sam was alone. Sam brewed a pot of strong coffee to help with his hangover, and poured himself a cup. While he drank it, he skimmed Thursday morning's *Globe,* almost afraid of what he might find. But there was no mention of his missing wife. Sam set down the newspaper and, cup of coffee in hand, cooked breakfast, a duty he and Kaye had always alternated. Odd that something as simple as preparing a meal brought home to him the reality of her absence even more than sleeping alone had. Humans were such creatures of habit; they took comfort in routine, in knowing what to expect, in maintaining the status quo. Even the smallest disturbance in daily routine, the tiniest blip on the radar screen, was enough to cause anxiety in most people. It was why, when the world was crumbling around you, sometimes those daily routines were all you had left to hold on to.

After breakfast, he headed for the college. In the tiny patch of asphalt that passed for a faculty parking lot, he ran into Vince Tedeschi, climbing out from behind the wheel of a shiny new sports car. Sam stood by the open driver's door and tried to summon some enthusiasm for the car's sleek lines, its burnished copper paint, its charcoal leather interior. "Nice," he said. "Great color."

Vince emerged with his oversize travel mug in hand, the morning paper tucked into the crook of his elbow. "They call it Sunset Pearlescent," the math professor said. "Sounds a hell of a lot classier than coppertone, doesn't it?"

"It does. Mitsubishi, is it?"

"Mitsubishi Spyder. Ellen finally broke down and let me have it. I've been wanting one for years. She kept saying it wasn't family-friendly. Too much work to wrestle the baby seat into the back. But now that Deidre's outgrown the baby seat, she can climb in and out by herself. Problem solved."

"You're sure this isn't just your response to some kind of midlife crisis?"

Vince was several years older than Sam, and this was a running gag between them. They began walking together toward the building. "Nice try, buddy," Vince said, "but no. The car isn't red, in case you didn't notice. Isn't that supposed to be the determining factor for a midlife crisis? Bright red convertible, flashy blonde named Jennifer who's young enough to be your daughter?"

"I wouldn't know. In case you forgot, I'm way too young for that kind of thing."

"Right. In your dreams." Beside him, Vince grew somber. "Any news about Kaye?"

Sam squared his jaw. "No. But just in case I don't have enough stress, some yahoo decided to make a prank call to my house at two-thirty this morning."

"Jesus Christ. What kind of dick-headed fool would do that?"

Sam knew exactly what kind. For an instant, he considered spilling everything to Vince. But neither of them would benefit from that kind of disclosure. This was a burden he had to carry alone.

"Oh," he said vaguely, "you know. People like to get their jollies by making other people miserable."

"Did you star 69 the guy? Put the fear of God into him?"

"I, uh, to tell you the truth, it never occurred to me."

It was the truth. Even if it had occurred to him, there was little point to it. He might not know who was calling him, but he knew why. "It was the middle of the night," he said by way of explanation. "My faculties weren't exactly running at optimum speed."

"It probably won't happen again." They climbed the stairs to the side door together. "It was probably some kid, dialing random numbers. Or picking names at random from the phone directory."

"Right. That's probably it."

He and Vince crossed the lobby and nodded to Claire, the receptionist, who shot them a sharp glance and continued talking into her headset. They parted outside the Arts and Sciences office.

Inside, Maureen was typing about a hundred miles an hour. "Morning," Sam said to her. She stopped typing abruptly and stared at him as if he'd just landed from another planet. "What?" he asked, quickly and discreetly checking to see if his fly was unzipped.

"Nothing," she said, and went back to typing.

His mailbox was already full. The damn thing always seemed to be full. He got more junk mail at work than he did at home. Brochures from textbook publishers. Committee meeting reminders. Announcements about campus events, the ubiquitous and anal-retentive memos from the

administration, and the inevitable scrawled notes from panicked students. Just like a balanced meal, all the food
groups were represented. He quickly sorted through it,
saved a note from one of his Friday evening students and
the one piece of real mail sitting there (definition: the envelope had a handwritten address and a genuine postage
stamp) and tossed the rest without reading it.

"Is Lydia in?" he said.

"Not yet." Maureen didn't look at him. Instead, she
seemed utterly fascinated by something on her computer
screen.

"You know when she'll be in?"

Still focused on the monitor, Maureen said, "She had a
meeting. Could be all day." She sneaked a brief glance, saw
that he was looking at her, and quickly returned her attention to whatever it was she was having trouble tearing her
eyes away from.

"I'm leaving these graded exams in my mailbox," he
told her, "in case anybody's looking."

"Okay. Fine."

He stared at her for a minute, then grabbed his coffee cup
and the overdue library book he'd brought with him, and
left her office. He was a big boy, too big to go crying to
mommy because he'd been snubbed by the department secretary. If Maureen didn't know what to say to him, he could
understand, since he no longer knew what to say to himself. She might be in line for a little sensitivity training, but
that wasn't his call; it was up to Lydia to run her own department. He had more important things to worry about
than the fact that Maureen found it too awkward to speak
to him now that his life was fodder for the six o'clock news.

At the far end of the corridor, Nikki Voisine stood outside an open classroom door, engrossed in conversation with a student. The young French professor glanced in his direction, and he could have sworn she saw him. He nodded, but instead of responding, the usually gregarious Nikki turned away, said something to the student and went back into the classroom.

He was starting to feel like Alice in Wonderland. Nothing had made sense since he and Vince walked through the door together. He and Nikki were buddies who shared coffee and gossip on a daily basis. Could it be possible that she hadn't seen him? Or had she, too, suddenly discovered a deep and abiding interest in something that was just too engrossing to allow her to acknowledge his existence?

Maureen's cool reception had puzzled him, but Nikki's outright avoidance ticked him off. What the hell was going on here? On his way to the library, he passed a couple of students in the corridor. He didn't know them, but he could have sworn they knew who he was. They averted their gazes and quickly walked past. Sam stopped, wheeled around and watched them retreat, their heads close together and their hands gesturing wildly as they carried on an animated conversation. He was too far away to hear what they were saying, but the excited rise and fall of their speech was unmistakable. Were they talking about him?

An attractive female student leaned over the water fountain. She straightened, shoved a hank of long brown hair behind her ear, gave him a wide smile and lowered her head for another sip. *Okay,* he reasoned with himself. *She didn't look at you as if you were a three-headed ogre. Maybe you're imagining this. Maybe people aren't snubbing you to your face and talking about you behind your back. Maybe what you need is a good shot of Valium to make this all go away.*

He paused at the door to the library. Penelope Weller, the head librarian, who was older than dirt and had been working here nearly as long, glanced up from her perch behind the circulation desk and froze when she saw him. Behind her, Becky Swanson, the reference librarian, did the same. "All right," Sam said, striding forward and slamming down his overdue book on the counter. "Enough. What the hell is going on?"

Mrs. Weller—he'd been raised to respect his elders, and he just couldn't think of her as Penelope, not at her age—stood, her spine ramrod stiff. "I have no idea what you're talking about," she said archly, "but this is a library, Dr. Winslow, and I'd appreciate it if you'd keep your voice down. There are students here trying to study!"

Behind her, Becky Swanson folded a section of newspaper and awkwardly shoved it into a file folder, then turned and leaned against the desk with her hands clasped. The picture of innocence. "What was that?" he said.

Becky turned the color of a ripe tomato. "What was what?"

He gestured. "Whatever you're doing such a lousy job of hiding in that folder."

"Dr. Winslow," Penelope Weller said, "I really don't think—"

"I just bet you don't," he retorted, and her mouth fell open as he strode to the end of the circulation desk and rounded the corner. Becky gasped and leaped aside, while Mrs. Weller sputtered and fumed.

"Dr. Winslow," she said, "if you don't stop right there—"

He reached the desk and opened the folder Becky had been guarding. Inside was the folded piece of newspaper.

"—have to call security—"

He unfolded the newspaper and shook it out. It was the

front section of this morning's *Boston Tribune*. The newspaper was a sleazy tabloid, reviled by one and all, yet read with clandestine delight by the same people who were so fond of criticizing it. On page one, just below the masthead, appeared a grainy copy of his official faculty photo, taken from the school's Web site. And beside it, in bold black print a good three inches high, the headline shouted out like a beacon to anybody this side of legal blindness: **IS THIS THE FACE OF DOCTOR DOOM?**

"Jesus Christ Almighty," he said.

"Jesus Christ Almighty," Lorna said as she slapped down the newspaper Policzki had tossed on her desk two minutes earlier. "Wouldn't it be peachy-keen if Malone let us solve our own crimes once in a while?"

With cool efficiency, Policzki peeled open a tiny plastic creamer and poured the contents into his coffee. He stirred it with a wooden stirrer. Picking up a napkin from his desk, he proceeded to carefully wipe his hands. Only then did he deign to drink his coffee.

"Jesus, Policzki, could you be any more anal retentive?"

He paused with the coffee cup halfway to his mouth. "Don't blame it on me," he said. "I'm not the one who blabbed to Malone on the telephone."

"Oh, no. You're not hanging this on me. I didn't tell him a damn thing. He got it all somewhere else."

"Well, then." Policzki took a sip of coffee and in his most rational tone, the one that drove her absolutely bug-fuck, said, "There's no sense in getting worked up over it. What's done is done."

If there was one thing Lorna didn't need right now, it was rational thinking. "If you don't shut your mouth," she said, "I swear to God I'm going to pull out my service revolver and shoot you."

"No, you won't," he said with that same maddening calm that could send her diastolic blood pressure into triple digits. "In spite of your best efforts, you like me too much to shoot me."

It was the truth. A dozen times a day he infuriated her. A dozen times a day she let him know it. But for some reason, she had a soft spot for him. She couldn't explain why. It was simply one of life's great mysteries, like the question of why it was that every time you put a pair of socks in the dryer, only one of them came out.

"That's not the point," she said. "The point is that I was trying to finesse Winslow, not flatten him with a ten-pound maul. Listen to this." She picked up the newspaper, skimmed it until she found what she was looking for. "'According to an unnamed police source, there are no other leads in the case. At this point in time, police are focusing their investigation on a single suspect. Only one person knows the truth about what happened to Kaye Winslow. Is that person her husband?'"

She flung down the newspaper in disgust. "Is this guy a drama queen or what? I keep expecting Malone to pop up, wearing a black hooded robe and carrying a sickle, and point his bony finger directly at Winslow's heart. What does he think this is, freaking *Masterpiece Theater?*"

"Bet it sells a lot of newspapers."

Lorna snorted. "Doctor Doom, my ass. Malone isn't capable of separating fact from fiction. I suppose now I have to call the turkey and thank him for spooking my prime suspect. If Winslow ever had it in his mind to skip town, this should be enough to convince him it's now or never."

"Winslow's not going anywhere," Policzki said.

"And you know this because?"

Swiveling in his chair, he took a sip of coffee. "If he's guilty, he knows we're onto him and we're watching him. If he's innocent, it would just make him look guilty. There's no benefit to running. It'd just screw things up worse than they already are."

"It didn't stop Scott Peterson."

"True, but he didn't get far, did he?" Still swiveling, her partner sipped his coffee and eyed her over the rim of the cup. "So do you want to hear about my evening?"

"With Miss Iowa? Lay it on me, kid. I'll try not to blush through all the salacious details."

"Forget Miss Iowa. I'm talking about the latter part of the evening, in which Gracie Winslow handed us another suspect, all neatly gift-wrapped."

"Excuse me?"

Policzki filled Lorna in on his late-night visit with Sam Winslow's daughter. "Damn kids," she said when he was done. "I don't think they develop brains until they're twenty-five. They meet up with these sickos and wind up in hot water. The girl's damn lucky this came out when it did, before something happened."

"So now I'm trying to track down this Carlos." Policzki indicated the telephone book, which lay on his desk, open to the Yellow Pages. "Trucking companies, delivery services, courier services. It's a stab in the dark, but I have to start somewhere."

"Shouldn't be hard. There can't be more than five or six hundred guys named Carlos between here and East Boston."

"Let me put it this way. Did you ever get down on your knees in the sand and search for one specific little grain?"

"Geez, Policzki, you're just a fount of good news this morning, aren't you?"

"Hey, I did you a favor this morning, Abrams. I stopped by the Beachcomber on my way to work."

"Really? You managed to ignore the roaches and the sticky menus and the six inches of grease on the kitchen walls? What'd you have, a tofu omelet and a mineral water?"

"Cute. I caught Slattery's two witnesses just as they were getting to work. Separately. According to both of them, he was at work all day Tuesday. He put in a twelve-hour shift, with a half-hour break for lunch. Which he ate sitting at the counter and reading the sports section of the *Globe*."

"Doesn't necessarily rule him out. Our friend Mickey has known associates who'd kill their own granny for a six-pack and a Red Sox ticket."

"So he stays on the list."

"The very short list."

"Quit complaining. At least we made it a little longer."

"So why am I not happy?"

"Not my department. You need to take that up with Ed."

She'd just settled down at her desk when Isabel flounced by and dropped a stack of mail on top of the rubble that already littered her desktop. "Gee, thanks," Lorna grumbled.

"You think that's bad?" Isabel said. "Try delivering it all. Everybody wants to shoot the messenger. Do I ever get any thanks? No way, Jose. They're all grumpy like you. All except Douglas." She flashed the young detective a brilliant white Pepsodent smile. "He's a nice boy, that Doug. I bet he brings his mother flowers even when it isn't Mother's Day."

"Spare me," Lorna said, shuffling through the mountain of mail Isabel had given her. "Oh-ho," she said to nobody in particular. "Here's the report from forensics on the prints." She tore open the envelope, skimmed the boring stuff. Names, DOBs, criminal records, driver's license photos or mug shots for every set of prints they'd been able to identify. Most of them were probably real estate agents or house hunters. Wealthy house hunters. There were a couple of Worthingtons in the bunch. The rest of the names she didn't recognize. When she reached the end, she realized she hadn't seen Kaye Winslow's name. What the hell? She'd watched with her own eyes as O'Connell lifted a couple of decent prints from the handle of Winslow's briefcase. Puzzled, Lorna went back through the names and photos, this time more slowly.

When she reached a familiar face, she paused. Across the way, her partner hung up the phone after yet another futile call. "Hey, Policzki," she said. "I think I just figured out why your background search on Kaye Winslow hit a brick wall five years ago. Come take a gander at this."

He marked his place in the phone book and rolled his chair across the floor. "Look at this picture," she said, "and tell me what you see."

Policzki studied it for about three seconds before he stated, "Kaye Winslow. With a few years shaved off. Her hair was different. Different style, different color. But it's definitely her."

"And what's the name that goes along with the picture?"

He peered more closely at the piece of paper in her hand. And said, "Sheila Cunningham."

They looked at each other for a minute, then they both looked back at the unmistakable likeness of a younger Kaye Winslow. "Well, well," Policzki murmured. "Hello, Sheila."

Fourteen

Sam read the article all the way through, then read it again in case he'd missed something. Tommy Malone had painted him as a modern-day Jack the Ripper, a man whose footsteps were dogged by suspicious deaths and inexplicable disappearances. It was all wild speculation. Speculation and slander, designed to hook readers. Sam could demand a retraction, but what was the point? The damage was already done. The *Trib* could print a dozen retractions, but once people started doubting him, trust could never be reestablished. Malone was clever, like a defense attorney instructing the jury to disregard the comments that had just been struck from the court record. Once those words were out there, forgetting them was an impossibility.

At least now Sam knew why everybody was treating him like a leper.

He folded up the newspaper and set it back on Becky Swanson's desk. Both women still stood there regarding him with what he now recognized as fear. Doctor Doom. It had a certain alliterative quality that was sort of catchy. Maybe he'd get a name tag made up, wear it while he lectured. That would raise an eyebrow or two. He might have found the title clever, if it didn't mean his career was over, blown out of the water by some gung ho newspaper reporter who'd taken the simple facts of his life and embellished them into a bloody mess that bore no resemblance whatsoever to truth. All in the name of selling newspapers. Whatever happened to journalistic ethics?

Sam left the library without another word and moved on down the corridor. When he reached the faculty lounge, he stepped inside and let the door slam shut behind him. It wasn't until he'd collapsed onto one of the rock-hard, puce-colored couches that he realized he was trembling. Rage had his heart racing at twice its normal speed. There was a part of him that wanted to track down this Tommy Malone and rip him apart for so blithely destroying what was left of his life, while another part of him just wanted to crawl in a hole until it all went away.

That wasn't likely to happen anytime soon.

Doctor Doom. The nickname made him sound like some kind of supervillain, capable of bringing down the likes of Superman with one hand tied behind his evil back. All he needed was the kryptonite.

The door to the lounge opened and Nyles Larsen strolled in, carrying his lunch in a paper sack. He passed Sam without seeing him, went to the refrigerator and found a place on a shelf for his lunch bag. It wasn't until Larsen closed the door of the fridge that he noticed Sam slumped on the couch. When he did, his face curved into a smile.

"Well, well," he said. "If it isn't Doctor Doom himself."

Sam gazed at the literature professor through bleary eyes. "Shut up, Nyles. I don't need to hear it right now."

The smile broadened. "I always knew there was something special about you, Winslow. Something unique that set you apart from the rest of the faculty. Now I know what it was. You're a cold-blooded murderer."

"You know, Nyles, I'm surprised. A man of your stature reading the *Trib?* That's the literary equivalent of a Big Mac and fries. With botulism. I'm surprised you're not in the men's room, upchucking your breakfast. You know what they say. Garbage in, garbage out."

Larsen chuckled. "Say what you will, but it's not my career that just crashed and burned. Face it. You're finished on this campus. And considering how quickly news travels, I suspect you won't be welcomed into any other academic circles in the near future, either."

"And I bet that just tickles you pink, doesn't it, Larsen?"

"You'd better believe it does. And the best part is that I didn't have to lift a finger. You managed to implode your career all by yourself. Quite spectacularly, I might add. It's just a shame about poor, sweet Kaye. What did you do, Winslow, bash her head in with a tire iron and toss her in the river? That woman should never have married you. I could never understand what she saw in you. You're shallow, self-serving and stupid. You were never man enough for a woman like her."

"And I suppose you are?"

Larsen had never tried to hide his admiration for Sam's wife. He'd seen her at a number of faculty functions and, like most men, he'd been dazzled by her blatant charms. He'd once been overheard describing her to Vince Tedeschi as a goddess. If he only knew, Sam thought. If he had to live with the woman, the bloom would quickly fade from the rose of his schoolboy crush.

"At least I could have appreciated her," Larsen said,

moving toward the door. "That's more than you've ever done. It's dangerous, you know, to neglect a beautiful woman like that. You learn very quickly who your real friends are. You can tell by the stab wounds in your back."

"You want my wife, Nyles?" Sam laughed, but there was more bitterness than humor in it. "Hell, man, you're welcome to her. Of course, I'm not sure she'd go for you. Kaye doesn't seem to have much interest in cerebral guys. As far as I can tell, she prefers the sweaty and dangerous type."

Larsen's brows drew together, lending his face a thunderous expression. "Neanderthals like you? That's a laugh. Go on deluding yourself, Winslow. It just proves what I already knew about you—you're an idiot. Oh, and before I go, there's one last thing. I intend to clarify this right now, just in case you're still harboring any futile hopes. This morning, I shredded your tenure application. Don't bother with a replacement. As long as I draw breath, you'll never earn tenure in this institution." He opened the door, paused at the threshold to glance back. "Or any other, for that matter. Not if I have anything to say about it."

When he released the door, it slammed shut behind him.

It was a nice day for a drive. There was nothing like a cloudless blue sky, abundant sunshine and some spectacular fall foliage to make a guy feel good about life. While Lorna drove north on I-95 and crossed the Piscataqua River Bridge into Maine, Policzki, cell phone in hand, continued his Yellow Pages search for the elusive Carlos. The final leg of their journey took them over a secondary road so loaded with potholes that even with the cruiser's heavy-duty suspension, he wasn't sure he'd make it to his destination with all his teeth intact.

Trowbridge, Maine, was a shit hole. Little more than a wide spot in the road, the town center consisted of a municipal office and library, an elementary school designed and constructed in the 1950s by someone with very little imagination, and a general store that sold pizza and Italian sandwiches, live bait and premium unleaded for three bucks a gallon.

Rolling Meadows Mobile Home Village wasn't hard to find. It sat on the highway a half mile north of the town office on a barren patch of dirt where pigweed grew tall but the grass had given up all hope. Doug wasn't sure where the name had come from, since there was no meadow and the ground was unapologetically flat. Most of the homes were old relics, lined up like dominoes, so close together that if one had ever caught fire, the flames would have just leaped from trailer to trailer, and the whole place would have gone up like a tinderbox.

They parked in front of number 38 and got out of the car. A half-naked child of indeterminate gender was playing in the dirt. The kid's diaper was drooping halfway to his ankles, and when they stepped over him—or maybe her—the kid didn't even look up, just kept on making *vroom-vroom* sounds and pushing a tiny red car around in the dust. The yard was littered with garbage, some of it in bags that looked as if they'd weathered more than one Maine winter.

He tried to imagine Kaye Winslow living here, but couldn't. Everything he knew about the woman, everything he'd learned about her, from her taste in decorating to her shrewd business tactics to her highly educated college professor husband, told him it was an impossibility. Yet this had been Sheila Cunningham's last known address.

The trailer door was open. No screen to keep insects out. Inside, a television droned. Lorna rapped briskly on the wall of the trailer. "Hello?" she shouted. "Anybody home?"

The woman who came to the door wore cheap plastic flip-flops and carried a lit cigarette. Her hair was lank and greasy, and she might have been attractive once, but any prettiness she may have once possessed had been buried beneath a mountain of Big Macs and KFC hot wings. She studied them through blue eyes that were surprisingly clear, glanced at the unmarked cruiser and back at them. "Yeah," she said. "What do you want?"

"Abrams and Policzki," Lorna said. "Boston PD. You got a minute?"

The cigarette had burned down to the woman's fingertips. She took a quick drag and tossed it out the door. "Boston police?" she said. "You must've took a wrong turn somewhere."

"We're working a homicide case," Policzki said. "We ran across a name and address that interested us."

"That right?" She studied him with the same frank interest he saw in too many women. Sizing him up, in every meaning of the word.

"We're looking for Sheila Cunningham," Lorna said. "You know her?"

Still looking at Policzki, the woman said, "I ought to know her. She's my sister."

Policzki handed her a copy of the photo he'd lifted from the Web page. "This her?"

The woman peered at the photo. "Wow," she said. "Looks like my little sister's done all right for herself."

"You got a name?" Policzki asked.

"Deb," she said, and smiled. Her teeth were yellowed from smoking and God only knew what else. "Deb Rideout."

Lorna said, "Have you seen your sister lately, Deb?"

Rideout reluctantly dragged her attention back to Lorna. "I ain't seen her since she lit out of here back...hell, it must've been six or seven years ago."

"Know where she went?"

"She didn't leave a forwarding address. We didn't exactly part on the best of terms."

"Family squabble?"

"Something like that," Rideout said. "She in trouble?"

"Could be. She get into trouble a lot?"

"No more than anybody else, I suppose. But she had an attitude. Always thought she was better than the rest of us. To tell you the truth, it didn't break my heart none when she left. Good riddance to bad rubbish is what I said then, and I still haven't changed my mind. She was never satisfied. Always wanting more. One day, she just up and walked out on Charlie. Didn't even leave a note. I figured he was better off without her."

Lorna and Policzki exchanged glances. "Charlie?" Lorna said.

Rideout stole a sly glance at Policzki. "Charlie Cunningham," she said. "Sheila's husband."

Sam picked up his own copy of the *Tribune* on the way home. He wasn't sure whether he wanted to frame it or set it on fire. Maybe he just wanted to torture himself with it. *Doctor Doom.* He felt as though the entire population of Boston was staring at him. It was probably just his imagination. Still, he was tempted to buy some kind of disguise. Maybe a patch to cover one eye. With his long hair, he'd make an outstanding pirate. Or maybe he could dye his hair blue. At least then he wouldn't feel so conspicuous.

Sitting at a red light on Boylston, he glanced over at the car in the other lane. The driver looked back at him, his face slack with boredom. Good. There was at least one person in the city of Boston who didn't recognize him. There was still hope that he wouldn't be tarred and feathered and run out of town on a rail.

He would have to relocate. When this was all over, when all the hoopla died down, he would have to yank Gracie out of Bellerose Academy and move her somewhere else, someplace clear across the country, where, hopefully, his Doctor Doom moniker wouldn't follow.

His cell phone rang. Now what? He checked the number, but didn't recognize it. He flicked a button. "Sam Winslow," he said.

"Dr. Winslow, I'm so glad I caught you in person. This is Felicia Marlowe. From Bellerose Academy?"

"Yes. Of course. What can I do for you?" He'd met the academy's director once, when they first enrolled Gracie. She was one of those butter-wouldn't-melt-in-her-mouth types, awash in the kind of smarmy insincerity you could recognize at ten paces. He'd always let Kaye deal with her because he had no patience for phonies. His internal bullshit meter was permanently set at a low level. It was easier for Kaye, who worked in sales and dealt with that kind of stuff on a daily basis, to contend with all that artificial sunshine.

"I'm afraid we have a situation here," she said, "that needs to be dealt with right away. I realize you're a busy man, and…" she paused, and when she started up again there was just the tiniest warble in her voice, as befitted the occasion "…you have my deepest sympathy on the unfortunate situation you find yourself in."

Which situation would that be? he wondered dully. The

missing wife? Having his face splashed all over the biggest gossip rag since *Weekly World News?* Or was there more that he didn't know about yet? At this point, nothing would surprise him. For whatever reason, it had turned into Pick On Sam Week, and he was just sitting here in his car, waiting for the next bomb to drop. He was beginning to feel like poor, long-suffering Job, who'd been forced to deal with boils, locusts and pestilence. That was pretty bad, but at least Job had never seen his own face on the front page of a tabloid beside the words *DOCTOR DOOM*.

"—and of course, any issue that might affect the safety of our children—"

"Stop," he said, suddenly tuning back in. He hadn't realized he'd tuned her out until he heard the word *safety*. "Has something happened to Gracie?"

"Oh, no. No, of course not. I'm sorry if I frightened you. Gracie's fine, but—"

His heart rate, which had doubled, gradually began to slow. Much more of this and he'd wear out before he ever got to forty. "Then what is it, Ms. Marlowe? You've been beating around the bush for the last five minutes. Can we get to the point before we're both too old to care?"

At the other end of the phone, there was a moment of silence. "We have an issue," she said, her voice several degrees frostier than it had been. "We need to discuss it. Right away, if possible."

"What the hell," he said. "It's not like I have anything else to do."

He hung up the phone, checked his mirrors and darted into the left lane inches ahead of a green Subaru Outback. Behind him, brakes squealed and horns honked, but he managed to make the turn onto Dartmouth without a rollover. His Volvo might not have the horsepower of Kaye's Beemer, but when he needed speed, the old girl was always ready, willing and able. Sam followed Dartmouth to Commonwealth, where he took another left turn—this time without nearly causing a twenty-car pileup—and headed west, toward Newton.

Somehow, he knew his day was about to get a little worse.

Felicia Marlowe stared at Sam over the rims of her glasses. "As I'm sure you can imagine," she said, "given the salacious article that ran in this morning's *Tribune,* gossip has been running rampant on campus. It's put your daughter at a distinct disadvantage. There've already been a couple of incidents—"

Sam, who was slumped on his tailbone, sat up a little straighter. "What kind of incidents?"

"In the cafeteria, right after breakfast, a group of children ganged up on your daughter and—"

His pulse began a rapid thrumming. "I thought you said Gracie was okay?"

"Words were exchanged, but it never escalated into anything physical. In her defense, I would like to say that Gracie handled herself with remarkable maturity. But since your wife disappeared, there've been other incidents. Yesterday, Gracie was caught trying to sneak into the media room without a hall pass. And according to some of her instructors, her behavior lately has been a little—shall we say odd?"

He thought about what Mia had said last night. "There's nothing wrong with my daughter," he said stonily.

"That may well be. Nevertheless, I'm sure you can understand why her continued presence here would be disruptive."

"You're throwing her out? You're expelling my daughter from Bellerose Academy?"

"*Expulsion* is such an ugly word, Dr. Winslow. I prefer to say we're asking her—asking both of you—to accept a difficult decision that was based on what we all know is for the greater good." She adjusted her eyeglasses and assumed an expression of selfless martyrdom. "You're an educator yourself. Surely you can understand that we only want what's best for our students."

"The greater good? My daughter, Ms. Marlowe, is one of those students. What about what's best for her?"

The director steepled her fingers on the desktop. "Sometimes," she said, studying her nails instead of meeting his eyes, "what's best for the majority must override what's best for any individual student." Her glance moved to Sam's face. "Gracie's a smart girl. An A student, as I'm sure you know." The look she gave him clearly conveyed her belief that he had absolutely no idea what kind of student his daughter was, given his nominal involvement in Gracie's life. "She'll do fine no matter where she goes."

"So you'll just toss her to the sharks and hope she knows how to swim. Big of you."

"The bottom line, Dr. Winslow, is that Gracie is no longer welcome here. It's not personal. But I've already had five phone calls this morning from hysterical parents, threatening to remove their children from our school if your daughter remains a student here. They don't want them exposed to this sordid affair. Don't want them exposed to—" She paused abruptly.

You, he thought, mentally finishing her sentence for her. It seemed incomprehensible that these parents should be afraid of him. Afraid of his daughter. But afraid they were.

And because they were voting with their dollars, Marlowe and company had caved. Why was he not surprised?

"Now I get it," he said. "It's the money. That's what it's all about, isn't it, Ms. Marlowe? All that lost revenue if parents start yanking their kids out of Bellerose Academy because they don't want them associating with the daughter of Doctor Doom."

Her expression didn't change, but her lips thinned enough to tell him he'd hit a nerve. "Where's Gracie?" he demanded.

"She's in English class right now, but—"

"Go get her."

"There's really no need to disturb the class, Dr. Winslow. Gracie is welcome to stay here until the end of the school day."

He stood abruptly. Gripping the edge of her desk with both hands, he leaned over it. "I said, *go get her!*"

Her bottom lip quivered ever so slightly. Without taking her eyes off him, Felicia Marlowe picked up the phone on her desk and pushed a series of buttons. She cleared her throat. "Marie?" she said evenly. "Could you please get Gracie Winslow from Mrs. Marshall's class? Have her bring her things. Thank you."

She dropped the telephone receiver back into its cradle and regarded him steadily, her chin held high. But her eyes gave her away. She was afraid of him, too, afraid of the notorious wife-killer Doctor Doom.

"You know," he said in a casual, conversational tone, "I thought I cared what people thought of me. Right up until I walked through the door of your office, I thought I gave a damn. But I've just now realized that I don't. Let people say what they will. It can't hurt me. But I'll be damned if

I'm going to let this insanity harm my daughter. She had nothing to do with this situation. It's not her battle to fight. It's mine. You're right. Gracie doesn't belong here. She belongs someplace where people won't hold her parents' failings against her. Someplace where people will realize what a terrific kid she really is. All I can say is, if the rest of the people running this institution are as small-minded as you are, Ms. Marlowe, then you just did us a big favor."

Gracie paused at the door of Miss Marlowe's office. She took a deep breath, raised her hand and knocked.

"Come in."

The dragon lady's expression was even more sour than usual. Gracie stepped into the torture chamber, saw her dad sitting there and froze. Oh, shit. This couldn't be good. Dad and Miss Marlowe in the same room? Talk about a recipe for disaster. She looked from one to the other of them, trying to discern the atmosphere, but it was impossible. Her dad looked irritated. Miss Marlowe just looked like Miss Marlowe. Enough said. Was this about her trying to sneak into the media room? Or had they finally found Kaye?

"Dad?" Gracie said. "What are you doing here? Is something wrong?"

Her dad smiled, but it came out looking more like a grimace. "Nothing's wrong," he said. "Everything's fine. But you're coming with me. Where's your locker?"

Gracie glanced at Miss Marlowe, but the academy director was staring out the window instead of looking at her. "Come on," her dad said, and walked out the door without even saying goodbye.

Grim-faced and silent, he accompanied Gracie down the deserted corridor to the bank of lockers, then helped her empty her stuff into her backpack. Papers, pens, note-books, all the detritus that filled her day-to-day life. What the hell was going on? Was she finally getting sprung from this hellhole? Her dad neatly stacked all her textbooks and hoisted them into his arms. Gracie slung her backpack over her shoulder and closed the locker.

"It's no wonder half of America's teenagers have back problems," he said. "You're toting home fifty pounds of paper every night."

They walked together back down the corridor. When they reached the front office, her dad dropped the heavy stack of books on the counter with a bang. Carmen Souza, the school secretary, looked up from her computer termi-nal, startled by the noise. "These are yours," Sam said curtly. Without waiting for a response, he steered Gracie out of the office and through the lobby doors.

Outside, the grass was springy underfoot. They crossed the velvety green lawn, kicking through fallen leaves all the way to the parking lot. Sam unlocked the Volvo, Gra-cie tossed her jacket and backpack into the rear, and they climbed in. He slid the key into the ignition, but instead of starting the car, he just sat staring at the dashboard.

"I've been a really lousy father," he said, "haven't I?"

A fierce loyalty bubbled up inside her chest. It wasn't his fault that he lived on a different planet from the rest of the people she knew. It wasn't his fault that he never knew the right thing to do or say. "You're a great dad," she said. "The best." Then added, "They booted me, didn't they?"

His eyes, when he looked at her, were red-rimmed and tired looking. And apologetic. "They booted you."

"Dumb-asses."

Still, he didn't start the car. His hands on the steering

wheel, he said, "When you have kids, you do your damnedest to ensure their safety. You bleed for them. You'd lie down and die for them if you needed to. But sometimes, no matter how hard you bleed, you can't protect them. Some stupid, random, shit thing happens in your life, and before you can blink, it's started to swallow you up and pull you under. And no matter how fast you dog-paddle, you just keep going under. Do you understand what I'm talking about?"

She didn't have a freaking clue what he was talking about, but because she loved him, she said, "Sure, Dad."

"And if you haven't been careful enough, if you didn't supply your kids with the right kind of flotation device, they'll go down right along with you."

As usual, he was talking in some foreign language, some bizarre dad-speak that didn't translate to any human tongue she'd ever heard. Gracie wondered if there was some foreign language institute out there somewhere that gave lessons in speaking Martian. It might be as close as she'd ever come to understanding her father.

"It's because of me," he said. "I'm the reason they suspended you. Felicia Marlowe is a horrible woman. I told her off."

Gracie looked at him with new respect. "Go, Dad."

"I don't think you understand the seriousness of this, Gracie. That school is one of the best—"

"That school blows."

"You need a good education. The kind you can't get in the public school system."

"Dad, I hate to break this to you, but I'm not planning to go to Harvard." Actually, she already had her eye on a small art school in Chicago whose students were turning out some amazing stuff. But she still had three years of high school left. Who knew what might happen before graduation?

"I've made bad decisions," he said. "They had a detrimental effect on you. I wish I could go back and change them, but I can't. I'm going to try harder in the future. Once we get past this mess, I intend to start doing it all right. It's not too late. You're only fifteen years old. I still have time to turn this thing around."

This probably wasn't the time to tell him about Carlos. But she'd promised that detective she would, and she suspected he would check up on her to make sure she kept her promise. Doug. The guy was pretty hot, considering how old he was. Way too old for her, even if he did have sexy eyes. Besides, even while she'd been spilling her guts to him last night, she'd seen the way he kept looking at her aunt Mia. And the way Mia was looking back. Something was definitely going on there.

Gracie took a deep breath. "Dad?" she said. "There's something I have to tell you."

Fifteen

Mia had a Thursday morning crammed with back-to-back meetings, so she didn't get into the office much before noon. Bev had already gone to lunch, but she'd left Mia a stack of pink message slips and a handwritten to-do list half a mile long. Beneath the stack, neatly folded, was a news clipping, attached to it a yellow sticky note on which Bev had scrawled: "Sorry to spoil your day, but if you haven't already heard about this, I thought you'd want to know. P.S. No news about Kaye yet. P.S.S. Do not, I repeat DO NOT skip lunch!" It was signed "Mama Bear."

Holding back a smile, Mia riffled through the messages. Most were from clients, but she'd received several calls from the media. The *Globe* had phoned, and the *Herald*, not to mention WBZ news radio, WHDH and the local CBS affiliate. What the hell was going on? Yesterday had been rough, but today, she hadn't expected a media onslaught. Kaye was well known in the real estate community, but she wasn't exactly a local celebrity, just one more successful businesswoman in a city of thousands of successful businesspeople. Why should the media be so interested in her?

Mia peeled the sticky note off the news clipping, tossed the note and unfolded the article. When she saw Sam's face, her heart sank. The day tanked even further when the Doctor Doom headline accosted her. "Shit," she said. "Oh, shit." This was bad. This was really, really bad. This was going to affect every facet of her brother's life. Not to mention Gracie's.

The phone on her desk rang. Mia ignored it. It was probably just some bloodthirsty reporter looking for something to print in tomorrow's newspaper, and she wasn't about to give them the satisfaction. She skimmed the article to see how damaging it really was. The picture Tommy Malone had painted of Sam wasn't pretty. He'd taken a series of unrelated events and stacked them like bricks, mortaring them together with speculation and innuendo. The end result made her brother look guiltier than bin Laden.

At least it explained all the calls from the media. Setting down the news clipping, Mia sorted through the pink message slips, saving the business-related ones and tossing the rest in the trash. There. That took care of that. Goddamn vultures.

Taking a deep breath, she picked up the phone and dialed her brother's number.

She was saved, at least temporarily, by a busy signal. He was probably being bombarded with telephone calls. If the media had been phoning her all morning, she could only imagine how bad it must be at his house. She'd try again later. In the meantime, she had work to do. Voice mail and e-mail messages that would only breed like rabbits if she ignored them. Opening her desk drawer, she rummaged around until she found the package of Twinkies Kev had left there last week. Did Twinkies qualify as lunch, or would Bev read her the riot act when she returned? Mia checked the date, saw that they hadn't yet gone out of code, and peeled open the cellophane wrapping. God forbid Kevin should ever catch her eating junk food, after all the lectures she'd given him. But the Twinkies would have to do until she could get something more substantial.

She fired up her computer. While it loaded, she ran through her voice mail, scribbling notes on her desk blotter and deleting the messages from reporters. Once the computer was up and running, she opened her e-mail program, and while she lunched on gooey cakes and crème filling, she waded through the two dozen e-mails she'd accumulated since yesterday.

Aside from the obvious spam—Give your wife what she really wants tonight!—she opened every one to make sure she didn't miss anything. The useless stuff she deleted. The requests for information she forwarded to Bev. The rest she sent to the laser printer.

When she was done, instead of diving into the pile of work she'd just created, she pulled a steno pad from her drawer and began making notes. Doug Policzki was thirty years old. He'd probably been on the job for less than ten years, which meant he most likely took in a modest salary. Mia wrote down a starting figure, did some mental computations, ran a few numbers through her calculator, factoring in interest rates and monthly payments for upkeep and association fees, and came up with what seemed a reasonable price range. A young, single guy like Policzki would want to live in the city, near his job, near restaurants and theaters, and within a couple blocks of the T, so she jotted down the neighborhoods she thought he'd find most appealing.

Would he want a view? She chewed on the end of her pencil while she considered the question, finally concluding that with the erratic hours of a homicide cop, he probably wouldn't spend enough time at home to appreciate a view. So unless he told her otherwise, she'd leave the high-rises off the list. Policzki struck her as the type to value practicality over aesthetics. He'd want something solid, something affordable, something that suited the lifestyle of a young, single man with a demanding career.

This was the part of her job she liked the best, matching people to homes they would fall in love with, homes that fit them like a second skin. She logged into the Multiple Listing Service and began a search using the criteria she'd established. She quickly ruled out most of the listings she pulled up. Too big, too small, wrong neighborhood. Finally settling on a half-dozen listings that seemed like possibilities, Mia sent them all to the printer. She gathered them up and put them in a file folder along with her notes, labeled it with Policzki's name and tucked it into a drawer.

The phone rang again. As much as she hated to answer it, she couldn't avoid the damn thing. She had a business to run, and hiding from the world wouldn't help her sell houses. She picked it up. "Winslow & DeLucca."

"Mia DeLucca, please." The voice was female, unfamiliar.

Guardedly, Mia said, "This is she."

"Mrs. DeLucca, this is Emily Olson. Michelle's mother."

It took her a minute to make the connection. When she did, she sat up straight and raked her free hand through her hair. "Yes," she said. "Of course. Thanks for calling."

"Kevin told me you wanted to talk with me before we leave tonight. I can't say that I blame you. I'd do the same thing if it were my daughter heading off to Florida with people I don't even know."

"Then you don't think I'm paranoid? Overprotective? All of the above?"

Emily Olson's laugh was wonderful. "I suspect you're a lot like me. I know it's time to start letting go, but for the life of me, I can't figure out how. My husband thinks I'm a nutcase. But time goes so quickly, and we have our children with us for such a short time. It's incredibly hard to think about what it'll be like when they're gone."

Mia let out a sigh of relief at recognition of a kindred spirit. "Yes," she said. "That's exactly how I feel."

"Michelle's my last of four kids, and I've gone through it with every one."

"How do you do it? How do you survive letting go?"

"Honey, if I had the answer to that, I'd be a rich woman. You start out with this perfect little person, you spend every day with him for eighteen years, watching him grow. Teaching him, giving him so much of yourself that there's damn little left over for you. Then one day, you wake up and he's taller than you. And you wonder if it happened while you were asleep. Next thing you know, he's gone, leaving you wondering where the hell the years went to.

"This one's harder than my others. Michelle's my last. And my only girl. She'll be going off to college next September, and I have to admit that I'm terrified. What will I do with all that free time? Even worse, where will I put all that emotion? All that love and caring and tenderness? My husband's a great guy, but he's busy with his own life. I don't want to smother him. I suppose I'll just have to find something else to fill that empty spot inside me. Maybe I can take up ceramics. Or basket weaving."

Understanding completely, Mia said, "Or golf."

"God help me," Emily Olson exclaimed. "Anything but golf."

They laughed together, lapsing into a comfortable silence. "Can I be frank with you?" Mia asked.

"I wouldn't have it any other way."

"I know this is probably just my paranoia speaking, but I'm worried about how close our kids are getting."

"Ah, yes. The big *S*-word. Let me tell you, I've been through this three times already. When they decide it's time, nothing short of a nuclear explosion's going to stop them. I know it doesn't help you to sleep any better at night, but it's the simple truth. Sure, you can talk to them about the joys of abstinence. You can talk until you're blue in the face. And they'll listen, until those hormones kick in, and then nature will override any ideas about waiting until they're ready. As far as they're concerned, they are ready. So you teach them about responsibility, about the dangers of STDs, about safe sex, and then you lie awake at night and pray that some of it sank in. Enough of it, anyway, to keep them safe from AIDS and unwanted pregnancy. At that point, there's nothing else you can do."

"You make it sound so easy."

"Are you kidding? It's one of the hardest things I've ever had to do. But I told myself with every one of my boys— and I'm trying hard to tell myself the same thing with Michelle—that there are a lot of worse things they could be doing. When you look at it that way, it doesn't seem so awful."

"I suppose you're right."

"You have to give up the reins. Otherwise, it'll make you crazy. Listen, there's one other thing I'd like to say. My husband and I really like Kevin. He's a great kid. I know you've raised him alone. He told us about his dad. I just wanted you to know that as far as we're concerned, you've done a really amazing job with him."

"Thanks…" Mia paused, twirled a strand of hair around her index finger. "Can we talk again?" She hoped she wasn't being too forward, but something told her that she and Emily Olson could be friends.

"Absolutely. Considering how tight our kids are, I suspect we'll be having plenty of opportunity to talk in the future. How about I call you when we get back from Florida? We'll do lunch."

"I'd like that."

She disconnected the call. Emily Olson was right, of course. Once a child reached a certain age, a mother's influence was pretty much over. You had to hope you'd done right by them, had to hope you'd instilled the kind of moral values you wanted them to live by. Just like little birds leaving the nest, you had to let them go, had to push them out into the world and let them fly on their own wings. Guided, presumably, by the foundation you'd laid for them during those formative years.

Mia discreetly dabbed at the corner of her eye with a tissue. It was pointless to brood, pointless to dwell on a mother's worries. The important thing was to keep on moving. If you kept moving quickly enough, the gremlins couldn't catch up to you. It had worked for Johnny Winslow. It would work for her.

She picked up the phone and dialed Sam's number again. Still busy. This was getting her nowhere fast. She dropped the phone into its cradle and returned to scanning the e-mails that had come in while she'd been putting together the property listings for Policzki. First was a request from a client to view a property that interested him. She hit the print button and moved on. The following two messages offered her ownership of a fragment of paradise in the form of Costa Rican land, and preapproval for a twenty-thousand-dollar line of credit. Maybe she could use the pre-approved credit line to finance the Costa Rican land deal. She rolled her eyes, deleted both e-mails and opened the last message on the list.

Somebody had been creative with their HTML. In bloodred lettering on a black background, neatly centered and in the largest font her e-mail program would handle, were the words STAY OUT OF IT.

Stay out of what? With all the craziness that had gone down in her life the last two days, it could have referred to any number of things. Her life was a smorgasbord of disaster from which to pick and choose. Who the hell had sent the message? And why were they trying to intimidate her?

Not that their scare tactics were particularly effective. As threats went, this one was pretty lame. Like something a kid might write. Stay out of it or what? The sender hadn't bothered to elucidate. Stay out of it or I'll come and get you? Stay out of it or I'll unleash a nasty virus on your computer? Stay out of it or I'll be really mad at you? Any threat this vague lacked teeth. Mia checked the header to see if it was possible to tell where the e-mail had come from. The sender was listed as John Smith—now there was an original name—and it had come from one of those anonymous, easy-to-obtain free e-mail accounts. Mia would bet dollars to doughnuts that the account had been cancelled about three seconds after the e-mail was sent. As an experiment, she hit Reply and sent a blank e-mail back to the sender. Just to see what happened. She waited a couple of minutes, then checked her incoming. Sure enough, like a little swallow to Capistrano, her message had bounced back as undeliverable. No such recipient, it said. Surprise, surprise.

She wondered momentarily how they'd gotten her e-mail address, but of course it was right on the agency Web page, available to anybody with access to a computer. That was why she received so much spam, but it was impossible these days to run a business without a Web page and an e-mail address. E-mail was quickly replacing the telephone as the preferred means of communication for the twenty-first century, and the Web was like the world's largest telephone directory. She supposed that anybody with some computer tech skills and a few contacts could probably track down where the e-mail had come from. The police, for instance. But if she went to Abrams and Policzki and told them she wanted to utilize police resources to trace an e-mail that said something as innocuous as "stay out of it," they'd laugh their asses off.

She sent the e-mail to the printer and tried Sam's number again. That damn busy signal was annoying as hell. Who could he be talking to for so long? Was it possible he could be online? Not many people these days still used dial-up. Most of them had DSL or cable, and she couldn't imagine Kaye settling for anything as archaic as 56k. Maybe he'd simply gotten fed up with all the calls and taken the phone off the hook.

The minute she hung up, the phone rang again. Mia stared at it in dismay, then sternly reminded herself that the telephone was a splendid invention and the business-woman's best friend. *Right,* she thought, and answered it.

"Mia? Doug Policzki."

A burst of heat blossomed somewhere in her midsection, rose up her chest, passed her shoulders and shot up her face. She fumbled the phone receiver and almost dropped it. What the hell was wrong with her? Maybe she was having a stroke. She was certainly too young for hot flashes.

Ignoring the fine tremor in the hand that held the telephone, she ran her tongue over suddenly parched lips and said, "Detective."

"How's Gracie?"

"Humbled." Mia picked up a pen and began doodling on her desk blotter. "Don't worry, that's a good thing."

"You told me to call during business hours. About the condo." His voice sounded scratchy; wherever he was calling from, the cell phone reception was lousy.

"Actually," she said, opening her desk drawer and removing the file she'd put together for him, "I already looked through the MLS and pulled a few properties I thought you might be interested in. If you're game, we could schedule some viewings."

"What's your availability? I'm out of town right now, but I might be able to free up a couple of hours tonight. That is, if you're—" Static obliterated his next few words. "And if you don't mind working after hours."

"I'm a real estate broker," she said. "My job's a lot like yours. We work evenings, weekends, whatever it takes to get the job done."

"How about I give you a call? Sevenish? With the understanding that—" another break in reception "—comes up, we'll have to reschedule."

"Do you have my cell phone number?"

"Hang on. Let me get something to—" She pictured him fumbling in his pockets for a pen and a piece of paper. "Okay," he said. "Go ahead."

She gave him the number and he repeated it back to her. "Got it," he said, and hung up without saying goodbye.

Mia slowly returned the phone to its cradle, shoved a hank of damp hair away from her face and wondered what the hell she'd just agreed to.

When Lorna came out of the general store carrying two Dr Peppers, a meatball sandwich and a couple of greasy hot dogs, Policzki was leaning against the side of the car, cell phone in hand. It was no wonder the women were all after him. Long and lean and soaking up the sunshine, he looked good enough to eat. As she approached him, a truck wheeled into the parking lot, raising a rooster tail of dust. Policzki closed the cell phone in his hand and tucked it into its belt clip. "I decided to take your advice," he said. "I'm buying a condo and moving out."

"That, my friend, is what you call progress. Where are we eating?"

"Picnic table at eight o'clock."

They crossed the parking lot and settled on opposite sides of a wooden table that was gradually succumbing to the elements. Policzki frowned, brushed an unidentifiable object off the tabletop and muttered something about sanitation.

"Try not to think about it," she said. "You'll sleep better at night."

"I sleep just fine." He cautiously unwrapped the foil from his meatball sandwich. "I don't suppose they gave you a fork with this thing?"

Lorna took a bite of hot dog. "It's somewhere in the bag."

He fished around in the take-out bag until he located a plastic fork that would probably snap in two the minute he poked it into one of those meatballs. They didn't make plastic forks the way they used to. Sawing his way through a meatball that surely was made of rubber, he said, "Hard to believe that she's Kaye Winslow's sister."

"I wonder if Sam knows about her."

"I'd be willing to bet he doesn't. Or about the trailer."

"Or even about this town. So what is it with you? I had to practically kick you to get you to give the woman your card."

"Did you see the way she was looking at me? She wanted to eat me up."

"Nothing new, Policzki. They all want to eat you up."

"Doesn't mean I have to like it."

She grinned. "A little nervous, are we?"

"Damn right, I'm nervous. The woman was terrifying."

"There's a method to my madness. She liked you. She hardly noticed I was there. Ergo, I wanted her to have your business card instead of mine. If she comes up with anything, she's more likely to call you."

"That's what I'm worried about. Thanks for using me as shark bait." He gave up on the fork, picked up the sandwich and ate it like a man.

"Geez," she said. "After everything I do for you, you can't even show me a little gratitude."

He swallowed, took a second bite. "Thank you for the sandwich," he said around it. "Is that what you wanted to hear?"

"It'll do for now. You just dribbled tomato sauce on your tie."

Policzki glanced down. "That's why I tried to use a fork." He picked up a paper napkin and swiped ineffectually at his tie.

"Dry cleaner'll get it out. Better hurry up there, kid. We have places to go, things to do, people to see."

"And miles to go before we sleep. I've heard it all before." He took another huge bite of the sandwich, chewed and swallowed. Dug around in the bag for a clean napkin and wiped his mouth, then folded the foil around the remains of his sandwich and dropped it into the bag. "Let's roll."

Charlie Cunningham lived in a modest ranch home with a lawn that hadn't been mowed in a while. An old Ford pickup truck sat in a patch of goldenrod and milkweed beside the driveway. There was a doghouse, but no dog. The place wasn't much, but compared to Rideout's trailer, it was a palace. "Looks as though our friend Charlie's moved up in the world," she said.

There were no front steps, so they walked up to the side door and knocked. After a minute, Lorna knocked again, this time more loudly.

"Doesn't look like anybody's home," Policzki said.

"Rideout said she hadn't seen him in a while."

"Wonder what that means."

"I dunno. You thinking what I'm thinking?"

They wandered around the property, checked out the backyard, peered through the dusty windows of the ramshackle little garage. Then they got in the car and drove back to the town center, to the whitewashed cinder block building that served as town office and public library. Both facilities were housed in the same room, with a single counter where you could pay your taxes, register your car or check out books. One-stop shopping. The woman behind the counter was watching a soap opera on a twelve-inch black-and-white TV. The nameplate on the counter in front of her said Temple Hopkins. Hopkins glanced up at them, studied their faces for an instant, then turned back to the TV, just in case anything crucial had happened in the two seconds it had taken her to give them the once-over. "Can I help you?" she said.

"We're looking for Charlie Cunningham," Lorna told her. "You know him?"

The TV went to a commercial and Hopkins finally tore her eyes away from *The Bold and the Beautiful.* "Everybody knows Charlie Cunningham," she said. "Why are you looking for him?"

Lorna held up her badge. "You seen him around lately?"

"Not for a week or so. I drive by his house every day on my way to work. His car hasn't been there."

"Any idea where he might be?"

"I don't know him that well. We went to school together, but we didn't run with the same crowd."

"What do you know about him?" Policzki said.

"He's quiet. Keeps to himself. His folks died a few years back. Cancer took his mother, then his dad followed along behind her a few months later. Charlie was the only kid, so he inherited the house. He drives an old rust bucket, a '68 Pontiac Tempest. There's not much more I can tell you."

"He work somewhere?" Lorna asked.

"He's self-employed. He does odd jobs, carpentry work. Whatever it takes to put food on the table."

"There a lot of call for that kind of thing around here?" Policzki said.

"Enough to keep him busy, I guess."

"He ever get into trouble?" Lorna said.

"Not that I know of. There was a little dispute with a neighbor a couple years ago. Charlie's dog was barking all day while he was at work. My husband's the town constable. He had to go over and settle it."

"Yeah?" Lorna said. "So how was it resolved?"

"Charlie took the dog out back and shot him."

"That would certainly resolve it," Lorna stated. "He got a wife?"

"Not anymore. They split up a few years back. Sheila Rideout. Man, was she some piece of work."

"Why do you say that?" Policzki asked.

"She had delusions of grandeur. Sheila thought she was headed for Hollywood or something. She went off to college for a couple of years, up to Orono, majored in drama. But she flunked out. Too much partying is what I heard. So she came back home and married Charlie. It must have been one hell of a letdown."

"You wouldn't happen to know," Policzki said, "where we might find a picture of Charlie Cunningham?"

"The library has a yearbook. Of course, it's fifteen years old."

Lorna exchanged glances with Policzki, saw that they were on the same wavelength. "Good enough," she said.

Hopkins came around the counter and entered the library stacks, walking directly to the shelf that held the high school yearbooks. She perused the spines until she found the one she wanted, then pulled it out and flipped it open to the senior section. She riffled through the pages, paused. "Here," she said, tapping the book with a fingernail, "here's Sheila."

Even with the poufy hairdo, Sheila Rideout had been an attractive girl. Lorna skimmed the list of activities beside her photo. Drama Club, Varsity Cheerleading, Senior Chorus, French Club. "Where's Charlie?" she said.

Hopkins shuffled through the pages, found the one she wanted, and pointed again. "There you go."

Charlie Cunningham. A good-looking guy with sandy hair and freckles, a goofy smile on his face, and the world laid wide-open ahead of him. Back in high school, he'd been on the basketball and wrestling teams. He'd played trumpet in the school band, and he'd been a member of Future Farmers of America. He'd had the same dreams as any kid, had lived the same humdrum, ordinary life as every other small-town jock who'd discovered that the real world was a whole lot tougher than high school. But somewhere along the way, Charlie Cunningham had hit a snag. Somewhere along the way, he'd taken a detour, one that had ended with him lying on the cold tile floor of a Back Bay mansion with a bullet in his head.

"Doug?" Lorna said.

Policzki cleared his throat and said to Temple Hopkins, "Could we have photocopies of these two pages, please?"

Sixteen

Sam and Gracie were just finishing up lunch when the doorbell rang. Gracie paused halfway to the sink, her empty Diet Pepsi glass in one hand, her plate, still holding half a tuna sandwich, in the other. That was one more thing they were going to have to talk about. His daughter's eating habits. Or, more accurately, her habit of not eating. Which he would never have noticed if his sister hadn't pointed it out to him. It had been a rough morning, culminating in Gracie's reluctant confession that she'd sent some guy she'd met on the Internet—the Internet, for Christ's sake—to chase after Kaye with a camera. Sam's life was edging ever closer to the *Twilight Zone*.

The doorbell rang again. It better not be another of those pain-in-the-ass reporters. Everybody and his uncle wanted an exclusive interview with Doctor Doom. So far, none of them had gone so far as to walk right up to his door, but they certainly hadn't been shy about calling. Could face-to-face visits be far behind?

"Wait here," he told Gracie. "I'm not in the mood for any more surprises."

The minute he opened the door, he wished he hadn't done it. The urge to flee, to slam the door and bolt it and run for cover, was overwhelming. But it was too late; his security had been breached and the enemy stood so close he could see the whites of her eyes. While her husband parked the car, she stood on his doorstep, wearing pearls and Chanel, a mink stole dripping off her shoulders and righteous fury in her eyes. A woman on a mission. "Evelyn," he said in resignation. "How nice of you to drop by."

"Where's my granddaughter?" Rachel's mother swept past him and into the foyer as though she owned the place. Which, of course, she once had, so perhaps her proprietary manner was justified. Behind her, Jack Wise climbed the steps slowly, a man who'd spent his life following in his wife's considerable wake. "Sam," he said. "How are you holding up?"

"Jack." He nodded. "I've been better."

"Where is she?" Evelyn demanded. "I know she's here. We stopped by Bellerose Academy and they told us she wasn't there. They said she no longer attends Bellerose."

Sam hoped that Gracie had been smart enough to go into deep hiding. She'd always been a little intimidated by this harridan who, by some accident of birth, was her grandmother. "Bellerose Academy and I," he said stiffly, "are currently experiencing philosophical differences. We came to a mutual agreement that it was no longer beneficial for Gracie to continue attending."

"I just bet you did." Evelyn glanced past his shoulder and caught sight of his daughter hovering in the kitchen doorway. "There she is! Gracie, darling, come see Grandma!"

Gracie crept down the hall and paused beside Sam. "Hi, Grandma," she said. "Hi, Grandpa."

Jack Wise opened his mouth to speak, but his wife beat him to it. She swooped down on her granddaughter and caught her up in a fragrant bear hug. "You poor thing," she said, clinging as Gracie struggled to free herself. "This is so terrible for you."

The teen finally managed to break free. She took a step back, looped her arm through Sam's. "Don't worry about me," she said. "I'm fine."

"You're such a brave little girl. And I can understand your loyalty to your father—" Evelyn glared at Sam as she grudgingly acknowledged his existence "—but you don't need to pretend for my sake. I know how devastating this has to be for you. That's why we're here."

"What the hell does that mean?" Sam said.

His former mother-in-law looked down her aristocratic nose at him as though he were something vile and rank. "Surely even you realize how damaging it is for your daughter to be exposed to something so sordid." She sniffed, as though his very presence was offensive.

"My wife's missing, Evelyn. Exactly how do you characterize that as sordid?"

"You may be able to fool other people," she said, "but I knew what you were the first time I ever laid eyes on you, and nothing you've done since then has changed my mind. You're a dangerous man, Sam Winslow. You've been a danger to every woman you've ever been involved with, and you're a danger to my granddaughter. God knows what irreversible damage your influence has done to Gracie since her mother died. Why the authorities have continued to allow you access to your daughter is beyond my comprehension. You're clearly an unfit parent, and I intend to do something about it. That's why we're here. Gracie, sweetheart, go get your things. You're coming home with Grandma and Grandpa."

Sam heard Gracie gasp, and her grip on his elbow became viselike. In that moment, Sam hated the woman enough that if he'd had a weapon handy, he might easily have used it to bash in her skull. So much for the evolution of humankind. No matter how tame a man might be, no matter how high the level of his education, beneath that thin veneer of civilization there beat the heart of a creature who acted on instinct, a savage beast who would stop at nothing when it came to protecting what was his. "My daughter," he stated, straining to rein in his fury, "is not leaving this house with you."

Evelyn stiffened. "Either you let her come with me," she said, "or I'll call the Department of Social Services and insist that they remove her from what is clearly an unsuitable environment for any child."

His fury, dammed for too long, overflowed its banks and ran free. In a tight, deadly quiet voice, he said, "I've tolerated you for more than a dozen years for one reason only—because you were Rachel's mother, and because you must have done something right when you raised her, since she was the most amazing human being who ever walked this earth. But Rachel's gone, and this is my house now, and I won't allow your poison to fester here any longer. Get out, or I'm calling the cops and having you thrown out."

He had to give the old girl credit. She wasn't afraid of him. She stepped forward until they were nose to nose and said, "Not without my granddaughter!"

"Gracie," he said, "go to the kitchen and call 911. Tell them we have a trespasser."

Evelyn sucked in a breath. "You wouldn't," she said.

"Watch me."

Gracie hesitated, not sure whether he was serious. For the first time, Jack spoke up. "Evelyn," he said, "why don't we just—"

"Oh, shut up, you old fool!"

"Back off, Evelyn," Sam said, "or you'll live to regret it."

"He threatened me," she said to her husband. "You heard that, didn't you?" She stood a little taller and shook her index finger in Sam's face. "You'd better believe that I'll be taking this to the police. You'll be locked up for so long that by the time you see the light of day again, Gracie won't even remember you." Her voice softened slightly as she addressed her granddaughter. "Gracie, darling, hold on for just a little longer. Grandma will have you out of this place soon." She straightened, met Sam eye to eye and said coldly, "I'll be calling the Department of Social Services this afternoon, immediately after I've filed an official complaint with the police. I can guarantee that DSS will come here to investigate, and when they do, I intend to come with them. Once I've gotten Gracie out of this repugnant situation, I intend to call my lawyer and sue you for permanent custody. And make no mistake about it, Sam, I *will* win." She turned to her husband. "Jack? Let's go now." With her nose raised imperiously, she swept back out the door, past her long-suffering husband, who stood with his hand on the doorknob, his shoulders slumped.

"Sam," he said, "I'm sorry. I told her this was a bad idea, but when in forty years of marriage has Evelyn ever listened to me?"

"You have to stop her, Jack. You can't let her do this to me. You can't let her do this to Gracie. If she cares one whit for her granddaughter, she won't tear her away from me."

"I'll try," Jack Wise said. "But you know how Evelyn is. Once she gets an idea in her head—"

From the street, a horn blared, two short, angry bleats. "I have to go," he stated. "Gracie, you be a good kid and help your dad, okay?"

Gracie's hold on her father relaxed a little. "Okay."

The Cadillac's horn blew again. "For Christ's sake," Jack called, "I'm coming!"

Sam stood in the open doorway and watched them drive away. "Way to go, Dad," Gracie said. "I've never seen you like this."

He closed the door, pressed his palms flat against it and took a deep, shuddering breath. "Things are going to change around here," he announced.

"That woman is severely delusional if she actually thinks I'm going anywhere with her," Gracie said. "I don't suppose you have any garlic to hang over the door?"

He locked the door and threw the dead bolt. "In spite of her personality flaws, I believe Evelyn has your best interests at heart. Or what she perceives to be your best interests."

"She's an awful woman."

"Yes," he said, "she is. But try to look at it from her point of view. She lost her daughter, her only child, and you're all she has left of her."

"How did Mom survive her childhood?"

Thinking of Johnny Winslow, Sam said, "Believe it or not, there are worse things."

"She can't really do what she threatened, can she? Can she really come back with the DSS people and take me away?"

He didn't want to answer her question, because he was afraid that under the circumstances, the answer was yes. If DSS was somehow convinced that he was an unfit parent and that his household was an unsuitable place to raise a child, they had every right—legally—to come in and remove his daughter from his home. It might take a court order, but it could be done.

And there wasn't a damn thing he could do about it.

Lorna gripped the steering wheel tightly, checked her mirrors and changed lanes to pass a slow-moving Toyota Camry. "So what the hell do you think this means?"

Policzki closed the telephone book on his lap. "Well, for starters, it means that Kaye—or Sheila, or whoever the hell she is—was still in touch with her ex-husband."

"Who just happened to drop in for a visit while she was working. And just happened to end up dead."

"While she just happened to vanish off the face of the earth."

"I don't like this," Lorna muttered. "The more we learn, the less we know."

"The lady certainly did have a lot to hide."

"Damn it, I was so sure that Rachel Winslow was tied up in this somehow. What if I'm wrong?"

"You mean what if Sam isn't guilty?"

"Bite your tongue, Policzki." Lorna blew out a hard breath. "Okay, so what if he isn't?"

"Then I'd say Kaye is our next best bet."

"You think she killed the ex and then took a powder?"

"I'm just thinking out loud. Tossing out ideas. If she did, there'd have to be a reason. What do you suppose that might be?"

"There are plenty of reasons to kill a husband. I've thought about every damn one of them at one time or another."

"Ex-husband."

"Even better. They're the worst kind of husband to have."

"Are you speaking from experience?"

"I have two divorced sisters and a horde of divorced friends. I know whereof I speak."

"On the other hand, maybe she was fooling around with the ex. We know she has a history of fooling around. Maybe Sam found out about it and decided to implement a permanent solution."

Lorna's phone rang. She flicked it on, said briskly, "Abrams."

"Oh, good, I was afraid I wouldn't get you."

"Isabel," she said. "What's up?"

"It's this woman. She's been calling and calling and calling. Please, will you phone her back before I go one hundred percent loco?"

"What does she want?"

"She won't tell me. I'm just a lowly servant. She won't talk to anybody but you. But she says it's urgent. She's called nine times in the last hour."

"She's not a reporter, is she?"

"Who knows? She says her name is Evelyn Wise. Does that mean anything to you?"

Evelyn Wise. Rachel Winslow's mother. Sam's former mother-in-law. "It does," Lorna said. "You got her number handy? Hang on. Policzki, write this number down. Isabel?"

When the secretary read it, Lorna repeated it aloud. "You got that, Policzki?"

"Got it."

"Finally," Isabel said. "Maybe now I can actually get some real work done." And she hung up.

Despite her flirtatious and insolent manner, Isabel was

a crackerjack secretary. One of these days, some good-looking young buck would sweep her off her feet and take her away to scrub floors and make babies. When that happened, Lorna was officially going into mourning.

She dialed Evelyn Wise's number. "Lorna Abrams," she said. "Boston PD. I understand you've been trying to get in touch with me."

"It's about time you called back. I've phoned several times, and that little Mexican girl you have working for you was very snippy with me. You might want to give her a talking-to about her telephone skills."

"I'll be sure to do that," Lorna said. "Is there something I can do for you?"

"Yes. You can arrest my son-in-law. Although I suppose he's not my son-in-law any longer, now that he's married to that blond bimbo. Oh, this is an unacceptable situation. Absolutely unacceptable!"

"Mrs. Wise, would you like me to come and see you? This doesn't sound like something we can really resolve over the phone."

"That's what I've been trying to tell you, Officer. I need to file a formal complaint against Sam Winslow. I was told you could help me with that."

A Southwestern stucco and red tile McMansion that looked out of place among the capes, the colonials and the New Englanders that surrounded it, the Wise home stood on a huge plot of land out in Andover. At the head of a long paved driveway sat a late-model Caddy and a slightly older Lincoln Town Car. A seventyish gentleman in a zip-up cardigan sweater was raking the lawn beneath a red maple that had begun shedding its leaves. He stopped and leaned both gloved hands on the rake handle. "Can I help you?" he said as they climbed out of the cruiser.

"Mr. Wise?" she said. "I'm Lorna Abrams, and this is my partner, Doug Policzki. Boston PD. We're looking into Kaye Winslow's disappearance. Your wife called and said she had something important to discuss with me."

"Damned awful thing," he muttered, and Lorna wasn't sure if he was talking about the disappearance or his wife's phone call. As far as she was concerned, it was a toss-up as to which was worse. "She's in the house," he told them. "Just knock. I'm sure she's watching for you."

Lorna met Policzki's eyes, sent him a telepathic message. "Nice place you've got here," he said to the older man. "How many acres do you have, anyway?"

The kid was sharp. Lorna shot him a wink and continued on to the house alone.

Jack Wise was right; his wife must have been watching, for she flung open the door before Lorna could knock. She was a solidly built woman, her hair permed into rigid, steel-gray curls that wouldn't have budged in the worst hurricane. "Come in," she said. "This is just so dreadful. You have to do something about it. The man threatened me!"

"You're talking about Sam Winslow?" The terra-cotta-tiled foyer opened onto a great room with soaring ceilings, warm wood and glass everywhere. The afternoon sun streamed in a burnished puddle on the hardwood floor.

"I am. And I'm furious," Mrs. Wise said, settling on the couch and primly tucking her hemline down over her knees.

Lorna waited for an invitation to join her. When it didn't come, she sat anyway. "With Sam?" she said casually, curling her ankles together, just two gals sitting down for tea and conversation. Minus the tea.

"With Sam, with the police, with this entire situation. I have my rights, you know, but nobody seems to care. That poor little girl. It's just not right."

Outside the atrium window, Lorna could see Jack Wise talking a blue streak, pointing and waving while Policzki hung on his every word. "You're talking about your granddaughter, I presume. Gracie?"

"Of course I'm talking about Gracie. Are you having trouble following me? That man is an unfit parent. He has no business raising a child. And Jack and I have so much to offer Gracie. All the things he can't give her. If she lived with us, she'd never want for anything. My husband has more money than God. And you know what they say—you can't take it with you. He might as well spend it on our granddaughter. We could make sure she was introduced to the right class of friends. We could give her dinners at the country club. She could take tennis lessons. We have our own court. And horseback riding lessons. Little girls love horses. We have plenty of room for her to play. And a swimming pool. She could have pool parties, invite all her little friends. Sam can never give her those things."

Lorna could have pointed out that if they were really so altruistic, they could provide those things for their granddaughter even if she did live with her father. But she held back. Instead, she pointed out the obvious. It probably wouldn't win her any brownie points, but it had to be said. "She is his daughter." *And not yours.* But she didn't say that out loud.

The woman eyed her coolly. "I thought you were here to help me."

"I'm here," Lorna said, "because you seemed upset and you were determined to talk to me. I'm pretty flexible. Just ask anybody who knows me. But I'm having a real hard time trying to figure out what it is you're asking me to do."

"Arrest him! The man threatened me not more than two hours ago, and—"

Lorna leaned forward eagerly. "How did he threaten you? Did he have a weapon? Did he threaten bodily harm?"

"He told me that if I didn't leave his property, I'd be sorry!"

"Did he explain what he meant by sorry?"

"He threatened to call the police and have me arrested for trespassing. Can you imagine? In my own house!"

"Now I'm confused. What do you mean, your own house?"

"I lived in that house for thirty years! Now that Rachel's gone, he says it's his place. The gall of the man. But in my eyes, it'll always be my house."

"Mrs. Wise," Lorna said, trying not to show her exasperation, "is Sam Winslow the legal owner of the property?"

Evelyn sniffed. "I don't see how he could be. We gave the house to Rachel. But according to our lawyer, the house became Sam's property when she died. I think it's a travesty, but Miles Lawson—he's our attorney—assures me that Sam inherited the place rightfully."

A headache began just behind Lorna's left eye. "All right," she said. "Let's backtrack a little here. Back to his threatening you. Was that all he said? He didn't threaten any kind of physical violence?"

"What do you mean, was that all? That's not enough? I was threatened! Threatening is illegal. Surely even you're aware of that."

She was beginning to understand why Winslow would have wanted the woman removed from his property. Or maybe from the planet. She was truly the mother-in-law from hell. If Ed's mother had been anything like Evelyn Wise, Lorna's marriage would have lasted about five minutes. And instead of carrying a badge and a gun, she probably would've ended up spending twenty-five to life in a prison cell for using the old bat for target practice.

"I'm sure it must've been upsetting to you," she said. "But I'm afraid it's really not specific enough a threat for us to take action. If he'd pulled a weapon on you, or threatened you with bodily harm, then we could arrest him. But threatening to have you removed from his property—I'm afraid he's well within his legal rights."

Evelyn Wise spluttered and turned such a violent shade of red that Lorna worried she might be having a stroke. "The man is dangerous!" she said. "He was responsible for my daughter's death, and now I'm sure he's killed his new wife. The child needs to be removed from his home immediately."

"There are channels for that," Lorna said, "but—"

"I realize there are channels, you nincompoop! I've already spoken to DSS! You're not listening to me!"

"I'm listening," Lorna said coolly. "But you haven't said much of anything. You claim he was responsible for Rachel's death. Do you have any kind of evidence to back up your claim?"

"He was never good enough for her. Sam Winslow is nothing but white trash, from a long line of white trash. His father was a mill worker, for God's sake! Sam took one look at my daughter—and her father's bank balance—and he set out to brainwash her. I tried to tell her he was bad news. But do you think she would listen? Of course not. She was in *love*." Evelyn spat out the word as though it were something vile.

Lorna glanced openly at her watch. If she'd hoped to get anything juicy from Evelyn Wise, she'd been sadly mistaken. The woman was spouting hot air. She didn't have a thing on Sam Winslow.

"Mrs. Wise," the detective said, "unless you can come up with something concrete, I'm afraid we're both wasting our time. Do you have any evidence that Professor Winslow was involved in your daughter's death? Did you ever see him mistreat her? Was he ever physically violent? Controlling? Did your daughter ever tell you that she was afraid of her husband?"

"Of course she didn't say she was afraid of him. I'm telling you, the man had her brainwashed!"

Trying a different tack, Lorna said, "What about Kaye Winslow? You also seem to believe he killed her. Can you tell me why?"

"Patterns," the woman replied. "Don't you get it? Didn't you read this morning's newspaper article? The man has established a pattern. Every woman he's been involved with has met an untimely and suspicious end. I don't want the same thing to happen to my Gracie."

"What do you think he'd do to Gracie?"

"Oh, I don't know! I'm just a housewife. Isn't it your job to figure out these things?"

"You drive." Lorna practically flung the keys at Policzki. He looked at her oddly, but didn't question her, just got behind the wheel, backed the car around and headed down the driveway.

Lorna reached for her seat belt, locked it, then leaned her head back and stared at the ceiling. "Oh, my poor, aching head," she said. "I think it's about to explode. I've just revised my theory about Rachel Winslow's death. I think she shot herself, just to get away from her mother."

"That bad?" Policzki said.

"Worse. Worse beyond your wildest imaginings. I feel like I've just been fed through a paper shredder. Alive. Do you suppose it's too late to change my career track? I should've listened to my mother and gone to secretarial school."

"I don't know," he said. "I hear it's a jungle out there in corporate America."

"God, what a waste of time this was! Evelyn Wise—Christ, just the sound of her name makes my teeth ache—doesn't have zilch on Sam Winslow. All I got out of our go-round, besides the desire to never lay eyes on the woman again, was that she hates her former son-in-law. As in she detests the very ground he stands on. As in she thinks he's the biggest demon who ever walked this earth. Worse than Hitler, worse than Mussolini, worse than Beelzebub himself. She hates him so much, I actually found myself wanting to defend the guy."

"Any particular reason why she feels this way?"

"Hell, yes. His daddy was a mill worker, an occupation which the laudable Mrs. Wise has placed at the top of her personal list of all-time most evil professions. Numero uno. I guess Viking pillager and IRS agent were already taken. Furthermore, when her precious daughter died, Sam Winslow had the audacity to inherit what was Rachel's. Including the house where he now resides, which apparently belonged to the Wises before they handed it over to their daughter. Oh, and that threat he made? The one she wants to file a complaint about? He told her to get out of his house or he'd call the cops and have her thrown out. Hell, if he'd called me, I would have helped him escort the lady through the door. The woman's a nutcase. A dangerously pissed-off, certifiable nutcase."

Policzki cleared his throat. "Well, then. I guess you probably don't want to hear what I got from the lady's husband."

"If it's more of the same, spare me."

"I think you'll find it interesting, if only for the contrast."

"Fine. Hit me."

"They built the Andover house as a retirement home on three acres—we walked the property together—about nine years ago because Mrs. Wise didn't want to live in the city any longer. The Union Square house they turned over to Rachel, since it seemed obvious that, A, she wasn't going to leave her husband and come back home anytime soon, and B, she and the kid needed a decent place to live, and Sam Winslow wasn't able to care for her in the manner to which they'd like her to be accustomed.

"Sam and the old lady have never seen eye to eye on anything, especially his marriage to her daughter. Mrs. Wise was always convinced that Winslow was after her husband's money, despite evidence to the contrary—he never asked them for a penny, and he and Rachel lived exclusively on his income. Aside from the house, of course. According to Jack Wise, Winslow was madly in love with Rachel—Wise said he could see it in the guy's face every time he looked at her—and apparently it was mutual. Winslow might not have been his first choice for a husband for his baby girl, but the man made Rachel happy, which, as far as Wise is concerned, was the main priority. He said Winslow's a decent sort of fellow, maybe wrapped a little too tight, but then, there are worse faults.

"When Rachel died, the guy went to pieces. It took him a while to recover, with Kaye's help, although Wise says he knew that relationship wouldn't last from the moment he first met her. She was a little too greedy, a little too grasping, and not at all Winslow's type. Said he was a little surprised when Winslow married her, but he had a twelve-year-old daughter to consider, and he was having trouble raising her alone, so it made sense for him to hook up with somebody. And of course, Kaye was a real looker. That didn't hurt any. But Wise says he never trusted her. There was just something a little too hard about the woman. A little too calculating. He doesn't believe Winslow was involved in her disappearance. However, if she did come to a bad end, he wouldn't be at all surprised."

Lorna just stared at him, her mouth hanging open. "You got all that," she said, "in twenty minutes?"

"I also learned the best methods for mulching flower beds and the name of the most effective weed killer on the market. And I bet you didn't know the difference between Bermuda grass and Kentucky bluegrass."

"You don't have a lawn, Policzki."

"Not yet. But I might someday."

"So now we have a dual picture of Sam Winslow. Saint and sinner. Just depends on whose point of view you're looking at."

"Yep. That's how it lays out."

"Damn it, I didn't intend to ask this, but I have to. How'd you get all that out of Wise in such a short time?"

"Easy. I just put on my best choirboy face, asked the right questions at the right times and *yes-sirred* him to death."

* * *

The Olsons swung by around five-thirty Thursday night to pick up Kevin. Michelle bounced through the front door, eyes sparkling with excitement. "Hi, Mrs. DeLucca," she said, then bounded up the stairs, yelling, "Kev! Get your scrawny butt moving! We'll miss our plane!"

A minute later, she came back with Mia's son in tow, his sneakered feet thundering down the creaky staircase. Eyeing the backpack he'd slung over his shoulder, Mia said, "That's all you're taking?"

"I'm a guy. We don't need much."

"You have everything? Clean underwear, socks, swimsuit, cell phone—"

"Mom," he said, "I can handle it."

Back off, Mia, a little voice inside her said. So instead of pushing it, she held the door open for them and said, "Have a great time in Florida."

"We intend to!" Michelle trilled, already halfway to the car. "Bye!"

Kev started down the stairs and paused on the bottom step. He turned and looked at her standing there, then bounded back up and opened his arms. "Bye," he said.

She returned his hug. Through a tear-clogged throat, she managed to say, "Bye, sweetie. Have a safe trip. Call me!"

And he was gone. She watched him get into the backseat, waved as the car pulled away from the curb. And held in her tears until he'd disappeared from sight.

He was seventeen years old. Sooner or later, she had to let go. Intellectually, she knew this. But it was harder to make her heart understand. Until Michelle had entered their lives, they'd been inseparable. He'd been so young when his father died, and because Mia had raised him alone, Kev had become her entire world. In the absence of a husband, it was her son who'd become her significant other. He was her best friend and companion. If she rented a movie, Kev watched it with her, even if it was a chick flick. If she ate out, Kev was right there. He even went shopping with her, although he generally disappeared into the electronics department while she tried on clothes.

Then Michelle had come along, and something had happened. Mia's relationship with Kevin had changed. A door had closed between them, a door she knew would never reopen. It was Michelle who had become his significant other, Michelle who was the person he wanted to be with, Michelle who took up most of his time and all of his thoughts. And suddenly Mia was left to fend for herself.

She realized that her dependence on her son was unhealthy. The break was necessary to his growth, and probably to her own. It was the natural order of things. But every time he walked out the door with Michelle Olson, his mother went green with envy.

It was a terrible thing to acknowledge. Even more terrible to know that soon he would be gone, away at college, and if she didn't want to fall into some dark abyss when he left, she needed to start preparing herself now. Certainly she could throw herself more deeply into her job. But she couldn't work twenty-four hours a day. She needed something, or someone, to help her fill the rest of those twenty-four hours and keep her from losing her mind.

At least for tonight, she had something. She rolled up her sleeves and pulled out the file she'd put together for Policzki, and sat on a stool at the kitchen counter to study it. The places she'd chosen were all airy and modern, with great amenities like in-house security—which, as a cop, he should appreciate—and on-site laundry and fitness facilities. He looked like the kind of guy who worked out. Lean, but rugged, with everything in all the right places. The kind of guy who undoubtedly had women swarming over him. The kind of guy who could date a different woman every night of the week if he wanted to.

So why hadn't some woman snatched him up by now? It was a question worth pondering. The man was nearly thirty-one years old. Yet he had no wife and no steady girlfriend, at least not if his date with the lovely Melissa was any indication. Could he be gay? Mia considered the idea for about five seconds before she discarded it as ridiculous. There'd been too much heat in his eyes when he looked at her. And that throwaway comment on the phone, when she'd asked him if he knew what brand of lingerie she wore and he'd told her he didn't know her well enough… yet. The man had deliberately stepped over the line. She might have incited the comment, but if she were of a litigious bent, she could have sued him for sexual harassment.

Instead, she'd gone so hot the phone had nearly melted in her hand.

"Enough," she said out loud. Doug Policzki's sexual inclinations were none of her business. Her job was to help him find a condo. And maybe, while she was at it, convince him that her brother wasn't guilty of murder.

Sam. There was a whole other kettle of fish. She'd finally reached her brother this afternoon. He'd been in surprisingly good spirits, considering that his wife was missing, some reporter at the *Trib* had splashed his face all over the front page of the newspaper and nicknamed him Doctor Doom, and his former mother-in-law was threatening to take his daughter away from him. In the increasingly bizarre world that had become Mia's brother's life, it was just one more ordinary day.

She ate a cup of soup for dinner, then showered and changed into a snazzy black business suit. She was standing at the bedroom mirror, trying to insert a very stubborn obsidian earring into her ear, when her cell phone beeped. It must have rung while she was in the shower. She finished putting in the earring, then picked up the phone and dialed her voice mail.

His voice was soft and laced with apology. "Mia? It's Doug Policzki. I hate to do this at the last minute, but I'm tied up tonight and I have to cancel. Can I get a rain check? I hope this won't complicate your life any more than it already is. I'll try to catch up with you tomorrow to reschedule." He paused for a single beat, then added, "Have a nice night."

Well. She tried to shake off the feeling that she'd been stood up, but the letdown she felt was all out of proportion to the situation. It was a business meeting, for God's sake. Not a date. She told herself she was disappointed because she'd put so much time and effort into finding him the perfect property. But she still felt like the only girl at school without a date to the prom.

She took off the obsidian earrings and the business suit, threw on jeans and a T-shirt, and went downstairs. As long as she had the evening off, she might as well continue what she and Gracie had started the night before. So she carted the boxes to the kitchen, which was her favorite room in the house even though it wasn't finished, grabbed a Diet Pepsi and went to work.

Even after all the work she and Gracie had done the

night before, the job took hours. Mia skimmed every file, putting anything connected to First Boston Savings in a separate pile to be looked at more closely later.

Kev called around eleven. "It's so cool," he said. "This place is amazing. It's right on the beach. And I mean *right on the beach*. You'd love it, Mom. My room has a balcony and everything. Listen." There was a distant soughing sound, which she took to be the surf. "Did you hear that?" he said. "That was the sound of the ocean. You should see the waves. Man, this place is paradise."

They chatted for a few minutes, and when she hung up the phone, that dateless-prom feeling was gone. Policzki might have stood her up, but her number one son was still dependable.

Another hour passed before she reached the last file. When she opened it, she was puzzled. This one wasn't like the others. It held a single manila envelope crammed full of papers. Mia pulled out the wad and unfolded it. Every sheet looked alike, and it took her a minute to realize what they were: credit reports. Dozens of credit reports, on different individuals. What the hell?

It wasn't unheard of for her or Kaye to run a credit report on a client, especially if that client showed an interest in an expensive property and seemed a little shaky financially. It was preferable to wasting time on somebody who wouldn't qualify for a loan, anyway. It gave her a better idea of who'd be able to prequalify. But it wasn't something they did with all their clients.

Mia began slowly thumbing through the reports, but didn't recognize any names. Wondering what the hell it meant, she got up from her chair, stretched her aching muscles and made herself a cup of tea. She carried it back to the table and drank it slowly while she paged through the reports again and thought things over.

"Okay," she said aloud, looking from the credit reports to the Grant Ashford files and then back. "I know there's something here. What am I missing?"

Inspiration struck. She gathered up the reports and began putting them in alphabetical order. This was probably a waste of time, but the only thing in danger was her night's sleep. It took her twenty minutes, and then she began going through the First Boston Savings mortgages, one file at a time, looking for names that matched.

It was long past midnight and her eyes had gone bleary when she finally found a match. The buyer's name was Stuart Landers, and if his credit report was any indication, the man was loaded. The property he'd purchased had sold for a whopping nine million dollars. And the roster of people attending the closing read like a Who's Who of the local real estate community. His Realtor had been Kaye Winslow. The title attorney was Greg Dubrowski. And his financing had come from Grant Ashford of First Boston Savings.

Puzzled, Mia paged slowly through the file. She should have known about a sale this big. Kaye should have been crowing over her coup. And the agency bank account should have swelled to epic proportions.

But Kaye hadn't crowed. There'd been no huge infusion of cash. And Mia had a bad feeling about it. A really bad feeling.

There was only one thing she could do. In the morning, she'd run it by Marty. If there was something rotten in Denmark, he'd smell it a mile away.

She went to bed with her head spinning, and fell into a

deep and dreamless sleep. When her phone rang an hour later, she was groggy and disoriented. She fumbled on the bedside table and brought the receiver to her mouth, her head feeling as grainy as a bag of sand. "Hello?" she said.

"Mia? It's Dan Liston."

As fuzzy-headed as she was, it took her a minute to recognize the name of her downtown landlord. "Dan," she said thickly. "Is there a problem with the building?" Last year, there'd been a water leak in one of the upstairs apartments and it had caused quite a mess in her office.

"I'm sorry to wake you so late," he said, his voice somber. "But I thought you'd want to know. The building's on fire."

Seventeen

They'd been up until all hours Thursday night. There'd been paperwork to be done, phone calls to be made, next of kin to be tracked down and notified. This morning, Lorna felt like Wile E. Coyote after he'd been steamrolled one too many times. Yet there Policzki sat, bright-eyed and bushy-tailed, phone book open to the Yellow Pages, his dialing finger busy on the telephone.

"Don't you ever go home?" she said, dropping her briefcase, her pocketbook, her bag lunch on top of her desk. "When I left last night, you were sitting there. And this morning, you're in the exact same spot. It's like déjà vu. If you hadn't changed the wrinkled shirt for a fresh one, I'd think you slept here."

"A little grumpy this morning, aren't we?" Policzki hung up the phone and swiveled around to look at her. "Seen the morning *Trib* by any chance?"

"What? Oh, shit, now what's Malone done?"

He picked up a folded copy of the paper and tossed it to her. She caught it in midair. "Read it and weep." Policzki opened a white take-out bag, removed a steaming cup of coffee and a muffin. "You want half of my bran muffin?"

"Only if it has chocolate chips." Lorna opened the newspaper, read the headline and groaned. "Missing Realtor's Sordid Past Exposed. Christ Jesus. Is Malone trying to derail our entire case?"

"Keep reading." Policzki peeled back the little plastic tab on the lid to his coffee cup and took a sip. "It gets better."

"'In an exclusive interview with the *Tribune,* Deborah Rideout, sister of the missing woman,' yadda yadda yadda…"

"Keep reading. The good stuff's in the third paragraph."

Lorna shifted her attention southward. "'According to Rideout, Kaye Winslow's real name is Sheila Cunningham, and she grew up in a trailer park in the tiny town of Trowbridge, Maine, where she lived with former husband, Charlie Cunningham. Yesterday, police identified Cunningham as the unidentified male who was found inside the house from which—'" Lorna folded the newspaper. "Oh, shit. I can't read any more. My eyes might start bleeding."

"I figured you'd like it."

"Where does he get this information? My own lieutenant's barely had time to hear it, and Malone prints it in the fucking newspaper for the entire world to see. What the hell does he think he's doing?" She picked up the phone and punched a button. "Isabel?" she barked. "Get me Tommy Malone's number at the *Trib.*"

For once, Isabel didn't talk back. Maybe she'd read the damned article, too. She was back on the line in about thirty seconds with the number. Lorna wrote it down, then said, "Thanks, kid. *Hasta la vista.*"

Malone was his usual chipper self this morning. Lorna didn't even bother to identify herself, just launched into her tirade. "Have you lost your mind?" she said. "Even for you, Malone, this is going a little too far."

"And a fine good morning to you, too, Detective."

"What the hell were you thinking? We're in the middle of a goddamn homicide investigation here. Are you really that intent on fucking it up?"

"The woman came to me, Lorna. Did you really think I'd turn down a story this juicy?"

"Goddamn it, Tommy, there's a time and a place. This isn't it. We're mucking around in this mess with blinders on. Somebody knows where Kaye Winslow is. Somebody put a bullet in her ex-husband. We're trying to keep things down to a dull roar in the hopes that sooner or later, we might solve this goddamn case."

"What can I say? You do your job your way, I do mine my way. While you're doing it, I'll be sitting on the sidelines, eating popcorn and watching the fireworks. Have a nice day."

Lorna stared in disbelief at the dead phone in her hand. The little shithead had hung up on her. "Fuck a duck," she said. "I changed my mind. Give me half of that muffin, Policzki. Maybe it'll help straighten out my sour disposition."

The damn thing didn't have much flavor—who the hell eats bran, anyway?—but the chewing was therapeutic. While she ate, she reread Malone's article, half listening while Policzki continued his relentless search for Carlos, Man of Mystery. How he could keep it up, call after call, mystified her. "Don't you get tired of it?" she said. "I'd think by now you'd have developed carpal tunnel of the dialing finger."

"I'm not giving up until I find him. I made a promise to Gracie."

"And you always keep your promises. Christ, Policzki, you're too good to be true. Don't you have any vices? There has to be something. Nobody's that perfect. Not even you. Let me guess. You're a closet alcoholic."

"Wrong." With his finger, he marked the next number in the phone book, cradled the phone between his ear and shoulder and punched in the number with his free hand.

"You have a harem of wives hidden away somewhere."

"Wrong again."

"You're secretly addicted to Internet porn?"

The man actually cracked a smile in the instant before he turned his full attention to the telephone. "Good morning," he said. "Detective Douglas Policzki, Boston Police Department. How are you today? Fine, thanks. I'm trying to track down a gentleman who might be an employee of yours. First name is Carlos. That's C-A-R-L-O-S. Right. Unfortunately, I don't know his last name. But this fellow is in his twenties, brown eyes, brown hair, currently sporting a shaved head, may or may not live in East Boston." He listened for a minute. "Right…right. Really? Yes. That's true." He wrote something down, paused. "Uh-huh. Uh-huh. Of course, I realize that kind of thing is confidential. I wouldn't want to get you into trouble. How about I give you my badge number? You can call and check it, and then—sure, I can hold on for a minute."

He was doing it again, that thing he did, the Dudley Do-Right sincerity thing that made women of all ages blush and tee-hee and give him whatever he asked for. No matter how many times Lorna watched, she couldn't figure out how he did it. But she'd seen him in action enough times to know without a doubt that the person at the other end of the phone line was female, and that she was practically peeing her pants in her eagerness to provide him with what he wanted. Maybe they'd been playing the game backward all this time. Maybe he was the one who should be playing good cop to her bad cop. The minute he turned on the charm, people looked past the somber face.

"Uh-huh," he said again, and began writing once more. "That's *R-I-V-E-R-A.* Got it. Thanks, Earlene, you're a peach."

He hung up the phone and swiveled around in his chair. "Carlos Rivera," he said. "Twenty-two years old. Works for Northeast Freight Services. Lives in East Boston. He has a shaved head, and he didn't report to work on Tuesday morning. Or Wednesday. Or Thursday. His sister finally called yesterday afternoon to say he's been sitting in a jail cell since Monday night."

"Amazing," Lorna said. "Fucking amazing."

"No," Doug said. "It's called diligence."

"It's called if I had your fucking patience, I could've made lieutenant."

Her phone rang, and she eyed it with the same distaste she'd have given a fish that had been lying around dead for a while. Reaching out, she picked it up. "What?" she said.

"Good thing for both of us that I'm not the commissioner," Conor Rafferty said. "I just had a call from a Lieutenant Gerrish of the New Hampshire State Police. They have a positive ID on that BMW you've been looking for."

Her day, which had started so bleakly, took an immediate 180 degree turn. "I knew it!" she cackled. "I knew it! Did I or did I not tell you we were about to get a break in this case?"

"As much as it pains me to admit it, you did. Want to stop jumping for joy long enough to hear the rest?"

"Be still, my beating heart. You have something better?"

"Lots better. It must be your birthday or something. Congratulations, Abrams. You'd better get your ass up to New Hampshire. They popped the trunk and found something pretty interesting."

Mia didn't function well on three hours of sleep. She'd raced down here last night, but it hadn't done her any good. She'd had to park three blocks away, and then the firemen hadn't let her anywhere near. Just one more spectator hovering at the fringes of the crowd, she'd stood at a distance, shivering in the cold October night, and watched it burn. Everything she'd worked so hard to build, gone in an instant, swallowed by the flames. She'd stayed and watched until they had the fire out, and then she'd driven home, her movements mechanical and automatic, tears blurring her vision. Only after she'd fallen into bed had she allowed herself to cry. It poured out of her in jagged paroxysms of sobbing that left her spent. Afterward, she'd fallen asleep and dreamed of flames surrounding her, circling ever closer, trapping her with nowhere to run.

This morning, she'd called Bev at first light and told her the news. Now they stood side by side on the sidewalk across the street from what had been their office, currently gutted and blackened, its windows turned to yawning black holes. Gone were the firemen in their fluorescent gear, gone were the trucks and the ladders and the snaky hoses. The air was heavy with the smell of burned wood. The night had been just cold enough to freeze the thin layer of water left by the fire hoses, and now the pavement was a skating rink. Across the street, men from the fire marshal's office picked through the debris, looking for God only knew what.

Bev slipped an arm around Mia's waist. "None of it's irreplaceable," she said. "It's only wood and paper and plastic. We have insurance. I know it looks bleak right now, but we'll get through this."

God bless Bev for saying "we" instead of "you." She was a loyal employee, a loyal friend. "That's what I keep telling myself," Mia said. "But when I think about it, my heart breaks. I loved this place. I painted the walls myself, did all the decorating. It was an extension of me."

"I know, hon."

"Goddamn that Dan Liston. If he'd had a sprinkler system installed, it might have saved us. I bet the wiring in this place hasn't been updated in a hundred years." She saw Mr. Li, who owned the seafood market next to her office, talking with one of the fire investigators. Mr. Li had a wife and three daughters who depended on his market to keep a roof over their heads. His business hadn't been damaged as heavily as hers. Mia suspected it had sustained mostly smoke and water damage, as had the flower shop on the other side. It didn't take a trained investigator to figure out that the fire had started in her section of the building. Anybody with a brain could see that this was where it had burned hottest.

Mr. Li came over to them, sliding across the icy ground, shaking his head. "Bad," he said. "Very bad."

"Do you think anything inside your shop can be salvaged?"

He shrugged. "No insurance," he said.

"I'm sure Dan has insurance on the building."

"Insurance on building," Li stated. "No insurance on business."

"Oh, no. What will you do?"

Again, he shrugged, as if it were all too much to take in. He walked away with his shoulders slumped like an old man, and Mia cussed under her breath. "What about the people who live upstairs?" she asked. "Margo, on the second floor? And the Garcias? I haven't seen them around. Please tell me they got out."

"They got out," Bev said. "There were working smoke alarms in the apartments, and they suffered mostly smoke damage. I heard a couple of the investigators talking when I first got here. The Red Cross took care of the tenants."

"Thank God." The Garcias had small children. It would have been unbearable if anything had happened to one of them. And thank God for the Red Cross. Too bad there wasn't some organization that put Band-Aids on small business owners who'd lost everything. Someone to give Mia a warm blanket and a cup of chicken soup and the reassurance that within a few days, she'd be back up and running.

It wasn't going to happen. Her section of the building was a total loss. She would have to start over again at square one. All those files gone. All that paperwork lost. Mia couldn't even think about how this would affect her clients. Right now, the only things she had left were Kaye's files and the folder she'd put together for Policzki.

Something sparked inside her muzzy brain, some faint connection. She tried to follow it, but lost it completely when she saw Marty Scalia slipping and sliding his way to where she and Bev stood. "I just heard," he said.

"Marty. Thanks for coming down."

His embrace was warm and solid and comforting. "Tough break, kid," he said. "Christ, you're a block of ice. Why aren't you wearing a jacket?"

Mia looked down in surprise at her bare arms. "To tell you the truth, I didn't notice."

"Here." He took off his ugly tweed suit coat and handed it to her. She wrapped it around her shoulders, grateful for its warmth in spite of the fashion statement it made.

"Thanks," she said. "Marty, what am I going to do?"

"You're gonna get some sleep is what you're gonna do. You look like shit. Once you throw off the zombie look—which, by the way, doesn't do a thing for you—you'll come over to my place and I'll fix you up with an office you can use until you get back on your feet."

"Marty Scalia," she said, "my savior. Who'd have thought?"

"Hey, I'm proud of what you've accomplished, kid. I'm not letting some piddly fire wash Winslow & DeLucca down the drain. You can work out of my agency for a while. You, too," he said to Bev. "I have a couple of empty offices. Computers are already there. You can use my phones, or run your own lines with your own number. Whatever you need, it's yours."

"God bless you, Marty." He'd just handed Mia the equivalent of that warm blanket and cup of chicken soup.

"The least I can do." He swung around, studied the burned building across the street. "They got any idea how it started?"

"I haven't talked to anybody yet. Even if I had, they probably wouldn't tell me anything. Mr. Li already tried, and I don't think he got a thing out of them."

"There's not much you can do here. Why don't you go home and get some sleep?"

"I already slept," she said. "For three whole hours. I can't go back to bed. I have too much to do. Clients to call.

The insurance company. The phone company. Christ, is it Friday already? I have a closing at one-thirty."

"Nobody would fault you for missing it."

"I'm not missing it. I have to go." She started to give him back the jacket, but Marty held up a hand.

"Keep it," he said. "You can give it back to me later."

"I'm coming with you," Bev told her. "If ever you needed me, now's the time."

"You don't have to do that."

"Don't listen to her," Marty told Bev. "She needs somebody to keep an eye on her. Gotta watch her all the time or she gets into trouble."

They made it to New Hampshire in thirty-five minutes, which was pretty good, considering that the first twenty minutes were spent fighting their way out of Boston. Once they reached Peabody, it was a straight shot up I-95, throttle wide-open and siren screaming as the unmarked passed everything on the road. The rest stop was located just north of the state line, in a picturesque setting of green lawns, evergreens and autumn-hued deciduous trees. Lorna pulled in, tires squawking on the pavement, and parked beside a Rockingham County sheriff's vehicle.

The place was crawling with cops. She and Policzki flashed IDs and, stepping over the yellow crime scene tape that was keeping the tourists at bay, made their way to a group of people clustered around the rear of a bright red BMW that sat with its trunk open. In spite of the strong breeze, the sun was warm, and as she approached the car, Lorna could smell a telltale odor. "Morning, boys," she said. "Abrams and Policzki, Boston PD. What do we have here?"

The tallest of them, the guy in charge—she could always tell who was in charge from a quarter-mile away—stepped away from the group. "Farris," he announced, introducing himself, shaking her hand and then Policzki's. "Why don't you take a look for yourself."

Lorna crossed the pavement to the car. Standing next to the bumper, she peered down into the trunk and saw a balled-up wad of fabric. A piece of clothing. Bright red, it looked like the jacket to a woman's business suit.

And it was saturated with blood.

"Whoa. That's a lot of blood."

"Pretty, isn't it?" Farris said.

Beside her, Policzki said, "Who found the car?"

"Groundskeeper came in to work this morning and saw the car, remembered it was here yesterday morning when he came to work. It didn't feel right to him, expensive car like that, sitting here that long with nobody in it. So he called in the plate number. It matched up with your APB, so we drove on over to check it out. Opened the trunk and found this."

Lorna examined the trunk lid. There were no pry marks. "How'd you get the trunk open?"

"With the button in the glove compartment."

"Say what? The car wasn't locked?"

"Nope. Maybe whoever left it here was hoping somebody'd take it for a joyride."

"Or maybe somebody did take it for a joyride, and abandoned it when they identified that pungent odor wafting from the trunk."

Policzki said, "Is that enough blood to mean—"

"Good question."

"Here's another. If it is, then where's the body?"

Farris said, "We have people out beating the bushes.

Could've been dumped off anywhere. There's one other thing you might want to see."

He led her around the side of the car. Lorna knelt and looked closely at the single bloody thumbprint on the left rear fender, so perfect it might have been left there deliberately. "Hot damn," she said.

Could the professor have pulled off driving the missus all the way out here on Tuesday afternoon and then getting back to BBCC in time for his four o'clock class? He would've had to plan it right down to the last minute. He would have needed a getaway car, and probably an accomplice.

The logistics were questionable enough to make her uneasy. Kaye Winslow had left the realty office around two. It would have taken her a few minutes—say ten or fifteen—to get from there to the Worthington house. Another five to go inside, deposit her personal items on the kitchen island. If hubby had shown up at, say, twenty past two and killed his wife and Charlie Cunningham right away, then somehow managed to get her body out the door of the house and into the trunk of her own car—in broad daylight, no less—he'd have had about a ninety-minute window. Ninety minutes, in weekday traffic, to get out of Back Bay and onto the highway, drive north to the New Hampshire state line, stopping somewhere to discard Kaye's body— again in broad daylight—swap cars, and get back to BBCC in time for class.

It was possible. Depending, of course, on traffic. After all, she and Policzki had made it up here in thirty-five minutes. Thirty-five up, thirty-five back would still leave twenty minutes, if you were driving at the speed of light. But it was cutting things damn close. Granted, the Beemer could do it. But it was still risky, even in Massachusetts, where speed limit signs were treated as little more than suggestions. If he'd been pulled over for speeding and the officer had looked in his trunk, it would've been curtain time. And if traffic was bad—and when was Boston traffic anything but bad?—he might have been late to class. A man would have to be pretty desperate to take that kind of risk.

Of course, he could've killed his wife and hidden the car, with wifey in the trunk, until later that night, after she and Policzki had questioned him. Under cover of darkness, he could easily have driven up here at a sedate speed that wouldn't draw attention, dropped her off and swapped cars, and driven back to Boston at a leisurely pace. He could've been back at home, watching Jay Leno, by midnight.

But if he'd done either of those things, the Beemer would have been here on Wednesday morning. Why the hell hadn't the witness noticed it sooner? Kaye Winslow had disappeared on Tuesday afternoon. It was now Friday. If the car hadn't been here since Tuesday afternoon, where the hell had it been?

"Where's the groundskeeper?" she said. "I'm going to want to question him."

"He's inside. Emilio Alonso. Young fellow, Puerto Rican. Looks like he's FOB."

"FOB?"

"Fresh off the boat. Let's just say his grasp of English leaves a little to be desired."

"All right." She paused to survey the scene. "You might as well call off your people. I have mine on the way. They should be here any minute now." Policzki had spent most of the thirty-five-minute drive up there making phone calls.

"Not necessary," Farris said. "My forensics crew's ready. We were just waiting for you to get here."

"No offense, but I'd rather have my own people process the scene."

"None taken. But it's my crime scene, so it's a nonissue."

Her hackles rose instantly. "Wrong," she said. "My investigation, my crime scene."

"Which just happens to be sitting smack in the middle of my jurisdiction. Or maybe you missed that Welcome to New Hampshire sign back there."

"Listen, Farris, I've been working this case since Winslow disappeared, and if you think I'm about to hand it over to a bunch of bumbling fucks from the state of New Hampshire, you've got rocks in your head."

His eyebrows went sky-high. "Bumbling fucks?"

"Let me put it this way. How many homicides do you see a year in the bucolic little state of New Hampshire? Ten? Twelve? Last year, in Boston alone, we had seventy-five. So I think we happen to have a little more insight into homicide investigation than you do."

He planted his feet apart in a confrontational stance and leaned down into her face. "Are you insinuating, Detective, that I don't know how to perform my job?"

She held her ground. "What I'm insinuating, *Detective,* is that my people will be the ones processing the scene. Winslow lived in Boston. She disappeared from Boston. If that bloody trunk is any indication, I'd say she may have been killed in Boston. If this car had been found a quarter-mile south of here, you wouldn't be dealing with it at all because it would've been left in the Commonwealth of Massachusetts. Now unless somebody can give me one hell of a convincing argument that

Kaye Winslow was killed right where we stand and tossed into the puckerbrush out back, she's mine. Any questions?"

Farris squared an already rigid jaw. "If it was up to me," he snapped, "I'd hand the whole thing to you gift-wrapped, with a big red bow. I have enough headaches of my own without taking on any of yours. But it's not in my hands. I'm just following procedure. You want the case, you take it up with my lieutenant."

He turned and walked away, leaving her there sputtering. "The nerve of that guy," she muttered. "Arrogant ass. Did you hear that, Policzki?" She wheeled around to gauge his response and found him standing a few feet away, talking on his cell phone.

"Right," he said. "Farris. That's *F-A-R-R-I-S.* Correct. With an *A.* Thank you, Lieutenant. We'll wait to hear from you."

He hung up the phone, returned it to his belt clip. "Ten minutes," he said. "Give Rafferty ten minutes, and he says he'll have it straightened out."

"Keep an eye on things. Nobody makes a move until we hear back from Rafferty. Not our people, not theirs." She glanced toward the entrance ramp, where the first of the BPD vehicles was pulling in. "I catch anybody touching anything before we get this mess straightened out, I'll personally chop off their hands at the wrist. I'm going inside to question the groundskeeper."

Emilio Alonso was a little guy, no more than five-three, with snapping dark eyes, a thick head of black hair and a swarthy complexion made darker by a summer spent doing outdoor work. He sat on a bench, a cup of water in his hand

and a damp cloth pressed to his forehead. "Mr. Alonso?" she said.

He glanced up, gave her the once-over, then glared at her. *"Sí,"* he said.

She knelt so that they were eye to eye. "I'm Lorna Abrams, Boston PD. Can I ask you a few questions?"

He carefully folded the wet cloth into a neat little square, looking at a nearby park ranger for help. When it didn't come, he returned to glaring. "Questions," Lorna said. "I. Need. To ask. You. A few. Questions."

"Preguntas. Sí." His chest rose and fell with his breathing. Those piercing eyes studied her with distrust, but he seemed to be waiting for her to continue.

"All right then," she said briskly. "When did you first notice the car?"

He just looked at her blankly. *"El auto,"* she said, and made a driving motion with her hands. "When—" she tapped her wristwatch "—what time did you first see it?"

Alonso just gave her an apologetic shrug. Lorna racked her brain for the few phrases she'd managed to carry away from twelfth grade Spanish class. But it had been two decades, and trying to pull them out of the muck that crowded her mind was like unearthing the lost continent of Atlantis. *"Cuándo,"* she said, mentally patting herself on the back for remembering the word.

"Cuándo?"

"Yes. *Cuándo.* When? When did you—" she pointed to him, then to her eyes "—see *el auto*—" again the driving motion "—for the first time? *Primera vez?*"

He let loose with a rapid stream of Spanish that was so vehement, she was nearly blown over backward. This was hopeless, she thought, scrambling to regain her balance. They might as well have been from different planets. Tugging at her skirt to adequately cover herself, she rose to her feet. Getting up from a crouching position wasn't as easy as it used to be. Standing, she eyeballed the park ranger. "Is this man a state employee?" she asked him.

"Subcontractor."

"Oh, well, that makes all the difference. How in bloody hell did he manage to make a 911 call?"

"He got lucky," the ranger said. "There was a Spanish-speaking dispatcher at the other end."

"Shit." While she stood there, trying to figure out what to do, Alonso looked from her to the ranger and back, his head swiveling like a spectator at a tennis match.

Maybe she could recruit a little help. There were at least a dozen people milling about, most of them wearing uniforms. Nobody seemed to be doing much. Lorna cupped her hands around her mouth and bellowed, "Hey!"

The room went silent as every head in the place turned to look at her. "Anybody here speak Spanish?" she said.

She was greeted with blank stares, a few shakes of the head. All of them negative. Within seconds, everybody in the room returned to whatever important task they'd been in the middle of—drinking coffee and yakking being high on the list. Leaving her nowhere. "Jesus Christ," she muttered, "has the state of New Hampshire ever heard of diversity?" Pulling out her cell phone, she called Policzki. "What's going on out there?"

"Rafferty just called with our clearance. I'm about to give the forensic team the go-ahead."

"Who's here? Tavares isn't out there, is he? Or Morales?"

"No. Why?"

"I'm looking for somebody who can speak Spanish."

"I speak Spanish."

"Right. I suppose you took a semester or two in high school." It would be better than nothing, she supposed. After all, he was a hell of a lot closer to his high school days than she was.

"Actually," he said, "before the police academy, I went to college in Arizona for three years. I majored in Spanish."

It took an instant for his words to sink in. And then she jumped on them. "Does the department know this, Policzki? Why the hell didn't you ever tell me?"

With his customary maddening logic, he said, "You never asked. And yes, the department knows about it."

"Nice of them to tell me. Geez, is there anything you can't do? If there is, I haven't found it yet. Get the forensic team to start processing the scene. Then, if it's not too much for you, do you think you might get your ass in here and help me out?"

Eighteen

"He's not happy," Policzki said, "that we—that would be all of us law enforcement types, I presume—kept him sitting for hours, cooling his heels, when he's supposed to be doing his job. He gave me a lengthy lecture about the inefficiencies of the justice system."

The forensics people had finished with the crime scene and the car had been towed away for further processing. Lorna wheeled the cruiser into a turnaround, waited until there was no oncoming traffic, and pulled smoothly into the southbound lane of I-95. Accelerating, she said, "Maybe when this case is over, I can hire him to teach my twelve-year-old about a solid work ethic. Can't even get the damn kid off the couch long enough to mow the lawn. What'd Alonso say about the car?"

"He says it wasn't here on Wednesday. It showed up sometime during the night. Claims he noticed it first thing Thursday morning. They get a lot of fancy cars through here, but this one in particular caught his eye because it's the very car he aspires to own someday."

"Of course. The good old American Dream. A chicken in every pot and a Beemer in every garage."

"And streets paved with gold."

Lorna drummed her fingers against the steering wheel. "What time did he come on shift Thursday?"

"Seven a.m. Alonso's pretty sure that he would have noticed the car if it'd been there on Wednesday. Since it's the car of his dreams and all. And while you were outside making friends with the local constabulary, I questioned everybody who was on duty both days. Nobody saw anything. Problem is, even if the car showed up during the day shift, those guys are stuck indoors all day. They're too busy answering questions from tourists to see anything that's going on outside. That's grounds crew territory."

"Which right now happens to be Alonso."

"Correct. The other guy who usually works with him has walking pneumonia, so he was working alone yesterday. And he spent a big portion of the afternoon mowing at the far end of the property."

"Damn." Lorna chewed on her lip. "I don't get it. Kaye Winslow and her car both disappeared on Tuesday afternoon. Thirty-six hours later, give or take, the car shows up at a rest stop fifty miles north of Boston, with a shitload of bloody clothes in the trunk, but no body. If it wasn't driven there Tuesday night—"

"Then where the hell was it those first thirty-six hours?"

"Exactly."

"I have another question. The New Hampshire state police must patrol that rest area regularly. There was an APB out on the car. How come nobody saw it during a routine overnight patrol?"

Lorna eyed him thoughtfully. "Oh, shit," she said. "This case is giving me another headache."

* * *

Back at home, Mia's first call was to her insurance agent. Since it was Friday, he promised to send an adjuster down to look over the damage before the day was out. Her second call was to Yolanda Lincoln, her part-time employee, to tell her what had happened and where their temporary office would be located. After that, she called the utility companies and got things settled with them. She had all calls temporarily forwarded to her home number, then scheduled a time to have a new phone line installed at Marty's place. Then she and Bev got to work calling everyone they regularly did business with to notify them of the situation and to let them know she'd be back up and running in a few days.

That took the rest of the morning. While Bev ran out and picked up a couple of sandwiches, Mia showered and dressed and applied makeup to try and disguise the hard evidence of her sleepless night. It didn't work. She still looked like something the cat dragged in. She hated looking unprofessional, but there was little she could do about it. Until she got a good night's sleep, she'd be carrying around bags under her eyes so heavy she'd need a forklift to pick them up.

After lunch, she finally managed to break free of Bev. "There's nothing left for you to do," she told her assistant. "After this one-thirty closing, I'm coming back home and sleeping. It's Friday. You might as well start your weekend early. Get rested up. Next week, we have to start putting our lives back together."

Bev made motherly noises, but Mia could tell how much the idea of a long weekend appealed to her. "Are you sure you'll sleep?" she asked.

"I'll sleep. I'd probably skip this closing today and go to bed now, except that I want the check in my hot little hands to deposit before the bank closes. Meet me first thing Monday morning at Marty's. We'll look over the situation and then we'll figure out our next move."

The closing moved along quickly, and Mia drove from the title company directly to the bank, where she deposited the check into her account and ordered new business checks to replace the ones that had been destroyed in the fire. So many little details. So much to do, so much to replace. Just thinking about it gave her a headache.

It was midafternoon when she got home, so tired that her brain was having trouble functioning. Mia dropped her briefcase in the center of the kitchen table and checked her answering machine. There was a message from her insurance agent, saying that the adjuster had checked out the damage and now he wanted her to make up a list of everything she'd lost, with approximate dollar values. Oh, and could they have it by Monday morning?

She kicked off her shoes, tiptoed upstairs and peeled off her panty hose, leaving them in a pile on the bedroom floor. The scourge of the modern businesswoman, the goddamn things were like sausage casings, squeezing her so tightly they'd probably done irreparable damage to her internal organs. Freed at last, she took a deep breath, reveling in her ability to breathe again, and envying the young girls she saw on the street every day in all their bare-legged glory.

After she hung her business suit and dress shirt in the closet, she wrapped herself in the soft flannel robe that had been a birthday gift from Sam and Gracie. She had promised Bev that she'd sleep, but Mia was too keyed up to do so. Instead, she went back downstairs, found her reading glasses, curled up on the couch and picked up the Stuart Landers file. Mia opened it and began reading, but she had trouble focusing. She took off the glasses, rubbed her bleary eyes and put them back on.

It didn't help much.

If only she weren't so tired. There was so much to be done. So much to worry about. Sam and Gracie. Kaye's disappearance, and her possible involvement in real estate fraud. The fire and all the headaches it brought. Doug Policzki, who'd somehow managed to get under her skin and now was stuck there like a burr, refusing to be dislodged no matter how hard she scratched.

Mia closed her eyes. Just for a minute. Then she'd get back to the file.

She fell asleep within seconds, still clutching the file in her hands.

There were a half-dozen voice mails waiting for him. Policzki sat at his desk and worked his way through them, making notes on a lined pad as he went. The first two could be dealt with later, but the third was too intriguing to ignore. "Policzki?" a gravelly voice said. "Tim Maroni, Arson. I'm working on a case and your name just happened to come up. I have some information you might find useful. Give me a call."

He wrote down the number, dialed it. "Maroni?" he said. "Doug Policzki."

"Policzki, yeah. You're working that case where the real estate lady disappeared, right?"

"I am."

"I thought you might like to know that somebody torched her office last night."

His stomach went into free fall. Trying to keep his voice steady, he said casually, "Anybody hurt?"

"Nah. Middle of the night. Downstairs businesses were closed for the night, and the upstairs tenants got out okay."

Some of the knotted feeling left his stomach. But not all of it. Mia hadn't been there. She hadn't been hurt. At least not physically. He wondered if her business would survive a blow like this. "You're sure it was arson?" he said.

"Oh, yeah. It was definitely set. By amateurs. They didn't try very hard to cover their tracks. We found traces of accelerant, and an empty turpentine can in the Dumpster out back. Don't know if it's connected to your case, but after a few years in this business, you just get a feel for things. I thought you should know."

"Thanks," Doug said. "Thanks for the information."

He hung up the phone and sat there for a while. Thinking. Puzzling it out. There was some kind of connection, he was sure. A woman disappeared, leaving the dead body of her ex-husband behind. A few days later, somebody burned down her office. The next morning, her car was found with her bloody clothing in the trunk. Policzki was a cop. He didn't believe in coincidence. And that was just too many coincidences. Something here stank worse than seaweed at low tide.

He was dying to toss it around with Lorna, but she'd gone down to the lab to try to push them on the prints. His partner was a master of pushology. So instead, he got back on the phone and made a few calls until he found out where Carlos Rivera was being held. He wrote Lorna a note and left it on her desk: "Gone to check on a couple of things. Back later. Call me if anything comes in on the prints."

The rest of his voice mails could wait. Policzki grabbed

his car keys from the desk drawer and headed for the jail to have a little chat with Carlos Rivera.

Rivera stepped into the interrogation room, dressed in a bright orange jumpsuit, his brow drawn low and his lips pressed hard together. He flopped onto a metal folding chair and propped his elbows on the table, then treated Policzki to one of those long, insolent stares that he'd seen a hundred times before. The kid was trying to look fierce, but his bravado was little more than a bluff. On the surface, he might appear cool and indifferent, but beneath the table, his size twelve feet were drumming almost convulsively against the tile floor.

The guard left them alone. When he closed the door behind him, Policzki pulled a photo of Kaye Winslow out of his pocket and set it down on the table in front of Rivera. Lining it up squarely in front of the kid, he said, "You know this lady?"

Rivera glanced down at the photo, then returned to staring. "Who wants to know?"

"I want to know."

"Who the fuck are you?"

Policzki pulled out his badge and set it on the table. "That answer your question?"

"I don't know her," Rivera said.

"She's a classy lady," Policzki said. "Drives an expensive car. Wears expensive clothes. Maybe you thought she'd be an easy mark."

"I told you, I don't know the lady."

"So what, you and a couple of buddies planned it? Only you ended up in here, so they had to take care of her for you? Was that it?"

"Man, I don't have any idea what you're talking about. I didn't have nothing to do with this lady. Whoever the hell she is."

"You know, Carlos, you're already in a lot of trouble. I hear you've been making a few special deliveries along with your regular ones. Bad news, buddy. You're maybe looking at a little time inside. You ever been to prison, Carlos? It's not like this place. Young, good-looking guy like you ought to be real popular in there."

"Fuck you, man."

"I'd say you're the one who's fucked. I checked your record. Since this is your first offense, if you smile and keep your head down and kiss major ass, the judge might be persuaded to be lenient with you. But throw in a couple more charges—oh, I don't know, maybe invasion of privacy, stalking, online solicitation of minors—"

"Give me a fucking break, man. I didn't do none of those things."

"Which is why I'm giving you a second chance to look at the picture. Take a good, close look, Rivera. Think about that prison cell before you answer."

Rivera glared at him, then snatched up the photo and pretended to study it through heavy-lidded eyes. "I maybe seen her."

"I hear they have communal showers. Big, hairy guys, and communal showers. You know what communal means, Carlos?"

A trickle of sweat ran down the kid's temple. "All I did was take her fucking picture, man! Last time I heard, that wasn't against the law!"

"So you admit you know her."

"Jesus, man, I only followed her for like an hour one

day. I gotta work for a living, you know. I can't be going around doing volunteer work. Gracie asked me to follow her around. See if I could dig up any dirt. I felt sorry for the kid, so I said I'd do it. That's all there was to it!"

Policzki reached out, caught Carlos Rivera's shirt in his fist, and hauled him halfway across the table. With deadly calm, he said, "That kid is fifteen years old. If I ever catch you with her again, or with any other underage girl, I'll cut off your nuts and stuff 'em down your throat. Got that?"

Rivera yanked himself free. "I didn't know she was fifteen," he whined. "She didn't tell me."

Policzki stood. Tucking the photo of Kaye Winslow back into his pocket, he said, "Well, then, Carlos, if I were you, I'd start carding all my dates."

While he navigated the hellish Friday afternoon traffic, Policzki called Gracie Winslow. "Hey, Gracie, it's Doug. Got a minute?"

"Am I in trouble?"

Squeezing into an opening between a transit bus and a duck boat, he said, "You're not in trouble. I found Carlos."

"You actually found him?" She sounded amazed. "How?"

"I have secret powers. Did you tell your dad about him?"

"I didn't have much of a choice, did I? I figured if I didn't, you'd cuff me and send me up the river."

Policzki held back a smile. She was really something, that Gracie. "And yet you're still alive to talk on the phone with me."

"It wasn't as bad as I'd thought it would be. Um... there were a few other issues going on that sort of softened the blow."

"So you hit him while he was down."

"You could say that. What about Carlos?"

Policzki stopped for a red light. "You're in the clear. Carlos couldn't possibly have had anything to do with Kaye's disappearance. He was unavoidably detained at the time it happened."

"Unavoidably detained," she said. "That's a euphemism for something you don't think I'm old enough to hear. I hate euphemisms. Just come out and say it."

"He's in jail, Gracie. He's been there since Monday night."

There was a moment of silence before she said, "Should I be relieved?"

"You should definitely be relieved. He's not a particularly nice guy."

"He was my friend."

"Kiddo," Policzki said, "you need to find a better class of friends."

He double-parked in front of Mia's house and activated his blue dashboard light. It took her a few minutes to answer the door. Sleepy-eyed and wrapped in a turquoise flannel robe, she sported a red ridge on one side of her face from whatever she'd been sleeping on. She looked like she'd been to hell and back, but she was alive and walking upright, and that was what mattered.

At the sight of her, all those knotted-up places inside him began to relax. Until they did, he hadn't realized how tense he was. "Detective," she said in a voice that was smoky from sleep. "Sorry. I was napping."

"I can tell. I'm sorry I woke you."

She raked a hand through her tangled hair. "'S okay. What are you doing here?"

"I just heard about the fire. I wanted to check in on you. Make sure you were all right."

"I guess that depends on your definition of all right. Come on in."

He stepped into the foyer and was immediately accosted by her scent. It might have been perfume, might have been shampoo. Whatever it was, it was wispy and delicate and undeniably female, and it wrapped itself around him and sucked him in. He followed her to the kitchen, studying the subtle sway of her hips as she walked. Dressed in business attire, she was one classy lady. In her flannel robe, barefoot and with her hair a mess, she looked softer somehow. More approachable. In his line of work, he met a lot of women. Most of them took second looks at him. He was used to it, but it had been a long time since he'd looked back. He was looking now, looking hard, thinking things he had no business thinking. Not with this woman. He was in the middle of a homicide case, and her brother was his prime suspect. Policzki had no business being here, in her house, alone with her.

"I found Carlos," he said.

"Oh?" She swung around, and he caught a flash of thigh as the robe parted. She cinched the belt tighter. "And?"

"He's been in jail since Monday night. There's no way he could've been involved in any of this."

"Does Gracie know?"

"I called her and told her."

"That has to be a weight off her shoulders. Can I offer you a cup of coffee?"

"I can't stay long. Mia…there's something I need to tell you."

She paused, coffeepot in hand, and eyed him quizzically. "What?"

"Have you talked to anybody about the fire?"

"Anybody as in who? I've talked to friends. Coworkers."

"As in fire investigators."

"No." Her gaze sharpened. "Why?"

Closely watching her face, he said, "I had a call from Tim Maroni with the arson squad. The fire was deliberately set."

"What?" She went so pale, Policzki thought he might drop the coffeepot. Moving quickly, he pried the handle from her fingers and set it back on the burner. "Arson?" she said.

"That's what Tim told me. They apparently found evidence."

"Those dirty rat bastards. Who the hell would do this to me?"

"I don't know. And that bothers me. It bothers me a lot. Somebody's behind all this. They could decide to come after you next."

"Oh, gee, thank you, Detective, for that comforting thought."

"I'm not trying to scare you."

"Good, because I'm not scared. I'm royally pissed off, but I'm not scared. If I find out who's responsible for this, I'll string them up by the neck."

"Careful. You're talking to a homicide cop."

"I'm serious. When I think of the headaches this is causing me—God, it just makes me steam."

"I'm serious, too. I don't suppose you could take a vacation for a few days? Go stay with a friend or something?"

"Are you crazy, Policzki? My business was just destroyed. My livelihood. I have to start putting my life back together, and damn fast. I have money in the bank. I'm far from destitute, but what I have won't go far, not when I have to pay mortgage installments and save for college tuition and put food on the table for my kid. I have two employees, and they count on the regular income, too. None of us is independently wealthy. And I have clients who depend on me to guide them through the real estate jungle. I can't just leave them hanging. We have pending deals, scheduled closings. I can't walk away from that. Especially with Kaye gone. I have responsibilities."

He wanted to tell her the rest of it. Wanted to tell her what they'd found in New Hampshire. But he couldn't. It was evidence. He couldn't talk about evidence. It would be a breach of professional ethics. They could take his badge over something like that. It was probably a breach of professional ethics just walking through the door of her house, because no matter how many times he'd told himself he was here in a professional capacity, the truth was that he'd come here because he couldn't get her out of his head. And that was a dangerous thing for a cop.

"What'll you do? About the business?"

"A friend of mine is loaning me office space at his agency until I can get back on my feet. I should be back up and running, in a limited capacity, by Tuesday. It's not an ideal situation, but I'm grateful for his offer."

"If you can't leave town, why don't you take a room in a hotel for a while? Just until Lorna and I figure out what's going on."

"Look, Doug, I'm not running away. That's not my style. You're a nice kid, and you mean well, but I'm staying put."

It was the first time she'd used his given name. Why had it felt like a put-down? He narrowed his eyes and took a step forward. "I'm not a kid," he said. As a matter of fact, he was coming dangerously close to showing her exactly how much of a kid he wasn't.

She took a step backward and pressed her spine against the granite counter. "I'm too old for you, Policzki."

"Five years, Mia. Five lousy years."

"Tell me this. When I graduated from high school, what grade were you in?"

"Seventh. But that was—"

"See what I mean?"

"—half a lifetime ago."

"When I was in high school, I was babysitting kids your age."

"Give it up, Mia. We're both long past high school. Those five years don't matter anymore."

She opened her mouth to speak, then slowly closed it. Policzki looked into her eyes, and what he saw held him there. Scorching heat simmered just beneath the surface as they stood frozen in time and space, barely a breath apart. Her lips might be saying no, but her eyes were signaling *yes oh God please yes*.

He took another step forward. It brought him close enough to give him a clear view down the front of her robe and into the shadowy valley between her breasts. He tried not to peek, but it was impossible to resist that kind of temptation. In a soft, silky voice, he said, "Just what brand of lingerie do you wear, Mia?"

She clutched at the front of her robe and drew it closer together, obliterating his view. But the message in her eyes remained the same. He lifted a hand, brushed her cheek with his knuckles.

Beneath his suit coat, his cell phone rang.

They both froze. It rang a second time. A third. On the

fourth ring, he dropped his hand from her face and took the phone from its belt clip. Cleared his throat. Still looking at her, he thumbed the On button and in a tight, hard voice, said, "Yes?"

"Wherever you are," Lorna Abrams said, "you'd better get your ass the hell back over here. We have an ID on the thumbprint."

He cleared his throat again. "And?"

"It belongs to Sam Winslow."

Nineteen

After he was gone, Mia paced the floor, arms folded across her chest, and wondered how something like this could have happened. Was it temporary insanity? She didn't even like the man. Up until she'd seen the photos of his nieces and nephews, she'd thought he was cold and un-feeling. Incapable of emotion. But she'd been wrong. Today, looking into his eyes, she'd seen a glimpse of what he kept hidden beneath that cool outer facade. Now, just thinking about it raised gooseflesh on her arms. Her thighs. Her breasts.

If his cell phone hadn't rung when it did, she and the wildly attractive Detective Douglas Policzki would have ended up in bed together. And she would have gone will-ingly. Eagerly. In just three days, she'd gone from intensely disliking him to—to—*this*. Whatever the hell *this* was. She didn't dare to look too closely at it, for fear of what she'd find.

She'd dated a few men in the years since Nick died. Men who ran in the same business circles as she did, men who dressed to kill and smelled nice and had impeccable manners. Men in Italian leather shoes, who drove expensive foreign cars and thought nothing of dropping several hundred dollars on dinner. She'd even kissed a few of them. None of those kisses had come close to moving her the way she'd been moved by Policzki's knuckles against her cheek.

And she'd certainly never invited any of those men into her bed.

Doug Policzki was a cop, earning a cop's salary. His shoes were polished, but she doubted they'd ever seen Italy. He'd left her house this afternoon driving a ten-year-old green Ford Contour. He didn't even have his own place, for Christ's sake. The man lived at home with his mother. Who the hell still lived with their mother at the age of thirty?

Mia had spent some time torturing herself with the numbers. He'd been born the year she started school. When she graduated from high school, he'd been in seventh grade. The year her son was born, Doug Policzki had turned thirteen years old.

There was a term for that: cradle robber.

And look at the way he'd run off just as things were getting interesting. He was a homicide detective. That meant his work hours were even crazier than hers. More unpredictable, subject to the whims of every homicidal maniac running loose on the streets. Was that the kind of future she wanted, with a man whose job interrupted all their intimate moments?

Oh, for Christ's sake. What was she doing, thinking about a future with a man she'd known for three days, a man who was a mere thirty years old, a man she'd never so much as kissed? Wasn't that putting the cart a little bit before the horse? She didn't know a thing about Doug Policzki, except for the way he made her feel. That was hardly enough to base a future on.

This was ridiculous. She had more important things to do than moon over Policzki like some lovestruck teenager. She had problems, serious problems. A life that had literally just gone up in smoke. A partner who was missing. A niece who might be anorexic. A brother who not only was a suspect in a homicide, but who knew more about his wife's activities than he was letting on.

Somehow Mia had awakened on Tuesday morning without realizing that sometime during the night, her life had been transformed into the *Twilight Zone*. Maybe she just needed to change the channel. Adjust the antenna a little. Try to tune back into her regular programming.

Work. That was what she needed to clear her head. Or what passed for work these days. So Mia made herself a pot of tea, picked up the Stuart Landers file once again and sat down at the kitchen table.

She paged through it slowly, her tired brain looking for something that just wasn't there. No dual settlement statements, nothing that looked funky. Every i was dotted, every t was crossed. There was nothing visible anywhere to make the transaction look questionable.

So why was her gut telling her something wasn't right?

Maybe it all meant nothing. Maybe Kaye had a valid reason for keeping that envelope full of credit reports hidden away at the back of her filing cabinet. Just because a buyer's name happened to match one of the reports didn't mean there was fraud involved. Maybe, in her sleep-deprived state, Mia was imagining things that didn't exist.

She picked up the phone and called Gwen Freeman, the Realtor who'd represented the seller. "Mia, honey," Gwen said, "talk about a run of bad luck. I saw Marty this morning, and he told me about the fire. This on top of Kaye going missing. You must be half out of your mind. Is there anything I can do to help?"

"Actually, there is. I'm calling to pick your brain about a sale back in May of this year. You represented the seller, a Dwayne Jordan. Kaye repped the buyer, Stuart Landers."

"I remember. What do you need to know?"

"I'm trying to reconstruct financial records. Taxes will be a nightmare, now that I've lost everything." It was the truth. Of all the headaches that would result from this fire, the IRS would be her biggest. "Can you look in your records and tell me the details? Sale price, commission split?"

"I don't have to look it up. I remember. Asking price was three-point-five mil, the buyer talked us down to three. Jordan was ecstatic to get that much, because the property was just about ready for the wrecking ball. It was a great space with tons of commercial potential, but it was old and tired. It needed new plumbing, new wiring, new everything. The commission was a straight seven percent, split fifty-fifty between your agency and mine."

This wasn't what Mia wanted to hear. It was what she'd been looking for, but until the proof was dropped in her lap, she'd held on to a thread of hope that she'd been wrong. "Listen, Gwen," she said, "could you do me a huge favor? Could you fax me a copy of the settlement statement? Here's my number."

She hung up the phone, feeling numb. *Damn you, Kaye,* she thought. *Damn you. How could you do this to me?* She'd taken Kaye in as a partner because she trusted the woman. What that said about her own instincts, she didn't want to think about.

Upstairs in her home office, the fax machine started to hum. Mia climbed the steps and caught the papers as they came through. She sat down at her desk and compared the two statements, then did a few quick mental calculations. The bank had paid out nine million dollars to finance the property. Dwayne Jordan, after paying the agency commission on the price he thought he'd sold the property for, had walked away with two-point-seven million. That left the other six million for Kaye and her cronies to split among themselves. Who was in on it? Kaye for sure. Greg Dubrowski. Grant Ashford. The buyer, whose real name she was willing to bet half a year's income didn't sound anything like Stuart Landers. And whoever had done the property appraisal. Six million dollars, to split among five people. That was more than a million dollars apiece. Tax-free.

This was enormous. There was no way Mia could ignore it. Whether or not it had anything to do with Kaye's disappearance, she couldn't let it go. If she did, if she failed to call the police and report her partner for real estate fraud, she might be the one who paid when the truth finally came out. It was her agency that was involved, her partner who'd committed the fraud. She'd have no way of proving her own innocence.

What had she done with Policzki's business card? Mia went downstairs and checked her briefcase, her purse, but didn't find it. She'd taken it to work with her yesterday, in case she needed to call him about the condo viewings. Had she brought it home with her, or left it there to burn? Frustrated, she upended her purse on the kitchen counter, rummaged through the mess until she found the card. She was just reaching for the phone to call him when it rang. She picked it up quickly, said, "Mia DeLucca."

She heard a sob, and then a wavery voice said, "Aunt Mia?"

"Gracie? Honey, what's wrong?"

"It's Dad." She hiccupped and took a hard breath. "The cops just came and arrested him."

"No. Oh, Gracie, no." Mia's heart began hammering as panic warred with fury. Threaded through their coupling, she recognized a thin sliver of dread. "What cops?" she said.

"It was Doug. I should've known better than to trust him. And that lady cop he works with."

Lorna Abrams. His partner. The phone call that had interrupted their little tête-à-tête and sent him racing off into the sunset. He'd walked away from Mia, had walked away from the emotions burgeoning between them, walked away knowing that he was about to arrest her brother for murder.

And he hadn't said a word to her.

"I'll be right there," she said, the cordless phone cradled between her ear and her shoulder as she rushed around in search of her sneakers. "Pack a bag. You can stay at my house tonight."

"I can't. I'm not at home."

She paused, sneaker in hand. "Where are you?"

"The DSS lady came with them. I'm in Andover. With my grandparents."

Mia felt as if she'd been kicked in the stomach. "That son of a bitch," she said. "That goddamn son of a bitch. When I get my hands on him, I'm going to kill him."

Winslow didn't put up any argument. He sat in the back of the cruiser, cool as a cucumber, staring blankly out the window as Policzki navigated the darkened city streets. In the passenger seat, Lorna was on the phone, talking a mile a minute as she filled in Rafferty on the status of the arrest. Policzki wished to God his stomach would settle. It had soured immediately after Lorna's call, had worsened as he listened to the rest of the evidence, and had tanked completely when Sam Winslow had held up both hands for Policzki to snap the cuffs on his wrists.

Policzki hadn't expected to be ecstatic; this was a lousy situation all around. Maybe his cop instincts were going soft. Maybe he'd been blinded to the truth by Mia's unwavering devotion to her brother. Or maybe he'd simply been sidetracked by Mia herself. There were reasons, valid reasons, why a cop wasn't supposed to become emotionally involved with anybody even remotely related to a case he was currently working. Emotional involvement led to mistakes, to dangerous distractions, to unreasonable biases and incorrect interpretation of evidence. It was at best an annoyance. At worst, it could prove lethal.

Whatever his reason, Policzki hadn't expected that evidence, when they finally uncovered it, to point to Sam Winslow. When it did, instead of the elation he should have been feeling at solving a case so quickly, he felt a huge letdown. Something about this just didn't feel right.

And then there was Gracie. Policzki didn't think he'd ever forget the way she'd looked at him when Loretta Ocasek of DSS led her away. She never said a word, but the betrayal she felt was evident in her eyes. He felt like a monster. Not one of the finer moments of his career.

Winslow was silent and cooperative through the booking process, which took awhile. When finally he'd been printed and had his mug shot taken, and the arrest report had been filled out, Policzki and Lorna led him into an interrogation room and sat him down at a table.

"Can we get you something, Professor?" Lorna was polite and solicitous. "A cup of coffee? Can of Pepsi? Drink of water?"

"No."

"Anything we can do to make you more comfortable?" Policzki said.

Winslow just looked at him with eyes that were so like Mia's, Policzki felt their impact deep in his gut. His sour, miserable gut. "Excuse me a minute," he said. Lorna looked at him strangely, but didn't question him as he left the room. He sprinted down the hall to the vending machines, pumped in a bunch of quarters and bought a roll of Tums. Policzki peeled back the foil and took three of them at once. And then he returned to the interrogation room.

He closed the door behind him, met Lorna's eyes, saw the curiosity there. And the concern. "Sorry," he said.

"Everything under control?"

"Everything's fine." He pulled up a chair and rested his arms on the table. "Do you understand the charges against you, Dr. Winslow?" he said.

"Yes."

Lorna said, "Did you kill Charlie Cunningham?"

"I didn't kill anybody. Who the hell is Charlie Cunningham?"

"Did you kill Kaye Winslow?" Policzki said.

"I just told you. I didn't kill anybody."

"What about the clothing we found in the trunk of her car?"

"What clothing?"

"The bloody suit coat. The red suit coat that your wife was wearing the day she disappeared."

"I don't know anything about any suit coat."

"Come on, Sam," Lorna said, "your prints were on the car."

"I don't know what you're talking about."

"We're talking," Policzki said, "about the bloody thumbprint we found on the fender of your wife's BMW. Your bloody thumbprint."

"I cut myself a few days ago. I was replacing a broken taillight and I accidentally cut myself on a piece of glass. That must be how it got there. You found her car?"

"That's a pretty weak story, Sam."

"It's not a story. It's the truth. Look, you can see for yourself." Winslow held up one finger, showing them a recent cut that had started to heal. "Why didn't you tell me you found her car?"

"We're asking the questions here," Lorna said. "What about the turpentine can? How do you explain that?"

Winslow looked befuddled. "What turpentine can?"

"The one that was used to set fire to your wife's office building last night."

"I don't know anything about this." He looked at Lorna, then Policzki. "The realty office burned?"

"The can had your prints on it. It came from your painting studio at the college." Lorna smiled. "Does that refresh your memory?"

"I have no idea what you're talking about." Winslow stood, rubbing his left wrist with the fingers of his right hand. "You might as well do whatever it is you're planning to do with me. I've said all I intend to say until I have an attorney present."

A half hour later, they met in the lieutenant's office. Rafferty looked tired; it had been a long day, and Policzki knew the lieutenant's wife was waiting up for him at home. "How'd it go?" Rafferty asked.

"About like we expected," Lorna said. "He kept insisting he didn't know what we were talking about, and then he got smart and lawyered up. I figure we'll let him cool his heels in a cell overnight. Maybe in the morning he'll be more interested in talking."

"Good work," the lieutenant said. "You've both done an exemplary job on this case. Now go home, people, and get some sleep."

Policzki and Lorna left Rafferty's office. "Walk out together?" she said.

"Go ahead. I have to finish up a couple of things before I leave."

"You heard what Conor said. Sleep, Dougie. That's where you lie down in an actual bed, close your eyes and go into a coma for eight hours. Or six, or four, or—"

"Good night, Abrams."

Policzki's desk was a mess. He couldn't work with a messy desk. He scooped up a stack of papers, slid open a drawer and shoved them in. He wouldn't win any awards for neatness, but tomorrow was another day. Saturday, according to his calendar. Something the rest of the world looked forward to. He'd been working homicide too long to believe in weekends. They were this mythical concept that he'd heard about once upon a time. Some people claimed they were real, but he'd never seen one.

Policzki turned on his cell phone. It beeped almost immediately. The digital readout told him that he had four messages. Grimly, he dialed into his voice mail and cued up the first one. Took a deep breath and pushed the button.

Her message was succinct. Short and to the point. "Call me. Now!"

It was amazing how much fury one small woman could

inject into three little syllables. The message had come in four hours ago. He couldn't wait to hear the rest of them.

The second message was a lot like the first. "Call me, Policzki. The minute you get this."

His stomach knotted up again. Policzki unwrapped the package of Tums and chewed a couple more. Screwed up his courage and listened to the third message. "I changed my mind," she said. "What I have to say to you can't be said over the phone. Get your ass over here, Policzki. Face me like a man."

Great. He'd hoped that with the progression of time, her anger might have leveled off. It seemed like he was wrong. Feeling like a prisoner about to face the executioner, he pressed the button and listened to the fourth and final message. "I'm still waiting, Policzki. I don't care if it's three in the morning when you get this. I'm not going to bed until I've talked to you."

He was tired, he was cranky, and right now, he wasn't very impressed with himself. But he didn't have a choice. She intended to skin him alive, and he probably deserved it. He might as well get it over with. If he hurried, maybe he could still squeeze in five or six hours of sleep.

Déjà vu. Policzki turned off his desk lamp, took his jacket from the back of his chair and headed off to face the Wrath of Mia.

Twenty

She'd been dozing on and off, but when the doorbell rang, Mia woke instantly. She glanced at the clock, saw that it was nearly one in the morning. About time. She'd been calling him for hours. Barefoot, she marched to the door and flung it open.

At some point in the last couple of hours, it had started to rain, and a fine mist rose from the pavement. Doug Policzki stood on her doorstep, drizzle raining down on him. If she'd seen an ounce of regret on his face, the barest trace of guilt, she might have been able to forgive him. Maybe. But he stood there, tall and good-looking and barely wrinkled after a twenty-hour workday, wearing the cop face she hated, the blank expression and the shuttered eyes that made him look like a heartless, soulless alien.

She didn't even speak, just turned and headed for the kitchen, leaving him to let himself in. Hopefully he was smart enough to shut the door behind him. If he wasn't, then he could deal with any intruder foolish enough to walk in. The man carried a gun. Anybody he couldn't reason with he could just shoot.

When she reached the kitchen, Mia rested both palms on the edge of the counter and stood there stiffly. Words swirled inside her head, so jumbled that she had to chase them around and capture them before she could figure out where to start.

Behind her, he said, "Before you start yelling at me, there's something I—"

She wheeled around. "Shut up," she said. "How could you? How could you do this?"

"Mia. Listen to—"

"Do you have any idea how much damage you've done? Any idea at all?"

Stiffly, he said, "I did what I had to do."

"Because of you, my brother is sitting in a jail cell."

"Your brother is sitting in a jail cell because of his own bad choices. Don't lay this on me."

"And my niece has been incarcerated right along with him, in that pseudo Southwestern country club out in Andover."

Tightly, he said, "I'm sorry about Gracie. But this isn't my fault. Maybe you'd like to hear my side of the story."

"I'm not interested in a goddamn thing you have to say, Policzki. You're a two-faced, lying son of a bitch. If you weren't so much bigger than me, I'd take great pleasure in messing up that pretty face of yours."

"Would you, DeLucca?" He took a step closer. "Go ahead. If it'll make you feel better, go ahead and hit me."

"I don't want to hit you, Policzki. I want to pulverize you! I want to pummel you until you're bloody and raw, and then I want to stomp on top of you—preferably wearing stilettos—until your own mother wouldn't recognize you!"

"I think you have some anger management issues."

"I'll anger management your ass!" She opened a cabinet door and took out a coffee mug, slammed it down on the granite counter so hard it was a miracle it didn't shatter into a zillion pieces. "My brother will never make it in prison," she said. "Don't you get that? He's not strong like I am. He never was. He won't stand a chance in that place. They'll chew him up and spit him out!"

"Not my fault."

"No," she snarled. "Nothing's your fault, is it? What about Gracie? Stuck in that awful place with that awful woman. Gracie has issues, Policzki. Not that I'd expect you to notice!"

"You mean other issues besides the fact that she finds all her friends on the Internet and hasn't eaten a decent meal in two years?"

Goddamn it. She didn't want him to be perceptive. She didn't want him to be anything right now except the recipient of her righteous fury. "Score one for the Vulcan," she said. "Damn it, Policzki, I trusted you. Gracie trusted you. And you turned around and stabbed us both in the back!"

A muscle twitched in his cheek, and his fists clenched. It was amazing to discover that the perennially unflappable Doug Policzki had a temper. "Are you done?" he said.

"Nowhere near!"

"Too bad. It's my turn now. What did you expect, Mia? Special treatment? A dispensation from the Pope? Was I expected to ignore the evidence and give your brother a Get Out of Jail Free card because of this—this—" he stabbed an arm through the air in a vague gesture "—this *thing* we have going on between us?"

"There's nothing going on between us!"

"The hell there isn't. I'm a cop, Mia. It's what I do, and

I'm pretty good at it. I put bad guys behind bars. That's the bottom line. I take pride in my work. I have high standards. Not just for other people, but for me. Expectations of myself. I follow the rules. Your brother's sitting in jail because we have evidence, good evidence, that ties him to a major crime. And you know what? I should be dancing a jig right now because I just took another creep off the street and put him where he belongs. But instead, I feel sick to my stomach. I've been feeling that way ever since I snapped those cuffs around Sam Winslow's wrists. You want to know why? Because the minute I put him under arrest, I knew I'd just blown the only chance I'd ever get with you!"

There was an instant of shocked silence, as if the universe itself needed a moment to process his words. Eyes narrowed, she took a step forward. "Oh," she said, "so that's what you think, is it?"

"Yes, goddamn it! That's what I think!"

"Then you're an idiot. One more clueless jackass who needs to be led by the hand like a little child!" She marched across the room to him, reached up and took his face between her hands, and yanked his mouth down to hers.

He sucked in a breath, and then he hauled her into his arms and kissed her so hard the ground beneath her feet rocked. It was a spectacular kiss, propelled by fury and lust and exquisite pent-up sexual tension. Mia locked her arms around his neck and gave as good as she got, lips and tongues tangled together in a divine battle of wills. He backed her across the room until she bumped up against the island. Gasping, they broke apart for air. "Still think I'm a kid?" he said hoarsely.

"I never said that, Policzki. You must be thinking of someone else."

He tilted her head back and kissed the sensitive spot just beneath her chin. Mia made a soft sound of pleasure. He ran his tongue down her neck to her collarbone and buried his face in the vee of her robe.

"I hope you understand," she said, "that this doesn't change anything."

He raised his head and studied her in silence.

"I'm still furious with you."

"Yeah," he said. "I can see that."

She reached for his necktie, tugged it loose and pulled it off over his head. Tossing it on the floor, she said, "So you'd better make this good. It won't get you out of the doghouse—" She pushed the suit coat off his shoulders and he shrugged out of it. It landed on the floor with a soft swooshing sound. "But it might soften my hard edges a little."

She studied the shoulder holster, trying to figure out how to get him out of it. He brushed her hands aside and unbuckled it himself, then set it on the granite island. "We definitely want to soften your hard edges," he said.

"Good. Don't disappoint me, then."

She unbuttoned his shirt, peeled it off, discovered the snowy white T-shirt beneath it. There was something so incredibly sexy about a guy in a white T-shirt. Mia pressed her face against the fabric, reveling in the smell of laundry soap and man. Policzki pulled the shirt off over his head and dropped it on the floor, and she just looked at him.

His body was amazing, smooth and sleek and hard. Mia couldn't help herself. She had to touch him. With all ten fingertips, she traced random patterns on that rock-hard, muscled flesh. He felt as good as he looked. Maybe better. She ran her hands over his chest, up his shoulders and down his arms. When she touched her mouth to the hollow at the center of his chest, Policzki untied the belt to her robe and wrenched it open. He took his time looking at what he'd revealed before his hands bracketed her hips, their warmth sliding down to cup her ass. Mia twined her arms around his neck, he hoisted her up and she wrapped her legs around his hips.

She pressed against him, naked flesh to naked flesh. He found her mouth again, and they devoured each other, frantic now that they'd tasted a glimpse of paradise. Mia undid his pants, worked them and the boxers down over his hips. His mouth still clinging to hers, Policzki helped her, kicking off his shoes, peeling off his socks, stepping out of his pants.

He broke free and they both took a breath. "Bedroom?" he said.

"Upstairs."

"The hell with it. Too far." He lifted her to the kitchen island and sat her on the hard granite edge, stood between her thighs and slid the open robe down off her shoulders. She freed her arms from the soft flannel and it fell to the granite countertop. Her gaze locked with his, she ran her hands down his chest, his abdomen. Circled his navel and moved lower, found what she sought, rock-hard and ready for her.

Wrapping both hands around him, she said, "I'm thirty-six years old, Policzki. I'm too old to have sex on the kitchen counter at one-thirty in the morning, with the curtains open and the lights blazing."

"Nobody's looking," he said, sounding breathless. "Nobody's up this late."

"Easy for you to say." She stroked him, fingers sliding up and down as they learned the feel of him, his damp heat, his size and shape. "You're not the one who has to live with the neighbors."

He lowered his head, tasted the side of her neck. "Mia?" he said near her ear.

She touched the tip of him to the place where she was wet and waiting. "Yes?"

"Will you please shut up?" And he buried all that heat inside her.

When he left her, it was still dark, and he was running on four hours of sleep and a surfeit of sex. He peeled himself away from her warm, sticky flesh, planted a kiss on her shoulder and tucked the blanket back around her. Naked, he went downstairs and gathered up his scattered clothes, pulling on his pants and yanking the T-shirt over his head. He crammed his feet into his shoes without benefit of socks, then buckled on the shoulder holster over his T-shirt because he felt naked without it. He rolled up the rest of his clothes—his dress shirt and suit coat, his necktie, his socks and boxers—and carried them out into the chill October morning. He started his car, shivering in the thin T-shirt while he waited for the windshield to clear.

The sun was just coming up when he pulled into his driveway and turned off his engine. The world had just begun to stir. Across the street, old Mr. Tucci was dragging his trash cans out to the street. Feeling like a fool carrying his clothes wadded up into a ball—hey, why not just flash a neon sign that read I Just Had Sex?—Policzki waved, then strode up the driveway and let himself into the house.

His mother was already up, sitting in her chenille robe, reading the morning paper and eating a sticky bun with her morning cup of decaf. "Well," she said, peering at him over the top of her paper. "I was going to ask where the hell you've been, but I guess I don't need to."

Heat raced up his face. Jesus H. Christ. He was almost thirty-one years old. He'd been a cop for ten years, had worked Homicide for the last five. Along the way, he'd seen most of the inhuman things human beings were capable of doing to each other. He'd dealt with drug dealers, pimps and a serial killer. Five years ago, he'd taken a bullet in the line of duty. He was tough as nails. Yet he was still capable of blushing because his mother knew he'd spent the night with a woman.

"Ma," he said, "I'm moving out."

She turned a page in her newspaper. "About time."

Had he heard her right? "You want to get rid of me," he said, "all you have to do is say so."

"Touchy, aren't you? No, I don't want to get rid of you. But you're thirty years old. I can't imagine you find it very fulfilling, living with a sixty-year-old woman whose idea of excitement is watching the Home Shopping Network. You need your own life, Doug. So what's her name?"

"What's whose name?"

"Don't try to bluff your way past me. You come in carrying your underwear instead of wearing it, that's a pretty good indication there's a woman somewhere." His mom turned another newspaper page. "You moving in with her?"

"I'm getting my own place. I'm buying a condo."

"So why aren't you moving in with her?"

"It's complicated."

His mother lowered the paper and looked at him. "That's all you ever say. She's not married, is she?"

Policzki sighed. "No. She's a widow."

"An older woman?"

"What are you, psychic?"

"How much older?"

"She's thirty-six."

"That's not older. Hell, your father was ten years older than me. So why's it complicated?"

"For starters, I just arrested her brother for murder."

"Shit. You don't just stick your toe into the water, do you? You jump in headfirst. So what's her name?"

"Mia."

"She pretty?"

"Ma, she's a goddess."

"So am I gonna like her?"

He thought about it. "Yes," he said. "I'm pretty sure you will."

Policzki was dragging ass big time this morning, and he looked like shit. "You got a cold or something?" Lorna said as she slung her briefcase onto the desk and flicked the power switch to her computer.

"Just tired." But he was hunched over his coffee cup like the end of the world had just arrived.

"You're not pissed off at me, are you?"

"No."

"Then what gives, Policzki? You're not your usual chipper self this morning."

"I need a doughnut," he said. "Something sticky and gooey, loaded with sugar and saturated fats and a chemical or two thrown in for good measure."

"Now you're really worrying me. Since when do you eat doughnuts?"

"Once in a while," he said irritably, "I like to pretend I'm a regular person."

Yikes. Talk about hostility. "Come on, Pollyanna," she

said. "Let's go get you a doughnut before you chew somebody's head off."

He brought his coffee with him, and they wrestled with the vending machine to get him a stale honey-dipped doughnut wrapped in cellophane. Lorna wouldn't have eaten the damn thing on a bet, but the kid wasn't himself this morning, and she didn't dare to say too much for fear of having some crucial limb cruelly amputated.

"Let's take a walk," he said. "I need to talk to you."

Now they were making progress. In Lorna's book, talking it out was always preferable to holding it in. Whatever it was. There was nothing like a good heart-to-heart to clear the air.

They left the building and ambled along the sidewalk. Policzki peeled open the cellophane and bit into the doughnut. "Jesus Christ," he said. "Why didn't you warn me?"

"It thought it'd be better to let you figure it out on your own. You should be careful what you ask for. Sometimes you actually get it."

"I thought my mother was a lousy cook, but this defies belief."

"Okay," Lorna said. "You got your doughnut. It was DOA, but you got it. Now will you please tell me what in bloody hell is wrong?"

"I'm asking Rafferty to pull me off the case."

"Oh, shit," she said. "You're sick, aren't you? Listen, kid, you're young and strong. There's no reason to believe you can't beat it. Did you get a second opinion?"

"I'm not sick."

She didn't look too closely at the vastness of her relief. "Then why would you ask Rafferty to take you off the case?"

Staring straight ahead, he said, "I did something I

shouldn't have done. Something that could compromise the whole case. Something that was wrong on so many different levels, I can't even count them."

"Get out of here. You're the consummate choirboy. You couldn't do anything wrong if you tried. You're just not programmed that way."

"I must be programmed that way, because it happened."

"*What* happened? What in hell did you do that's so bloody awful?"

"You have to understand that I didn't intend for it to happen. It wasn't planned. I'm not even sure how it happened—I mean, of course I know *how* it happened. That's pretty obvious to anybody past the age of nine. I just don't really understand—"

"For Christ's sake, Policzki, get to the point!"

He looked at her then. "Mia and I—" he said. "Mia De-Lucca? We, uh…"

Understanding dawned. "Holy mother of Mary," she said. "You had sex with Mia DeLucca?"

He closed his eyes and swallowed. "I did."

"About time you had sex with somebody. Although I could've recommended a better choice."

"You weren't available at the time for a consultation."

"Goddamn it, Policzki, when I told you to get laid, I was talking about Miss Iowa. What happened to her? Was she a dog?"

"She was gorgeous. It just…wasn't there."

"What wasn't there?"

"The chemistry, Abrams. You either have it or you don't."

"And you and DeLucca have it."

"Oh, yeah," he said. "In spades."

"This is bad," Lorna said. "This is really bad." She raised an eyebrow and studied him. "I'm impressed. Appalled, of course, but also impressed. DeLucca's a classy lady."

"Yeah. She is."

"In spite of the fact that her brother's sitting—oh, boy."

"That's just one of those levels I was talking about."

"Okay, we have to think this through carefully. You're not intending to have sex with her again, are you?"

"Not unless the opportunity presents itself. If it does, all bets are off."

"Oh, fuck. Dougie, Dougie, Dougie. Tell me you're not in love with her."

"It's a distinct possibility."

"Hon." She laid a motherly hand on his arm. "You have a promising career ahead of you. You can't let it be derailed by a woman."

He took a sip of coffee. Swallowed. "It's a little late for Monday morning quarterbacking."

"Can you manage to at least stay away from her until this case is resolved?"

He just looked at Lorna with those big, brown eyes of his. "Okay," she said. "Scratch that idea."

"There's only one solution. Rafferty has to pull me off the case."

"You're not being pulled off the case. What would I do without you?"

"Get another partner?"

"Damn it, Policzki, I don't want another partner."

He raised both eyebrows in an expression of surprise. "Why, Abrams," he said, "I didn't know you cared."

"Yeah? Well, don't spread it around, because I'll deny it with my dying breath. Who else knows about this?"

"Just you, me, Mia, and—" He glanced heavenward. "Oh, and of course my mother, who just happened to be waiting in the kitchen when I came slinking in this morning carrying my boxer shorts under my arm."

Lorna tried not to laugh, but it was hard. "I doubt the Big Guy up there is going to give you a ration of shit about it. As far as your mother's concerned, you're on your own there, toots. Listen, Policzki, you're a good cop. You're smart, you're levelheaded. It's why we work so well together. I have a tendency sometimes to jump into things."

"You think?"

Ignoring his sarcasm, she said, "You balance out my impulsiveness."

"Your point, Abrams?"

"You are not going to Rafferty. You are not telling anybody else about this. We're going to pretend this conversation never happened, and we'll both keep on keeping on with the case. And you will continue to act like the levelheaded cop you've always been. If you do something stupid that ends up with me getting my ass shot off, I'm going to regret this. Don't make me regret this."

"What about ethics? What about conflict of interest?"

"Are you hearing anything I'm saying? Maybe I should put it another way. If you take this to Rafferty, you'll go down. If that happens, I'll go to him and tell him I knew what you were doing and I failed to report your behavior. You go down, I go down with you. You want that on your conscience, fine with me. But you might have to explain it to Ed, because he may be wondering why they're foreclosing on our mortgage."

"That's dirty pool."

"It's the only deal I'm offering you."

"Sometimes you're a real bitch."

She grinned. "You say that like it's a bad thing."

When they got back, Rafferty was waiting for them, looking like he'd rather be anywhere else on a Saturday morning. "I just got a call," he said. "Winslow's ready to talk."

Twenty-One

Gracie was the only passenger that morning getting on the commuter train from Andover to Boston carrying a backpack and a cat in a plastic pet carrier. It was Saturday, so there weren't many other passengers. Which was a good thing, because she wasn't sure Ralph was even supposed to ride the train. But nobody questioned her, not even the sleepy MBTA cop riding at the front of the car with his morning cup of coffee in his hand.

Ralph hated the carrier. She was a cat. Cats didn't like being confined. She'd meowed pitifully all the way to the train station. Now that she was parked comfortably on the seat beside Gracie, instead of being bumped and jostled against Gracie's hip while she walked, the cat had finally settled down. Gracie stuck a couple of fingers through the wire door of the cage. Ralph sniffed them and began purring softly.

Her grandparents were going to be pissed. So was the lady from DSS. And probably Aunt Mia. But Gracie couldn't stay in that place. Grandpa was an okay guy, but her grandmother was a monster. Gracie and Ralph had only been there a few hours and already the woman was complaining about little white cat hairs on her expensive furniture. How much longer would it take before Evelyn packed Ralph up and left her at the pound?

This was all such a mess. As if Dad could have killed anyone. If he were capable of murder, he would have killed Kaye a long time ago. Sure, when he was pushed, he displayed a temper. Who didn't? But it was one long leap from yelling at Gracie about cleaning her room to picking up a gun and shooting someone. What was wrong with Doug Policzki, anyway? She'd really thought she could trust him. Thought he was one of the good guys, the guys with the white hats who came riding in at the last minute and saved the day.

So much for trust.

The train rattled into North Station, and Gracie and Ralph got off. Famished, she bought a breakfast sandwich at the McDonald's inside the station. She set down the cat carrier, sat on the floor beside it with her back against the wall and devoured the sandwich. It wasn't until she started licking crumbs from her fingers that she realized she'd inhaled the whole thing in about twenty seconds. Her thighs would never forgive her. But, man, she was just so *hungry*.

She crumpled up the sandwich wrapper, finished off her Diet Coke and tossed wrapper and cup into the trash. Then, her backpack slung over her shoulder and the cat carrier in hand, she set off for Aunt Mia's place in the North End.

It wasn't far, but it had rained overnight, and the sky was still overcast. A bank of heavy, dark clouds lay on the horizon, edging closer by the minute. Gracie hurried, praying she'd get to Mia's before those clouds opened up and dumped their heavy load of rain on top of her.

The closer she got, the more dread she felt bubbling up inside her. What would Mia say? She wouldn't be happy, that much Gracie knew. But this was where she needed to be. Here, where Ralph would be safe from the gas chamber. Here, where everything was happening. Not in some stuffy house out in Andover, where the only way she'd find out what was going on with Dad was if she read it in a newspaper that her grandmother hadn't stuffed deep enough into the trash.

Gracie marched up to her aunt's door and stood on the top step. Inside the carrier, Ralph meowed. Gracie took a deep breath and rang the bell. Waited a minute, then rang it again. From the other side, she could hear footsteps approaching. The lock turned and Mia opened the door. For an instant, neither of them spoke. Then Mia said, "Oh, shit."

At the same time, Gracie said, "Ralph and I are moving in with you."

"I can't believe you did this," Mia said. "What am I going to do with you, Gracie Lee? Your grandparents will blame this on me. I already have enough headaches. I don't need another one."

Gracie, perched on a wooden kitchen stool with her cat on her lap, said, "Don't tell me you're turning on me, too. You're the one person I always knew I could depend on."

The old guilt trip. It was the oldest weapon in a teenager's arsenal, and damned if it wasn't working. She was clever, that Gracie. A little too clever for her own good. "I'm not turning on you," Mia said. "Honestly." She ran a hand through her hair. "But I can't keep you here. The Department of Social Services placed you with your grandparents. If I let you stay with me, I could get into trouble."

"You're sending me back there?" The look on Gracie's face was so pathetic that Mia's heart broke for her.

"Just for now," she said. "But I promise you this. If your dad goes to prison—" She winced, closed her eyes and took a deep breath. "If your dad goes to prison, I'll petition the courts for custody."

"They'll win. They're loaded. Rich people always win."

"Not necessarily. Listen, sweetheart." Mia sat on the stool beside Gracie and took her hand. It was icy, and she rubbed at it with her thumb, trying to bring back some warmth to Gracie's pale skin. "You're fifteen years old. You have your own ideas about how things are supposed to be. You can tell the judge where you want to live. He'll listen, and take your feelings into account."

"Will he?"

"He will. I can't guarantee you'll win, but I think there's a good chance of it."

Gracie cradled the cat to her chest and buried her face in its fur. "What about Ralph?" she said. "Grandma hates her."

Mia had been a mother for seventeen years. She knew manipulation when she saw it. She also knew when she was beat. "Ralph can stay here," she said. "With Kev and me."

"Really?" Gracie opened one eye and looked at her.

"Really. But you have to let me take you back to Andover. And you have to promise to stay there until I can do something to get you out of there. Otherwise…" She paused, hating herself for what she was about to say. But it was the only leverage she had. "Otherwise, it's curtains for Ralph."

Gracie considered her terms, then nodded. "As long as Ralph's okay, I can survive Grandma and Grandpa for a while. I put up with those twits at Bellerose Academy for two years." She grew somber. "But what about Dad?"

"I don't know. I'm going to try and find out where they're holding him, and see if I can get in to visit him today. And I'm going to talk to the cops. See what I can find out."

That wasn't the only reason Mia needed to talk to Policzki. They'd been so busy jumping each other's bones last night that she'd never gotten around to telling him about the real estate fraud. He needed to know about it, and she needed to wash her hands of the whole thing. Turn it over to a higher power. One who wore a badge and carried a gun.

Gracie snorted. "As if you can believe anything the cops say."

How could Mia explain it to a fifteen-year-old kid? How could she make Gracie see that life wasn't all black-and-white, that it was a continuum with varying shades of gray in between those two extremes? "You can't blame them," she said. "It's not their fault."

"I trusted him," Gracie said bitterly. "But you know what? Doug's no better than anybody else."

That wasn't quite how Mia remembered it. Not that she had extensive experience for purposes of comparison, but upon recall, it seemed to her that he was considerably better than anybody else. She certainly hadn't been disappointed. As a matter of fact, if memory served, she hadn't been disappointed at least three times. She would never again look at polished granite in quite the same way.

Dragging her attention back to Gracie, she said, "No. He's not better than anybody else. He's no better, and he's no worse, than the majority of us." The words he'd said to her that night at the Skywalk, a million years ago, came back to her. "He's just a guy," she said, "doing his job."

"Yeah? Well, his job sucks."

"You know what? I bet there are days when he feels the same way."

The telephone rang. The damn thing was always interrupting her at the worst possible times. Mia wanted to finish the conversation with Gracie, but she didn't dare ignore the phone. Lately, it had been bringing her a new disaster each time it rang. God forbid she should miss anything important.

It was an unfamiliar voice. "Mrs. DeLucca? My name's Frank Patterson. My wife and I are relocating to the Boston area, and I'm interested in looking at one of your properties."

It took her an instant to remember that she'd had the phone company forward all her agency calls to this number. "Of course," she said with false brightness. "Which one?"

"It's a two-bedroom ranch out in Brighton. Revere Street? I'd like to see it this morning, if that's possible. I'm only here in town for a few days and I have a very small window of free time. I realize you're probably busy, but do you suppose you could squeeze me in?"

For an instant, she was disoriented. In all the chaos of the past twenty-four hours, she'd managed to forget about work, and it took her a minute to shift gears. For the first time since she had opened her agency, she was tempted to blow off a potential client. But God only knew how this thing with Kaye would turn out, and with the agency in flux because of the fire, she didn't dare to turn down a buyer. She needed the business.

She racked her brain, trying to remember the house. Two-bedroom in Brighton? Yes, of course. Now she remembered: 2300 Revere Street. One of Kaye's listings. The owners had moved to Atlanta, and the house had sat unoccupied for months. There'd been the occasional nibble of interest, but no serious lookers since August. The bedrooms were too small, and when it rained, the basement took on water. "I know the place," she said. "I can meet you there later this morning."

"That would be great. Actually—" He chuckled. "Actually, I'm calling you on my cell phone. I'm sitting in the driveway right now."

She checked the time and calculated the traffic she'd run into midmorning on a Saturday. "I can be there in about a half hour," she said.

"Thanks a bunch," Patterson said. "I'll be waiting."

Mia hung up the phone. "I have to go out and show a house," she told her niece. "I'm taking you with me. I'll drop you back off with your grandparents afterward."

Gracie sighed, one of those overly dramatic, put-upon teenage sighs. "Fine," she said.

Mia called the Wises to apprise them of the situation. Fortunately, it was Jack, instead of Evelyn, who answered the phone. "Jack," she said, "it's Mia DeLucca. I just wanted you to know that Gracie's here, with me. She showed up at my door this morning."

"That's good news," Jack said. "Evelyn's been frantic. Wanted to call the police, but I wouldn't let her. I told her the girl would show up sooner or later. Figured she was with you."

Jack Wise was a nice man. A really nice man. How the hell he'd managed to stay married to Evelyn for nearly forty years was beyond her. "Gracie's upset right now," Mia said. "She's worried about her father. She doesn't mean to be disobedient. Well, okay, she probably did mean to be disobedient, but it was a case of doing the wrong thing for the right reason."

"Of course she's worried. Wouldn't be normal if she wasn't. Should we come and pick her up?"

"I have to run an errand, so I thought I'd bring her by afterward. It might be an hour or so, but I'll have her back before lunchtime."

"No hurry," he said. "The poor kid needs to talk to somebody who understands her. God knows, that isn't us. Evelyn and I are just a couple of old fogies who've forgotten most of what we ever knew."

It was raining, a hard and vicious downpour that had come out of nowhere. With her umbrella open over her head, Mia raced for the Blazer, with Gracie right behind her. They climbed in on opposite sides and closed the doors. Mia shook excess water from the umbrella and tossed it on the floor in the back. Her feet were already drenched. There went another pair of shoes. How many pairs had she ruined since she'd started this job? Probably so many that the replacement cost would have bought her a shiny new car. "Who the hell looks at houses in this weather?" she grumbled.

"I don't know," Gracie said. "Who?"

"Some guy named Patterson. He's from out of town. Keep your fingers crossed. This one's been a hard sell. He sounded desperate. That could be a good thing. Maybe his desperation will charm him right into making an offer."

Traffic was a nightmare. In the driving rain, visibility was down to almost nothing. Why the hell anybody *would* want to look at a house on a day like this, she couldn't imagine. The house wouldn't show well on a rainy day. The interior was dark and dated, and with little to no natural light coming in, it would look like a tomb. Patterson would probably run away screaming. If he hadn't been in such a hurry to leave town, she would have rescheduled for a sunny day, when he could better see the quality of the woodwork and the built-in cabinets.

She almost missed Revere Street, a narrow side street off Commonwealth Ave. She took a quick right, drove past the apartment buildings populated mostly by college students, crossed an intersection and pulled into the driveway of a small gray ranch style next to a car that was already parked there. "You stay here," she told Gracie. "If you're not sitting right here when I get back, I'm going to take Ralph hostage."

"I'm not going anywhere."

Mia climbed out of the Blazer. When she popped open her umbrella, the wind nearly blew it inside out. She struggled with it for a moment, got it under control. But by then, she was drenched to the bone. Patterson got out of his car with a folded newspaper over his head to protect him from the elements, and together they made a run for it.

On the front steps, beneath the overhang, he lowered his soggy newspaper and she closed the umbrella. He held out a hand. "Frank Patterson," he shouted over the hammering rain.

He looked familiar. As a matter of fact, Mia could have sworn she'd met him before. Somewhere, sometime. But she couldn't place him. She met so many people. "Mia De-Lucca," she shouted back. "Nice to meet you."

"Awful weather," he said as she worked the key to the lockbox. "Appreciate you coming out in it on such short notice."

"No problem," she said as she turned the doorknob. "It's what I do." The door popped open and she stepped through it. The foyer was dark. "Watch your step," she said as he came in behind her on a gust of wind. She fumbled for the light switch, located it, flipped it on.

A dim yellowish glow fell on the living room carpet.

Standing in the middle of that pool of light was Kaye Winslow. She was holding a gun, and it was pointed directly at Mia.

Behind her, the man who called himself Frank Patterson closed the door and locked it.

"Hello, Mia," Kaye said. "I hear you've been asking a lot of questions about me."

Twenty-Two

Outside, rain hammered down. Inside, everything was a little too damp. Papers curled at the corners and then fell limp. The air was heavy and carried a slight scent of mold. The four of them—Abrams, Policzki, Winslow and his attorney, Andrew Meriwether—sat around a small table in a cramped interview room. Meriwether set his briefcase on the table. "My client and I," he said, "have conferred at length, and he's informed me of his intent to pass on to you information that might peripherally implicate him in criminal activity. As his attorney, I've counseled him against doing so. I'd like to propose a deal. We give you the information we have, and you agree not to hold Dr. Winslow criminally responsible for anything he tells you today."

"Stop dicking us around," Policzki said. "The man's been charged with murder. We don't do deals."

"Then maybe we should stop this before it even begins."

"No," Winslow said, and they all turned to look at him. "I need to say this before I lose my nerve."

His attorney gave him a long, level look. "You remember what we talked about."

"I remember. Damn it, Andy, I just want this over with."

"Do you really want this splashed all over the tabloids? Think hard, Sam. Think about Gracie."

"My life's in the toilet," Winslow said. "I'm living in a five-by-five jail cell. I'm sitting here with my hands cuffed. How much worse can it get?"

Meriwether threw up his own hands in defeat. "It's your funeral."

"That's right," Winslow said, "it is." He ran a hand over his chin, his mouth. Took a deep breath. "Six months after Kaye and I got married," he said, "she found out that for years, I'd been having, ah…discreet liaisons…with other men." He glanced up, saw that he had their attention. "It's not something I'm proud of, but it is what it is. When I met my first wife, Rachel, all those years ago, I fell head over heels in love with her. We were married for ten years, and I never cheated on her. But it was always there, this shadowy something that every so often came out of hiding to hit me hard in the gut."

The room was so silent that the only sound Policzki could hear was the whirring of an oscillating fan somebody had brought in to deal with the dampness. "I married Kaye two years ago," Winslow said, "and for the first few months, we were okay. Not like Rachel and I had been, but we had what I thought was a solid foundation. Until she found out the truth, and started using it as leverage against me."

Quietly, Policzki said, "How'd she find out?"

"I told her. Pretty stupid of me, wasn't it? I'm not a very good judge of character. I thought she'd understand. That was when I realized what kind of woman I'd married."

"But you stayed married."

Sam raised his head and looked Policzki in the eye.

"Living alone," he said. "It's damn lonely." He ran a hand through his long hair. "I guess Kaye had her reasons for staying, although I'll be damned if I knew what they were. It wasn't long after my big confession that she started cheating on me. I guess I wasn't man enough to keep her at home."

Across the table, Lorna leaned forward and opened her mouth to speak. Policzki pursed his lips and shot her a quick glance, and she closed her mouth and sat back in her chair.

"Two weeks ago," Winslow said, "I brought in a big stack of mail and accidentally opened something addressed to Kaye. It was a statement from some bank in the Cayman Islands, and when I saw the account balance, I thought I'd read it wrong. She had more than a million dollars stashed in an account she hadn't told me about. When she got home, I confronted her about it. At first, she denied doing anything wrong, but when I persisted, she finally admitted to me that she and some of her colleagues had pulled off a huge real estate scam. She didn't tell me all the details, just that they'd pulled off a real coup, and now she had all this money. We argued over it. Even ignoring the legalities of what she'd done, it was an idiotic move. I asked her how long she really thought it would be before somebody—the IRS, some bank auditor—found the discrepancy and uncovered what she'd done. She told me she'd take her chances. When I threatened to go to the authorities and turn her in—" he glanced up, met each of their eyes in turn "—she played her trump card. She said that if I told on her, she'd do the same to me."

Policzki said, "So she blackmailed you."

Winslow studied him through bleary eyes. "You have to understand. I've kept this secret for thirty-nine years. I have a teenage daughter. I'm up for tenure. Or I was, anyway." He laughed, but there was little humor in it. "I guess I can kiss that goodbye. Even in the academic world, which prides itself on being so liberal, homophobia is alive and well. I come from conservative people. My parents are gone, but I have aunts and uncles. Cousins. Even my sister doesn't know. I couldn't tell her. I was so afraid of disappointing her. And Gracie. How does a kid like that deal with having someone like me for a father? So I kept my mouth shut. Kaye knows me well. She knew I didn't have the guts to live with myself if the truth came out. She knew I'd keep my mouth shut forever, if I had to."

Quietly, Lorna said, "Where is she, Sam?"

"I don't know."

"Did you kill her?"

"No. But there's more. Ever since Kaye disappeared, I've been getting these phone calls. People calling and then hanging up. Leaving cryptic messages implying that they're keeping an eye on me, or that I better not forget to keep my mouth shut. Once, all they did was play a few bars of an old Village People song." Again, that humorless smile. "Wonderful symbolism, wouldn't you say? Hell, once they even called my sister."

"They called Mia?" Policzki said sharply. "When?"

"A few days ago. They told her to give me a message, to tell me that they're watching me."

She hadn't said anything. Her partner was missing and involved somehow in a homicide, her brother was in hot water, and Mia hadn't said a goddamn word to Policzki about getting strange phone calls.

"I was furious when I found out Kaye'd filed for divorce. We'd talked about it, you see. She'd agreed to wait until my tenure came through. I thought it would look better to the committee if we seemed like a normal family."

"In other words," Lorna said, "you used her as a smokescreen."

He squared his jaw. "Call it what you will."

She leaned forward over the table. "Why'd you burn down the realty office?"

"I didn't burn down the goddamn realty office. Why would I do something like that?"

"Maybe to cover your wife's tracks. Maybe there was some kind of evidence there that would have pointed the finger of guilt at both of you."

"I didn't have anything to do with the fire."

"Come on, Sam. The can of turpentine had your prints on it."

"We've already been through this. Anybody at the college could have had access to it. It's kept in the painting studio."

"Who has a key to the studio?"

"The maintenance crew. Maureen, the department secretary. My lab assistant, David Briggs."

Policzki said, "Would any of those people have a reason to start a fire and implicate you?"

"I can't imagine why they would."

"What about David Briggs?" Lorna said. "Does he have any grudges against you?"

Winslow's mouth thinned. "David had nothing to do with it."

"How do you know that, Professor? Are you and David Briggs lovers?"

Winslow's fist clenched on the table, and his color went instantly from pasty white to bright red. A vein throbbed in the side of his neck. "No," he said through gritted teeth.

"What about the phone call?" Lorna said. "Kaye called somebody at BBCC right before she disappeared."

"I told you before, and I'll tell you again. It wasn't me. Why the hell would she call me? We were barely on speaking terms."

"Did you kill Charlie Cunningham?"

"Goddamn it, I told you last night. I don't even know who the hell Charlie Cunningham is!"

"You should know. He used to be married to Kaye."

"That's ludicrous. Kaye wasn't married before."

"Obviously, you don't read the *Trib*. I'm going to ask you this one last time, Doctor. Did you kill Kaye Winslow?"

Winslow gripped the edge of the table so hard his knuckles went white. "I didn't kill anybody!"

His attorney rested a hand on his arm. "Sam," he said, "that's enough. Calm down." Glaring at Lorna, he said coolly, "Detective, this interview is over."

Gracie instinctively shrank back against the seat of the Blazer, even though she knew nobody could see her through the opaque black windows. You could see out, but nobody could see in. When they were younger, she and Kev had thought Mia's car was the coolest thing on four wheels. They used to pretend they were movie stars riding in some smoked-glass limo. Or a Mafia don and his favorite hit man.

Now, she was grateful for the anonymity those windows provided, because something was very wrong here. Mia had come to show the house to a Mr. Patterson. Except that the man who got out of the car and went inside with her wasn't Frank Patterson. He was somebody else, somebody Gracie knew well. She should; she'd spent enough time at his house, playing with his little girl, Deidre.

He was her dad's best friend. Or at least her dad thought he was. He might feel differently if he knew that Kaye and Vince Tedeschi had been sleeping together since July.

Something very odd was going on here, something that had Gracie's stomach tied up in knots. Kaye was missing, and a man was dead. Vince, who'd been carrying on with Kaye for months, was here, in this empty house, pretending to be a home buyer from out of town. Mia had brought home all of Kaye's files to look for evidence of fraud. The next night, the realty office had burned.

It didn't take a genius to figure out it was all related somehow. If Vince was in that house, chances were pretty good that Kaye was there, too. And if the two of them had tricked Mia into coming here, this home viewing wasn't going to end in a sales contract.

Gracie spent awhile thinking it over. Studying the facade of the house, the drawn blinds that hadn't moved an inch. She reached for the door handle, unlatched it and eased it open. Rain fell in fat drops on her face. Moving slowly, an inch or two at a time, she slid down from the Blazer and closed the door behind her. Not tight, just closed enough so the overhead light would go out. Mia had told her to stay put, but if she stayed put, she might never see her aunt again.

Cold rain drizzled down the back of her neck as she inched along the side of the Blazer to the walkway. She took a final look at the house, pulled the hood of her sweatshirt up over her head and shoved her hands into her pockets. Her head down, she began walking quickly away from the house, trying to look like just one more yahoo who'd been caught in the deluge.

The instant she was out of sight of the house, she broke

into a run. Gracie ran so hard she thought her lungs would burst. She reached Commonwealth Avenue and dashed through the door of a pizza shop. The guy behind the counter, who was probably a year or two older than her, gazed at her kind of funny. She probably looked like a drowned rat. She shot him a withering glance, and he quickly looked away. Wiping her hands on her sweat-shirt—kind of stupid, since the shirt was soaked through—she took out her cell phone and dialed 911.

There was no time to question her judgment, no time to question his motives. There was time only to act. "My name is Gracie Winslow," she told the dispatcher. "I need to speak to Detective Doug Policzki. He works in Homi-cide. It's an emergency."

Afterward, they met in Rafferty's office to dissect the interview. Lorna leaned back in her chair, kicked off a shoe and wiggled her toes. Policzki cleared his throat. "I have an alternative theory," he said.

Lorna stopped wiggling her toes. Rafferty looked pained, as if he already knew Policzki was about to toss a monkey wrench into the middle of what looked like a nice, neat case. The lieutenant glanced at his watch. "How long will this take?"

"Five minutes. Ten at most."

Rafferty sighed. "Make them worth it. I'm meeting my wife for lunch."

"What if he's telling the truth?" Policzki said. "What if Winslow isn't guilty?"

"Oh, come on, Policzki," Lorna said. "Don't tell me you fell for his sob story."

"That's not up to us to decide," Rafferty said. "You

know that. We just gather evidence. Guilt is determined by the judicial system. And in this case, the evidence is pretty damning."

"That's my point," Policzki said. "Just hear me out. I've given this a lot of thought. I realize you've both worked Homicide longer than I have. But I have good instincts. If Winslow really wanted to kill his wife, it seems like he'd have gone to a little more trouble to cover his tracks."

"Come on, Doug," Lorna said. "Criminals do stupid things. And the guy isn't exactly experienced with crime. Inexperience leads to mistakes. So does the smug belief that you're above the law."

"I haven't seen any evidence of smugness. What I have seen is frustration, bewilderment and what looks a lot like forthrightness. He's also scared shitless."

"You would be, too, if you were standing in his shoes."

"The guy may have good reason. What if somebody's trying to set him up?"

"Christ Almighty, Policzki, this is the real world. Not *Days of Our Lives*."

"Lose the cynical cop persona for just a second, Lorna. Look at this objectively. What's the biggest thing you see here?"

"I'm too old for guessing games, Policzki. You tell me."

"Overkill."

"Overkill?"

Looking directly at Rafferty, Policzki said, "Kaye Winslow disappears three days after a big, noisy fight and one day after filing for divorce. She leaves behind one very dead ex-husband. Her disappearance—and the discovery of the corpse—conveniently coincides with a time of day when Winslow's not in the classroom and doesn't have an alibi." He turned to Lorna. "Some anonymous citizen sends you flowers, adds a card to helpfully point you in the direction of Rachel Winslow's unsolved murder. In turn, leading us to take a closer look at Sam Winslow. Funny, isn't it, how dead bodies keep following this guy around? A little bird feeds Malone confidential information he shouldn't have been able to get his hands on. We find Kaye's car, with a blood-soaked jacket in the trunk that matches the one she was wearing the day she disappeared. Her husband's bloody thumbprint just happens to be on the fender. Then, somebody torches her office, using a can of turpentine they left in the Dumpster directly behind the building. Amazingly enough, that has Winslow's fingerprints on it, too. Come on, people. Think about this. Doesn't it seem a little bit over the top?"

He had the lieutenant's attention. Lorna was still looking skeptical, and maybe a little miffed, but Rafferty was listening. "Now we find out that the professor has this deep, dark secret. One his wife was threatening to blab if he told anybody about *her* secret. Why would he tell us this if he was guilty? He sure as hell didn't want it to get out. And as far as murder goes, it's just one more nail in his coffin. It adds teeth to his motivation for wanting Kaye out of the way. If she's dead, she can't tell the truth about him. Don't you think he'd have considered that before he told us? Don't you think his lawyer would have considered it? What possible benefit could he reap from telling us if he's really guilty?"

"Smokescreen," Lorna said. "That's all it is."

Ignoring her, Policzki leaned over the table and spoke directly to the lieutenant. "Every goddamn shred of evidence points directly to Sam Winslow. When was the last time you worked a case where the evidence is so obvious it's like being hit over the head with a sledgehammer? I can't remember when I ever did. Guilty people try to cover up their tracks. They hide evidence. They don't leave it lying around in plain sight, like Hansel and Gretel with their trail of bread crumbs. He's either the most incompetent killer I've ever met, or somebody's going to one hell of a lot of trouble to make it look like he is."

Rafferty drummed his fingers on the desktop. "This case," he said, "has not endeared itself to me."

"But are you hearing me? Do you understand where I'm coming from?"

"I wish I could say no. I really wish I could say no. I can't say no."

"For Christ's sake, Conor," Lorna said. "His theory has more holes in it than a slice of Swiss cheese."

There was a knock on the door. "What?" Rafferty said.

The door opened. Gail, the weekend dispatcher, stuck her head in, located Policzki and said, "I have a phone call for you. It's a little girl who says her name is Gracie Winslow. I told her you were busy—" she arched a brow in Rafferty's direction "—but she insisted you'd want to talk to her. She says it's an emergency."

Policzki found himself on his feet. "Put it through to my desk," he said. "Lieutenant?"

"Go. My brain's about to explode. We'll talk later."

Policzki trotted back to his desk and picked up the ringing phone. "Gracie? What's up?"

"I know where Kaye is," Gracie said. "She's with Vince Tedeschi. He's a friend of my dad's. They're in a house in Brighton, and Mia's in there with them. You have to come, Doug. I think they're going to kill her."

* * *

While Policzki rode shotgun, Lorna drove erratically, splashing through puddles, dodging trucks and taxis, nearly mowing down an old woman and her poodle who were crossing the street illegally on a green light. The woman jumped out of the way, yanking the leash so hard the dog's feet left the pavement. Hunched over the wheel, Lorna missed them by inches. She kept on driving, ignoring the rude gesture the woman made at her as she passed.

"The phone call," Policzki said. "It wasn't Sam she called, it was Vince Tedeschi. She got herself into a pickle with Cunningham, and she called Vince for help."

"You were right," Lorna said. "I goddamn hate it when you're right."

"Watch out for that—Jesus H. Christ, Abrams, I think I just got ten new gray hairs. If you kill us both, I'm never speaking to you again."

"You're too young to have gray hair."

"Want to take a look?"

"You have a problem with the way I drive," she snarled, "you do it! It's your girlfriend whose ass I'm trying to save."

"Just keep moving. Tedeschi could have had access to the painting studio, you know. He's a tenured faculty member. Who would question his right be anywhere in that building? He could probably waltz right into the department office while Maureen's at lunch, borrow the key, go upstairs and steal the can of turpentine, then put the key back, and nobody'd ever know."

"So you're smarter than me," Lorna said. "Stop gloating." Ahead of her, a traffic light turned red. She turned on the lights and the siren and ran it at fifty miles per hour in a thirty-five. When they reached the other side of the intersection, they were still alive. In Boston, where the custom was to ignore emergency vehicles, that was a miracle.

"My daughter called this morning," she said.

"You mean Bridezilla?"

"The wedding's back on. She says she and Derek were both so stressed over planning for that three-ring circus that they couldn't take it anymore. That's what they were fighting about."

"Intersection coming up. So now what?"

She blipped the siren a couple of times. "So they cancelled most of the hoopla and decided on a small wedding. Thirty, thirty-five guests. Nice family dinner afterward instead of a big reception." Lorna tried to read a street sign as they passed, but couldn't make it out. "Are we there yet?"

"We must be getting close. I think it's the next—there she is! That's Gracie."

Lorna got a quick glimpse of a too-thin young girl, standing in the pouring rain in a sopping-wet hooded sweatshirt that was five sizes too big. Lorna wheeled the cruiser into the right-hand lane, cutting off a taxi, and came to a skidding halt on the wet pavement. Policzki scrambled to reach over his seat and open the back door, and the kid ducked in.

"Man," she said, "am I happy to see you guys."

"You okay?" Policzki said.

"Yeah, but I'm freezing."

"Here. Take my jacket." He peeled it off and handed to her.

"Where to?" Lorna said.

"Take a right here. It's on the second block, h॰ down on the left. A gray ranch house."

Looking in the rearview mirror, she told the g॰

down. It could blow the whole thing if Kaye or Tedeschi see you with us."

Gracie disappeared from sight. Her eyes focused straight ahead, in case anybody was looking, Lorna drove sedately past the house, not a mile over the speed limit or a mile under it. "Policzki?" she said.

"The Blazer's in the driveway. Gray sedan next to it. Looks like a rental. Garage is attached to the house by a breezeway. Drapes are drawn, but I could see a sliver of light peeking out from the picture window in the living room. Neighbors fairly close on both sides, but hidden by rows of lilac and something else that might be forsythia. Neighbors across the street have a bird's-eye view. Oh, and the For Sale sign's lying on the ground beside the driveway."

Lorna stopped at the end of the block, signaled and took a left turn. "You missed one thing, Policzki."

"What's that?"

"You forgot to tell me if it was Chinese or Thai fast-food containers in the kitchen trash." She took another left and started down the street that ran parallel to Revere Street. "Can you see the back of the house?"

"Almost. Slow down a little. Yeah, there it is. Pull over here."

She stopped the car, and together they studied the rear of 2300 Revere Street. The back of the house had three windows and a single door leading into the breezeway. It a typical in-town house lot, small and square, with nal landscaping and four sagging wooden posts sup- a clothesline that took up a quarter of the backyard. blew this, Mia DeLucca would die. If she wasn't ad. Lorna stole a quick, fearful look at Policzki.

He was a good man, and this was the first time in a long time that he'd let a woman get past that natural reserve of his. There had to be something pretty special about De-Lucca. If she died, he'd spend the rest of his life blaming it on Lorna. If she died, Lorna would spend the rest of her life blaming herself.

There was just one solution to the problem. They couldn't let her die.

Lorna turned off the car. Policzki studied the house intently, with what appeared to be his customary composure. Looking at him, anybody who didn't know him would have seen a calm, unruffled guy without a care in the world. But Lorna knew him well. The signs of stress were there, if you knew where to look. Like those telltale rings of sweat beneath the arms of his dress shirt.

In all the time she'd known him, she'd never seen the man sweat.

"Being partners," she said, "it's a little like being married. You have to trust each other with your back. Be willing to follow each other into hell."

He didn't respond.

"When this is over," she said, "I'll buy you a dozen jelly doughnuts. You've earned the right to live dangerously."

He still didn't respond.

"We're in this together. I'm trusting you, Policzki. Trusting that you won't get my ass shot off. You remember that little conversation we had?"

Still not looking at her, he said, "I remember."

"Good. Then let's roll." She glanced into the back where Gracie sat shivering, Policzki's jacket w around her. "Do I have to handcuff you to the wheel to keep you in the car?"

"I'll stay."

"See that you do. If you don't, I'll find a way to make sure you're grounded for the next hundred years." Lorna got out of the car, popped the trunk, took out a blanket, and gave it to the kid. Crouching by the open back door of the cruiser, she said, "If anything happens—anything bad— you're to stay put until help gets here. Understood?"

Gracie nodded. "Good," Lorna said. "I'll see you in a few."

Guns drawn, she and Policzki crept through backyards, fighting their way through a tangle of wisteria vines and brambles, jumping over a small brook and drenching their feet. It was a frigging miracle that somebody didn't come outside and ask them what the hell they thought they were doing, skulking about in broad daylight, guns in hand. Of course, on a day like this, most people weren't too keen on making that kind of effort. More likely they'd just stay inside where it was dry and call 911, and wait for the cops, who'd show up with sirens shrieking and lights blazing. That would help with the stealthy arrival they were aiming for.

Policzki touched her arm, nodded his head in the direction of the house, and they took off running, low, along the shrubbery. They reached the place and pressed their backs up against the old-fashioned asbestos siding that had been so popular in the 1950s. Breathing hard, Lorna rested her hand against her midriff and waited to see if somebody was going to come out and blow their heads off.

When it didn't happen, she followed the kid along the wall of the house until he stopped so suddenly that she bumped into him. Finger over his lips, he pointed at something low above his head. "What?" she whispered.

"Screen," he whispered back.

She looked up at the window, then at all the others. He was right. It was the only window here without a screen. "I'll hoist you up," he whispered. "See if it's locked."

Lorna holstered her gun, and they fumbled around like a pair of teenage virgins trying to figure out the steps to the horizontal tango. She somehow managed to climb onto his shoulders, and he lifted her up so she could peer in.

"What do you see?" he whispered.

"It's a bedroom. Let me try the window."

She reached up and pushed at it. To her amazement, it slid open effortlessly. Soundlessly. Fuckin-A. It couldn't be this easy, could it? Was Allen Funt about to jump out and tell her she was on *Candid Camera?* "You gotta be kidding," she muttered.

"Can you get through?"

"Almost." She reached both arms up and was able to grab the sill, but couldn't quite get the leverage she needed. "A little higher," she said, and he lifted her right up off his shoulders. The kid was strong, she'd give him that. Good muscles. Must be the bran muffins. Or the yogurt with wheat germ. She caught hold of the sill, lay flat across it, panting, and looked around for something she could grab on to so she wouldn't fall on her face.

"Hold on." Policzki pressed both hands hard against her rump and pushed her a little higher, just high enough so she could swing one leg over the edge of the sill.

She lay there for an instant, straddling the sill, her skirt bunched up around her thighs. "If you look up my dres Policzki," she whispered, "I'm sending my husband c to visit you. He's six foot seven and weighs two hur and sixty-two pounds."

It was only a slight exaggeration. Ed was at le

ten, and probably close to two hundred, especially with those love handles he'd spent the last couple of years cultivating. She drew her other leg in, slipped, and fell onto the bed with a thud they should have heard in New Hampshire.

Oh, shit, she thought, and lay there for a moment, stunned by the impact and waiting for imminent death. Or for her breath to return. Whichever came first. While she waited, Policzki hoisted himself through the window and dropped to the bed with the grace and silence of a swan floating on water. "Sometimes," she whispered, "I really hate you."

The place was sparsely furnished. Nobody was living here. But they'd left a few things behind. A clock radio. A couple shelves of books. A poster on the wall of a cat hanging by a thread, with a caption that read Hang in There, Baby.

Policzki crawled off the mattress, took a single step away from the bed, and his shoe squeaked. Behind him, Lorna froze. Without making a sound, he toed off the wet shoes, and Lorna did the same. Gun in hand, she followed him to the bedroom door, where they both stopped to do a quick recon. It was a typical 1950s ranch, a center hallway with bedrooms on both sides, and the kitchen and living room at the other end. Voices came from the living room. Policzki took a step backward, bumped into her and veered off to take a look around the room. He moved silently to the bookcase, picked up a couple of different books and weighed them in his hand before deciding which one he wanted. It was a dictionary, a heavy one. Since this was hardly the time to take up the study of linguistics, Lorna figured he must have some kind of plan for it. But what would he do with a dictionary?

"Who the hell do you think you are," she whispered. "Fucking MacGyver?"

"Well, well," Mia said. "So you're alive, after all."

"Very much alive," Kaye said. "Surprised, are you?"

"I'm already beyond surprised. I've gone right past it, straight to furious. Do you have any idea of the headaches you've caused me?"

"Believe it or not," Kaye said, "most of it wasn't intentional. Things just got out of hand. I had to do something about it. If Charlie'd stayed out of it, none of us would be here today."

"Who the hell is Charlie?"

"My ex-husband. He wouldn't leave me alone. If he hadn't been so greedy, he'd still be alive. He was squeezing me for money, Mia. I already gave him his share, but the materialistic son of a bitch wanted half of mine. Tell me, is that fair?"

"It wasn't your money in the first place." Mia tried to ignore the business end of the gun Kaye was pointing at her. "You tarnished the good name of my agency. Left me holding the bag. And then you burned the place down."

"I had to destroy the evidence. Sam scared me when he started talking about auditors and IRS agents. I figured they wouldn't find anything if it wasn't there to be found."

"You screwed up. Your files didn't burn. They're sitting in my living room. I already found it, Kaye. I found the Stuart Landers file."

"I know. Word travels fast in the real estate communit doesn't it? I wish you could have left it alone. I've alw liked you, Mia. You were the closest thing I had to male friend. Women don't like me." The gun in he wavered. "This wasn't what I wanted," she said. "I was going to divorce Sam. Vince was going to leave his wife, and we planned to get married and live comfortably on all that money. Right, baby?"

The man stepped out of the shadows behind Mia and slipped an arm around Kaye's waist. "Right," he said. "Until it all fell apart."

"So we had to make new plans," Kaye said. "Fake my own death, make it look like Sam was to blame for everything. Start over again somewhere else, as somebody else. It's not the first time I've had to do it. Except that this time, I have a nice little nest egg to tide me over."

"No matter who you had to screw to do it."

"I didn't intend for you to be hurt. That's your own damn fault. The agency always meant more to you than it did to me. I knew you'd still have that. You'd survive financially. Eventually people would stop wondering what happened to me, and move on with their lives. Even if Sam blabbed, by the time he opened his mouth, we'd be gone."

"Sam knew?"

"He found out. But I knew he wouldn't tell. I had him by the short hairs. Your brother has a few secrets of his own."

"What the hell does that mean?"

"Sam Winslow is gayer than a three-dollar bill," Kaye said. "He's so far in the closet, the light doesn't even reach him when you open the door. I figured you knew, but if that look on your face is the real deal, I guess you didn't."

She hadn't known. But it made a strange kind of sense. ~~oo~~king back, Mia realized she had a lot of unanswered ~~que~~stions about her brother. About his life, and about some ~~of the~~ decisions he'd made. This answered so many of them.

~~"I f~~igured it out a long time ago," the man named Vince

said. "A long time before he married Kaye. But I didn't say anything. I figured it was his own personal business, so I kept my mouth shut."

Mia looked at him more closely. "I know you," she said. "I've met you before."

"Vince Tedeschi," he said. "Professor of Mathematics."

"You work at the college with my brother." Her eyes returned to her sister-in-law. "You cheated on my brother with one of his friends?"

"Sam didn't give a shit," Kaye said. "All he cares about is his reputation. A girl has to get her kicks somewhere. I certainly wasn't getting them with him."

"So now what? You'll kill me, and the two of you can run away together? You'll never be able to outrun what you've done, Kaye. It'll just follow you around forever. Sooner or later, somebody else will read that file. Somebody else will look at those two settlement statements, and they'll come after you. My brother will break his silence and tell what he knows. You'll have to spend the rest of your life in hiding."

"Sweetie, I have beaucoup bucks. Enough to keep me in style for a very long time. Vince and I will be so far away, nobody'll ever find us."

"Is that true, Vince? You're leaving your entire life behind for this…this—whore? It's not much fun, living on the run. You have kids, don't you? You'll never see them again. Is that what you really want?"

"Kaye and I are in love. That's all that matters."

"I see you've wrapped one more sucker around your finger, Kaye. How do you do it?"

"Shut up."

"See how long that love lasts, Vince, once the money

runs out. With her expensive tastes, it won't last long. You'll have to go back to working for a living just to keep up the payments on that hacienda in Mexico."

"Shut up!" Kaye said. "You're starting to piss me off."

"So why don't you just shoot me? Is your trigger finger a little shaky? I realize it's a bit messy when you're forced to kill your in-laws. It makes for awkward conversation around the dinner table at Thanksgiving and Christmas."

"Fine. That's what you want, I'll be happy to—" Behind Kaye, something hit the floor with a thud that nearly sent all three of them through the roof. She wheeled around and pumped a bullet into the *Webster's Ninth Edition* that had just landed from the middle of nowhere.

"Police!" Lorna Abrams shouted. "Nobody move!"

Gun in hand, Kaye swung back around. While Mia watched in horror, Doug Policzki tackled her sister-in-law. They fell to the floor and struggled for possession of the firearm. It flew out of Kaye's hand and skittered across the floor. Vince Tedeschi, looking a little shell-shocked, bent to pick it up, then froze when he felt the muzzle of Lorna's gun pressed against his temple. "Touch that," she said, "and my itchy trigger finger might just slip."

"I want a lawyer," Vince said. "I'm not saying a goddamn thing without a lawyer."

"Yeah, yeah, that's what they all say." Lorna cuffed him, turned him and shoved him hard. "March your ugly ass to the couch and sit. *Now!*"

Across the room, Kaye was flat on her back on the floor, with Policzki straddling her. He forced her flailing arms above her head and snapped his handcuffs on her wrists. "Pig," she said through narrowed eyes. "Lousy son of a bitch pig."

"Haven't heard that particular epithet in a while," Lorna said. "What, did your parents meet at Woodstock?"

"Up, princess." Policzki, sweating profusely, hauled Kaye to her feet. His hand clasping her elbow, he guided her none too gently to the couch. "Sit."

While Lorna called for backup, Policzki turned his attention to Mia, who still stood trembling, one hand clutching the door frame beside her. There was a cut over his left eye, and his shirt was torn. When she saw the blood on his face, her legs went weak. Policzki swiped his bloody nose on his shirtsleeve and slowly crossed the room to her. "You're bleeding," she said.

"I've bled before. I'll bleed again. Welcome to my world. You ever do anything that stupid again, I'll strangle you with my bare hands."

"What did I do?"

"Nobody ever told you it's dangerous to deliberately provoke somebody when they have a loaded gun pointed at you?"

"Oh," she said. "That."

"Goddamn crazy woman."

"I liked the dictionary falling out of the sky routine."

"Yeah," he said. "I thought you would."

"I won't give up my independence for you, Policzki."

"Neither will I. I'm still getting my own place. You can help me decorate it."

"But I'm willing to—that is, I'd like it if we could—"

"Yes," he said, his knuckles brushing her cheek. "I'd like it if we could, too."

"—you know. Give it a try. See what happens."

"So does this mean we're going steady?"

"I think it does."

"I'd kiss you to seal the deal," he said, "but I'm on duty. It's against the rules."

"What time will you be off duty?" she said. "In case you wanted to kiss me then?"

He looked around, ran a hand through his hair. "It'll be a few hours. I'll come over. When I'm free."

"I'll be waiting, Detective."

"You have your cell phone on you?"

"I left it in the car with—oh, my God. Gracie."

"She's okay. She's waiting in the cruiser. If it wasn't for her, you'd be dead." Policzki closed his eyes for a minute. When he opened them again, she saw a peculiar sheen in them. Ignoring it, he unclipped his cell phone from his belt and handed it to her. "Here," he said. "Use mine. Call her." His knuckles brushed her cheek again. "I think," he said, "she's waiting to hear from you."

New York Times
bestselling author

HEATHER GRAHAM

On a weekend vacation, Beth Anderson is unnerved when a
stroll on the beach reveals what appears to be a human skull.
As a stranger approaches, Beth panics and covers the evidence.
But when she later returns to the beach, the skull is gone.

Determined to find solid evidence to bring to the police,
Beth digs deeper into the mystery—and everywhere she goes,
Keith Henson, the stranger from the beach, seems to appear.
Then a body washes ashore, and Beth begins to think she
needs more help than she bargained for....

THE ISLAND

"Another top-notch thriller
from romance icon Graham."
—*Publishers Weekly*

*Available the first week
of March 2007, wherever
paperbacks are sold!*

New York Times bestselling author

CARLA NEGGERS

The largest uncut diamond in the world, the Minstrel's Rough
is little more than legend. Brought into the Pepperkamp Family
in 1548, it has been handed down to one keeper in each
generation. Juliana Fall has inherited its splendor from her
uncle—and, unwittingly, its legacy of danger.

There are others who seek the Minstrel's Rough: a U.S. senator,
a Nazi collaborator and a Vietnam war-hero-turned-journalist,
among them. Now Juliana has only two choices: uncover the
past before they do...or cut and run.

Cut and Run

"No one does romantic suspense better!"
—*New York Times* bestselling author
Janet Evanovich

*Available the first week of March 2007,
wherever paperbacks are sold!*

USA TODAY bestselling author

JENNIFER ARMINTROUT

In the two months since I was attacked in the hospital morgue and turned into a vampire, I've killed my evil sire Cyrus, fallen in love with my new sire, Nathan, and have even gotten used to drinking blood. Just when things are finally returning to normal, Nathan becomes possessed by one of the most powerful and wicked vampires alive—the Soul Eater. And then he slaughters an innocent human. With the Soul Eater and my possessed sire on the loose, I have a lot to fear. Including being killed. Again.

blood ties book two: POSSESSION

"This fast, furious novel is a squirm-inducing treat."
—*Publishers Weekly* on *The Turning*

MIRA®

*Available the first week of February 2007
wherever paperbacks are sold!*

www.MIRABooks.com

MJA2418

REQUEST YOUR FREE BOOKS!

2 FREE NOVELS
FROM THE ROMANCE/SUSPENSE
COLLECTION PLUS 2 FREE GIFTS!

YES! Please send me 2 FREE novels from the Romance/Suspense Collection and my 2 FREE gifts. After receiving them, if I don't wish to receive any more books, I can return the shipping statement marked "cancel." If I don't cancel, I will receive 4 brand-new novels every month and be billed just $5.49 per book in the U.S., or $5.99 per book in Canada, plus 25¢ shipping and handling per book plus applicable taxes, if any*. That's a savings of at least 20% off the cover price! I understand that accepting the 2 free books and gifts places me under no obligation to buy anything. I can always return a shipment and cancel at any time. Even if I never buy another book from the Reader Service, the two free books and gifts are mine to keep forever.

185 MDN EF5Y 385 MDN EF6C

Name _____ (PLEASE PRINT)

Address _____ Apt. #

City _____ State/Prov. _____ Zip/Postal Code

Signature (if under 18, a parent or guardian must sign)

Mail to The Reader Service:
IN U.S.A.: P.O. Box 1867, Buffalo, NY 14240-1867
IN CANADA: P.O. Box 609, Fort Erie, Ontario L2A 5X3

Not valid to current subscribers to the Romance Collection,
the Suspense Collection or the Romance/Suspense Collection.

Want to try two free books from another line?
Call 1-800-873-8635 or visit www.morefreebooks.com.

* Terms and prices subject to change without notice. NY residents add applicable sales tax. Canadian residents will be charged applicable provincial taxes and GST. This offer is limited to one order per household. All orders subject to approval. Credit or debit balances in a customer's account(s) may be offset by any other outstanding balance owed by or to the customer. Please allow 4 to 6 weeks for delivery.

Your Privacy: Harlequin is committed to protecting your privacy. Our Privacy Policy is available online at www.eHarlequin.com or upon request from the Reader Service. From time to time we make our lists of customers available to reputable firms who may have a product or service of interest to you. If you would prefer we not share your name and address, please check here. ☐

BOB07

MIRA®

www.MIRABooks.com